Billy Old
Arizona Ranger

Keith,

Hope you enjoy the book,
and thanks for the
promo-

Geff Moyer

BILLY OLD
ARIZONA RANGER

A HISTORICAL NOVEL BASED ON A TRUE STORY

GEFF MOYER

SUNSTONE PRESS

SANTA FE

Sunstone books may be purchased for educational, business, or sales promotional use.
For information please write: Special Markets Department, Sunstone Press,
P.O. Box 2321, Santa Fe, New Mexico 87504-2321.

Book and cover design › Vicki Ahl
Body typeface › Baskerville Old Face
Printed on acid-free paper
∞
eBook 978-1-61139-476-4

Library of Congress Cataloging-in-Publication Data

Names: Moyer, Geff, author.
Title: Billy Old, Arizona ranger : a historical novel based on a true story /
  by Geff Moyer.
Description: Santa Fe : Sunstone Press, 2016.
Identifiers: LCCN 2016019250 (print) | LCCN 2016021037 (ebook) | ISBN
  9781632931399 (softcover : alk. paper) | ISBN 9781611394764
Subjects: LCSH: Murder–Investigation–Fiction. | Revenge–Fiction. |
  Arizona–History–To 1912–Fiction. | GSAFD: Western stories. | Historical
  fiction.
Classification: LCC PS3613.O924 B55 2016 (print) | LCC PS3613.O924 (ebook) |
  DDC 813/.6–dc23
LC record available at https://lccn.loc.gov/2016019250

SUNSTONE PRESS IS COMMITTED TO MINIMIZING OUR ENVIRONMENTAL IMPACT ON THE PLANET.
THE PAPER USED IN THIS BOOK IS FROM RESPONSIBLY MANAGED FORESTS. OUR PRINTER HAS RECEIVED CHAIN OF CUSTODY
(COC) CERTIFICATION FROM: THE FOREST STEWARDSHIP COUNCIL™ (FSC®), PROGRAMME FOR THE ENDORSEMENT OF FOREST CERTIFICATION™
(PEFC™), AND THE SUSTAINABLE FORESTRY INITIATIVE® (SFI®).
THE FSC® COUNCIL IS A NON-PROFIT ORGANIZATION, PROMOTING THE ENVIRONMENTALLY APPROPRIATE, SOCIALLY BENEFICIAL AND
ECONOMICALLY VIABLE MANAGEMENT OF THE WORLD'S FORESTS. FSC® CERTIFICATION IS RECOGNIZED INTERNATIONALLY
AS A RIGOROUS ENVIRONMENTAL AND SOCIAL STANDARD FOR RESPONSIBLE FOREST MANAGEMENT

WWW.SUNSTONEPRESS.COM
SUNSTONE PRESS / POST OFFICE BOX 2321 / SANTA FE, NM 87504-2321 /USA
(505) 988-4418 / ORDERS ONLY (800) 243-5644 / FAX (505) 988-1025

Dedication

This book is dedicated to the memory of
George F. Moyer who instilled in me a love for
American history and the West.

Acknowledgments

Special thanks to Tom, Paul, Richard, Steve, and Jim

Prologue

She couldn't remember the last time she tasted meat, let alone what type of meat it was. Maybe it was the trout Kelsey had cooked up for her several weeks ago. He was always good for at least a few meals a month. Especially if he was horny. He had asked her to marry him three times, but she didn't need or want a man in her life. She hoped he'd return from his current outing with a deer and share a shank with her. "Share" being the key word because she sure as hell couldn't pay for it. Until she caught up on her grocery bill, turnip and onion sandwiches would be a staple. Mustard usually helped. Corn was plentiful and cheap, but never sat well with the shrapnel still floating around her innards.

Standing shin deep in mud with a dozen other women who had volunteered to serve as nurses with the Red Cross in France, she was told that her work would be safe and far behind the front lines. The Germans didn't get the telegram. Sixteen years later whenever a thunder storm would crash across the mountains and attack Taos, she'd find herself cowering under the large table in her work area reminded of how strange life is. It took a war to give her purpose. From its maiming and slaughter she found a calling. From her calling she got her dream: This gallery. But it had been over a month since a customer had entered, two since she had sold a painting. Original art wasn't at the top of the list of people's purchases at this dour time. She wondered how many starving artists would end up dead ones before this Depression finally ran its course. She had sworn she wouldn't be one of them. She had been through too much hell to give up now.

The snow was late and that worried her. Snow brings skiers. Although there had been less and less of them the past few years, she figured the ones who could still afford to come might also be able to afford a painting. Her part time shift at the local clinic rarely helped because she was paid only when the customers could pay, and the local Taos natives were hardly any better off than the struggling little art community. If this place does survive she figures it will be a goddamn miracle.

The chugging of a car engine broke the mid-October silence. Peering out the window she expected to see another local returning from a fruitless job search, or Kelsey's pickup truck. It was neither, but it did park in front of her gallery. The age of the old Ford was her first hint that the man driving wasn't a buyer. When he got out wearing a Sears and Roebuck mail order suit, she was sure of it. At least he wasn't toting a Bible. It angered her how this Depression had given birth to hundreds of door-to-door Bible salesmen all trying to convince millions of hopeless people that buying the Good Book will somehow put food in their children's bellies.

She left the gallery area and retreated to her work shop to give the stranger a few minutes to browse the paintings. All of which were horses. That was her fervor. She grabbed a rag and wiped the smudges of paint from her hands and face, then released the ribbon to allow her hair to tumble free and cover her missing left ear, courtesy of a vicious Mexican policeman. The bell over the door announced the man's arrival.

When he saw the subject of the many paintings on the walls of the small gallery he knew he had the right place.

"Anyone here?" he called.

"Yessir," she answered out from the back room. "Be with ya in a minute."

The man roamed the small gallery studying the paintings. They were stunning. Dozens of different breeds and colors with every muscle captured. Some were standing on hilltops. Some were rearing. Some were running. Some were grazing. A few had colts by their sides. Some were sweating and foaming with the sun glistening off their hides. Some stood in snow with the cold air puffing from their noses. One he particularly liked showed three of them emerging from a misty fog and running full speed straight at him. It was like they were going to leap out of the painting, stampede through the gallery, and burst out the door. That was also when he realized that none had a rider. Not one human interacted with any horse in any painting. These were free spirits of a time long gone.

Returning to the gallery she eyeballed the man studying her work. He was handsomely familiar but she didn't know why. In his late twenties or early thirties, she guessed, and a good twenty years her junior. For the first time she noticed he was carrying a flat object about one-foot square wrapped in newspaper and immediately assumed he was just another goddamn door-to-door salesman.

"What can I do fer ya?" she asked impatiently and with an obvious hint of disappointment.

Apparently the man must have been absorbed in the paintings. She could tell her voice had startled him. That pleased her.

"These are wonderful paintings," he stated.

The woman he was looking at was easily twenty years his senior. Her hair hung loose to her shoulders. She wore little or no make-up, but was still attractive in an earthy way. Her nose had a slight crook to it. He figured it must been broken, probably a childhood accident, but it seemed to give her character. Even under her loose fitting smock he couldn't help but notice an ample set of breasts, still strong enough to rest high.

"Thank you," she said, but thinking, "Get yer fuckin' sales pitch over with!"

Without any further chit-chat the man removed the newspaper from the object he was holding and placed it on the counter in front of her.

"Here it comes," she warned herself with a sigh.

"Did you paint this?" he asked.

Looking down at the painting she felt the wind leave her chest. The man watched her face form into a pallid expression of both pain and pleasure.

"Where the hell'd ya get this?" she asked.

Sonora, Mexico, 1910

La Bandera was hot enough to melt a lizard's toenail. Piss in the dirt and it would suck it up before it could make mud. It felt like August, but was probably March. Maybe still February. The street was empty. That was good. No bystanders. He figured it might be Sunday. Since there was no whorehouse in sight he knew the cantina played double duty, like so many others he had searched. That was good, too—less walking. Every time his boot heel struck ground a shard of pain would whip through his jaw. The toothache that had been making unwelcomed social calls for many moons had finally become a full-fledged squatter.

He had no idea of how many of these pestholes he'd dirtied his boots in. His fifth grade education wouldn't let him count that high. The towns, barrios, villages, and grottos had all become a blur of baked adobes waiting to see which one would be the first to cry *tio* and knuckle under to the dead Sonora earth. Their only differences were the size of the bone orchards and the amount of dog shit in the streets.

The sombrero he had donned a few weeks earlier felt like he was balancing a platter of beer mugs on his skull. The *serape* was a heavy, itchy burden that made him sweat and stink all the more, but did provide a soft landing for the critters that lost their grip and nose-dived from his beard and shoulder-length hair. Staring at the bleached and cracked outside walls of the cantina he knew how its guts would look. A bar would rest a few feet from the back wall. Most times it was simply a few boards ripped from a dying neighbor and stretched across two large, empty barrels that still reeked of rancid rain water. A handful of small tables would be scattered about, each covered in a layer of dust deep enough for a fellow to write his name. Providing anyone in there could write. The only unknown was how many other *hombres* might be hanging around and if any of them would prove to be a problem.

He hitched Orion by a trough of scum covered water. Not pleased, the testy horse snorted and spewed a glob of snot onto the dry ground.

"Quit bitchin'!" Billy groused at the black stallion with the white star on its forehead. "It's wet, ain't it?"

This prickly banter between man and mount dated back to 1905, when both were part of the disbanded Arizona Rangers. The two had just had traveled one-hundred-and-sixty miles southeast from Pedro Conde, very deep into Sonora, deeper than his plan ever intended on taking them. Close to two back-breaking-sore-ass weeks were spent getting to this pus-bucket of a town, costing him the majority of his supplies. He sucked in a mouthful of *mescal* from his flask, blanketed it around the angry tooth, then spat it onto the ground and watched the dirt inhale it with a wink and a thank you.

Like countless times before, his former captain's warning rattled through his head: "Only a fool goes into a hostile place 'lone." He wondered if his close friend and fellow Ranger Jeff Kidder had heard those words before he stepped into Lucheia's *cantina* in Naco, Mexico two years ago. Was he nervous as he waited for his eyes to adjust to the dark room?

"No!" Billy whispered. He knew Jeff was too fast to be nervous—too smart to be foolish. After all, he was the one with the brains.

"Knowin' yer surroundin's," bellowed Captain Harry Wheeler, "that's an advantage! A hidden belly or boot gun, an advantage! Shotgun, advantage! When in doubt, shoot first! Ain't nothun wrong with none of 'em things. It ain't cheatin.' It ain't bein' a shitwad. It's bein' smart. God knows 'em shit buckets yer goin' up agin will have no misgivin's 'bout takin' advantage of you."

He pulled the Smith & Wesson from its holster and slid a round into the one empty chamber that rested under its firing pin then returned it to its home. Next, he released the thin leather strap that secured a Colt Model 1905 .45 caliber with a seven-round clip in a shoulder holster tucked under his left arm. It was a weapon he had picked up during his Rough Rider days and had come to appreciate for its penetrating prowess. Reaching around to the small of his back he gave the bowie knife a slight tilt to the right so its handle was propped for fast freedom. Years ago a breed taught him the Comanche way of knife fighting. Staying balanced and calm was the key, because panic in a blade fight would get a fellow gutted quicker than shit through a goose. He

12

scooped up a handful of dirt and rubbed it around to best the sweat on his palms.

"Sorry, Cap'n!" he repeated for an untold time, closed his eyes, and stepped into the dark *cantina*.

The room reeked of urine mixed with the foul odors of warm, stale beer and whores who rarely bathed. Opening his eyes, Billy surveyed the room. The bartender stood at the end of the bar tossing the bones with a fat, drunk *puta* who needed to lean on its wooden slats to stay upright. Another whore was alone at a table, one foot propped up on a second chair, tinting her toenails. She looked at Billy and winked then returned to decorating her digits. A somewhat fancy dressed man sat at a corner table playing solitaire. His eyes never lifted from the cards. No problem there. Gamblers mind their own business. At another table were the usual two old men playing checkers and nursing smelly warm beers. Dead center of the bar, eating the worm from his empty bottle of *mescal*, stood a Mexican policeman in a soiled uniform.

"Moises Alvarez?" Billy called out, expecting the policeman to turn and reply.

Moises turned alright, but he turned skinning his shooter and firing.

The speed shocked Billy. The bullet punched a hole in the left side of his *serape*, missing his ribs so closely he could feel the heat as it hissed past and violated the adobe wall behind him. Billy's first shot went wild, smashing the empty *mescal* bottle on the bar. Before Alvarez could pull off a second round, a chunk of flying glass pierced the policeman's right eye. He screamed and cursed in Spanish, then leveled his *pistola* for another shot. His last statement, in English, "Fuck you, grin..." was cut short with a bullet to his mouth, taking out the back of his skull and planting pieces of it and brain matter on the already filthy dress of the fat, drunken *puta* at the end of the bar. Everything happened so fast that no one in the *cantina* had even made a move for cover. The gambler was frozen in mid-deal. One of the old men held a checker suspended in the air ready to jump a foe. The whore painting her digits had smeared a bright red streak down the length of her big toe. The bartender couldn't take his eyes off the blood and chunks of brain splattered on the fat *puta's* dress. She didn't seem to notice them.

Keeping his Smith & Wesson in his right hand, Billy pulled a five dollar gold piece from his pocket and held it high in the air with his left.

"Diaz Pasco?" he demanded, turning in a slow circle and brandishing the glittering gold coin. "Diaz Pasco?" he again demanded.

The gambler was the first to regain his voice.

"Back in Naco, Ranger," he managed to choke out.

Billy squinted. Did he know this man? "You 'Merican? he asked.

"Used to be," replied the man. "Ain't sure now, Ranger."

"Ain't no Rangers no more!" stated Billy. "How'd ya know Pasco's back in Naco?"

"He owes me money and went there to get it from one of his whores. I'm stuck here 'til he gets back or my luck hops to the better side of the stick. So if yer after him, it'll save me some ass blisters."

"It won't get yer money," stated Billy.

"Ya kill him, it'll make me smile," declared the gambler. "And there ain't too much to smile 'bout 'round here."

"*Señor!*" the barkeep exclaimed. "*La policía viene!*"

Billy flipped the five-dollar gold piece to the gambler and slid a silver dollar down the length of the bar.

"Plant him," he ordered the barkeep, backing towards the door.

"If you leave a dead man in a town down there," explained Captain Wheeler during one of his briefings, "always leave a silver dollar fer his funeral. That'll at least be 'nough fer a pauper's burial. It helps keep good relations."

"Good relations!" Billy spat as he hopped on Orion. "No such fuckin' thing!"

Before any of Moises' fellow policemen could stir from their *siestas*, Billy and Orion were heading north for Naco.

April 3, 1908

Hunkered down in the corral on the Arizona side of the border town of Naco, Ranger Jeff Kidder was beginning to worry that his informant had sent him up a false trail. Dying men don't always talk true. Back in December he and fellow Ranger Freddie Rankin had flushed the territory of two gun-running bandits who bequeathed them a shitload of illegal weapons and over 10,000 rounds of ammunition. One of the *hombres* lived long enough to gurgle out a couple of his cohort's names. To no one's surprise it was two Mexican policemen by the names of Delores Quías and Tomás Amador. Lucheia's *cantina,* right across the short, wooden bridge from the corral, was said to be their favorite watering hole. So Kidder waited, alone, and that was how he wanted it to come down. Billy was off safe on an assignment in Patagonia, several miles north. Sparky was sleeping soundly back in the Nogales barracks. Jeff purposely did not tell Captain Wheeler where he was headed. He knew the man would insist on him bringing along another Ranger, but he had to do this on his own hook.

Just as the sun burned orange his hot, sweaty wait was rewarded. Quías and Amador strolled out of the alley next to Lucheias and entered the *cantina.* Jeff drew his fancy Colt with the mother-of-pearl handle and slid a cartridge into the empty chamber that always rested under the firing pin. He counted the bullets in his cartridge belt—sixteen—plenty enough for two men. Taking a grip on Vermillion's reins, he led the horse across the bridge that granted the border town of Naco two identities. Simply a dozen weathered wooden planks with a split log railing on each side were all that kept Arizona from flushing into Mexico. Under it was just more of the same rock and sand and dirt that painted the entire landscape. It was simply a symbol, a marker, of where one world ended and another began. He tethered Vermillion to a post in front of an empty water trough. At first he considered entering Lucheias with his Colt holstered. "Maybe," he thought, "just maybe, they'll come peacefully." After all, even though Quías and Amador were gunrunners they were still Mexican police. But a gut feeling said these men placed no value on any oath. He kept the Colt in his hand.

Mexican General Luis Torres, an honest man when it benefitted him, had given a few of the Rangers the permission to enter and perform their duties within the district of Sonora. That few included Billy Old and Jeff Kidder. That didn't bode well with the Mexican police who were tangled in some shifty side businesses. The only thing that pleased Amador and Quías when Jeff walked into Lucheia's was that he was alone.

Before his eyes could adjust to the dark a voice shouted, "Kidder!" A gun fired and it felt as if someone had slapped a hot branding iron across his left forearm. He fired at the muzzle blast. The cry that came from the darkness told him he had struck meat. Two more rounds exploded. One bullet splintered the bar just inches from his hip as the other sizzled past his shoulder. Again he fired at the muzzle blast. Meat again! Both policemen were down. As his eyes adjusted to the dark room he slowly approached the two wounded men. Quías was unconscious from the bullet that had grazed his skull. Amador was crouched in a corner clamping one hand over his bloody rib cage.

"Fuckin' Ranger, fuckin' Ranger!" screamed the wounded policeman.

Just as Jeff reached for the handcuffs looped in his belt, the back door to the same alley Quías and Amador had just come from burst open. Two more men ran in with weapons blazing. A round slammed into Jeff's stomach, ripping a large exit hole in his back and catapulting him over a table. From flat on the floor he emptied his Colt into the two new fighters. Even with eyes burning from the sulfur clouding the small room he was able to see that both were hit, and that both also wore soiled police uniforms. One was face down on the floor, the sawdust beneath him turning a gooey brownish red. The other, oddly enough, was perfectly seated in a chair with a stunned expression on his face and a red hole in his forehead. It was almost a comical sight, but Jeff knew if he laughed his insides would flood through the growing hole in his belly. It felt like he was dying of thirst, but knew gut shots put a fellow in that state. He also knew that drinking anything with such a wound would simply hurry The Reaper. So first things first: stuff his bandana into the hole in his belly to curb the stream of blood that was darkening his shirt and Levis. Next: reload, which left ten rounds in his belt. Third: get his feet back under him and get the hell out of there. Using chairs and tables as crutches he stumbled and groped his way to the door. The outside steps fooled him and he spilled down them and out into the dusty street.

Darkness was coming, but he wasn't sure if it was the beginning of nighttime or the end of his own life. It was twenty yards of open ground back to the bridge and across to the safety of the Arizona side of Naco. Vermillion whinnied and stirred and stomped his hooves. Jeff struggled to his knees and tried to grab the nervous horse's reins. Then a hailstorm of bullets pinged and thudded all around him.

Three more policemen, Moises Alvarez, Diaz Pasco, and the mysterious man Billy knew only as Victoriano, came running down the street, eagerly joining the fight. They, too, knew their target. Jeff rolled behind the empty water trough as a barrage of lead splintered and punctured the rotting wood.

16

arrived in Naco before dawn, April 5. When Billy saw the rat hole his friend had been put in and how he had been left, it took both Wheeler and Foster to keep him from air holing every Mexican policeman in sight.

As he gasped for breath Jeff keep repeating the names "Amador, Quías, Alvarez, Pasco, Victoriano...Amador..." He had half of them out for the fifth time when he went quiet, looked square at Billy and said, "Remember?"

Billy wiped a tear from his eye and replied, "Ya got it!"

Jeff gave his friend one of his tobacco stained smiles then exhaled the little life that was left in him. The three Rangers placed Kidder's body in a wagon. Billy drove it as Wheeler rode to its left and Foster to its right. The lumbering twenty yards to the Arizona side of Naco was accompanied by several taunts, in Spanish of course, by a small gathering of Mexican policeman lined on their side of the bridge.

Wheeler glanced over at Billy and saw the rage on his face and the tears in his eyes. "Easy, Billy. Ain't nothun we can do on this side a the bridge."

"The day'll come, Billy," stated John Foster. "The day'll come."

"Yer fuckin' right it will," declared Billy as he whipped the reins to speed up the lazy wagon team. He wanted out of Mexico, out of the sight and earshot of the scumbags lining their way. As the horses hoofs struck the first board of the old bridge he repeated in a harsh whisper, "Yer fuckin' right it will."

Jeff's body was sent by train to his mother in Los Angeles for burial. Less than three days later the greasy Mexican gears were put into motion. The five killers were magically whisked off to various unknown Sonora towns. Someone had helped the scum suckers vanish into seventy-one-thousand square miles of mainly desert. Since it happened below the border, no charges were ever made. Arizona couldn't and Mexico wouldn't.

April, 1902

The train screeched, jerked, grunted, and belched smoke as it strained to stop at the Nogales, Arizona depot. Jeff Kidder removed his horse from a boxcar and led the animal from their fourth and final train since leaving Vermillion, South Dakota. Even three wretched days in stuffy and soot-filled passenger cars hadn't dampened his furor. He had waited a long time for this chance, much longer than most bucks that had the itch to head west. He was twenty-six-years old and college educated. Yet even with all that learning it was the colorful bullshit of the Dime Novels that stirred him. For years he had practiced the quick draw and was fast with the mother-of-pearl handled Colt holstered at his right side. His dream of being a lawman was just a few city blocks away in the headquarters of the Arizona Rangers.

As Captain Harry Wheeler glanced up at the fellow entering his office, his first thought was here's a shiny new coin that needs a little smudging up.

"Harry Wheeler," he said as he rose from behind his desk and extended his hand.

"Jeff Kidder," the coin answered and watched his hand disappear within the big man's grip. Kidder topped out at around five-foot-ten-inches, but had to crick his neck up to meet the hard eyes in Wheeler's leathered face. A face he figured had earned every line in it.

"Have a seat," the captain ordered, pointing to the chair in front of his desk, which just happened to be the only other one in the room.

Wheeler returned to the comfort of his high back swivel chair as Jeff sat down in a stiff, hard-backed wooden chair that was as unpleasant as it looked.

"It's green up in the Dakotas, ain't it?" asked the captain.

"Yessir, 'cept when it snows," answered Kidder with a slight grin as he shifted to find a tolerable position in the chair.

"So why the hell ya wanna come down to this shithole?"

The blunt question caused Jeff to shift a little more in the hard chair. His back told him to not do it again.

"To make a difference," he finally managed to say.

"A difference in what?" asked Wheeler.

Jeff watched a clump of grey cigar ash tumble onto the man's tan shirt. He didn't bother to brush it off.

"In the life of people who live on the right side of the law," he replied, pleased with his quick response.

"Ya ain't one of 'em shitwad fools who think they're gonna 'tame the west,' are ya? That ain't ne'er gonna happen."

"If it were tamed, Captain, there wouldn't be any need for men like us."

A little smile formed on Wheeler's lips. Jeff assumed his answer pleased the man. For a long moment the captain just stared at the anxious recruit, puffing so hard on his cigar that he almost disappeared behind a cloud of smoke. Jeff shifted. Wheeler stared. He had eyeballed this type of fellow before—all shiny and half-cocked with eyes that had never seen the type of trouble he would face as a Ranger.

"Ever kilt a man?" the captain finally asked.

"No sir."

"Think ya could?".

"If it comes down to it, yessir!"

"Oh, it'll come down to it. How's yer draw?"

"Some folks say I'm fast," Jeff answered with a confident grin.

Wheeler stood and adjusted his gun belt, stepped out from behind the desk, and crossed to within five feet of Kidder.

"Let's see it."

"Right here?" asked Kidder as he gratefully rose from the hard-backed chair.

"Good a place as any."

"Against you?"

"Ain't no one else here, son. Let's see it. Just don't shoot me."

Jeff took note that the captain wore his six-shooter up high on his right hip with the butt facing left, which meant he was southpaw. He remembered that the Dime Novels called that a "border draw." He also recalled that executing such a cross draw usually takes the iron a split second longer to leave leather.

"Uh, should we count to three or anything before..."

"Just draw, son!"

Kidder reached for his fancy pearl handled Colt. Before he even had it drawn and raised to four o'clock, Wheeler's pistol was winking at his belly button.

"Jesus," he muttered.

"Some folks say I'm slow," the captain said with a grin then spun his weapon to bed, turned, and with two long strides was once again seated in his padded swivel chair.

"Anyone ever passed that test, Captain?"

Putting pen to a sheet of paper and not even looking up at Kidder, Wheeler replied, "You just came purty near, but all 'em questions ya was asking 'fore you finally decided to pull told me ya think too much. When ya gotta draw, son, just do it! Don't give the other shitwad an advantage." The captain finished writing on the sheet of paper. "Here's what I'm gonna do, Mr. Kidder," he continued. "You take this note to the sheriff in Nogales." He handed the paper to Jeff. "His name's Donny Austin, friend of mine, good man. Work with him awhile. Salary'll be shit, but enough to live on fer a spell."

"How long of a spell?" Jeff asked, concerned about the limited amount of funds in his pocket.

The captain's eyes squinted slightly as he answered, "Til I decide if and when yer fit to be a Ranger."

The Dime Novels had told Jeff all he needed to know about "Nasty Nogales." Inside he was grinning. He was headed for the streets of one of the most vicious towns in the west and he'd be wearing a badge.

It took eight months of dealing with drunken cowboys, bank robbers, murderers, rapists, angry whores, inebriated Indians, wet stock and wetbacks before Kidder found himself planted back in that ass-hard chair in Wheeler's office. The captain had finally inquired of his progress with a note to his friend Donny Austin. The Nogales sheriff scribbled on the back of the same piece of paper and returned it to Wheeler.

"The man is not reluctant to pull and use that fancy Colt, barrel or butt end, whichever the occasion requires, particularly on an Injun. Killed one."

Wheeler noticed the shine he had seen eight months ago had dulled. The recruit's eyes were colder, more penetrating, more focused. The once clean-cut fellow from Dakota now sported at least a month's worth of face stubble and was in bad need of a haircut.

"Here ya kilt a man," the captain finally stated.

"No choice, Cap'n. Him or me."

"How'd it feel?"

"It was a drunk Apache, Cap'n, and he came at me with knife in hand."

Twenty-four hours later he was sworn in as an Arizona Ranger and given his first assignment.

January, 1903

The Arizona border town of Pirtleville was just stirring when the Mexican *bandito* Doroteo Arango and his men ravaged it. They were in and out in less than fifteen minutes with all the money in the town's bank, a couple dozen new Winchesters, and a corral full of horses. In their wake they left two burning buildings and three people dead, one of them a ten-year-old boy. For years the notorious robber and murderer had been raiding U.S. money shipments and rustling cattle, always targeting the wealthy. Then he'd slink back across the border and share a little of his loot with the poor. Very little. That sharing also included the Yaquis, which made him an instant *amigo* to the local tribes. In turn, they showed Arango just about every back trail and shortcut in and around the entire District of Sonora, especially in Yaqui country. He was dubbed by the locals as their "Robin Hood," though most of them had no idea who "Robin Hood" was.

Captain Wheeler ordered Billy Old, William "Sparky" Sparks, Alex MacDougal, J.J. Brookings, and the newest Ranger Jeff Kidder to track and perforate the slippery eel and as many of his men as possible.

"Rumor has it the oiler seems to frequent the area 'round the town of Cuauhtémoc," Wheeler briefed the small group of Rangers just before they were to set out. "In Aztec Cuauhtémoc means 'He who descends like an eagle.' The fool likens himself to an eagle soarin' down on its prey. In this case, places like Pirtleville. Since Cuauhtémoc is southwest of there but southeast of here, ya fellas might be able to cut the beaner off. Ifin so, nail the shitwad and as many of his boys as ya can."

A day later the small group of Rangers had Cuauhtémoc in sight. They crossed to the east of the town in an attempt to pick up the trail of a body of horses coming from the northeast.

"Whatta ya think, Sparky?" Alex MacDougal asked.

William "Sparky" Sparks was off his mount and down on one knee studying the ground. With his palm hovering about two feet above the earth, he slowly moved it left and right like he could feel the heat from the hoof prints.

"Least a dozen riders," answered Sparky as gazed to the southwest. "They skirted southwest, probably headin' fer 'em cliffs."

"How long ago?" inquired J.J.

"Ground's still warm."

"What color were the horses?" Billy asked with a grin.

Sparky chuckled and spat back, "Kiss yer grandma's butt!"

That was about the foulest thing Sparky would ever say. He never cursed. He never visited the whore houses. Besides an occasional shot of red eye, his only true vice was he could chew and spit as much tobacco as any two men combined. Head scratching the clouds at six-foot-ten-inches tall and crushing the scales at two-hundred-seventy pounds, some folks thought he was two men. He lifted one long leg over his horse, settled into the saddle, and stared southwest.

"Only five a us," he stated. "Ain't good odds."

"Guess we'll have to surround them then," answered Jeff Kidder as he spurred his horse.

"Appears that new Ranger don't believe in the dem'cratic process of votin'," stated J.J. Brookings as he watched Kidder trot off to the southwest.

Alex MacDougal turned his mount to the southwest, dug in his heels, and said, "Cap'n did say perf'rate as many as we can." He wasn't about to let the new fellow have all the fun.

Billy, Sparky, and J.J. looked at each other and sighed, then reluctantly followed the two rambunctious Rangers.

The trail was hot. The *banditos* couldn't be more than an hour ahead. With hearts' pumping and eyes wide, the Rangers picked up their pace. Forty-five minutes later that pace came to an abrupt halt.

"I don't like this," Sparky muttered.

The hot trail suddenly led straight into a narrow, winding gorge. All five animals nervously twitched, twisted, and turned in circles as their riders studied the tight entrance.

"Yeah, well, if ya liked ev'erthin' 'bout yer job ya wouldn't have nuthun to bitcha 'bout," replied Alex as he boldly entered the skinny cranny with Kidder tight on his tail.

Nodding towards the gorge Sparky said, "Could be hot grease in thar!"

"Been in it afore," stated Billy as he allowed his horse to slowly follow Alex and Jeff into the split in the rock.

"Keep yer eyes skinned!" warned Sparky.

"And yer asshole tight!" added J.J.

The jagged cranny was barely wide enough for two horses abreast, but quickly gave way to more open area, enough for three or four mounts side-by-side. Billy lightly spurred Swiss, his chocolate gelding, to get up alongside the new Ranger.

"Slow down, Kidder," he stated. "We all wanna git there t'gether." He scanned the sheer rock walls and said, "Feel like we're ridin' into a tomb."

"Might be," Jeff replied with a half grin.

Billy watched the new Ranger slip a cartridge into the empty chamber that rested under the firing pin of his Colt, then spin the fancy pearl handled revolver back into its holster. He'd seen calves like Kidder before—bucking for a fight. Most times they wound up feeding worms.

The gorge had opened up even wider, but they rode slow, keeping their eyes glued to the rocks above. At twenty yards in it twisted to the right then made a wide, lengthy turn back to the left. The walls on each side were a good fifty feet high and lined with perfect pockets for hiding a man with a rifle. After a straight stretch of about thirty yards, one more tight turn took them back to the right. There they came face-to-face with a large, bowl-shaped box canyon surrounded by solid rock walls.

"Where the hell'd they go?" shouted Alex, turning his horse in circles

With his gut instincts boiling over Sparky turned his horse and shouted, "GIT!!" His voice echoed through the rock walls as he spurred the animal like a man dancing over a rattlesnake. With his warning still bouncing off the enclosure, bullets roared down, kicking up dust and ricocheting off rocks. As he waved his hand and yelled "GIT!" once again, a bullet took off the top half of his thumb.

In seconds the Rangers were riding like hell to escape the deathtrap. At every twist and turn lead rained down. Billy felt a hot, stinging sensation cross his calf. Three rounds struck J.J. almost all at the same moment. One removed part of his ear as two others smashed into his right forearm, shattering bone and defiling his tattoo of Ol' Glory.

When they turned the final corner of their narrow grave they found the entrance blocked by burning debris. Horses whinnied and panicked and turned in circles. Another bullet creased Billy's forehead, almost knocking him from his saddle. Sparky took a second round in the soft spot of his shoulder. The men fired blindly into the rocks above. Alex MacDougal's collarbone exploded, twisting his body and throwing him from the saddle, but with his foot hung up in the stirrup. His terrified horse bolted straight for the fire and tried to leap the rising flames, dragging Alex along with it. Neither made it. The horse's mane and tail instantly ignited. Alex's dry, dusty clothes went up like a piece of paper in a campfire. He was screaming, his horse was screaming. The blazing animal bolted back into the gorge, dragging a burning Alex along with him. Kidder looped his lasso around a half-burning stretch of timber and pulled it aside. That was all they needed. Billy saw a round blow a hole in the new Ranger's side. It didn't even slow him down. They rode out of the cranny fast and hard with Kidder being the last to leave.

Twenty minutes later Billy cried out, "The horses are baked!"

They slowed to a trot.

"I'm bleedin' like a stuck pig," JJ stated with a painful groan.

Darkness was coming. Their clothes and saddles were caked with blood, but Sparky wanted them to push on just a little bit farther.

"Feather Yank done tol' me 'bout some moss 'at grows in marshes," explained Sparky through gritted teeth as he fought the pain from his wounds. "Says it's good fer healin'."

"You believe an Injun?" Jeff asked, gritting his teeth and holding his side. "What if we bleed out before we find this magic moss?"

"Ain't gonna happen," replied Sparky. He pointed to their left. "Thar be the marsh!" Although the stagnant water was unfit to drink—and no Ranger was yet willing to light a fire—it did help in cleaning their wounds. "Not the dark stuff," instructed Sparky. "Feather Yank says the light stuff be best."

The moss is sphagnum—though Sparky didn't know that—a healing agent Mother Nature kindly provided for as long as man had been collecting wounds. He didn't know that either, but he did know Feather Yank.

Cringing in pain as he scooped up a handful of the moss Jeff said, "I hope your damn Injun's right. Lucky none of our horses were hit. Raised Vermillion from a colt"

"Tweren't luck," declared Sparky. "Em Yaquis wanted our mounts. What they couldn't ride, they'd et!"

"You mean those were Injuns up there," asked Jeff, "not Arango's men?"

"Arango must've given 'em some of 'em Winchesters he stole to hold us off," explained Sparky. "Make a friend with a Yaqui and he's a friend fer life. We was lucky they weren't good with 'em rifles yet or alla us mighta still be layin' back in that canyon with po' Alex.

J.J. Brookings was first to try the sphagnum. He spread some on his ear then gingerly applied more to his damaged forearm. "I'll be damned!" he grunted. "It do cut down the burnin,' but look how 'em fuckers ruined my tattoo."

Billy helped J.J. prepare a sling.

"Have to dig this one out when we get back to the barracks," said Sparky as he pushed a wad of moss into the hole in his shoulder. Then he covered his half-of-a thumb with the healing substance and wrapped a cloth around his shaking right hand. "Good thing I'm left-handed."

"Now ya can only count to nineteen-and-a-half," teased Billy.

"How the hell'd they git outta that canyon?" asked J.J.

"Must be a slit or somethun' in 'em rocks," answered Sparky. "Yaquis prob'bly showed it to 'em!"

"Go back and find out, Sparky," Billy teased again.

"Kiss yer grandma's butt!"

Jeff was studying a handful of the moss as he voiced his concern to Sparky. "You sure this shit isn't gonna make the wound fester all up and just get worst?" he asked. "I don't trust no Injun's remedies."

"Don't use it then," Sparky flatly replied.

"It works, Kidder," insisted J.J. "Don't be a pucker-ass!"

They all laughed then grimaced at the pain it caused. Jeff finally began to doctor the wound in his side. He was stunned by how quickly the moss stopped the burning.

"Thought I was gonna go the way of my uncle that time," Jeff said to Billy, who was next to the new Ranger tending to his own wounds.

"How's that?" asked Billy, as he gingerly plunked pieces of boot leather from a flesh wound in his right calve. The graze on his forehead was minor, but the blood kept seeping into his left eye.

"My Uncle Lyman was a Calvary lieutenant," Jeff explained, grunting as he shoved some of the sphagnum into the hole in his side, just inches below his rib cage. "Lucky! Damn thing went clean through." He covered the moss with a folded piece of cloth, also pushing it slightly into the wound and continued his story. "My Uncle Lyman, along with ten soldiers and an Injun guide, was hauling dispatches to Fort Wallace when they were ambushed by a band of Cheyenne and Sioux, July first, eighteen sixty-seven. Killed every man! Chopped them up so bad Custer couldn't even recogni..."

"Custer?" interrupted Billy. He finally got his forehead dressed enough to stop the dripping irritation into his eye. "*The* Custer?" Seeing Jeff was struggling to get a long swath of cloth wrapped around his waist he said, "Lemme do that!"

"Appreciate that!" he said to Billy and cringed as he raised his arm to allow the cloth its access.

Billy pushed some moss into the round's exit hole that Jeff couldn't reach, then wrapped and tied the temporary bandage.

"Ya stretchin' my blanket," asked Billy, "bout Custer?"

"No. It was George Armstrong himself! He and his men found the bodies. They were so chopped up they just buried all the pieces in a big hole right there on that Kansas prairie. Well, 'cept for my Uncle Lyman. They were able to spot his remains by the calico shirt he was wearing. My grandma had made it for him. His pieces were sent home to his pa, my grandpa. Can ya imagine that? Gettin' a box with pieces of yer son in it? History books call it 'The Kidder Massacre.'"

"So yer famous?" asked Billy.

"Me?" replied Jeff. "Naw!" With a grin he added, "Not yet!"

Even though his uncle had died eight years before Jeff was born, at every family gathering the brutal incident would experience a rebirth. An uncle, a cousin, any relative with too much hooch in them would regurgitate it.

"Them savages couldn't just kill a man," declared a cousin while gnawing on a turkey leg and using it to point and put emphasis on his ramblings. "Them poor soldiers were sliced and hacked up into a hundred pieces, and each piece was punctured with dozens of arrows and all of them left to rot on that prairie."

Every time Jeff heard the tale it was more brutal than the last. He saw pieces of men scattered about a red-soaked Kansas prairie. Each piece riddled with arrows, making them look more like dead porcupines than anything akin to humans. He saw drunken Indians in his hometown. He saw the jails constantly filled with them. He saw their filthy reservations and how they lived. They disgusted him.

Touching the firmly wrapped dressing, Jeff said, "Thanks! I've never been shot before."

"Hurts, don't it?" Billy said with a forced smile.

"More than I thought. How 'bout you?"

"Second time—first time ri'chere." Billy tapped his chest. "Bullet went straight 'tween my heart and lung, missin' both of them by a horse hair."

"Lucky! Did you get the shooter?"

"Nope," answered Billy. "She got away."

"Oh," Jeff said with a little smile.

"Ya know, just ridin' hell bent straight into a gorge like that...well, we were lucky this time...might be wise to talk things out first. Don't wanna get famous fer bein' dead, do ya?"

Jeff smiled and said, "Good thinkin'."

It was a response that surprised Billy. No one had ever accused him of being a good thinker.

Two days later the bloodied and exhausted Rangers limped back in to Nogales, but the moss had lived up to its reputation. Rangers Langston Penny and Freddie Rankin were in the open training area to greet them.

"Ya fellas git on over to the infirm'ry," ordered Freddie. "Langston and me will take care a yer mounts."

J.J. Brookings was half conscious and began to slip from the saddle.

"I got 'im," cried Langston as he caught his fellow Ranger. Looping J.J.'s undamaged arm around his shoulder, he helped him to the small hospital.

Jeff stretched and twisted as he carefully removed the dressing from his waist. The air felt good. "Guess even a dumb Injun can be right once."

"Feather Yank ain't dumb," said Billy. "And I wouldn't ne'er call 'im that."

"You telling me you know a smart Indian?"

"Smarter 'en me."

"I find that hard to believe."

"Quit my schoolin' in the fifth grade," Billy admitted with a hint of embarrassment.

"That's still five more grades than any Injun," replied Jeff as the two walked to the infirmary. "Try livin' near one of their reservations for twenty years; enough to make you sick."

Born and raised in south Texas, Billy knew the loathing folks had for the Comanche. Working in New Mexico he witnessed that same hatred for the Utes, Pueblo, Zuni, and others. Now, in Arizona, it was the Apache, Hopi, Papago, Pima, Yaqui, Navajo, and many, many other tribes that held the wrath of the white man. But he had heard this new Ranger was supposed to be an educated man. He had gone to college. It made Billy wonder how someone with so many smarts could be so bent on putting a whole type of people into one big pile of hate.

"You can read and write, can't you?" asked Jeff.

"Smidgen," Billy said as the two slowly limped towards the infirmary.

"Smidgen is still more than none," replied Jeff, releasing a stream of tobacco juice into the dirt. "Injuns don't even have a written language."

"They got pitchers on rocks and an'mal skins."

"Pictures leave too much up to a man's eye. The written word says it, right there, in black and white."

"Written words ain't always true. Look at them broken treaties."

Jeff stopped and looked straight at Billy. "You a bleedin' heart Injun lover, Billy Old?"

Having to stop and think for a moment before he answered, Billy finally said, "No, but I respect them. Ifin ya don't, they can kill ya sure as snot from a bull."

April, 1908

It was a stormy Monday night when Sparky entered the barracks to find Billy sitting on his bunk, a half empty bottle of whiskey in his hand. The two friends had hardly spoken since Jeff's death. Sparky slipped out of his wet duster and shook it. He slowly undressed, stealing an occasional worried glance at his *compadre*. He stretched out on his bed of two mattresses placed end-to-end on the floor to handle his six-foot-ten-inch frame. For a long moment he just watched Billy sway back and forth on his bunk, his eyes half-closed, drool dripping down his chin.

30

"Ya thunk 'bout goin' to church, Billy?"

"Why?"

"Sometimes it helps."

"Won't help me none," Billy slurred.

"Ya ne'er know 'til ya try."

Standing quickly he hissed at his friend, "Well, I ain't gonna try, god-damn it." He rose and headed for the door.

"It's rainin' frogs and fish out thar, Billy!"

Stomping towards the door Billy threw his words back at Sparky. "All the hate I got in me right now, Sparky, that rain'll just sizzle offa me."

He walked out into the wet night and headed for the whorehouse. It was the one place where he could shake his head loose of "Amador, Alvarez, Quías, Pasco, Victoriano..Amador..." He even had a favorite whore, which wasn't unusual. Many fellows did. Some even ended up getting hitched to them. Jeff's was a short, thick nineteen-year-old woman from Colorado named Abbie Crutchfield.

Although she preferred Abbie, her papa had named her Abigail after the wife of John Adams, his favorite president. Widower Leo Crutchfield had a small wheat farm in the eastern Colorado flatlands, spitting distance from the Kansas border. At sixteen Leo's only daughter ran off with a roving gambler. It was no surprise to him. Knowing Abbie had a wild hair he didn't even consider going after her. Besides, he'd had his turns with her and his wheat needed tending.

The gambler took the young girl to Dallas. One week later he had his neck stretched by some angry cowboys when they discovered an extra ace up his sleeve. Another gambler took pity on the well endowed teen and whisked her off to Corpus Christi. While the two were skinny dipping in the Gulf a jellyfish stung him in the ball sack. Three agonizing days later he threw in his cards. Sure enough, along came another big-hearted gambler with eyes on those bosoms. He made the mistake of taking her to Nogales where history repeated itself. For reasons never determined, which was common in the notorious border town, the fellow was gutted in an alley less than a week after they had arrived. Alone, a thousand miles from Leo Crutchfield's wheat farm, Abbie turned to the only thing her papa ever taught her. Aware of the hazards her chosen occupation could bring, the first thing she did was purchase a boot gun.

Billy's favorite was a saucy Mexican bobcat named Retta. Since business was always slow on Mondays, especially rainy Mondays, it ended up being a very drunk night.

"Yo'no lea'me, too, Billy, *sí*?" Retta slurred as the two entered her tiny depressing room.

Laughing, he swept her up and tossed her onto the bed. "Why would I leave ya, Retta?"

"You buyme *ni'sings*, Billy?"

"Sure!" he replied, unbuckling his gun belt. "I'll buy ya nice things."

"Tomás, son-of-a-pig, he promise me *ni'sings* then he lea'me," she ranted and hopped up on her knees to reach the bottle of tequila on the night stand.

"Tomás?" Billy asked. Even drunk the name stirred some dark waters.

"Tomás *puerco*!" the whore spat in a drunken stupor. "He promise me *ni'sings* then he go 'way." She smiled, reached up and wrapped her arms around Billy's neck. "You promise me *ni'sings*, Billy?"

"Sure, Retta." He pulled her arms from his neck, placed a hand on each side of her face, and asked, "Who's Tomás?"

"Amador!" she replied, as if Billy should've already known.

His hands recoiled from her face and he found himself rapidly sobering as the names "Amador, Quías, Alvarez, Pasco, Victoriano...Amador..." plowed through his head.

"Fuck me, Billy," she demanded, writhing on the stained sheets. "Then buy me *ni'sings*."

"Where did Tomás go, Retta?" asked Billy, his hammer already soft and his mind already out the door.

"To fuckin' *putas* in Los Pozos!" the girl vehemently spat, then downed a long pull on the bottle of tequila, splashing much of it on the soiled sheets.

He had been sharing a whore with one of the murderers of his best friend. His guts tumbled. He whipped his gun belt back around his waist.

Retta sat up and asked, "Whachoo do, Billy?"

"I gotta go!" he answered, too disgusted to look at her face.

"*Ahora*?" she bellowed, rolling out of the bed and staggering towards him. "But I need you, Billy." She smiled and reached for his privates.

Pushing the whore away he hissed, "Ranger business!" He was out of the tiny, ugly room in a heartbeat, slamming the door behind him.

Retta threw open the door and shouted, *"Vuelve a mi, Billy! Vuelve a Mi!"*

Without even the slightest of a backward glance he was down the stairs to the back door. With her potential for *"ni'sings"* gone again, Retta kicked her room door closed, forgetting she was barefoot.

Billy aired his paunch the second he hit fresh air. Three times, maybe four. He stopped at the saloon and bought a two-bit bottle of the strongest, cheapest, nastiest rot gut they sold and toted it into the Ranger complex. It was late. Everyone was asleep. The place was surrounded by a weathered-grey wooden fence that featured a gate with hinges so rusted it no longer closed. A wide training area was in the center. Stables and a corral were to the north. The south side featured Captain Wheeler's office, the armory, and the small infirmary, while a run-down barracks filled the east. It was akin to a decade-old, abandoned military post in both size and rotten condition.

Standing in the open training area Billy slipped out of his high-top leather Justins and put them aside. Then he stripped down to bare skin and tossed his clothes in a heap. Uncorking the retched whiskey, he dumped most of it on the clothing. He filled his mouth with the vile liquid, but didn't swallow, just swished it around to rinse out the tastes of vomit and Retta then spat it out. He poured the remainder on his private parts. It burned like hellfire, but was an atoning burn. He stepped back from the pile of whiskey-soaked clothes and slipped back into his Justins. Then he lit a match and dropped it on the pile.

Something stirred a sleeping Sparky. Maybe the igniting whoosh of the liquor soaked clothes. Half awake and groggy he raised his six-foot-ten-inch frame and peered out the barrack's window. There was a naked Billy Old standing in front of a small fire.

"Ma, Billy's necked!" he mumbled and plopped back down to sleep.

Billy dug a small hole and buried the ashes. It took every ounce of control to not leap on Orion and head for Los Pozos, but he couldn't. He was still a Ranger. He couldn't take off on a one man vendetta. Captain Wheeler would never allow it. He had taken an oath and respected it. Besides, all he had on were his boots.

Knowing his men as he did, for two full months the cagey captain gave Billy no assignments, just kept him around headquarters doing horseshit tasks.

He kept asking Wheeler if anything was going on in or around Los Pozos, hoping he could get an assignment that would take him down there.

"Why there, Billy?" Wheeler asked, having a pretty good idea.

"Uh, there's a whore down there I'd like to see agin." He was not a good liar.

Wheeler scoffed, "Shit, ain't got enough of 'em here fer ya to unload yer baggage?" In very firm words the captain also reminded him that no charges were ever brought against any of the Mexican policemen. No warrant was ever issued. No "special permission" was given by General Torres to go after them. "I hate it as much as you, Billy, but 'em's the cards and we gotta play 'em!"

So Billy stopped asking and started waiting. For how long he had no idea, but it didn't matter. He knew the hatred inside him for the *hombre*s who took his friend wouldn't die soon and wouldn't die easy. Neither would they. Still, whenever he'd cross paths with a Mexican policeman he'd study his face to make certain he wasn't "Amador, Alvarez, Quías, Pasco, Victoriano... Amador..." but hoped he was. He knew all of them except Victoriano. That was the only face he couldn't see. The only name he'd never heard. He'd find out though. All he had to do was get his hands on one of them. And according to Retta, that "one" was enjoying the whores down in Los Pozos.

For weeks he shoveled horseshit, fed and brushed down livestock, cleaned every rifle in the armory more times than he could count, and swept repeating layers of dust from the barracks. It wasn't until mid June that he was finally given an assignment. To his dismay it would take him north to the old San Xavier Spanish mission, not south near Los Pozos. Rumor had it that the Mexican priest at the mission was once a notorious cattle rustler named Acosta Benito.

"Ya want me to a'rest a priest?"

"I want ya to find out if it's him," replied Wheeler. "If it ain't, fine! If it is, I'll leave it up to you."

It wasn't like Wheeler to give vague orders. When he sent a Ranger after a man it was damn certain he was to bring him back in the saddle or over it. Another strange part of this assignment was that Billy was sent alone. Rangers where usually sent out in pairs. He had left Nogales late in the day so he and Orion camped outside the barrio of Amado, about half way to the old Spanish mission. The captain's words kept running through his head. "I'll leave it up to you." Again he wondered why he was sent alone. For six years his friend was at his side, ready to defend him, ready to make him laugh, and always dropping little kickshaws of knowledge that Billy would store up like a squirrel. He lit his pipe and stared at the stars.

"Think Jeff is on one a them stars by now?" he asked Orion. The black snorted and bobbed his head. "Prob'ly up there watchin' us, don't ya think?" Orion snorted. "Wish I could figger whichen he's on."

He knew his pa was on the one at the top corner of the cup in the Big Dipper. His friend Henry Anderson was on one he saw only four times a year just before sunrise. His ma was on the first one he saw every night. That comforted him.

Two days later he walked back into Wheeler's office. The captain looked up from his paperwork and asked, "Well, was it him?"

"I asked him flat out, Cap'n, ifin he was Acosta Benito," answered Billy. "He hung his head a second then looked me square in the eyes and said, 'Si, Ranger. I have taken the vows of a priest and cannot lie. I hope God can forgive my past.'"

"The law don't forgive, Billy."

Ya said yer were leavin' it up to me, so I leaved him be. Want me to go back up there and bring him in?"

"No," Wheeler replied. "I needed to see how much hate was still cookin' in ya, Billy....if ya could still do yer job." The tall captain sat on the corner of his desk. "Ain't ya ever wondered why I teamed ya up with Jeff in the first place?"

Confused, Billy replied, "Use to! After 'while it didn't matter much. We got to be pals. He was the best man at my weddin'.

"Jeff liked the quick draw," explained Wheeler. "He was a damn good Ranger, Billy, don't get me wrong, but quick to pull. Yer not. Ya reason things out. He wanted to be famous. You just want to be a Peace Officer. I figgered it might've been a good balance.

A moment passed as a confusing fog lifted from Billy's head and he asked, "So ya knew that there priest was Acosta all the time?"

"I also figgered ya needed a day or so away from shovelin' horse apples," the captain grinned.

Billy stood for a long moment, not knowing exactly what to say. He knew the words that finally left his mouth were probably not what his captain wanted to hear.

"Cap'n, I ain't forgivin' them assholes who put Jeff under." He turned and left the office.

February, 1909

Several of the fat asses up at the territorial seat had their greedy fingers in many pies, always seeking ways to feather their nests if the territory ever became a state. Many didn't like that the Rangers were being used to break up strikes, even though many were the ones who ordered the Rangers to do just that. Instead of trying to reason things out, they just tore down a wall that stood between the good and the bad. They disbanded the Arizona Rangers.

It was a dark day when Captain Wheeler crammed the remaining seventeen Rangers into his small office. The men knew right away that something was haywire. Wheeler had never ordered all seventeen men back at headquarters at the same time. Billy saw men he hadn't seen in years. Some he thought were dead.

"Em legislature fellas say we done accomplished our jobs, men." Shocked groans and hisses came from men who had put their lives on the line for the past eight years. "Maybe if 'em fat assed shitwads would spend a day down here 'round the border, they'd sing a different tune." Agreeing shouts filled the room. "But we can't fight the gov'ment, boys. Orders are orders! All of ya are gettin' two months pay. He knew that amount would run dry before many found other work, simply because many of them had never known any other kind of work. "I want ya all to know, I'm proud of ya," he said, finding it difficult to raise his head and look at the men. "One thing I ask of ya: Never forget yer brothers—the ones who died, and the ones in this room right now." He shook every man's hand and gave each a personal flask with an engraving that read, "Arizona Rangers, 1901-09." The men were touched, grateful, saddened, and angered. They dispersed quietly, no one certain of which emotion they should chew on the hardest.

Billy stormed into the barracks. He had given eight violent years of his life. He had lost friends, including his best friend. It had cost him his marriage and contact with his two boys. He yanked the skinny mattress off his bunk and flung it across the room, knocking the piping from the pot belly stove and adding black soot to the layers of orange dust. He had thought his time with the Rough Riders had been the worst in his life, but this day trumpeted over every one of those mosquito filled jungle days. This was his home, his life, his reason for being, the only thing that made him feel worthwhile and not just some asshole taking up space.

Sparky walked in a minute later and grinned at the mess Billy had created.

"Good thing we ain't gotta clean this place no more."

"What the hell ya smilin' at, Sparky? Ya happy 'bout this shit?"

"Course not. Ain't nothun we can do though. Sometimes ya jist gotta move on, Billy."

"Move on to what, goddamn it? What the hell do we move on to?"

"God'll guide ya, Billy."

"Shit," Billy mumbled.

Then Jeff's voice bounced around his head and five names flashed across his mind: "Amador, Alvarez, Quías, Pasco, Victoriano...Amador..." hated names that were tattooed on the insides of his eyelids. He let that hate cool the burning in his guts and shake his brain back into focus.

Billy looked at his tall friend and said, "I think maybe He just did, Sparky."

Using the Ranger's private wire service he sent messages to every Arizona border town that had a sheriff, repeating the names..."Amador, Quías, Alvarez, Pasco, Victoriano...Amador..." Then he sent a wire directly to the local policeman in Los Pozos. He knew that was risky. If Tomás Amador was there, it could alert his prey, but he played a hunch. Knowing the Mexican police, he figured the original one in Los Pozos wouldn't take kindly to another one being forced on him, especially in such a small town. The last thing the man would want is a pissing contest over who was in charge. Besides, there might not be enough whores to go around. Within an hour he got an answer.

The telegram read, "Still here, still a *puerco*."

It was a little over seventy miles from Nogales to Los Pozos. He went to the bank and withdrew the money he had been squirreling away for ten months and turned it into silver dollars and five dollar gold pieces, along with a couple of twenty dollar pieces. He stashed the coins in a hidden pocket on the underbelly of his saddlebags then gathered a five day supply of oats, beans, bacon, coffee, jerky, and tobacco for his pipe. He was well aware of the little bugs in Mexican water that would knot up a man's guts and leave him shitting and puking at the same time. He didn't even trust the well water in the center of the small towns across Sonora. The only safe water down there came from springs, and they were as rare as a flea-less hound. He filled six canteens with fresh water and draped them over the lizzy on Orion's saddle. The ornery animal snorted a complaint about the added weight.

"Deal with it, shithead!" he scolded. "Yer a goddamn horse!"

Their first night on the trail was cold, but he didn't dare anything but a small fire. No sense in attracting the wrong guests. Even though it was the twentieth century in the rest of the world, Mexico hadn't figured that out yet. He slipped on his *chaqueta* and turned up the collar to protect his ears. He pulled out his pipe, tamped in some tobacco, and lit it with a burning twig. Puffing lightly, he leaned back and stared into the small flame. It reminded him of how his mother would sit and pray late at night while staring into the hearth in their farm house. Each night she'd repeat the same words: "I praise good thoughts, good words, and good deeds. I reject all bad thoughts, bad words, and bad deeds." He always felt those were good words, but it wasn't until years later that he'd find out why his mother only spoke them into the face of a fire, and only after his father was asleep. He thought about his own two boys, and how it had been quite a spell since he'd seen them. He wondered if they would even recognize him, or he them.

"When this is over," he told himself, "gotta go see 'em." Then he warmed his palm around the heat from his pipe's large bowl, a fancy buffalo head carved from a single chunk of ivory.

March, 1902

"That's quite a pipe you got there," Jeff remarked.

Wheeler had sent the two up to Flagstaff to escort the murderer and rapist Calhoun Small Toe from a holding facility and down to Yuma prison. Because of the fat asses' tight budget the two Rangers had to make the eight day ride up to the northern town on horseback, but were allowed to take the train back down to Yuma with their prisoner. This was their first assignment with just the two of them together and their first night on the trail. Billy wondered why Wheeler had paired him up with this new Ranger. Usually on long trips he'd be partnered with someone familiar, like Sparky or Freddie, maybe even Feather Yank.

"Hand-carved ivory," Billy proudly stated and held the pipe up for Jeff to see.

"You carve it?"

"Naw!" answered Billy as he stretched out on his bedroll. "My pa won it in a horseshoe match. Only thing he left me."

"Sorry!" Jeff replied.

"Yer Pa leave ya anything?"

"Hope not. Last I heard he was still 'bove ground."

"Up in the Dakotas?"

"Up in Oregon. My folks divorced and he moved up there. My ma moved to Los Angeles. She got tired of all the snow and cold. Made her bones ache. Gets pretty damn cold up in the Dakotas!"

"Like tonight?" Billy asked.

"Colder."

Billy shivered and said, "Wouldn't like that!" He tightened the blanket around his shoulders. Nodding towards Jeff's holstered Colt stretched across the saddle next to his head he asked, "Why ya pack such a fancy piece?"

"So a certain low element of our society can plainly see I'm wearin' a gun." He pulled out the fancy Colt and handed it to Billy. Its metal was darker than usual, but not from age, gunpowder or dirt. It was made that way so the mother-of-pearl handle would glow like an Indian moon.

"Nice weight!" remarked Billy. He spun the weapon once and returned it to the new Ranger. "Ever use it on a man?"

"Barrel-cocked a drunk Apache back in Nogales," answered Jeff. "Thumped him two good ones. Heard he died a day later."

"So ya didn't see him die? Ya weren't close up?"

"Nope! But I imagine I will."

"Ya won't like it."

"What about you?" Jeff asked. "How many?"

"One. Just one. Wounded a few—don't know if they made it—but I do know one didn't, saw the life leave his eyes. Ain't easy snuffin' out a man's lamp—ain't a good feelin'—like ya lose a little chunk-a-yer own soul." Billy's eyes momentarily wandered up to the sky full of stars. Then he added, "I notice ya ain't totin' a long rifle."

"Wild Bill Hickok once said there are two times when you need to look a man in the eyes: when you thank him, or when you kill him," explained Jeff. "Oh, I got nuthun against using a long rifle against a band of crazy, drunken, reservation Sioux. Don't want those fuckers anywhere near me. Not only do they stink like no other Injun, they're too damn good at knife fighting. And I'll use one when I go huntin'—picked off a mule deer at a hundred and sixty yards once—one clean shot, two inches above his brisket."

"How'd ya know Hickok said that?"

"Read it in a Dime Novel."

"Shit," spat Billy. "Them things are best used to wipe yer ass."

"Maybe so," Jeff said with a grin, "but they're fun readin'. Besides, a fella can't get famous by shootin' from a distance."

"Why do ya wanna get famous?"

Jeff bit off a chunk of chew and replied, "Hundred years from now I don't wanna be just another name on a cracked tombstone in some bone yard overgrown in weeds."

"Most folks are," Billy replied with a chuckle.

"But the ones who aren't, the ones who leave a mark, are the ones who did something to keep from being forgotten, and most of the time it's something good, something worthwhile."

Billy had to give that some heavy thinking. He'd never thought of himself as someone to leave a mark. He was just another fellow doing his job. A long silence followed as both men stared at their small fire. Finally Jeff broke the stillness.

"Where ya from, Billy?"

"Uvalde, Texas."

"Uvalde, Uvalde," pondered Jeff. "Why do I know that name?"

"Beats me! Only thing there is goats—goats here, goats there—whole damn town smells like goats."

"Goats! Sure! Angora goats! That's it! A big bunch of all the mohair made in the U.S. comes from there. That's why I've heard of it."

"Mohair?" What the hell's mohair?"

"Well," it's kind of a silk-like material made from the hair of Angora goats. Makes nice sweaters! Real soft! Women folk love them!"

"What's a Angora goat?"

"A special kind of goat from Tibet!"

"What's Tibet?"

"Little bitty country next to China."

"China? Ya mean them goats I growed up with were chinks?"

"Well, their eyes are a little slanted."

After their laughter died Billy asked, "How the hell'd ya know that, 'bout them goats?"

"Few years back my pa bought six of them for our farm. I didn't know much about raising them so I read a book."

"A book?" Billy was amazed. "There's a damn book 'bout raisin' goats?"

"It was just a little one," answered Jeff as he held up his index finger and thumb and separated them by less than a quarter-of-an-inch. "Only 'bout yay thick. We didn't have them long. Winter took two, wolves took three, and pa gave the last one to our half breed worker. He probably ate it."

Billy chuckled and said, "A book 'bout goats."

"Hell, they even got books about raisin' dogs."

"Dogs? And folks read that shit?"

"Yeah, folks do."

"Do you?"

"I read the one about goats, didn't I?"

Their laughter was followed by another long silence. Billy leaned back on his saddle and relit his ivory pipe, studying this smart yet congenial fellow sitting on the other side of a fire barely big enough to roast a frog leg.

"How'da ya 'member all that shit?" asked Billy. "That's crammin' a lotta stuff inna small space; gimme a headache."

"There's a lotta room up there."

"Guess I'm too stupid to grab it."

"Where do Angora goats come from?"

"Teebet, little country next to China."

"See! Ya ain't stupid! Ya learned that."

"Dropped my book learnin' in the fifth grade."

"You don't learn everything from books. I had a history professor in college named Colin Temple—old coot, well into his sixties, maybe seventies. Kept a spittoon right in the classroom and could hit it dead center from six feet or better. He'd spit, that wad would ping into that spittoon and when he made it he'd say, 'Andy Jackson!' his favorite president. When he missed, which wasn't often, he'd say, 'Ulysses S. Grant!' his least favorite president. Just from those shots at that spittoon we learned the goods and bads about those two presidents. He told us some things about history a fella could never learn from books. Some of the best learnin' comes from just listenin'."

Billy watched Jeff toss a few more small twigs into the flame then cup his hands over the rising heat for a moment. Maybe it was the way this fellow from Dakota talked, or the way he shaped his words, or the calmness in his voice—smooth, clear, soft, never top-lofty. Whatever it was, Billy liked it.

"Maple?" asked Jeff as he sniffed the aroma from the pipe.

"Yep."

"Nice! Covers up the horse shit!"

"Use to watch my pa make it. He'd take tobacco leaves, we grew a little on our farm, soak them in maple syrup and let them sit in the sun fer two days. Then he'd grind them up and smoke 'em."

"You do that, make your own?"

"Naw!" All store-bought anymore!"

Another long moment passed.

"Think you'll ever go back?" asked Jeff, once again being the one to crack the silence. "To Uvalde?"

"Maybe. Heard they built an op'ry house in ninety-one. Kinda like to see it."

"The house or an opera?"

"I guess if ya see one, ya gotta see t'other, doncha?"

"Good thinkin'!"

A few quiet moments passed then Jeff asked, "How long since you been home?"

"Left in eighty-eight. Was fourteen!"

"Damn! You're a year older than me but look five years younger. What's your secret?"

"My ma always said I got a baby face. Hated that! My pa always said I look like my ma. Hated that, too! Ain't it better that a boy look like his pa?"

"Depends on whose traits are stronger," commented Jeff. "Yer pa's or yer ma's."

"Well, them traits done decided wrong. Like I said, a boy should look like his pa. Anyways, truth is I think all that keeps me lookin' young is beans, beer, and whores."

It felt like their laughter lasted close to a minute, but was again trailed by another long silence.

"Fourteen's pretty young to leave home," Jeff finally remarked, hoping it might spur an explanation, but Billy just sat there puffing out clouds of smoke. Then he asked, "How long you been a Ranger?"

"Year!"

"What'd you do before?"

"Just cowboyed 'round. Did a short hitch as a deputy 'til I signed up with the Rangers. Well, 'cept fer some time with the Rough Riders." He wasn't sure why he made that last statement. It angered him that his tongue had pushed it from his mouth.

"You fought down in Cuba?" asked Jeff, sitting up on his bedroll and freeing another stream of tobacco juice.

"Yeah!" Billy took a double pull on his pipe and made an uneasy shift of his body.

"With T.R.?"

Again slightly shifting his position, Billy huffed, "The fuckin' ol' bear himself!"

Jeff sensed this was a sore subject. There was reluctance, maybe disgust in Billy's voice, but his curiosity was fired. "What was it like?"

"Hell, Jeff, yer the college boy who's read all them fuckin' books, ya should know!"

The irritation in Billy's voice was clear as glass. If the fire would've been brighter Jeff probably could've seen the hair go up on his neck. Reclining back on his bedroll he said, "Well, I know we had four times as many killed and wounded than the Spanish."

"And the dumb shits still called it a victory!" blurted Billy. "All them men chargin' up that fuckin' hill and gettin' cut down like hay under a sickle! It started out fine, the enlistment, I mean. We were called the First U.S. Voluntary Calvary. It was just some good ol' boys, Texans, cowboys, Buffalo

Soldiers, even a few Injuns. All of us were decent horsemen. Had to be! When that fuckin' T.R. came on board, though, we started gettin' in all them Eastern bluebloods. Some of them still wearin' 'em silly lookin' choke-bored breeches. There was athletes like football players, baseball players, fellas whose only ridin' was in them fuckin'—whatcha call 'em?—poolo games! Even golfers and tennis players, and goddamn Glee Club singers! Yeah! Can ya fuckin' believe that? Glee Club singers! Shit!" With his rant beginning to subside, Billy took a few long pulls on his pipe and just shook his head in disgust. "Buncha kno-theaded dumb shits!" But that fuckin' ol' bear led them up that hill anyways! None of them knew how to fight. None of them knew how to die."

He couldn't understand why he had let those words pour out to this new Ranger. For years his time with the Rough Riders had been a heavy stone lodged in his gut. He couldn't puke it up, couldn't shit it out.

"Hell," Billy added, I still see them legless football players and jawless glee singers in my dreams."

Jeff stirred the fire and said, "That ol' professor I told ya about—Colin Temple—he fought in the 'War of Northern Aggression,' as he used to call it. He told us about other fellows who fought in it who hadn't had a full night's sleep in twenty years, fellows who'd fall to the ground at loud noises, fellows who used to wake up stabbing their wives with a rusty bayonet in the middle of night. Things like that can fuck you up in your head. But you made it back in one piece and you won. That's what counts." Jeff warmed his hands again and began humming "Red River Valley."

March, 1909

A church with a recent bath of whitewash was the first thing that welcomed Billy to Los Pozos. It gave off an eerie angelic glow in the afternoon sun. He also noticed there was no trash in the streets, not even dog shit. A few children were counting and playing *escondidas*. He saw that many adobes had also been freshly whitewashed. The corral was placed on the north side so the pushy south wind would carry its stench away from town. He couldn't imagine a pig like Tomás Amador being content here. It was too clean, too nice, and far too quiet.

Then a bullet blew off his hat.

He dove off Orion and landed hard on his belly, but with gun in hand. Two more bullets struck the ground in front of his face, spraying dead earth into his eyes, nose, and mouth.

"*Vete al diablo, Ranger!*" screamed a policeman as he ran up the street towards Billy, a *pistola* in each hand. He fired wildly on the run and again screamed, "*Vete al diablo, Ranger!*" Tomás Amador had spotted the black horse with the white star on its forehead just minutes after the two had ridden into town.

The earth that coated Billy's tongue and filled his nose was turning to a choking mass. His eyes watered and burned as he kept spitting out more mud and dirt and firing wildly at the charging man. Amador was firing downward, which usually was an advantage, but what the Mexican policeman forgot was that running on an afternoon's worth of tequila wouldn't help his aim.

Billy had the advantage.

One of his bullets hit the beaner's left forearm. It didn't even slow him down. He kept coming, kept running, kept shooting, kept yelling. The tequila had deadened his pain.

Amador had the advantage.

Lead was striking all around him, pelting his face with more Sonora dirt. At a distance of about twenty feet he saw a red hole appear two inches above the bridge of Amador's nose. Since Billy was firing upward, a lucky shot had found the top of the policeman's forehead and cleaved his skull open clear down to brain matter. His entire body lifted two feet into the air, floated backwards, and plowed onto the earth with a heavy thud. Then all was quiet. Billy spat out a mouthful of mud and jumped up. Wiping the sweat and dirt from his face with his bandana, he hurried over to the very dead Mexican policeman.

"Goddamn me!" he shouted and kicked up some dirt. Trying to question this *hombre* on the whereabouts of the others, and just who the hell Victoriano was, would prove a hitch with half his head missing.

A voice came from behind. "Holster the weapon, *Señor!*"

Billy froze.

The voice sternly repeated itself. "Holster the weapon, *Señor!* NOW!"

Billy carefully bedded his Smith & Wesson and turned slowly. It was another Mexican policeman, but the man wasn't even holding a weapon. His *pistola* was buckled inside his service holster. He was also clean shaven, which was a rare practice with Mexican police. His hair was neatly trimmed and tucked under his cap. His uniform was crisp, not sweaty and soiled. He didn't even smell.

"Self defense, so a*dios, Señor*," the man insisted.

Billy realized this was the fellow who answered his telegram with the five word message, "Still here, still a *puerco*." He pulled a silver dollar from his pocket and flipped it to him.

"Plant him," he ordered.

With a half grin the officer flipped the coin back to Billy and said, "It is on me, *Señor*."

As Billy leaned over to pick up his newly ventilated John B a familiar pain shot through his jaw: that hellacious first sign of a tooth going bad. He'd had a few yanked before and wasn't looking forward to what could trail this ache. When he straightened up the pain fled. He sighed in relief. Climbing back on Orion, he stole a side glance down at Amador's body. A thousand flies had already turned his red cleaved head into a black, writhing mass. "Funny," he thought as he gazed at the dead policeman, "Just kilt a man and I ain't feelin' poorly 'bout it."

"*Adios, Señor*," repeated the policeman.

Holding on to Orion's reins, Billy turned the horse to the left, then to the right, then back to the left, and back again to the right. Then it hit him. His lack of smarts had left his ass puckering in the wind. He had plunged head first into this pursuit of Amador without even thinking about his next move. The word "knothead" swirled around his head. He knew he had just enough supplies to get back to Nogales, but none of the men he was after were there. They were cowering under the rocks that covered thousands of miles of Sonora County. He wanted to ask the clean policeman something, anything, but what, he had no clue. He scolded himself again, "Knothead, stupid knothead!" For the first time in years he had no assignment, no destination, no plan. Not even a home to return to. He knew Jeff would've planned his next move. Jeff was smart. Jeff would've wounded Amador just enough to bring him down, but he was a better shot and a quicker thinker, even flat on the ground. Orion snorted in frustration, anxious for a direction to take his rider.

Sensing his hesitation, the policeman repeated for the third time, "*Adios, Señor,*" and smacked Orion's butt.

By no choice of their own, Billy and Orion were heading south, deeper into Sonora County. Again he cursed his ignorance.

February, 1906

"Why the hell'd ya go and volunteer us fer this crap?" Billy bitched at his friend.

"What're ya complainin' about?" responded Jeff. "It's easy duty and we're inside. Besides, I thought you could use the extra pay now that you're a married man."

"Ain't I gone enough from Anna without you addin' an extra night?"

"Then look at it this way: we're learnin' somethin'."

"Learnin'?" miffed a frustrated Billy. "Learnin' what? I don't un'erstand a fuckin' word 'em flannel-mouthed fat asses are sayin.' Judikal recall? Woman's sufferin'? What sufferin's are bein' brung down on what woman, and who's bringin' it?"

He and Jeff were positioned inside the entrance of the Nogales town hall staring at the backs of about twenty well-dressed fat asses seated facing a small platform. On the platform were three other fat asses with hind ends overflowing their three chairs. The group had been palavering about Arizona becoming a state. The even fatter asses up in Washington had dubbed Arizona as "a crude land of scoundrels, ne'er-do-wells, and savages" and wanted to make New Mexico and Arizona one state. The people of the Territory of Arizona felt they had earned their own identity. Aware of the town's reputation, the men who had come down from the Territorial seat had requested some Rangers for protection. Captain Wheeler figured this could be something his only college-educated Ranger might find interesting. He offered the extra-duty-extra-pay job to Jeff, who readily volunteered Billy to come along.

"*Judicial* recall," explained Jeff, "simply means that we'd have the right to fire judges who aren't doin' a good job. *Women's suffrage* means givin' women the right to vote."

Billy was stunned. "Women wanna vote?"

"Sure!"

"Why?"

"Why not? They live in this country, too."

"Anna ain't ne'er said nothin' 'bout wantin' to vote."

"You ever ask her?"

"No."

"Do!"

After another moment Billy asked, "Whores, too?"

"Whores, too," Jeff answered with a chuckle.

"Then why the hell are 'em fat asses coyotin' 'round like that? Why don't they just spit it out in a way us stupid folks can un'erstand?"

"Damn it, Billy, you're not stupid! Stop sayin' ya are!"

"Fifth grade, Jeff," Billy fired back in a frustrated state of self-loathing. "Fifth fuckin' grade."

"See that?" declared Jeff. You knew right where to put the word 'fuckin.' Right after fifth and right before grade! Fifth fuckin' grade."

Baffled, he looked at Jeff for a moment then said, "Shut the fuck up!"

With a big tobacco stained grin, Jeff stated, "Got that one right, too!"

Laughing too loud earned the Rangers several chiding glances from various well-dressed fat asses. To one who held his nasty glare a bit too long, both Rangers presented their middle fingers. A week later they were summoned into the captain's office. Wheeler was mad as a pissed-on turtle as he waved a letter in their faces.

"That little gesture ya pulled at the meetin' last week got me this," he fired at them. "Do either of ya knotheads know who Henry Ashurst is?"

Billy and Jeff glanced at each other then gave Wheeler a clueless shrug of their shoulders.

"He's the Coconino Country District Attorney," hissed Wheeler, "and he don't 'preciate bein' given the high sign by two a my Rangers."

"Why are you upset 'bout what some fella clear up in Coconino County thinks, Cap'n?" asked Jeff.

"Ya know what they call him?" inquired Wheeler.

"Horse's ass?" responded Billy. Both Rangers burst out laughing.

"Shuddup!" shouted the angry captain. "They call him 'The Silver-Tongued Sunbeam of the Painted Desert,' 'cause he's such a smooth talker."

"That's quite a handle," remarked Jeff.

"Sure is," added Billy. "Must take a purty big biz'ness card."

The two men laughed again. Then the captain slammed his fist down on his desk and they quickly swallowed their amusement, remembering that Harry Wheeler could have them shoveling horse shit for days if he got the itch, and he appeared very close to getting it.

"People listen to what he's got to say, bellowed the captain. "And right now he's sayin' some purty shitty things 'bout us, and shitty things 'bout us can make others up in the territorial government cut our shitty fundin' down to even shittier than it is. To make things worse he's a shitty Democrat and they ain't ne'er liked the establishin' of the Rangers anyways. So yer dumbass stunt was just that...a shitty dumbass stunt that could cost us some jobs!"

"Sorry, Cap'n!" Jeff stated, struggling to hide a smile. "We didn't know how shitty he was."

"Yeah, Cap'n," added Billy. "All them shitty fat asses look alike in them suits."

Wheeler glared at the two men then finally said, "You will both write a letter of apology to the man. I want 'em on my desk 'fore the day's done. Got that?"

"Yessir," replied Jeff.

"Now git outta here," Wheeler clamped some angry teeth down on an innocent cigar.

"Uh, Cap'n?" asked Billy. "Could we write one letter and botha us sign it? I'm purty shitty at letter writin'."

The captain hesitated for a long moment, cold eyeing the two men before finally answering, "Alright!" Then he shifted his eyes directly to Jeff and added, "But it better be good!"

After the two Rangers left Wheeler's office Jeff stopped outside the door and turned to Billy.

"Yer not gonna get away with not addin' anything to that letter. I'm not doin' it all myself."

"Hell, Jeff," replied Billy with a devilish grin, "I don't even know how to spell 'pology.'"

Jeff's eyes tightened as he leaned in close to Billy's face and said, "I'll teach ya, goddamn it!"

"Fifth fuckin' grade!" Billy reminded his friend.

"That's a shitty excuse, Billy!"

March, 1909

He jerked Orion to a halt and said aloud, "Hold it!"

The black released a snort that sounded like "Why?"

"If that Gen'ral Torres is any kind of Gen'ral, he'd have punished them fellas by sendin' them to the towns with the most Yaquis." Orion snorted again, this time in agreement. "That's where the trouble'd be. But we'll need more supplies." Orion snorted in agreement. "San Moise," Billy declared.

The town was just a two day ride south and big enough for him to purchase more supplies. How many, he had no idea because he didn't know where they'd be headed after that, but at least it was a starting point. He gave Orion his head.

The land between Los Pozos and San Moise mirrored the rest of Sonora—bleak, dry, and hot. Pockmarked with bristly shrubs and creosote and jojoba bushes, it was like riding through a painting by an artist who only owned three colors: brown, yellow, and a small dab of green for the occasional cactus. No wildlife was in sight, at least not when the sun was hungry. It was on the third day when Billy saw the buzzards. About a dozen of the skin-eaters were circling and swooping down on something in the brush ahead. Orion snorted at the smell seconds before the hot south breeze pushed it into Billy's nose.

He patted Orion's neck and said, "Yeah, I caught it, too, Big O."

Carefully they pushed through the high thickets and underbrush and came upon a small clearing. The sight they saw caused Orion to snort and shake his head and Billy's guts to tumble. Eleven dead, half-eaten Apaches, five men, three women, and three children lay in eleven grotesque positions. The ground around each body had soaked up most of the blood, but couldn't hide a lingering reddish-brown stain. All had been scalped and left to be feasted on by the neighborhood occupants. The women had been raped, front and back, probably after they were shot. Apache women fight like hell. From the number of bullet holes in each body Billy figured at least four men had to have done this carnage.

"Scalp hunters," he mumbled in disgust.

August, 1903

"I tell ya," exclaimed Sparky as he knelt over the bodies of two children, "either 'em Injuns who done this scalpin' had some purty dull knives, or they was jista learnin' 'bout scalpin'!"

"Why?" asked Freddie.

"I seen a 'Pache take a scalp afore. Grab, slice and pull! Slick as a weasel! 'Em here kid's haids look like they done been hacked and sliced I don't know how many times."

Just as Jeff was turning away from the sight in disgust a shout came from behind the burned farm house.

"Got a woman back here!" cried Billy.

The men had been on the trail of some rustlers when they spotted wisps of smoke in the distance. Freddie, Jeff, and Sparky hurried to the other side of the smoldering structure. Billy was standing over the naked body of a woman laying face up in the high grass, obviously the two children's mother.

As they approached, Billy warned them, "It ain't purty!"

Again Jeff had to turn from the sight. He crossed back to his mount to fetch his E-tool. "Let's bury them," he insisted.

Right then Sparky called out, "Got some tracks o'chere!"

He had wandered several paces to the west of the empty corral. Billy and Freddie joined him to eyeball the tracks. Jeff kept moving towards a cottonwood. He wanted the bodies underground right this minute. Even with growing up hearing such morbid tales of Indian attacks and knowledge of his uncle's brutal demise, he had never seen a scalped body and didn't want to look at it any longer. He had three holes to dig; one large, two small. He dug in quiet fury, jamming his e-tool into the dry earth, chopping through tree roots, upturning rocks and tossing them aside.

"One horse," declared Sparky, "Headin' west! It ain't Injun though. It's shod."

"The husband?" asked Freddie.

"What?" asked Billy, "Ya thinkin' he hightailed it outta here and left his family to them Injuns?"

"Don't think it twere Injuns," declared Sparky, still studying the ground. "Don't think it twere Injuns at all. No Injun's gonna make such a mess a scalpin.' They just ain't! A scalp's too powerful a med'cine to hack up the ways thesechere folks bin done."

"I don't get it," said Freddie. "Whether Injuns did this or not, why ain't there more tracks 'steada just this one set?"

"Looky chere!" insisted Sparky, who was pointing at some disturbed dirt. Billy and Freddie hurried to him.

"See how the ground is mushed down?" directed Sparky. "I think whoever done this ragged their horse's hooves to cloud their trail. Em other tracks o'er there, the shod ones, be deep, meanin' that there fella took off like a bat outta hades. Question is, be it from bein' 'fraid, or bein' mad?"

"Well," exclaimed Billy, "while ya two figger that out I'm gonna help Jeff dig."

When Billy reached the cottonwood he saw that Jeff's cheeks and neck were pale, but his forehead was a steaming red hot. It looked as if he couldn't decide whether to upchuck in disgust or explode in anger.

"Never seen anything like that, Billy," Jeff stated without stopping his shovel from stabbing and scooping up the dry land. "Never seen anything like that anywhere."

The other two Rangers helped Jeff and Billy finish the graves and bury the woman and two children, all the while listening to Sparky try to unknot the mystery. They agreed to follow the single set of tracks for a spell. An hour later they wished they hadn't. Lying next to a small water hole were three dead Apache children, two boys and one girl, all around seven or eight years old. Their throats had been slit and they had been scalped in the same clumsy and crude manner as those back at the farm house. The trail of the single rider continued west.

"Jesus," muttered Freddie. "What the hell's goin' on out here?"

"Keep following the tracks," Jeff spat.

"Should we bury them kids?" asked Freddie.

"Let 'em rot," Jeff coldly stated. "Let their folks find them like we found those white kids."

"We don't touch 'em," warned Sparky. "Don't git yer scent on any of 'em."

The Rangers left the small, mutilated bodies untouched and continued following the lone, shod tracks. As they crested a hill blanketed in tall grass they spotted a camp by a stream.

"Jicarilla," noted Sparky. "Can tell by their wickiups."

The four men, riding side-by-side, Jeff to Billy's right, slowly descended towards the Indian camp. Before they were even halfway down the high grassy slope, eight braves came galloping out, all armed. They stopped about fifty yards from the Rangers, also lined side-by-side.

"Lemme go it 'lone," stated Sparky.

"No fuckin' way!" declared Jeff as he tightened the grip on Vermillion's reins.

With a jerk on his mare's reins Sparky turned directly in front of Vermillion, blocking Jeff's path. With eyes tight and teeth gritted he ordered, "Haul in yer horns!"

Billy saw Jeff's eyes tighten. He knew that look well so he quickly shifted Orion to his friend's right where Jeff's fancy Colt rested. With cold eyes Jeff leaned towards Sparky, having to look up into the big man's face.

"I see the slightest twitch from any of them red assholes I'm comin' down this hill a-smokin', Sparky. Ya better duck."

The three Rangers hung back and watched the tall Ranger descend the hill. They didn't do it because Sparky was in charge. They simply all knew when it came to dealing with Indians, no one was better suited.

"*Da go te'*," Sparky called out to the warriors as he raised one hand in the air and purposely zig-zagged his horse down the slope as a sign for a palaver. Billy chuckled to himself when he saw every Indian in that line mumble to one another about this huge man who made his mount look like a colt.

One brave muscled up some courage, spurred his pony a few steps forward, and yelled, "*Deeya, deeya!*"

Sparky knew that meant "leave," but he stopped his horse about forty feet from the Indians, climbed off, and slowly walked towards the brave, keeping both hands in the air.

"*Da go Te, Da go Te*," the big man repeated.

The brave finally dismounted and walked towards Sparky. While the tall grass was waist high to the Jicarilla, it barely reached Sparky's knees. The other Rangers could see the whites of the brave's eyes grow large at the sight of the giant man approaching him. If there was a Goliath in any of his Indian children's tales, that brave was about to meet him. When the two were only ten feet apart, Sparky tapped his chest.

"Sparks," he said, his deep voice resonating down the hill and causing the Indian ponies to stir.

"*Litso Chinii*," the brave stated loudly, also tapping his chest and trying to not show fear of this large white man, but the quiver in his reply said different.

After several loud sentences the small Apache's fears subsided enough to allow the two to come within five feet of each other. That also brought their conversation down to a level out of earshot of either group of tense onlookers. The Rangers watched the brave point back towards the camp, then gesture up the hill. Sparky listened and nodded his head. Just like that the palaver was over.

Taking a step backwards, Sparky raised his hand and said, "*A-key-yeh!*"

The brave took a step backwards, raised his hand and said, "*Egogahan!*"

The brave climbed back on his pony and the warriors headed back to their camp. Sparky stepped onto his mount and returned to the Rangers.

"Well," he explained, "it ain't good. They done got the farmer down there in the camp. Said he came ridin' in screamin' and shootin', kilt a squaw and 'nother brave afore they could stop 'im. Said he was all crazy mad killin' fer no reason. I told Yellow Dog, that was that fella's name, 'bout the farm and the woman and chillin. He says they din't do it. I believe him."

In a caustic tone Jeff asked, "Why?"

"Paches hate lies. Oh, they might twist the truth a bit, but I could see from the look in that brave's eyes when I told 'im 'bout the farm and 'em folks, they din't do it. Near as I kin figger 'em farm folks were killed whiles the farmer was away. He comes back, finds 'em all scalped and dead and figgers 'em 'Paches done it. Went crazy and charged into this 'ere camp."

"What about them Apache kids by the water hole?" Freddie asked.

"Din't tell Yellow Dog 'bout 'em. Jicarilla be very pertec'ive of their chillins. That might've riled 'em so they'd done took it out on us. 'Sides, that farmer din't kilt 'em kids."

"Who did?" asked Billy.

54

"Same skunks that kilt 'em farm folks," answered Sparky. "It'd take more than some farmer to sneak up on three 'Pache kids and cut their throats."

"So what's gonna happen to the farmer?" asked Jeff.

"Oh, it done happened. They cut off his Johnson and ball sack and let him bleed out."

"Jesus!" muttered Freddie.

Jeff exploded, "Godless pig-fuckin' animals! Can't they just kill a man outright?"

"Killin's killin'," responded Sparky. "Makes no never mind how it's done!"

Jeff gave Sparky a hard look and said, "How about a bullet to the head? Quick and clean!"

Although Sparky had trouble recalling a great many things, Jeff's feelings towards Indians wasn't one of them. He certainly wasn't going to argue with him on a hill overlooking an Apache camp that would soon realize they had three missing children.

"Well," Sparky said, "anyways ya look at it he's with his wife and kids now."

Jeff was livid. "So we're just gonna let them fuckin' Injuns get away with killin' a white man?"

"Yea, we are!" Sparky said forcefully. "We're gonna ride outta here, alla us!"

Sparky could easily pluck Jeff right out of his saddle, toss him to the ground, and simply sit on him until he cooled down. Billy watched his friend's tense body wisely ease. But the hate in his eyes didn't.

Ever the mediator and trying to ease the friction between Sparky and Jeff, Freddie asked, "So who kilt the woman and kids back at the farm?"

"Yer guess is as good as mine," answered Sparky, pulling his face from Jeff's and sitting up straight in his saddle. "Below the border ya kin still git five dollars a scalp, ya know! Don't much matter what color it be."

Sparky turned his horse towards Nogales. Billy and Freddie followed. Jeff gave one last glare down to the Jicarilla village then spurred Vermillion to join the other Rangers.

Chancing that the *restaurante* in San Moise was clean enough to not reacquaint him with that rascal Montezuma, Billy downed a sort of hot supper of *tamales* and rice. After the meal he sat sipping a mug of warm, skunky-smelling Mexican beer, offsetting its bitter taste by sprinkling in some salt and pulling several tokes on his pipe. At the same time he used his finger to trace out a crude map on the dusty table. His years with the Rangers had taught him that the best place to get information about the Mexican police is from the people who hated them the most: the peasants and the Yaquis. If the peasants had a problem, the police were only willing to help them in exchange for food, which they had little enough of already, or some private time with their daughters. The Yaquis had no love for any kind of authority. Unlike the Apache, who were basically roaming hunters, the Yaquis set up permanent villages, even towns. Like the Apache, though, they were fierce warriors. Their enemies had been coming at them for centuries—the Tolmecs, Aztecs, Spanish Conquistadors, Apaches, and now the Mexicans. Since they surrendered to Mexican rule in 1901, 15,000 had been rounded up and sold into slavery on Yucatan plantations. The Yaquis had no love for the Mexicans, especially the Mexican army and police. Since Yaqui country was a hot bed of trouble, Billy hoped General Torres had enough decency in him to plunk Jeff's killers down in the thick of it.

Recalling some of the towns along the route he figured if he didn't go straight west towards Yaqui country, but veered in various directions, he could resupply in those towns. Also, by changing directions, Orion might not be so damn cantankerous. One of the black's more frustrating quirks was that he disliked taking the same trail twice, and especially backtracking. Billy had never known a horse with such a keen sense of direction and such an irritating streak of stubbornness.

He wiped his finger on his vest and studied the crooked trail he had made on the dusty table top. Each change of direction was the location of a town. He knew the names of those towns, but had no idea how to spell them. So for each town he just made a little circle in the dust. He also had no clue of what supplies would be available so it left a pretty big unknown to his plan. But it was still a plan, and he'd concocted it. Just like Jeff would've done.

"We're not gonna just ride in all willy-nilly!" declared Jeff. We don't know which of those four buildings they're in, how many there are, or how well armed they are. "I don't think any of us want to be another ghost in that ghost town.

"Sparky," taunted Billy, "Go take a look!"

"Kiss yer grandma's butt!"

"So what's the plan?" Freddie asked.

Until Jeff Kidder arrived, Billy and Sparky had always considered Freddie as the thinker of the group. After a few assignments with the Ranger from South Dakota, Freddie gladly passed that burden to Jeff. Freddie was the most cautious of the foursome, probably because he had the most to lose: a daughter who lived with his parents. The girl's mother had died giving her life. That was eight years ago so no one knew Freddie when it happened. Billy assumed it must've stung him deep because he won't visit the whorehouses. He says he wants to "keep himself clean for the next mother of his daughter." Freddie's parents owned and operated a very successful dry goods store up in Bisbee. They had hoped their son would join the family business, but Freddie was never content standing behind a counter doling out feed and eggs and clothes. They feared yet respected his decision to become an Arizona Ranger. Along with Billy, Freddie was one of the first to enlist in the Rangers. He was twenty-six and the smallest of their group, standing at just a boot heel over five feet, but he was thick and solid. Billy had nicknamed him "Boulder."

Sparky was a bit more reluctant in accepting Jeff. Not as part of their small band, but as a leader or planner. Sparky was leery of Jeff always seeming to be at half cock, too ready to put his quick draw to the test. Born and raised in Nogales, along with two brothers and three sisters, Sparky had grown up witnessing his fair share of viciousness. He also knew many of those incidences could've been avoided if men weren't so anxious to kill. When he applied to be a Ranger, Captain Wheeler knew the simple-minded fellow would probably have trouble driving nails in a snow bank, but from growing up with such a collection of childhood friends, Sparky spoke Spanish, Apache, and Yaqui better than he did English. Since he had yet to find a flaw in any of Jeff's previous plans he rarely voiced a concern, but always kept a close eye on the newest Ranger's temperament. If Kidder seemed too spunky Sparky would speak. All would listen.

The four Rangers were hidden in some rocks on a small hill overlooking the ghost town of Trigger Point, which sat a half-day east of Redington near the Galiuro Mountains. It was an old silver town that managed to birth only four buildings before the pale gray metal was played out and the residents sought richer ground. Three of the buildings were on the east side. A single story attempt at a hotel was on the south end. Behind it were the collapsed poles that once supported the tents found in mining towns that sprang up overnight. The canvas had long rotted away. A saloon rested in the middle and a general store on the north end. The lone building on the west side was a livery next to a small corral.

Feather Yank, Wheeler's favorite Pima scout, had informed the captain of a gang of cattle rustlers that were using the town as a hideout to alter the brands on stolen beef. From there they would drive their misbegotten herd south to Willcox and peddle it. The problem was the Pima had no idea how many men were in the gang, so neither did the Rangers. Even from their vantage point they could see no movement in any of the abandoned buildings left to the appetite of that hungry old bitch Mother Nature.

"Wish that damn Injun would've stuck around long enough to get us something more useful," complained Jeff.

Peering through his binoculars, Freddie said, "I think we can whittle it down to just the three buildin's on the east side." He handed the glasses to Jeff. "Take a hard look at the livery."

Jeff scanned the building and asked, "What am I lookin' for?"

"Ain't no glass in them windows," Freddie pointed out.

With a hint of sarcasm Billy reminded him, "It's a goddamn ghost town, Freddie."

Ignoring Billy, Freddie said to Jeff, "Keep watchin' them busted out windows!"

A few moments later Jeff's body slightly stiffened. "Something's moving in there." He slowly lowered the glasses and exclaimed, "Cows! They're keepin' the stolen cattle inside that old livery."

"Usin' it as a crowdin' pen to cross brand them critters," added Freddie, "hidden away from pryin' eyes."

"Bet it stinks to high heaven in thar," said Sparky.

Freddie pointed down the hill and said, "They gotta be in one of them three buildin's on the east."

"Three buildings, four of us," said Sparky. "Which buildin' gets two of us?" The other men looked at Sparky. Baffled by their staring he asked, "What?"

Billy grinned and said, "That's pretty fast cipherin', Sparky!"

"I can count to twenty, durn it!"

"Nineteen-and-a-half," Freddie reminded him. "I say we go in two from the North, two from the South, aimin' only at them east side buildins."

"Work our way to the middle," nodded Billy in agreement.

"Let's work them to the middle," Jeff stated. "Get them all trapped in one place!"

"How?" asked Billy.

"We do like Freddie said, two from the north, two from the south, but we set torch to the two end buildings."

"Let the fire do the work' fer us," agreed Freddie. "Why not?" Then he looked at Billy and mimicked, "It's a goddamn ghost town."

"What if they gots more cows in 'em other buildins?" asked Sparky. "Hate to burn up some po' cows."

"Go down there and check, Sparky," Billy teased again. "We'll wait here fer ya."

"Freddie, let's you and me take the north," stated Jeff.

"Ya did take note of there bein' very little cover on that side, din'cha?" commented Freddie.

"Freddie," Sparky jokingly pointed out, "someone left a purf'cly good buggy on that end a town. Ain't got no wheels, but a lotta ripped up canvas fer ya to hide b'hind."

Jeff turned to Billy and Sparky and said, "You two gotta give us ten minutes to circle 'round and get in place. We need to light both fires at the same time to drive them into that center building." He pointed to the rocks below their hill. "Then squat down in those rocks and we'll have them in a cross fire when they come out."

"Sounds good!" replied Billy, dropping to his belly. "Let's make like snakes, Sparky!"

"We got rocks, Freddie," Sparky grinned and taunted as he laid his six-foot-ten-inch body on the ground and began crawling down the hillside. "Ya squat that little body of yers down in that ol' rottin' canvas, ya here?"

"Kiss yer grandma's butt, ya overgrown turd," replied Freddie. "Hope they shoot yer dick off."

"Too small of a target," Billy said as he punched up his crawling to stay clear of his big friend's crushing hands.

Twelve minutes later the four Rangers were in position. Each team stuffed dry grass and straw against the sides of the rotting buildings and lit it just seconds apart. In less than a hare's heartbeat the two weathered and cracked tinder boxes were blazing like they were soaked in lump oil. The speed of the spreading fire shocked them all. Sparky and Billy quickly squatted behind the rocks at the south end of town while Freddie and Jeff struggled to find any kind of cover behind the old buggy.

"This cover ain't fer shit, Jeff. Damn canvas ain't gonna stop a slug."

"Maybe they'll see Sparky and just give up."

Even though the flames were across the street they still scared the patties out of the mossbacks. They mooed, wailed, kicked, and banged against the walls of the livery. Three men hurried out of the former saloon to check on the ruckus. As soon as they reached the center of the street they saw the flames in the two end buildings eating the dried structures and already nipping at the edges of the building they had just left.

"Arizona rangers! hands up!" yelled Jeff from the north.

Almost simultaneously Billy yelled from the south, "Arizona rangers! Hands up!"

The men didn't oblige. All three drew and began firing in the direction of the demanding voices. They backed towards the former saloon, sending wasted ammo into the air, nowhere near the hidden Rangers.

"Ya damn fools," yelled Jeff. "Don't go back in there!" No Ranger had yet fired a shot.

The flames ate the rotten wood like giant termites. Smoke was already pouring from the middle building. The men inside fired wildly out the windows.

"They gotta come out," declared Billy. "They're gonna roast in there."

Suddenly a scream overpowered the sound of burning timber. A woman carrying a baby ran from the building. Her hair and dress were on fire. Before she even reached the center of the dusty street, so was the blanket around the infant.

"Oh no," Jeff found himself saying and started to rise and go to the woman. Freddie yanked him back.

"Ya can't help them," he said, as the woman and baby fell to the ground in a screaming, twisting, burning mass.

One of the rustlers ran from the middle building to help the burning duo, but failed. Dropping to his knees he pounded the ground. His hands and head lifted to the sky as if pleading and the Rangers heard him release a piercing scream. He then raised his gun to his temple and pulled the trigger.

"Jesus!" muttered Freddie.

A young boy about eight or nine ran out of the same building, his clothing also on fire. He was sprinting south, screaming and swatting at the flames, and straight towards Billy and Sparky. In just three long strides Sparky had ripped off his duster and reached the burning child. He wrapped him in his coat, threw him to the ground, and desperately tried to smother the blaze. Then the burning roof of the middle building collapsed.

For a long spell the four Rangers didn't speak. They had no idea how many cooked bodies were still in the building, and really didn't want to know. Since the woman and baby were fused together from the heat, they only had to dig two graves.

Just a half hour later Sparky buried the boy he tried so hard to save. Even though Freddie offered to help, the big man swallowed the pain of his singed hands and dug the fourth grave alone.

"How were we to know?" Freddie finally muttered.

"If that goddamn Pima would've done his job we would've known!" Jeff spat with venom. "How can you miss seein' a woman and kids, fer crissake?"

"It weren't Feather Yank's fault, Jeff," said Billy. "They were rustlers! They picked their callin', all of them!"

"You're okay with killin' a woman and kids, Billy?" Jeff fired at Billy. "Now that you got a couple of babies are ya really okay with that?"

"No, I ain't! But there ain't nothun we can do 'bout it now, is there? Sometimes, sometimes good plans just go bad."

"So it was my fault, huh?" asked Jeff defensively.

"Nobody said that, Jeff," interjected Freddie. "We all agreed to fire them buildings."

"But it was my idea, damn it." Pointing at the fresh graves Jeff added, "I have to live with this."

"We all gotta live with it," declared Sparky as he removed his hat. "I think we oughta say a prayer."

The other Rangers removed their hats and Sparky said The Lord's Prayer. While the others whispered "Amen," Billy hoped the man and woman and baby would end up on the same star. Without any more words the Rangers mounted their horses. It was a long, slow, quiet ride back to Nogales.

March, 1909

His room at the San Moise hotel was about the size of four one seater privies placed side-to-side and back-to-back, forming a perfect square. The small bed offered a straw-stuffed linen bag as a mattress. It rested on crossed leather straps attached to an old wooden frame that he hoped wouldn't collapse under his weight. Being an even six feet tall, he knew his feet would dangle over the end of a structure built for shorter people. The yellowed pillow cost him an extra ten pesos. A sharp pain punched his jaw. "Ain't got time fer ya now," he muttered to himself then pulled out his flask and soothed the tooth with a blanket of tequila. He was aware of the whereabouts of the many towns on his tabletop map, but had only actually been to a few of them. He knew his plan was a big gamble, and he hated gambling, but it was a plan, and he had made it. He wished he could hear his friend say "Good thinking." Finally the toothache calmed and sleep defeated the short bed.

Something was in his room. He felt a presence, but his eyes wouldn't open. From far away strange sounds began to fill his head. They started low and muffled then slowly increased in volume until they were raw and heavy and packed with pain. Muscling up some courage he finally opened his eyes. Eleven Apaches, five men and three women were standing at the foot of his bed. The men were moaning and swaying while the women were sobbing and holding the three limp bodies of their papooses. All were pointing to the tops of their heads, but none had tops of heads. They were bloody masses with no hair and pieces of exposed brain throbbing and oozing in the moonlight shining through the hotel window. He gasped, closed and opened his eyes again, then sat up quickly. The room was empty, but he could still smell death. It took him a good hour to fall back to sleep.

Early the next morning he purchased a week's worth of supplies, saddled Orion, and tossed them across the black's rump. The testy horse snorted and twitched at the excess weight. Billy grabbed Orion's jakoma and pulled his head low enough to whisper into his ear.

"Ya heard a the automobile, shithead?"

Orion let loose a defiant snort that sent snot exploding into the dirt, but wisely stopped his twitching.

Checking his six canteens of water Billy discovered a bullet hole in one that must have come from the weapon of Tomas Amador. He pulled the empty and ruined canteen from Orion's saddle. Shaking it, the lead slug inside sounded like a baby's rattle. He held it up in front of the horse and patted its neck.

"Yer lucky, Big O! This piecea lead woulda ripped up yer innards."

There was no sense in buying another canteen and filling it here in town. The bugs in the local water would leave him laid up and running at both ends for days. For now, five canteens would have to be enough.

One boot was in the stirrup when something caught the corner of his eye. He turned to see four men riding slowly into town. An old familiar tingle climbed up his spine and rested like a red burr on the back of his neck. He couldn't recall the first time he had it. All he knew was that it came every time he spotted a bad man and had yet to fail him. Right now that burr was itching like a fat bite from a thirsty Cuban mosquito.

Hanging from the lizzys on the rider's saddles were several pigging strings, each boldly displaying enough scalps to make wigs for a hundred bald easterners. A horrid odor trailed them. Billy wasn't sure if it came from the scalps or the rangy men themselves. One rode an Appaloosa, a rare horse down here. They were bred by the Nez Perce up in Idaho. There was no way these scalp hunters would venture that far from the safety of the Mexican border. Billy figured the man probably took the horse from an Indian he had scalped, and that dead Indian had probably traded for it or stole it from another Indian until the mount had finally worked its way this far south. He also noticed the hooves of the men's horses were blanketed with tattered burlap sacks to help cover their trail. They lumbered past him, staring straight ahead. Here was a *gringo* clad in *gringo* clothing, alone, this far south, and they didn't even give him a second glance. He was insulted. The town noises soon surrendered to the sound of the out-of-tune player piano in the *cantina*.

The Peace Officer in him was screaming for a rebirth, but had no right to one. He ached to just pull his Smith & Wesson and Colt .45 automatic and air-hole all four of them, even in the back if need be because they deserved no better. Then use his knife to add their hair to the hideous collections swinging from their saddles. He knew that was what Jeff would've done, regardless of their number. The four men tethered their mounts in front of the *cantina* and entered. He couldn't believe they had left their bounty unattended. These scum buckets had truly put the fear of the godly bullet into the people of San Moise.

He led Orion to the front of the cantina and tethered him to a post a few feet from the scalp hunter's mounts. Stealing a fast glance into the *cantina* he saw all four *hombres* were bellied up to the bar while the bartender frantically filled their glasses with rye. Quick as a whistle Billy snagged all the pigging strings of scalps, grabbed Orion's reins, and led him two buildings to the west. Even though he carried the strings at full arm's length the vile stench still drifted into his nose and caused Orion to snort in disgust. He tossed the bounty into a pile in the middle of the street so when the hombres left the saloon they'd be certain to see it. Then as he leaned over to light the disgusting swag a twinge of pain again shot through his jaw.

"Told ya I ain't got time fer ya," he stated and lightly smacked his jaw with the palm of his hand.

The hair torched fast. The smell from the burning pile reminded him of the foul odor of burning locusts when the farms around his home town had to clear their fields of the hungry insects. He spurred Orion to the northwest.

For two days he kept a tight look over his shoulder in case the assholes had caught wind of his doings. He was relieved when the town of Banori, the first one on his dusty table top map, came into view. He took a deep, satisfying breath. Even though the barrio was nothing but a hump in the earth so small a caterpillar could've crawled from end-to-end holding its breath, it meant the first part of his plan was in granite.

The tiny place didn't even have a policeman and apparently didn't receive many visitors because the one road through was suffering from an outbreak of fat, one-foot-tall, undisturbed anthills. Orion carefully dodged them, not wanting hundreds of angry, stinging little pests crawling up his legs. The only supplies Billy could scrounge up were a half-pound of oats and a few *tortilla* patties. The small *cantina* did have enough *mescal* to replenish his flask, but smelled like it doubled as a stable. The bar was a weathered, warped board balanced across two empty barrels. When leaned on it sported enough splinters to pierce even the most shirted of elbows. Two old men were at a table playing checkers, of course. The bartender was seated by them cheering on their moves and taunting their mistakes. A whore was passed out on the floor. She was so skinny it looked as if she could slip through the floor board slats and fall into the crawl space below. For a moment Billy thought she was dead. Then she groaned, rolled over, and he wondered how many anthills her grandchildren would be kicking down today.

The two camped for the night a few miles west by a small, fast flowing creek, water he felt was safe enough to refill a canteen. He unsaddled Orion and slipped on the nosebag of oats, then cooked himself a handful of beans and wrapped them in some tortilla patties. The cool, clean creek water made for good, strong coffee. Jeff's voice bounced around his head and made him smile.

"I swear, Billy, I could float a horseshoe in yer coffee."

Orion snorted and stomped his hoof so Billy removed the nosebag and rubbed his friend's nose. He crossed to his bedroll, relaxed and pulled out his pipe. After tamping down and lighting the maple flavored tobacco, he leaned back against his saddle and watched the stars slowly blink on. Usually they comforted him. They were steady, always there. Tonight, for some reason, they made him feel very much alone. It was nights like this when he and Jeff would talk until dawn. It troubled him that he hadn't been able to decide which star his friend was on. He knew it would have to be one that moved around a lot because Jeff wasn't a patient man. Maybe one of those stars that shot across the night sky in one direction then came back from another direction, always heading for some new adventure. He figured that was probably what Jeff would like. The man craved new assignments. If he wasn't chasing down a bad man, he was at the whorehouse or saloon. He'd groom Vermillion three times a day, practice his quick draw, clean his fancy

Colt, and sometimes just roam the streets of Nogales on the prod. Billy knew Jeff truly believed he was destined to become a Dime Novel hero, at almost any cost. So he made it a point to always be right alongside his reckless friend. He had taken it upon himself to keep this hotheaded temple of knowledge and good humor above ground. He'd lost a close friend in the past by not being around and he wasn't going to let that happen again. But it did. Once again he wasn't there when a friend was put under and it ate at his guts every day.

He stretched out on his bedroll and listened to the fast flowing water. He hoped he'd see one of those stars that shot across the night sky. At least then he'd know his friend was watching over him and knowing what he was doing. But it was a night without shooters. He let the sound of the creek lull him to sleep.

Retta was floating down the creek straddling a log. With her dress hiked up to her waist, he could see the often visited mound of dark hair snuggled against the bark. Spotting his campsite she began yelling for her *"ni'sings"* and frantically hand-paddled to the shore. The log slid smoothly onto the moist bank. She hopped off and began running towards him laughing and throwing off her clothes, but it wasn't the body he knew. This Retta was skinny, weathered, and old. So skinny she slipped right down into an anthill screaming.

He woke up the next morning with a rock solid boner. It angered him that the whore who was also servicing one of the killers of his best friend could still stir him that way. He thought the rot gut red eye had cleansed his privates and his mind of Retta. It seemed to have, until now. So why did he dream about her? Maybe he needed to unload some baggage. It had been several weeks. Maybe more. Standing by the small creek he dropped his trousers, knelt down, and doused his privates with a hatful of cool water and watched his member slowly collapse.

"Don't do that agin," he warned it.

Several days later, after making a swing to the southwest, Billy and Orion reached the town of El Veracruz. It was hardly any bigger than Banori. At the local *cantina* he was greeted by a jolly, kettle-bellied policeman with open arms who even treated him to a shot of tequila. In passing Billy mentioned the names..."Amador, Quías, Alvarez, Pasco, Victoriano...Amador..."

"Ah, *Señor* Ranger," the happy *hombre* said, "I know many men with those names, but no policemen."

Once again supplies were almost nonexistent, along with fresh water. He wondered what that policeman could be feeding on to have grown so fat in this nothing of a town. He did manage to procure a partial bowl of cold *pozolé*. Even though he figured it was possibly someone's leftovers, definitely not the fat policeman's, he downed it quickly. The stew was tasty and still a bit warm, but only padded his belly by a smidgen. More empty tortilla shells and a few beans again, that was it. The smithy did sell him a small bag of oats for twice its worth. He knew a man could last near a month without food, but Orion starts to bitch if his breakfast is late.

The bartender offered him the only room in the back of the *cantina*. When he went in to check it out he found a hole in the roof the size of a wheel barrel. The floor and the small cot were covered in piles of bat guano and bird shit. He thanked the man but declined the offer, making the excuse of how he liked to sleep under the stars.

El Gabino was northwest of El Veracruz and one of the few towns on his dusty map that he had visited several years ago on another of the Ranger's many fruitless pursuits of Dorotéo Arango. He was certain it was a place where he could replenish his supplies. They were getting low and he was tired of just beans, jerky, and tortilla shells. Perhaps he might even be able to sleep on something more pleasing to his back than the hard ground. As he shifted and stretched in the saddle to help relieve the stiffness, Orion started nervously twitching and snorting. They were at the outskirts of El Gabino.

"Easy!" ordered Billy, as he patted his friend's neck. "What's eatin' ya, shithead?"

Billy could feel Orion's muscles tighten under him. Something was stressing the animal. Usually this was a warning of danger, but there was no one in sight. The street was empty, not even a stray dog, just dead silence.

"Where the hell is ever'body?"

Without being spurred Orion snorted, bucked a little, and picked up his pace, anxious to get them clear of whatever danger he was sensing. Then Billy noticed the yellow flags hanging on the doors of practically every building in the town.

"Shit!" he muttered. "Cholera! Fog it, Big O!"

The black leapt into action. They were clear of the barrio within seconds. After another fifteen minutes of hard riding, Billy pulled Orion to a halt and climbed off. As the horse searched for some rare vegetation, Billy stooped down and tried to recreate his map in the dry Sonora earth.

"We're in a pickle, boy," he finally declared. "If we don't wanna be more parched bones in this shithole we gotta swing north to Colonia Reforma, and we're both gonna be purty damned hungry by the time we git there. Can ya handle it?"

Orion snorted and bobbed his head.

"And keep yer nose open fer some fresh spring water."

By the time they reached Colonia Reforma, they were in an endless duel of grumblings exploding from their empty bellies. Orion won with one loud enough to chase a scrawny, barking dog back into an alley. Billy stabled the black with a plentiful nosebag and then filled his own belly with close to a dozen *tamales* and several warm beers at a small *cantina*. Besides hard liquor, beer was about the only safe liquid to drink below the border. The *tamales* were tasty, but his temperamental tooth forced him to chew on just one side of his mouth. He figured he could live with that until he could find a dentist and get the damn nuisance yanked. Providing Mexico has such a person.

When trying to get a hotel room a surly clerk rudely informed him that they were all filled up. The man's demeanor told Billy he obviously didn't want a *gringo* defiling what he mistakenly considered a fancy facility. He was finally able to land a small shack at the south end of town from a bartender who didn't care whose money he got as long as it was money. It was a nasty, dirty, cobwebbed filled structure with barely enough room to turn around. It had a small cot with a yellowed mattress that smelled like year-old sweat and piss. But it did have a roof with no holes in it. He flipped the thin mattress over and placed his tarp on top of it so the occupying bedbugs would have to fight through an extra layer before they could feast on him.

Colonia Reforma offered two whorehouses, which was unusual for a town its size. Still, very few of the whores would even talk to him. When they did, it was all business. With the exception of the greedy bartender who rented him the shack, the remaining town folk chose to steer clear of this *gringo* stranger, too. Neither of the local policemen would even speak to him.

"*No habla!*" they'd reply and start to walk away. So he tried Spanish, and to that he got a cold and firm, "*No compréndé!*"

He split the next two days between the two brothels drinking and lounging in the parlors and studying faces. To insure himself of not having another dream about Retta, he unloaded some baggage with a big, feisty redhead with green eyes that could send a fellow into a trance.

After acquiring more beans, jerky, pipe tobacco, oats, a few airtights of peaches, beef biscuits, and tomatoes, and some withered yet edible carrots, he saddled Orion and left the unfriendly town.

It had been years since he had spent this much time riding alone and it was giving him too much time to think. He would hear things he couldn't see and see things that weren't there. Even though it had been many weeks since he had burned those scalps, he still found himself peeking over his shoulder. Were those scalp hunters hunting him with as much vigor as he was hunting his prey? No one saw him take the hair. At least he didn't think anyone did. Maybe some kid was hidden in one of the buildings peeking out a window. Maybe some drunk was lying in an alley and saw the deed. Maybe there's something about Orion's hoof prints that make them easy to track, but his path had been too erratic and twisting, mainly to keep the horse happy. Besides, they would've surely lost track of his hoof marks among all the others in the towns he had passed through. He wished his friend was riding on his right, covering his back like he did for six years, telling him stories, teaching him little tidbits of history and two dollar words, joking about anything and everything. Even his bitching about Injuns would be a grateful earful.

"Fuckin' knothead!" he mumbled. "If Jeff was here ya wouldn't be here anyways!"

He killed off the airtights the quickest, especially the ones with peaches. For the next several days it was jerky and hard sinkers. They barely filled his belly and would send his tooth into a throbbing frenzy that was only soothed when bathed in *mescal.* Looking forward to some soft food and beer, he was relieved to see the distant adobe buildings of Toritos to the southwest. A satisfying smile forced some of the dust on his face to tumble down on his vest. The town was right where his tabletop map said it would be.

It was a short lived smile. Barely more than fifty feet into the town he was greeted by three mounted and uniformed men. Not the usual soiled, tan colored police uniforms. Each of these men wore two ammo belts strapped in an X over dark blue shirts. Their brown breeches were covered by *chaparejos* lined with studded silver conchas stretching down the length of the leg and stopping just above identical shiny chiuahuas' with wide metal rowels. They even sported matching white sombreros. All three packed shiny new Winchesters.

Some Mexican towns established a Rural Guard known as Rurales. They were a no-nonsense bunch of well-armed vigilantes with military training. One of their jobs was to discourage any corrupt policemen from even considering their peaceful *barrio* as a possible haven. They also didn't care for any former Arizona Rangers hanging around, unless he was decorating a cottonwood. With three rifles pointed at him, Billy was escorted straight through to the outskirts of Toritos. They passed a *tasajero* where the smell of the smoking beef spilled from the building. His mouth watered. He could picture the carcasses slowly being smoked in large ovens. Even though he asked in polite Spanish if he could at least gather a few supplies, the Rurales simply shook their heads and guided him and Orion to a sign that read, "*Gracias por la visita Toritos.*" A Rurale said one word, "*Vamose!*" They showed him their mount's asses and spurred them back towards town.

"Obliged, assholes!" he yelled as the men rode off.

Without looking back, one of the Rurales raised his hand and extended his middle finger.

"Fuck!" Billy mumbled. "Some damn plan!" Orion snorted in agreement. Billy looked at the horse and said, "Oh, and I s'pose you could come up with a better one?"

It was a ten day ride to Quitovac, the next town on his crude map. It rests on the edge of one of the most inhospitable deserts in Mexico. To reach the Rio Yaqui, the river where many Yaquis established their villages and towns and where he hoped the Mexican police would be the thickest, he'd have to cross that desert. Problem was he had only three days of supplies. He figured he could stretch them out to last five, maybe six, but those last few days were going to be belt-tightening. He had lived off the land before, but usually in a place where the game was tastier than bony sage hare and rubbery lizard. He knew one of the most abundant meals in a place like this was rattlesnake. With all its venom in its fangs and not in its body, a man can eat its meat without croaking before dessert. Of course, the critters had to be pulled out of hiding, snagged, their heads cut off, and skinned. They didn't take kindly to that. And the goddamn head can still bite an hour after it's been hacked. Rattlers don't go under easy.

His calculations were close. He and Orion finished the last of the jerky, sinkers, and oats the morning of the seventh day. With no beans or vegetables to balance his diet he could feel his bowels becoming potgutted. He hadn't relieved himself in three days. Still being a far cry from Quitovac, he had to do something to loosen his innards. He thought the wild onions would help, but all they did was make his breath strong enough to down a fly in flight. So he turned to another desert treat. Prickly pears are small purple, grape-like objects that grow on the ends of cactus, but like rattlers, they also have a way of biting back. He had to wear gloves to pick them or they'd bless his fingertips with several nasty, little, painful thorns that felt like he'd just rested his hand on a red hot griddle. Next, they have to be rolled in the dirt and washed to completely remove the thorns, then sliced into strips and cooked. But even after devouring several of the bland tasting pears, his bowels wouldn't move. Every step Orion took jarred his innards. The only thing that briefly relieved the discomfort was a good, long fart. When the two finally reached Quitovac, he found himself in an odd state: starving yet plugged up stiffer than a new pair of boots.

He stabled Orion with a full nosebag. The small *restaurante* specializing in green chili might be the solution to his clogged bowels. He knew drinking the local water would help release his innards, but it would also lay him up in some seedy hotel room for near a week. He gobbled down two bowls of the powerful green mixture, which was made with the local water, but boiled to a slightly safer consumption. Twenty minutes later he was frantically seeking a public privy. The trots stayed with him for the rest of the day and dried up his innards to the point that he finished an entire canteen of his safe water.

Quitovac wasn't a large town. It only featured one cantina that, naturally, doubled as a whorehouse with no extra rooms to let. Once again, a friendly bartender came to his rescue. The young man owned two old tents at the edge of town. They were specifically for letting to travelers. He had a roof again, even though it was canvas. As in all the towns he had visited, the answer was the same though: No one knew any policemen by the names of…"Amador, Quías, Alvarez, Pasco, Victoriano…Amador…"

The young bartender told him the trip across the desert would take at least two weeks, if he didn't get lost. "No *pronto* desert," explained the bartender in broken English. "*Jornado del muerto.*"

Billy knew exactly what he meant: a journey of death. He had traveled his share of deserts and knew he could not rush across, especially the one he was facing. After a few more tequilas, a couple more beers, and some deep thinking, he determined five canteens would not be enough. He purchased a small pot and rigged up a fire pit outside the tent to boil enough water to get his canteen supply back up to five. He also bought two *tinajas* from an old woman at a street pottery booth. They were heavy, but he'd need them. With his canteens and necessary food supplies, and additional water in the *tinajas*, the load would be too much for Orion. Later that evening he returned to the cantina and the friendly young bartender.

"Need a pack mule," he stated to the bartender.

"*Mu…mu…?*" stammered the Mexican. "*No compréndé, senor.*"

"Ass," explained Billy.

The bartender smiled and pointed to one of the whores.

"No, no," Billy laughed then added, "Burro. *Grande* burro."

"*Ah, si, burro.*"

The bartender tore a small piece of paper from a yellowed wanted poster on the wall behind him. It featured the likes of the Apache Kid, who had been assumed dead for ten years. With a chunk of charcoal he drew a crude map. Then the grinning bartender pointed to his drawing and said, "Ass!" He started to laugh at his own humor, but cut it short as his eyes fell upon two *hombres* entering the *cantina*.

"Is there a trail across the desert to the Rio Yaqui?" asked Billy.

"No trail, *Senor, folla' sun.*"

Billy chuckled and said, "Just keep headin' west, huh?"

Smiling and pointing towards his right the bartender replied, "*Si, Senor,* West!"

Then Billy watched the bartender's expression rapidly change. He had seen that look in a hundred men. It was fear and danger. He turned nonchalantly, keeping one arm leaning on the weathered bar to not present a threat to some trigger happy new customers. The moment he laid eyes on the two new patrons that familiar tingle returned and the back of his neck started itching. Both men were filthy. He watched the dozen or so customers in the cantina quickly sink to about half that size.

"*Mierda!*" mumbled the bartender with a frown that quickly turned to a forced grin as he pulled two bottles of mescal from under the counter and placed them on the bar.

The two *hombres* approached the bar. Small dust clouds puffed forth from their worn *chaparejos* with each step. Both smelled like they had shit their pants. They gave Billy a hard stare, to which he returned with a smile and a nod. With a disgusted grunt they nodded back and scooped up their mescal, then crossed to a corner table that had been quickly vacated by two fleeing old men, leaving their checker game unfinished. One of the nasty *hombres* grabbed a reluctant young whore who Billy thought couldn't have been much older than Freddie's daughter. The man pulled her to the table and forced her down on his lap. She grimaced at their rank odor. An older whore across the room started to cross to the men, maybe in an attempt to take the place of the inexperienced and frightened young girl. She was quickly grabbed by another customer and hustled out the door of the cantina.

The bartender leaned over and whispered to Billy, "*Arango hombres.*"

The burning body of Alex MacDougal flashed across Billy's mind. He felt his hand slowly lower to his Smith & Wesson. He wanted to air hole the pus-bags, but there were still too many customers in the cantina. Besides, he wasn't a Ranger anymore. He knew what Jeff would've done. Ranger badge or not, as soon as he heard the word "Arango" his pearl handled Colt would've been out and blazing. Then two Mexican policemen burst through the door, each toting pump action shotguns. The men still in the cantina fell to the floor pulling screaming whores along with them. Billy turned and saw the bartender dropping behind the bar so he slammed his palms on the top, vaulted to the sober side, and squatted in the sawdust with the young man. At least eight shotgun blasts split and stung the ears of every other cowering person in the small room. Then just like that it was over. The cantina stopped bouncing and ringing and the whores stopped screaming. Billy and the bartender slowly rose. People began to slip out of their hiding places and wipe the lingering sulfur residue from their eyes. The two shit-smelling, perforated, and very dead *hombres* in the corner didn't get off a single shot. Their table, bottles, chairs, and the checkers and board were in a hundred pieces.

So was the young whore.

"I thought y'all liked Arango," said Billy, very confused.

"No, no, senor," explained the bartender. "Arango men fight for Madero. *Presidente* Diaz we like."

Although he didn't ask, Billy wondered, "Who the hell is Madero?"

The next morning he rose early to follow the bartender's map to the mule breeder's farm. As he led Orion out of the stable he heard the solemn music of a funeral dirge. A procession of people following a cold-meat wagon carrying the collected pieces of the dead young whore slowly passed. He removed his hat and waited for them to turn the corner towards the cemetery. The older whore who had tried to replace the young one was dressed in black with a veil covering her face. She walked alongside the coffin, sobbing, with her hand resting on it. He realized she was the dead girl's mother.

The farm was about two miles north of town. The breeder had a *mulada* of seven animals for sale clustered in a small corral. Billy eyed the group, wondering which one to select. He'd never bought a pack mule, never even ridden one. He wondered if he should check its teeth and legs like he would a horse. A strong back was an obvious, but beyond that he was clueless. In hopes of making the decision easier he entered the corral for a closer look. The smell almost knocked him over. As he stood examining a dull grey colored beast something nudged his back. He turned and was staring into the face of a big brown mule.

"Hi, fella!" Billy said and nodded to the brown animal. He continued on to another mule. As he lifted the second mule's head to inspect its teeth the big brown one again nudged him from behind. When Billy turned to face him for the second time the animal almost seemed to be grinning at him. As he started to move on to a third mule he was nudged again. This time hard enough to push him forward a foot or two. He turned and the same brown mule hee-hawed loudly.

"I'll take this one!" Billy told the farmer as he patted the head of the big brown animal. "Think he wants outta here."

"*Burros son animals curiosos.*" the breeder told him.

"*¿Como se llama?*" asked Billy.

"*Capitano!*" replied the breeder.

Billy chuckled. "Captain! Good name fer a mule."

He paid the man and led Captain over to Orion for a formal introduction.

"Shithead, Cap'n! Cap'n, Shithead!" Patting the mules neck he added, "His real name's Orion, but after a few weeks 'long side him ya'll be callin' him Shithead, too."

On the ride back to town Billy kept laughing at the way the two animals eyed one another. For the past several years Orion's trail buddy had been Vermillion. Now there was this odd smelling and odd looking creature almost as big as him trotting along side. He knew a mule is even-tempered and patient, and hoped some of those qualities might rub off on his haughty and stubborn partner, but doubted it. Even after four years he and Orion still quibbled over who was really riding who.

July, 1905

The big, black stallion was backlit by a full blue moon and glaring at them from atop a small rise. The two exhausted Rangers were returning from a wasted search for some slippery cattle rustlers up around McNeal. The black just stood there watching them. Even from that distance Billy and the stallion locked eyes. It was like the horse took a look at the two tired cowboys and thought, "Go ahead! I dare you."

"No horse looks at me like that," exclaimed Billy as he slipped the lasso off his lizzy and began to slacken the rope.

Jeff groaned and said, "Billy, I'm beat and my ass is already sore. Ignore the sumbitch."

"I want him, Jeff! Look at him! Standin' there like a statue!"

"It's a fuckin' horse, Billy, and what the hell's wrong with Swiss?"

For the past few years Billy had been riding a chocolate gelding appropriately named Swiss. He was a good horse and kept a good head, and seemed to like his rider. So even Billy wondered why he was so hell bent on snagging this stallion. Maybe it was because they had failed at their assignment and he didn't want to return to Nogales empty handed. Maybe he just needed a challenge. No. It was a connection. He felt it the moment their eyes locked, and he knew from stories heard over the years that a man knows when he has found the right mount. The animal becomes more than just his horse. They became one...like Jeff and Vermillion.

The black stomped his hooves several times as if saying, "What're ya waiting for?"

"He's darin' me," Billy said as he looped his lasso. "I can feel him laughin' inside."

Jeff sighed and readied his rope. "Alright," he surrendered, "just hope that big fella doesn't kill us both."

It was a painful pursuit filled with clever maneuvering from both the Rangers and the stallion, but they finally managed to pin the cunning horse down in Leslie Canyon.

Later that night Jeff pointed up to the sky and said, "See those three stars in a line there?"

Billy knew precisely where to look. "Ya."

"They're called Orion's belt—three bright stars in the constellation of Orion. Seeing your black has that white star on his forehead..."

Billy finished his sentence. "I should call him Orion."

He leaned back against his saddle, lit his hand carved ivory pipe, and pondered the suggestion as he stared at the night sky. Even though he never knew their name, those three stars and the Big Dipper had always been his favorites. Many a night he had watched them travel across the sky, wondering if some other fellow was up there watching him travel across the sky.

"Fittin'!" he finally declared.

Roped and lead back to the Ranger's barracks in Nogales, the strong and stubborn black fought them every step of the way. The only thing that seemed to temporarily calm him was when he would trot alongside Vermillion. If Billy put the black next to him and Swiss, the wild horse would get as agitated as a prairie dog spotting a rattler. When he thought Billy wasn't paying attention he'd suddenly jerk to one side in hopes that this strange being would lose the rope that kept him from breaking range and heading for the hills.

For the first few weeks the black was a beast with a bellyful of bed-springs. No one could stay on him. Finally, after five weeks of fart-knocking falls, and bruised tailbones Billy was able to stay in the saddle. But to this day he doesn't think Orion considers himself broken...just cooperating.

April, 1909

He stayed another day and night in Quitovac, spending most of his time in the cantina. The blood and the splintered pieces of chairs and table and checker board had been cleaned up, but the stubborn smell of death had yet to leave the room. He knew the next two weeks would be hell in the saddle, but to reach the towns where he hoped his prey could be cowering, it was a necessary hell. The friendly bartender had once again greeted him with a smile when he entered. Even in just the short time Billy had been in Quitovac he had grown to like the fellow. Outside of Sparky, this was the first time he had felt a liking towards anyone since Jeff's death, especially a Mexican. Before leaving the cantina to return to his tent, he gave the young man two silver dollars just for the hell of it.

"*Gracious, senor,*" exclaimed the smiling bartender. Then with a serious dip of his eyebrows he added, "*Trece días a Rio Yaqui.* No let desert eat you."

The next morning Billy loaded both animals with supplies, most on Captain's strong back. He had boiled enough water to fill the two heavy *tinajas.* He covered and secured their contents with rabbit hides and hung one on each side of Captain's midsection. Taking a last long look at his animals and checking his supplies, he decided they were as ready as they'll ever be. The newly formed trio set out across one of the deadliest stretches of ground in Mexico.

Desert, Day 1 of 13

The desert is a demon with a huge appetite. It cooks its meat in the daytime and freezes it at night. Billy, Orion, and Captain were nothing more than walking meals for Gila monsters, coyotes, rattlers, bobcats, buzzards, tarantulas, scorpions, centipedes, and things no one could even describe or imagine. Even the vegetation was their enemy. The Jumping Cholla Cactus will hook anything that makes the mistake of passing too close. Its spines jab and lock in under the hide of both man and beast. Getting shy of them is like pulling out dozens of tiny fish hooks. The agave plant is armed with long sharp spikes that shred clothing, puncture skin, and leave a bloody, burning hole the size of a ten-penny nail.

Feather Yank says the desert is a tricky coyote that fools a man into dying so the dry ground can drink his blood and the critters can have his meat. The sun gets his bones. Since moving too fast would drain their energy and kill them, and moving too slow would cook them and kill them, Billy had to find that safe pace that kept them moving and kept them alive.

It was a long day of struggling to maintain that steady pace while weaving in and out of underbrush that was as hungry as the critters he knew was watching them. As the sun was finally collapsing over a hilltop to the west he decided to make camp. After freeing both animals of their burdens he filled and slipped on their nosebags. While they ate he spent an hour plucking cholla thorns from their hides and from his own arms and legs. Since he knew a cold desert night was coming he built a large fire, cooked up some bacon and beans and wrapped them in a tortilla shell. He knew the fire would keep some critters at bay, but a fellow rarely sleeps alone in the desert. Something was always bound to try to snuggle up in his bedroll on a cold night. He purposely hadn't taken a piss all day, and for a reason: A Buffalo Soldier in the Rough Riders had told him about the *ditch and piss* trick: dig a shallow, skinny ditch around his bedroll and then piss in it. The urine was supposed to repel snakes, scorpions, and spiders. He figured this was as good a place as any to try it. He spread out his bedroll then slipped his e-tool from the packing. Every Ranger was issued an e-tool, a folding shovel with a handle about eighteen inches long and a blade eight inches wide. It was mainly for digging graves.

He shoveled out a thin ditch a few inches deep all the way around his bedroll, then he pissed in it. It felt good and he had enough stored-up piss to completely encircle his bedroll. A few hours later he awoke with a tarantula sitting on his chest, inches from his face. He could count the eight eyes staring at him. He had seen a great many of these furry devils, even eaten some at a *pansaje* with some Quechan Indians, but he never knew they hissed. He shuddered and whisked the beast off his chest, grabbed a rock and crushed it into a gooey mash, then sat up the rest of the night in case any relatives came looking for their missing kin.

"So much fer ditch n' piss," he muttered.

He watched the sun rise in the east. Since he hadn't slept since crushing the spider he figured the threesome could get an early start before that sizzling old bastard turned loose all of its heat. As he packed the supplies back onto Captain he spotted a hole the size of a ten-penny nail in the lower side of one of the *tinajas*. It was drained dry.

"Goddamn thorns," he yelped and tossed the ruined *tinaja* into the dry brush where it shattered. For a second he thought he heard the bushes chuckle at his ignorance. He pulled his S&W and sent a round into their midst. After the sound had rippled its way far off into the distant mesas his eyes narrowed and he scanned the other vegetation. "Got four more here, fellas," he warned them. Not one bush dared to even giggle.

Day 5 of 13

It was a hard sleep, his first in days. He thought he was dreaming when the whinnying, snorting, hee-hawing, snarling, growling, and yapping filled his head. He opened his eyes and saw it was still night time and he wasn't dreaming. Three coyotes were circling the campsite, keeping a fair distance until they decided on which animal to attack. All it took were a few chucked rocks for Billy to scatter them.

"What the hell ya wakin' me fer?" he shouted at Orion and Captain. "There was only three of them! They come back, ya kick the shit outta them desert hoboes, ya hear?" He released their tethers. He knew Orion wouldn't go anywhere and figured Captain was smart enough to not wander off in this deathtrap. "There! Now if they come back, show 'em who's boss! It's hard enough to get shut-eye out here without ya two chicken shits wakin' me."

Day 8 of 13

He needed a warm supper, something besides the jerky and hard biscuits that vexed his tooth. The odor of sizzling bacon could be smelled for miles, especially in the desert, but his stomach insisted on taking the chance of attracting unwelcomed guests anyway. He knelt by the fire and tossed some beans into the small iron skillet to simmer in the grease alongside the bacon. He leaned his face over the skillet and sniffed in the fine smell. Moments before the pork had turned to an edible color, his ears caught a noise in the distance. It was like a bunch of grunts, but high pitched grunts. He'd never heard anything like it, but could tell it was coming his way. The grunts soon became a piercing, gurgling, almost painful noise, obviously unfamiliar to the ears of the entire trio because Orion and Captain stirred and stomped and whinnied and hee-hawed as the sound grew louder and closer. He stood up and drew his gun, straining to see what was coming, but dusk in the desert before the moon blinks on turns everything into an inky blackness.

Orion and Captain were almost in a panic, shuffling and turning in circles, snorting and making sounds Billy had never heard them make before. He backed away from the fire and filled his left hand with the weapon from his shoulder holster. The sound seemed to be all around them. He was spooked. He expected to see the Reaper explode from the darkness, his red eyes glowing under a black hood and his skeleton arms swinging a bloody scythe as he slashed everything in his path. Now the air was filled with a shrill, gurgling clamor that was so loud he felt as if his head was going to burst like a melon. Then a terrifying sight blasted through the brush, causing him to stumble backwards and fall to the ground. A huge red camel thundered into the campsite. Steam was snorting from its nostrils, drool pouring from its wide open mouth. Its heavy hooves crashed down into the fire, flipping the iron skillet and spilling the bacon and beans into the coals. Orange and red hot cinders sailed into the air and danced around the camel's legs causing whisks of its hair to ignite and die like hundreds of tiny explosions. Billy was screaming and cursing. Then a chill shot through his body. He felt every muscle tighten and freeze like a frigid wind had iced him solid. Strapped to the camel's back, right between the animal's humps, was a headless human skeleton.

As fast as it struck, the camel trampled off into the desert night.

With cold sweat soaking his clothing and suffering from a case of the shakes like none he'd ever known, he realized he hadn't fired a shot from either weapon. Orion and Captain had run off into the darkness, but he knew they'd return. Gathering his senses he jumped up and screamed again, then began firing into the dark void where the beast had vanished. After emptying both weapons he dropped to his knees, panting and trying to catch his breath. Tears were spilling down his cheeks and he realized he had pissed himself.

"The Red Ghost," he gasped, and quickly reloaded both weapons.

He knew the legend but never believed it. The U.S. Calvary tried an experiment with camels in the Southwestern desert. In the 1880's, so the legend goes, a young Calvary recruit was having trouble staying on a camel, so in fun his fellow soldiers lashed him to a big red one and smacked its rear. It didn't end up being much fun for the recruit. The frightened animal took off, outrunning its pursuers and disappearing into the desert. The young recruit and the big red camel were never seen again. Alive, that is! From the Grand Canyon up north down to the deserts of Sonora, stories spread about a big red camel with a skeleton rider. Folks named it the Red Ghost. People began to spot the eerie twosome just lumbering through the desert. Stories were told about how it would turn, charge, and trample anyone who tried to catch it, how it would suddenly appear at night to lone campers and stampede through their campsites, and how bullets bounced off it or passed through it. He believed it now.

An hour later Orion and Captain came wandering back.

"Glad to see I can count on the two a you chicken shits," Billy spat at his companions.

The animals wandered over to where Captain's supplies were laying and began lapping at something.

"What ya got there?" Billy asked as he walked over to them.

On the ground he saw the second *tinaja*. It had been shattered in the animal's panic and the two of them were drinking up the last of its contents. They were back to five canteens.

Day 10 of 13

Once again he thought he was dreaming. Dogs were growling, barking and yelping. Horses were whinnying and mules were hee-hawing. He leaped out of his bedroll and drew his gun expecting to see the Red Ghost charging into his campsite again. What he saw in the moonlight was amazing. At precisely the same time Orion and Captain launched two coyotes into the air with swift kicks from their hind legs. Billy chuckled at the sight of the desert hobos twisting and spinning in mid air. They struck the dirt rolling and yelping then ran off. This time, though, they had brought some friends. Three other ones were snarling and circling the horse and mule. One coyote made the fatal mistake of coming straight at Orion, who reared up and brought his front hooves down on the scavenger's back. Billy heard a loud, sickening crack. The coyote yelped once then was dead silent. A second coyote, thinking it was clever, came at Captain from the side. Then Billy saw something that caused his jaw to drop—Captain's right leg flew out in a sideways kick striking the attacker square in the snout. The coyote flew backwards like it had just run face first into a locomotive, its snout mashed into its face. Billy had heard mules could do that—kick sideways—but had never seen it. The lone uninjured coyote and his pal with the crushed snout slinked off into the desert night, both whimpering in defeat. Orion raised his head then reared and snorted and stomped his hoof. Captain released a loud whinny that quickly turned into a proud hee-haw. Billy treated them both to a withered carrot.

Day 11 of 13

He knew the hills in the distance were the type created by a river. The Rio Yaqui was close. Pretty soon they'd be across this deathtrap. He wanted to speed up, but knew the hills were still days ahead. He was trying to keep their steady and safe pace when Captain suddenly stopped and stared off to his left.

"What the hell's wrong with ya, Cap'n?" The mule started walking south. "Hey, where ya goin'?"

Billy remembered what the breeder back in Quitovac had told him, "Mules are curious animals." Then Captain began snorting and stomping at an object sticking up from the ground. Billy and Orion crossed to him. For some reason an unusual boulder had earned the mule's curiosity. When Billy saw it, it also sparked his fancy. It was its shape that intrigued him—like a big bone. It was very long with much of it still buried under the shifting sand. He ran his hand along the object. It felt different, not like rock. It was smoother. He tapped on it. It didn't sound like stone. It felt like a strange combination of hard, hollow, and brittle at the same time. He had seen many unusual things in his roaming around Texas, New Mexico and Arizona, but never anything like this. He decided it was a bone, but a bone from what? It was huge. Even though he knew he shouldn't exert himself in this hellhole, he pulled his E-tool from the supplies suspended across Captain's back.

"Guess maybe yer curiosity done rubbed off on me," he told Captain.

He dug the sand away from part of the large bone. In a short time he had unearthed what appeared to be the lower leg bone of some animal, but it was about eight feet long. He dug a little more and uncovered part of what looked like the upper leg bone.

"Jesus!" he found himself stating aloud. "This thing's gotta be o'er twenty feet tall."

An elephant in a traveling circus was the biggest animal Billy had ever seen. He knew this bone didn't belong to such a beast. It was more like a lizard bone, but one hell of a big lizard. He wondered if more of these over-sized monster lizards might be romping around this desert. One could be watching him right now digging up the resting place of his dead pal. He wondered what would happen if he came across a live one. Could he kill it? Could Orion outrun such a gigantic beast? Could Captain? With legs as big as he figured this thing could have, it would take very long strides, snatching them up in minutes. To match the size of the leg bone meant the monster's head had to be bigger than two or three rain barrels. He shuddered as he envisioned the size of its teeth. It might even be able to spit venom like some lizards do, but a lizard that size could probably spit venom hundreds of feet. The threat of this new and deadly monster shook him to his toenails. This was worse than the Red Ghost. Over the next two days the screech of a hawk or buzzard would bugger him into pulling his Smith & Wesson and looking for lizards bigger than a house. He didn't sleep either night, just sat by the fire, guns in hand.

Day 13

The Rio Yaqui was a wet blessing. Orion and Captain grazed and drank and frolicked while Billy floated naked in the cool water. Then he spread his bedroll on the soft grass and slept. And he slept. And he slept. Orion nudged him with his nose. Captain hee-hawed and slobbered into his ear. When he finally woke up he had no idea how long he had been out, but a full bladder and growling stomach told him it had to have been quite awhile. He relit the campfire. At first he considered beans and bacon, but the river was so teeming with catfish he couldn't pass it up. It only took a matter of minutes to pull in two fat bottom feeders. He devoured every edible part of both of them. After supper he boiled enough river water to get his canteen supply back up to five. Then to his surprise, he actually fell back to sleep and woke with the sunrise.

The trio camped by the river for another two days. Refreshed and seeing both animals were grass bellied, and somewhat certain no giant lizards or the Red Ghost were sniffing at their trail, they began their journey to the villages and towns along the river. If his plan held water then his prey should be sipping tequila and unloading their baggage in at least a few of them.

Unless someone had given them reason not to be, like Dorotéo Arango, Yaquis were usually friendly to Rangers. Still, Billy knew riding into any town filled with Yaquis didn't always mean you'd ride out. He pulled the Ranger badge from his vest pocket and pinned it on his chest in plain sight, even though it had no authority and made a nice shiny target. He ran his fingers across the metal. He had forgotten how good it felt, how it gave him balance. That familiar, returning sense of pride caused him to sit up in the saddle and brush some of the desert from his clothes. He would let the glistening piece of tin guide him.

He spent weeks riding in and out of every village and grotto in his path. Eventually the trio came to the point where the Rio Yaqui forked, part going southeast the other northwest. Captain wanted southeast, Orion northwest. After staring at the fork for several minutes, he spat in his hand and slapped his palms together. The spittle shot to the north. Captain grunted and hee-hawed his displeasure, but that was their route, decided by one of the most tested methods in the West.

The spit-directed trail led them along the river to the town of Querob-abi. From there it was northwest to Altar, then northeast to Saric, then west again to Noche Buena. Days and weeks no longer existed. The land had become an endless canvas of the same boring shades of brown and yellow with a few coarse patches of green good only for giving shade to rattlers. He roamed in and out of villages and towns, almost reaching the Gulf of California. Then he dipped southeast, but soon looped back to the northwest to catch a few small *barrios* he had heard about from people in other towns. Always the same question, always the same answer: "No Amador, Alvarez,

Quías, Pasco, Victoriano...Amador..." He'd lost count of how many times he had to replace thrown or worn out iron from the hooves of both animals. He had more raw kack-biscuits on his inner thighs than a toad has warts, and they couldn't decide if they wanted to just make him itch or burn like hell, so they did both. His toothache kept coming and going like an adulterous wife. He would tell himself he was getting it yanked at the next town, but the moment he drew close to one the pain would hide. Probably because something in his head really didn't trust a Mexican dentist—if there even was such a thing.

For awhile he had placed a small pebble in a *maleta* hanging from Orion's saddlebags, one for each day, but now the rawhide pouch was over-flowing with more pebbles than he was capable of counting. He dumped out the tiny stones, threw down the *maleta*, and stomped it into the sand with his boot. His frustration was at a peak. All this time and just one man dead—Tomas Amador. Then he wondered why he was still including that name. The man was dead. Why was he still repeating the name "Amador?" Should he drop it? No! They'd become words that no longer spewed from his mouth like venom from a snake, but flowed like a fast stream of clear, fresh water. Like the words to a song. Like Red River Valley. "Amador, Alvarez, Quías, Pasco, Victoriano...Amador..."

He was cat napping in the saddle when Captain came to an abrupt stop and hee-hawed loudly. This also caused Orion to stop and whinny. Billy opened his eyes and gathered his senses. He was surprised to find the three of them in a small *barrio* standing outside a *cantina*.

Captain was staring at the building. Hanging over the door was a sign that read, "*Limpiénse los pies.*" Billy remembered it immediately. The first time he saw it he wondered why some run down *cantina* would have a sign that read, "Wipe your feet!" They had passed through this tiny village a few days ago. Besides a rundown corral and two empty adobes the only building still standing was this old cantina. He hadn't even wasted the time to go in it.

"How the hell'd we end up back here?" He asked Orion. The horse snorted and walked in a circle.

"I know, ya hame-headed fleabag, I know we rode in a circle! Why?" Turning his wrath to Captain he continued, "And you, dumbass, I thought mules were su'pose to be smart!" Captain replied with a hee-haw that almost sounded like a laugh. "Okay, fine! Just fer them smartass remarks I'm gonna go in and have a drink and ya two can bake out here in the sun." He tethered the two animals to a post by a trough of murky water and stepped up to the door of the *cantina*. "Figger out where we go next, dumbasses!" He threw the words back at the animals. Lying at the base of the door was a coarse, rectangular horsehair rug. He wiped his feet.

"*Sí, Señor?*" the bartender asked as Billy approached the bar.

"Tequila," he answered and scanned the room.

Two old men were seated at a table playing checkers. Every *cantina*, two old men playing checkers, always looking the same—loose fitting soiled yellow shirts that were probably once white, baggy *pantalones*, sandals, and long, grey-streaked hair covered by straw sombreros that didn't stop the sun from cracking their faces. An old whore was seated with them, trying to influence their moves. A couple of local *hombres* at the end of the bar momentarily eyed Billy suspiciously, but after he smiled and nodded they returned to their *mescal* and conversation. The bartender placed a glass, a bottle of tequila, and a salt shaker on the bar.

"Sorry, no lime," the bartender said. Then took a chunk of charcoal and made a mark on the bottle at the point where its contents currently rested.

Billy poured himself a shot, licked the side of his hand and sprinkled on some salt. He licked the salt and downed the shot of tequila in one swift gulp. It burned, soothed, and satisfied at the same time. Fortunately his flirtatious toothache had been playing hooky for a few days so he didn't have to waste any of the liquid by resting it on the enamel devil, just let it go where it was supposed to go. After the initial singe had waned he poured himself another. This one he would sip, take his time. Scanning the room again he spotted something he had originally missed: a man dressed in *gringo* clothing was asleep with his head on a table in a far corner.

"*¿Ese es un gringo?*" he asked the bartender, pointing to the man at the table.

"*Sí, Señor!* Ranger, like you!"

"Ranger? Ain't no Rangers no more!"

As he started to cross to see who this man was, the bartender voiced a concern, "*¡No problema, Señor! Por favor! Siempre está borrachos!*"

"No trouble!" Billy assured him and crossed to the sleeping man's table. The first thing he noticed was the man was missing his right arm from the elbow down. He tapped lightly on the table. "Hey, Ranger?" he said in a voice just above a whisper. No response. He tapped a little louder and repeated, "Hey, Ranger!"

In a sleepy, drunken stupor, and with great effort, the man raised his head slightly and garbled, "Ain't no Rangers no more! Lemme the fuck 'lone!" With a thud his head returned to the table.

Billy was shocked. It was J. J. Brookings, the Ranger who was with them on that deadly chase of Dorotéo Arango. He recalled how J.J. had caught two bullets in his right forearm during their escape from that gorge. He had been sent to the Nogales hospital for surgery and Billy had lost track of him after that.

"J.J.?" Billy whispered softly.

The man slowly raised his head and tried to focus his blurred eyes on this stranger. "Who be askin'?" he slobbered, wiping the drool from his chin with his remaining left forearm.

The moment Billy sat down at the table the foul odor hit him. J.J. smelled like he bathed in alcohol and shit. The stench almost forced him to rise and step away, but he knew he couldn't, shouldn't, and wouldn't.

"It's me, J.J., Billy Old."

J.J. raised his head up further, still trying to find vision through the milky haze that covered his eyes.

"Billy?" he muttered.

"Yeah!"

The man's face was dirty and bloated. Through his beard Billy could see open sores surrounding his mouth. He looked twenty years older than he was. His clothing was soiled, torn, and filthy, just like his body.

"Billy Old?" J.J. asked, confused.

"Yeah, J.J.! It's me!"

J.J. looked around and asked, "Am I in Nogales?"

Billy felt his heart break. "No, J.J.! No, this here ain't Nogales."

"Well, where hell am I then?" he asked, slowly gathering what few wits the alcohol hadn't burned away.

"What happened, J.J.? Why ya here in this shitsaken hole?"

"Ya don't know, Billy?"

"Why would I know, J.J.?"

"Well, hell, if ya don't know how the hell should I?" He laughed and exposed teeth that if not rotted were simply not there. Harsh, deep coughing quickly killed the laughter.

Billy grabbed the bottle of tequila and his glass from the bar and returned to the table. When he poured the man a drink, J.J. downed it like water. No grimace. No burn. It's a funny thing with drunks—Billy had seen it many times—they have moments of clarity during those first few drinks after waking from a passed out state. Almost like their minds are foggy when awakened, but the liquor chases away the fog, but only for a short time. Soon it rolls back in and the passed out state returns.

J.J. scooped up the bottle of tequila, eyed it lovingly, and said, "G'mornin', darlin'!" He poured himself a second drink and downed it as smoothly as the first.

"Ya gonna talk to me now?" asked Billy.

"Whata ya wanna talk 'bout, Billy Boy?" asked J. J. as he poured himself a third shot.

Just as he was raising the small glass to his lips Billy grabbed his hand.

"What the hell ya doin' here, J.J.?"

Anger flashed across J.J.'s face. How dare anyone come between him and his tequila! He glared at Billy for a long moment then raised his half arm. Billy released his hand.

"They sent me to that Nogales hospital," he explained, finishing his drink and pouring a fourth. "Couldn't save my arm so they tried me out in the telegraph office. Only needed one hand to poke a key." He chuckled, swigged down the tequila, and poured himself a fifth. "Couldn't learn all 'em dits and dashes though." With each drink he began to speak faster and clearer. "Can't throw a lasso or draw a shooter with my left hand, so deputy work was out, and it takes two arms to cradle a scattergun, and I ain't gonna stare down no plow mule's ass! Been on the drift since. Oh, they gimme a pissant little pension fer losin' my limb. Drank it up in no time." After his seventh shot he looked around the room. With words beginning to slur again he asked, "Where hell am I?" There was a long pause as he stared off into the distance. Billy knew the fog was returning. "How'd I get back to Nogales?" He squinted to see who was across the table from him. "Billy Old, damn it's good to see ya!" He poured himself another drink. "They got any whores in this shithole, Billy Boy? I could sure do with a fat whore right now with a big fat ass like 'em fat asses up at the ter-a-tory seat." J.J. stood awkwardly and shouted to the bartender, "Hey, *amigo*, where's the whores?" No one in the *cantina* even glanced his way. He fell back into his chair laughing. It took only seconds for the laughter to turn to coughing. His head dipped and slowly swayed side to side. The fog had rolled back in. Billy's guts ached knowing there was nothing he could do. He pulled two five dollar gold pieces from his pocket and placed one in J.J.'s hand.

"Now ya listen to me, J.J., and ya listen good! Ya take this and get yerself fed and cleaned up and outta this fuckin' hole. Ya hear me now?"

"Outta this fuckin' hole," slurred J.J., barely lifting his chin from his chest. "Right, Billy boy, outta this fuckin'...." J. J. He laid his head back down on the table. The fog had turned to sleep. Billy stared at his friend for a long moment. He rose and walked over to the bartender holding the second five dollar gold piece at eye level.

"*Habla inglés?*" he asked the man.

"*Sí!* Yes!" the bartender replied.

"I just gave my friend one of these to get hisself straightened out. This one's fer you!" He stuffed the gold piece into the bartender's pocket. "Help him or kill him."

He turned and walked out of the *cantina* knowing whichever the man did would put J.J. in a better place. Both Orion and Captain admonished him for leaving them tied out in the heat, but he was too angry to respond. How many other Rangers were in the same state as J.J. Brookings? He wished there was a hunting season on fat asses.

Date unknown

The sun was about to be swallowed by the horizon when he spotted the ruins. He thought it was a strange location for a village, and certainly not on his tabletop map. There was no sign of tilled land or a water source, just endless sunlight and heat. He also noticed these were not the usual decaying adobe dwellings he'd seen all over Sonora. Yet there was something familiar about them. Orion snorted at the ground and stomped his hooves. Billy looked down and realized they were no longer following a simple horse trail. They were actually on some type of *sendero* that led straight into the heart of the deserted pueblos. Looking behind him he was surprised to see that they had been on it for some time and he hadn't even noticed. The Jojoba bushes and drifting sand had all but swallowed it up.

Of course, the curious Captain headed straight for the ruins. At first Billy thought about calling him back, but then figured it could be a good place to camp for the night. First he'd have to chase out the rattlers and scorpions that called it home. The closer they got the more familiar the ruins became. Then he remembered.

"Chaco Canyon," he muttered.

He and his friend Henry Anderson had visited the strange ruins back in New Mexico years ago when both worked for a ranch in Alamogordo. This was a much smaller version of those same types of pueblos, but still the same. He strained his brain trying to remember the name of the Indians who once lived at Chaco, but couldn't.

Captain heard the chanting first and it stopped him in his tracks. Orion's ears twitched upwards when the sound reached them. Billy was the last to hear it, but recognized it immediately—an Indian death chant. Somewhere in those ruins an Indian was dying. Hoping not to interrupt the ritual he led Orion and Captain to a half standing pueblo with walls still high enough to help hide the glow of a fire and keep a respectful distance from where the death chant was coming.

"We'll let the fella take his goin' in peace," he told the two animals as he stripped them of their burdens and slipped on their nosebags.

He built a fire, not a big one, but strong enough to cook himself a hot meal. After eating he spread out his bedroll and pulled the ivory pipe from his pocket. Just as he began to light it the chanting stopped.

"I dream of you, white man," a graveled voice called from somewhere among the ruins.

Billy sat up and stiffened as the voice continued.

"I dream of pony with mark of star gods on head."

Billy could hear the age in the voice.

"I dream star on chest lead you to me. I am too old to come to you but want to see your face."

The first thing Billy thought of was a trap. Maybe the old voice had some young pals waiting to collect some coup.

"I am alone and too old to fight, no fear," the voice replied, seeming to read Billy's thoughts.

"No fight?" Billy finally called out.

"No fight, Ranger," replied the old voice.

"How the hell'd he know...?" Billy mumbled.

He had his gun drawn and was already creeping towards the voice when it spoke again.

"If you no come to me I will talk all night so you cannot sleep," the voice added with a chuckle, "or 'til I go to cloud gods, if that come first."

Billy saw the small glow of the man's fire first. He peeked around a half decayed pueblo wall and saw the Indian sitting cross-legged on several blankets in the middle of a small kiva, like the ones back in Chaco canyon. It surprised him that he remembered what the shallow pits were called. A painted lance decorated with feathers was standing straight up, stuck in the ground within easy reach of the old man. Encircling him was a carefully arranged gathering of clothing, beads, peace pipes, arrows, an unstrung bow, scalps, knives, tomahawks, necklaces, and a fancy headdress. It was probably everything the old fellow owned.

Before Billy even came into the man's view he said, "No *pistola*, Ranger. Fighting days long gone."

Billy stepped into full view of the Indian, but still maintained a safe distance. He knew how dying Indians liked to take a fresh scalp with them to the Happy Hunting Grounds. Through the glow of the small fire Billy could count the cracks and crevasses in the man's face. He knew this was one salty Indian.

"What ya doin' out here 'lone?" Billy asked.

"Dying," answered the Indian.

"Alone?" Billy asked, glancing around the decaying pueblo walls, still alert for any pals the old Indian might have hidden.

The man smiled and said, "No one jump at you, Ranger. I face death alone. My people grow weak, run from kachina in death mask. I will pull off mask and spit in face of wearer. I pray wearer is my fourth squaw—mean woman, grow big as bear, hairy, too."

Billy couldn't help but chuckle. "What tribe are ya?" he asked.

"Hopi."

Trusting the man wasn't a threat and had no hidden pals wanting to count coup, he holstered his Smith & Wesson. "Yer a long way from home," he stated.

"I begin here," explained the old Indian as he raised his thin arms and made a circling gesture. "My people move north from this place, follow star the gods put on Ranger pony. When time to go from this world, I come to place I begin nine hundred moons ago."

Billy knew there were twelve moons in a year, but couldn't handle the ciphering to figure the old man's age. He took comfort in a frog squat that still allowed him to spring to his feet if necessary.

"My people say before you die you see all you have done, good and bad—all arrows you shoot, all men tomahawk hit, all horses you have, all women you love." Then the old Indian grunted and added, "So far, no see shit."

Billy chuckled and said, "Yeah, my people say that, too. Seems to me though it'd make a fella happy to see all he's done, but I ain't ne'er seen a man die happy."

"Man should be happy to go the cloud gods."

"Cloud gods, huh? White man ever try to Christian ya?"

"Try," the Indian answered with a grin. "Me no *mansito*. You keep Christian god. Me keep mine. What you call pony?"

"Orion."

The old man smiled and said, "Good name." He sniffed the air. "You have burro?"

"Mule."

"Smell like strong one."

"Try standin' next to him," replied Billy with a chuckle that seemed to put both men a little more at ease.

"What they call you, Ranger?"

At last Billy sat down in the sand, but still kept a decent stretch between them. "Billy Old. You?"

"Páayo´ Taaqa...mean Three Man...I fight like three man...long ago, not now. Bones break if I fight now. Thought I die standin' up, but old bones no let me. Why Ranger Billy Old long way from home, too?"

"Lookin' fer some fellas."

The old Indian nodded his head in understanding and asked, "How many?"

"Four. Bad men, bad Mexican police."

"I look one time many moons back," stated Páayo´ Taaqa. "Three bad man. Mexican, too."

"Did ya git them?"

The Indian glanced at his surrounding items then pulled three dark scalps from a pile and held them up with a toothless grin. He placed the scalps back in the exact position they had been resting and reached for a peace pipe. For a moment Billy thought about asking what the men did to warrant being hunted, but since the Indian didn't pry into the nature of his hunt, he'd let common courtesy stand its ground.

"Smoke, Ranger Billy Old!" It wasn't a question.

Three Man lifted a fancy pipe to his wrinkled lips. It was painted in many colors and featured two eagle feathers hanging from the center of its long stem. After lighting it with a twig from the fire he puffed and pulled several times, taking its contents deep into his lungs. He expelled a long stream of white smoke then ceremoniously offered it to Billy with two hands. Scooting to within arm's reach, Billy nodded his thanks and took the pipe. After one puff and a deep inhale he realized it wasn't tobacco.

"Holy shit, Three Man," he coughed as he handed the pipe back to Páayo´ Taaqa. "This don't taste like kinnikinnick. Whatcha got in here?" He coughed again and again.

The Indian smiled, patted his stomach, and said "Help stop pain here."

"I got some jerky if yer hungry," Billy offered in a raspy voice still trying to clear his lungs.

"No, no, Ranger Billy Old. No hungry pain...dark demon eat belly... soon no belly...then go to cloud gods."

After a few more puffs the man offered the pipe back to Billy. He knew if he refused the offering it would be considered an insult, and even as old and frail as the Indian appeared, he was pretty sure Páayo´ Taaqa could still handle that lance stuck next to him with some deadly speed and accuracy. He took another puff and inhaled. It came easier the second time. After a moment he let it slowly drift from his mouth as he handed the pipe back to

Three Man. That was when he realized he was grinning, and the grin seemed frozen in place.

"Good stuff, hey, Ranger Billy Old?" He placed the pipe back in its original position among the many treasures surrounding him.

Billy blinked his eyes to regain his focus, but it refused to return. The one Hopi had magically turned into three.

"Uh, ya said ya dreamed of me and Orion?" he asked, the words seeming to echo in his head. He chuckled.

"Back when know I die, six moons ago," Three Man explained, "dream last man I see in this world is white man. Thought tricky coyote come into dream and made person white to anger Three Man. But this day I dream of white man with star on chest and pony with star on head. Then you come. My vision...and you come. Cloud gods must want white man to cover me with stone. Still not know why." The old man glanced around and said with a smile, "Plenty stone here."

Billy's head was spinning and what Three Man had just said made it spin even more.

"Wait a minute," he said. "You...you want me to bury you?"

"Cover with stone so coyote not eat, then spirit go to cloud gods and make rain for my people."

"Ain't ya got no family or no one to do that?" asked Billy, knowing he could not wait around this abandoned pueblo for the old Injun to finally go under. He had his plan, such as it was.

"All gone," replied the Indian. "This one live too long. Maybe that why gods curse me with white man puttin' on stones."

"Look, I'd like to help ya," Billy had to shake his head to get his eyes rattled back into place, "but I gotta move on first thing in the mornin'." It took him three tries to finally stand. "What the fuck ya put in that pipe?" The spinning in his head had advanced to somersaults. He wanted to lie down, but was still uncertain of his safety.

The Indian looked at him with a crooked grin.

"Okay to sleep, Ranger Billy Old," Three Man declared. "This Hopi not take scalp in sleep. No honor."

As much as his body wanted to accept the man's invitation, his mind kept returning to Orion and Captain.

"Gotta get nosebags offa my animals," he slurred. The sound of his own voice seemed deep and slow and again echoed around his head.

"Cloud gods call soon, Ranger Billy Old. I sleep now, too."

The old Indian lie back on his blanket and closed his eyes. Billy stared at him. He noticed what seemed to be a glow around the old man, but blamed it on whatever the hell was in that pipe. It took a several more moments until he remembered why he stood up: the nosebags. He glanced around to regain his bearings. His head felt like a balloon inflating larger and larger and trying to lift him off his feet and float him away. He chuckled at the sensation, but his voice seemed high pitched like a woman's. Once again he had to remind himself of the nosebags.

The journey back to Orion and Captain took very careful maneuvering over broken walls that seemed to quiver when he touched them, almost like they were breathing. Several times he stopped and gently ran his hand across an unusual stone. Each time he did the stone seemed to giggle and tingle beneath his fingertips. It felt good. After what seemed like an hour he finally reached the decaying pueblo where he had left Orion and Captain. At first it frightened him when he saw that their heads had turned a light grey color. Then he recalled the nosebags. He slipped them from their heads and let them drop to the ground. The bedroll lying ten feet away looked like a huge, inviting cushion stuffed with soft feathers. He stumbled over to it and collapsed in a heap.

April, 1890

Luckily it was the bottom strand of barbed wire that some fat heifer had pushed loose. Otherwise the arrow would have sunk deep into his spine instead of the fence post. He had squatted to double tack the wire back in place when the wooden shaft made a loud thud a foot above his head. The post vibrated.

"What the hell," he gasped, trying to turn and stand but fell back on his haunches.

Then he heard a sound people out west hadn't heard for years, one that Billy had never heard: the war whoop of a charging Indian. It reminded him of his crazy uncle who had fought for the Rebs and always screamed out the Texas yell when he was drunk, which was often. But the sight charging at him quickly erased that grating memory. Coming out of the morning sun was a warrior on horseback, riding full tilt straight at him, yelping like a wild animal. At first Billy thought it was joke. Indians don't do that anymore. Then a second arrow whistled by his left shoulder and thudded into the ground beyond the wire. Still perched in the dirt he drew his gun and fired twice in the air, hoping it would frighten away this cracked-brained or drunk Indian. It didn't. He kept charging. He veered his mount at the last moment, kicking up dry earth, close enough for Billy to see that his face and chest were covered in war paint. On the run, the Indian looped his pony back towards the lone cowboy with his ass still planted in the dirt. He notched another arrow and came galloping in for a third try. This time he would be close enough to hit meat. Billy reluctantly aimed his gun at the charging horseman, screamed for him to stop, but to no avail. The lunatic was headed straight at him, full speed, bow pulled taut. Billy fired. The Indian spun off his horse backwards and lay on the ground gurgling.

"What the hell's wrong with ya, ya fuckin' knothead?" yelled Billy, as he got up and ran over to the downed man just in time to hear his final death rattle and see the life leave his eyes.

"There ain't no damn injun wars no more!"

He saw the hole in the man's sternum bubbling and oozing life, and rapidly gathering flies. "Why'd you make me do that?" he screamed. Then he noticed this wasn't some young brave. It was an old man.

Henry Anderson came galloping up yelling, "What's all the shootin'?"

Billy was standing over the Indian's body, pale and shaking. At only sixteen years old he had just killed a man.

Henry leaped off his horse when he spotted the dead Indian. "Not another one," he sighed, shaking his head.

"Another what?" Billy asked, his voice nervously breaking into a high pitch.

"We get three or four a 'em old Ute warriors ever' year," explained Henry. "They get fed up with life on the Rez, paint themselfs up like the ol' days, chew some peyote, and make a su'cide charge, usually at one a us fence riders. Guess they figger 'cause we're mostly 'lone we make easy pickins. Ya done right by shootin' him, Billy. He'd a cut ya to pieces. He was aimin' to meet the Great Spirit with a purty new scalp. Yers!"

Fighting a sick feeling in his guts Billy stammered, "Should...should we bury him?"

"Hell, no!" declared Henry. "His pals know what he was doin'. They'll come find him." Henry slipped his arms under the Indian's shoulders. "Grab his feet," he ordered Billy.

"Why?"

"We'll carry him up to that pine on the hill and lean him agin it."

"Why?" asked Billy as he reluctantly grabbed the dead man's feet.

As the two carried the Ute up the small hill Henry explained, "Them Utes got some strange things they do with their dead, paintin' 'em up, dancing 'round 'em, weird shit. If ya bury thisa one it could just piss off the others and we'd have more of 'em chargin' at us. Besides, thisa way his pals will see him, and puttin' him on the 'tuther side of the tree you won't have to see him agin case they don't come and get him. They sat the Indian up against the far side of the pine. "Purfek!" Henry exclaimed. "Now even if they don't git him, the coyotes need to eat, too."

Henry hopped back on his horse and headed towards the west fence line, his responsibility. Henry was from Abilene, Kansas. He liked to tell folks that he was born on the same day Wild Bill Hickok shot his own deputy in that town. Billy had the north fence and Paulo Cacciattore the south. Paulo was the first real foreigner Billy had ever met. It took him a long spell to understand his patter and get used to hearing so many words end in A. The east was filled with the Dempsey's ranch house, barn, corral, and bunk house. Billy had been working there for several months.

His head kept turning back and forth from the pine hiding the dead Indian to the ass end of Henry's mount which was growing smaller in the distance. As soon he was certain his friend was out of sight he dropped to his knees and discovered how hard it was to sob and upchuck at the same time.

"Ya done right by shootin' him, Billy." Those words echoed in his head for months. Even though he never saw if the Indian was ever collected by his pals, he still saw the dead man almost every night for weeks in his dreams. The corpse would be leaning against that pine, but in each dream it would be more and more decayed. He could see and smell the rotting flesh dripping from the Indian's body, the hole in his chest layered with maggots. Sometimes he'd wake up and find his pillow and blankets soaked from sweat. Sometimes he'd just wake up crying.

Date unknown

Suddenly it was morning. His mouth was as dry as the ground under him. His tongue felt like a thousand tiny boots had stomped across it during the night. His head was pounding like a blacksmith's hammer on an anvil.

"What the fuck was in that pipe?" he groaned and rubbed his forehead.

To make things even worse, his tooth hurt. Fortunately one of his canteens was next to him, but he didn't recall putting it there. He guzzled half of it down before remembering he should conserve his safe water. Too late now. Pulling the flask from his vest he took a swig of mescal and allowed it to rest on the angry tooth for as long as the remainder of his mouth could handle the burn, then he spat it into the sand. Orion and Captain were restless, anxiously awaiting their breakfast.

Looking at the animals and frowning he asked, "Why don't ya two assholes fix me breakfast sometime?"

After refilling and replacing the animal's nose bags he relit his small fire and made his usual strong coffee using the last of his safe water from the one canteen next to him. It helped his head. Then he fried some bacon, enough to bring a few slices to Páayo´ Taaqa.

"Hey, Three Man," he called out as he carried the bacon to his neighbor in the kiva that didn't seem as far away as it did last night. "Can yer belly handle some bacon?"

Three Man didn't respond. Billy knew immediately that he was gone. The glow around him had vanished. For a good minute he just stared at the old Indian. He thought about all the fellow would have seen in his long lifetime. He wondered how many battles he had fought and how many children he had made...how many white men he had killed.

Orion snorted in the distance and Billy figured the animals were finished feeding and needed the bags removed from their noses. They could wait. He sat the bacon aside and covered the body with one of the Indian's many blankets. He gathered all the belongings surrounding Three Man and placed them atop or tight to his body. Then he turned to the stones.

Plenty of stones.

It took about ninety of them altogether. When he was finished he remembered the bacon, which he placed on top of the stones.

"This here's to et on yer trip up to them cloud gods."

Date unknown

The fat, jolly policeman was happily stirring the boiling contents of a large iron cauldron suspended over a roaring fire. The tantalizing aroma of the pork and hominy *pozole* made Billy's mouth water. The policeman grinned then handed him an empty bowl, inviting him to enjoy the tasty treat. Like a hungry orphan Billy grabbed the bowl and hovered over the contents of the cauldron, awaiting his helping of the stew. The fat man laughed as he churned and mixed the *pozole*.

Then Billy saw the arm.

A man's forearm with a tattoo of Old Glory was floating and bobbing in the steaming mixture. Repulsed, he stepped back and turned to the policeman whose face had now formed into that of Tomás Amador. Then it melted into the face of Delores Quías, then Moises Alvarez, then Diaz Pasco. Just as it was about to take the shape of the mysterious Victoriano, Billy kissed the ground hard. Flat on his back with the wind knocked from his lungs, stunned and groggy, he realized he had been sleeping in the saddle again. Before he dared to move he ran a quick check for broken bones. The sound of an angry rattlesnake shocked the remainder of his senses back into focus. The wind returned to his lungs. Then a second rattle sounded, followed by a third. Orion had walked right into the middle of a rattlesnake orgy. The horse had managed to buck and leap free of the snakes, but the move had thrown his sleeping rider from the saddle. Billy was spread eagle in the middle of their lusty ritual. He froze everything but his eyes. He peeked left and right, spotting a rattler on each side and just a few feet from his face. Both were coiled, ready to do away with this unwelcomed intruder in their bedroom. The third one was coiled somewhere out of his line of sight. If he rolled either direction they'd strike. If he reached for his weapon they'd strike. If he tried to get up they'd strike. Even if he remained motionless he knew they would soon strike anyway, just for the hell of it. Rattlers are like that.

Captain whinnied and hee-hawed then stepped right into the middle of the standoff. As the snake to Billy's left reared back to strike, the mule slammed his heavy hoof down on its head, mashing it into a slimy patty of dirt, blood, brains, and venom. Then the snake on Billy's right struck, but not at Billy. It flew into the air straight at Captain in an attempt to defend his or her mate. Billy watched the serpent's riveted underbelly sail a good two feet over his face like it was flying. Captain took a quick step backwards, raised his head, and slammed his teeth down on the soaring serpent, snatching it out of mid air. Dangling right above Billy's head, the snake twisted and hissed but couldn't free itself from Captain's crushing jaws. The mule shook his head violently, snapping the snake's body up and down and side-to-side. Then he whipped his head to his left and released his jaws. The smashed and broken snake flew into the brush. The third snake seemed to come out of nowhere. It struck the lower part of Captain's front leg. By that time Billy was up and drawing his Smith & Wesson. He fired and the remaining rattler's head exploded.

Captain was limping in fast circles and favoring his bitten leg. It took great effort for Billy to finally get the animal to the ground and lying on its side. He pulled some pipe tobacco from his bag, doused it with water, and squeezed and kneaded until it became a gooey poultice—a remedy he had learned from Feather Yank. He pressed it onto the snake bite. Captain groaned and grunted a soft hee-haw. Billy wrapped a cloth around the bite, securing the mixture to the mule's leg.

"Be still now, Cap'n! This'll draw out some of the poison," he said softly, stroking the animal's neck and trying to keep him calm. He knew if Captain decided to get up there was no way in hell he could stop the strong beast from doing so, so he made camp right there in the rattler's vacated bedroom. He dined on the snake Captain had smashed and the one he had shot. Every few hours he would change the poultice on the mule's leg, eventually using up an entire canteen of their safe water. It wasn't a guaranteed remedy, but since Feather Yank suggested it, Billy trusted it. Orion stood and watched, snorting concern over the state of his friend. Fortunately the mule didn't try to stand. He slept most of the time, which kept the poison from surging through his veins. Soon it would lose its killing powers. The morning of the third day Captain was up and hee-hawing again. That was also when Billy discovered the crushed canteen. The mule had been laying on it. They were now down to three canteens of safe water.

For Captain's sake Billy slowed their pace for that one day. Orion would occasionally nudge the mule's neck with his nose. Captain would shake his head up and down twice assuring his friend that he was going to beat the Reaper. Billy wondered if animals had names for Death, too.

A slight, prideful smile crossed his face as the town of El Plomo came into view, just in time and right where his dusty table top map said it would be. It was a decent little place and another day of rest would be good for Captain, and his toothache was making a vicious return visit. He was also out of pipe tobacco.

First he made certain the two animals were stabled and well-fed. He had noticed a barber shop with a sign in the window that said *"Dentista."* Reluctantly, he entered the small establishment. The barber was standing at the mirror trimming his nose hair, but immediately turned and dusted off his barber chair.

"Sí, Señor?" he asked with a grin.

"Dolor de muela!" explained Billy, pointing to his jaw.

"Sí, sí, Señor!" the man anxiously said and gestured to the chair. "Sit, *por favor!"*

Without wiping his hands of the nose hairs he began probing in Billy's mouth. After inflicting more pain the man removed his fingers. Billy spat out a few small hairs that had nested on his tongue as the barber tried to explain the situation.

"Tooth *torcído,"* the man stated with a gesture of tilting his hand at an angle.

Too impatient to recognize the word and too frustrated with the come-and-go pain, Billy ordered, "Just pull the goddamn thing!" He mimicked yanking out the tooth. The barber shrugged his shoulders, picked up a pair of pliers, and guided them towards his patient's wide open mouth. In the nick of time Billy noticed the dried, crusty blood on the end of the tool. "STOP!" he shouted. The barber leapt back in fear. "Ya ain't stickin' that dirty thing in my mouth!" He got up and walked out. There were still many towns and *barrios* ahead of him. Perhaps he'd find a barber with clean pliers and fewer nose hairs. He went straight to the nearest *cantina* and replenished his flask. After three shots of tequila the toothache dwindled to a tolerable level. He spat out the last of the nose hairs.

The *cantina* had three rooms upstairs and they actually allowed a *gringo* to use one. Not free, of course, but cheap. When he entered the room he realized why. Cockroaches that had been residing there didn't even bother to scurry for shelter. They just turned and looked at him as if saying, "What the hell are you doing in our room?" A face full of cobwebs gave him a tingling welcome and he immediately thought of the tarantula he had crushed with a rock in the desert, but couldn't remember how long ago. The room was obviously the former quarters of a resident whore who was likely dead or moved on to more lucrative parts, or fortunate enough to land a husband. Torn and yellowed wallpaper depicting various wildflowers clung desperately to the walls. Soiled doilies covered two small tables on each side of a bed hardly big enough for one, let alone a whore with a customer. A vase of very dead flowers rested on one of the tables. The slightest touch would crumble them to dust. On the other was a cracked and empty water bowl. No pitcher. The bed's thin mattress was stained and still carried the odors of hundreds of lusty encounters. He tossed it on the floor, spread his own bedroll across the leather straps, and stretched out his saddle sore body. He stared up at the roof and tried to recall the last one he had over his head. Before he could remember he was fast asleep.

The next morning Captain was steady and ready to travel. The blacksmith told Billy of a fresh water spring a short distance to the southwest of the small town, so he was able to get his safe water supply back up to his remaining four canteens. The smithy also sold him an ample supply of oats for the animals at a fair price. As far as his own sustenance, it was mule deer jerky, beans, and tortilla shells again, but he did manage to get his hands on a goodly amount of turnip greens to help keep his bowels flowing. He also replenished his pipe tobacco supply. It wasn't maple flavored, but would do. Thankfully the toothache had performed another of its vanishing acts. He recalled other ones he had suffered over the years. None would come and go like this one. They'd arrive and torture him until vanquished. It was like this toothache was purposefully tormenting him. His mother's words returned: "I praise good thoughts, good words, and good deeds. I reject all bad thoughts, bad words, and bad deeds." He wondered if he was being punished because his deed wasn't good. But it was. He was dealing justice to men who had escaped it and deserved it. That is the job of a Peace Officer.

"No," he said aloud. "My deed ain't bad. It's justa 'nother goddamn toothache."

The trio went west, then north, then east, then west again. Then south, then north again, veering, twisting, and baking in the sun. The land, the towns, the people, all looking the same, and fresh water was rare as gold. When he could procure a room or shed or tent, and stable the animals, he'd do it, but most of the time his bed was the hard Mexican ground. He'd visit every *cantina* and whorehouse in every town that offered one. Though the whores looked different, the insides of the houses were all the same, and smelled the same. There was a bar, a few tables, a couple of time-worn-moth-eaten parlor chairs filled by whores perched with one leg draped across the arm in an attempt to provoke business. But what fascinated him the most was the same painting of a plump, naked woman lying on her side in every whorehouse that could afford it. How bored that artist must have been painting the same portrait over and over and over, he thought. He wondered if any of the whores ever thought about the woman in the painting. Who was she, why was she posed like that, and why was her painting hung in dozens of whorehouses? Maybe she wasn't even a whore. Maybe she was the painter's wife. But who'd want a naked painting of their wife hanging in whorehouses? To any of the women who would listen, or were sober enough to listen, he'd repeat his mantra: "Amador, Quías, Alvarez, Pasco, Victoriano...Amador..." None wanted to talk, just take his baggage and his money.

Date unknown

There was no way to escape the dancing devils. The ground was too flat, dry, and barren. Several miles ahead and slightly to the north was a small mesa, but he knew they couldn't reach it before the devils would be on them. The whirling, twisting dust columns thrived on this type of land. They devoured dirt and sand, birthing one-hundred foot high twisting and churning pillars that rose and vanished into a turquoise sky. Billy had never seen this many at one time. It was like every devil across the entire county of Sonora had decided to rendezvous here. There were too many to avoid and they were spread too wide to go around. The sterile land had also made certain there was nothing the threesome could use as protection. Waiting them out was all they could do. The twisters weren't strong enough to scoop up the world and carry it away like a true Texas tornado, but this many could damage an animal's eyes, maybe even blind it. He hopped off Orion and pulled his last shirt from the saddlebag. After ripping it into two long strips he bound the eyes of both horse and mule. He pulled his bandana over his face, gripped the animal's reins, squatted in the dirt, and awaited the attack.

The dancing devils swarmed on them like the plagues he had heard Bible thumpers preach about in bunkhouses. He held the reins tight to keep the animals from panicking at the dust and noise around them. As fast as they arrived they were whirling off. He surveyed his two partners, then himself, and couldn't help but laugh. All three were caked in a burnt orange dust. They looked like three rusty statues. He removed the two pieces of his last shirt from their eyes, shook the earth from them, and used them to clean himself off. Both Orion and Captain snorted and shook their heads and bodies creating another flurry of dust and debris. Even as ridiculous as the threesome had appeared, Billy knew the devils had done their damage. The nostrils of both Orion and Captain were caked with orange dirt. Horses and mules can't breathe from their mouths. If their nostrils weren't cleared, the dust would mix with their snot and become rock hard, and they'd suffocate. He knew he'd have to use some of their precious supply of safe water. Of the five canteens hanging across Captain's haunches, only two were still full.

"Ya ain't gonna like this," he said to Orion as he grabbed the side of his bit, forced the animal's head upward, and quickly poured water into both nostrils.

Orion jerked backwards and shook his head. Snorting and sneezing the black expelled most of the dust and debris, a lot of it right back on to Billy. He did the same to Captain with the same results. For several minutes the two continued to react to the unpleasant remedy, snorting and shaking their heads. Neither animal would even look at him for the rest of the day. As he was setting up camp that evening, both remained a good twenty feet from him.

Date unknown

A high pitched, painful groan coming from some mesquite and granjero bushes to the north stopped the threesome in their tracks. Just as Billy was about to spur the animals onward, figuring it was some type of animal, another high pitched gasp filled his ears. This time it sounded human. Captain's curiosity, of course, was taking him straight into the high mesquite.

"Whoa, Cap'n!" Billy ordered. The mule obeyed. If it was a wounded animal in the bushes then its natural instincts would be to attack whatever approached. Billy climbed off Orion. "Ya two stay here! I'll take a look." He drew his Smith & Wesson and cautiously entered the thorny granjero bushes. He had heard no other sound since that last gasp, so whatever was in there could've gone under. A familiar odor invaded his nostrils, but he couldn't place it. It wasn't the usual smell of death, but had a slight rotting scent to it. He covered his mouth and nose with his bandana. It didn't help. Beyond the mesquite he saw that the ground was covered with the tracks of unshod Indian ponies and those of shod mounts of men obviously in pursuit. All were moving rapidly to the north. The ground around him was pounded into a hard crusty surface. He figured it was an old trading trail the Apaches were still using for raids into Mexico. From the depth and distance of the tracks the Indians must have been riding like hell to reach the U.S. before the Mexican soldiers or Rurales or Police, or whoever was on their tails could catch them. That led him to believe he'd find a dying Indian pony, shot during the chase. Maybe its rider. Instead, when he parted the bushes he discovered a dead squaw lying on her stomach with several bullet holes in her back. Shot from her horse, she had landed in the high mesquite along the trail, hiding her body from the pursuers. They must have been close to the raiders because an Apache would not leave a wounded squaw behind. Or perhaps she was at the tail end of the raiding party and none of the other Indians saw her fall.

She was young. Her head was turned sideways and her eyes and mouth were open and frozen in a hideous death mask of pain and fear. The next sight forced the breath from his lungs and his body recoiled in horror. Her buckskin dress had hiked slightly up above her buttocks and an infant's leg was protruding from her womb. The ground was still dark from her broken water sack. Now he recalled the rotting smell. He grimaced but couldn't turn away.

September, 1883

"Billy, wake up! I need your help."

A sleepy nine-year-old Billy sat up in bed and rubbed his eyes. "What's wrong, Pa?"

"The cow's birthin' and it's breech." Then Billy noticed the blood on his father's forearms. "I tried to turn the calf but couldn't. We gotta pull it out 'fore it tears up its momma's innards."

With that last statement his pa was out of Billy's room and headed back to the barn. Billy quickly realized the importance. While there were twenty or thirty goats on their small farm, they only owned one cow and they depended on her milk. He slipped on his trousers and shoes and ran to the barn. When he entered the small structure the smell smacked him in the face.

His pa tossed him an old rag and said, "Cover yer mouth and nose with this and grab the other leg!"

Under the yellow glow of a single lump oil lamp hanging on a wooden post Billy saw two legs sticking out of their milk cow's womb. His pa had hold of one of them. He froze.

"Come on, boy! We gotta do this pronto!"

Billy edged towards the standing cow, but the stench again stopped him.

"No time to upchuck, Billy! Grab the other leg!"

Billy tied the rag around his face and gingerly reached for the leg. He was instantly kicked in the chest and thrown backwards.

"Damn, boy! Muscle up! Grab the goddamn leg! We can't afford 'nother milker!"

"Will it hurt the calf?" asked Billy with tears welling in his eyes from the pain in his chest, the foul smell, and simply the terror of the moment.

"I'd rather lose the calf then its momma. Now grab it, son!" Billy did as he was ordered. "Now right with me, pull! Ya ready?"

Trembling and panting Billy replied, "Ya!"

"Pull!"

In a flash the calf slid from the womb. Billy fell backwards and the slime-coated newborn landed on top of him. As he rolled from under the slick animal his pa whooped in joy.

"Look at that, Billy Boy! We got ourselves a bull."

"It's a boy?" Billy asked as he struggled to stand. His clothes were drenched in a smelly, sticky substance.

"Sure is! Got yer pocket knife with ya?"

Billy groped at his pants pockets. "Ya. Why?"

"Git it out and cut the feedin' cord."

With his eyes wide and his body frozen in place all he could stammer was, "Huh?"

"Right here!" his pa ordered. "Right 'tween my hands."

Billy slowly pulled the knife from his pocket and freed the small blade. "Will it hurt him?"

"Hell, no! It's just a long flume that carries food from the momma to the calf."

"But ifin I cut it, how will he eat?"

"With his mouth, Billy. How the hell ya 'spect him to?"

"But you said..."

"Cut the damn cord, boy! I can't hold this forever!"

Tears were now streaming down Billy's face as he pushed the blade down on the cord.

"It's too hard."

"Cut from 'neath it, slice upwards! Put some muscle 'hind it! Ya ain't gonna harm him, son."

With his pa tightening his grip, Billy pushed up and severed the strong cord. A liquid shot from it and he almost passed out then and there. He watched his pa tie the end of the cord attached to the calf in a knot.

"That's it! That's all we can do." His pa stood, walked over to a bucket of water and began to wash his hands and forearms. "Clean yerself up, Billy. Better take them clothes down to the creek."

"Is Missy okay?"

"She looks okay." Right then Missy mooed.

"I think that was a thank you," his pa said with a smile as he pulled out his ivory pipe and lit it.

After a few comical attempts to stand, the calf finally gained his footing and wobbled over to its mother's teats.

"See, he's eatin'." He put his arm around Billy's shoulder and said, "It's all up to his momma from here. Ain't nothun we can do now."

Date unknown

Billy figured the Indians would circle back to find the missing squaw. As he started to return to Orion and Captain a movement caught the corner of his eye. At first he thought it was the hot breeze shuffling the mesquite.

Then he saw the infant's toes twitch.

"Just a muscle jerk," he told himself. Then the toes wiggled and another foot began to emerge from the womb. Again the breath left his lungs as he stepped back and shuddered. He watched more of the second leg struggle to leave its confinement. "Walk away," he told himself. "Ain't nuthun ya can do now."

He decided this was something he would keep dry, never tell anyone. No one ever needed to know. As he climbed back on Orion he thought, "We stink when we die and we stink when we're born."

Date unknown

Four empty canteens clanging against each other with every step Captain took was a taunting reminder of how thirsty they all were, yet he didn't dare discard them. Their pace was dangerously slow. His urine had turned to a deep yellow shade that he knew would eventually lead to the death of his kidneys, and then him. Shade was as rare as a virgin in a whorehouse. He wondered if the lack of water created the same headaches and dizziness in Orion and Captain as it did in him. Even his sweat had almost stopped, and he knew that wasn't good.

"Man no sweat," he recalled Feather Yank once saying, "man die."

He thought he was hallucinating when he spotted the cliff dwellings. They were far up the side of a mesa running parallel to them to the north. At precisely the same time, the heads of Billy, Orion, and Captain all turned to the right.

"Ya smell it, fellas?" Billy asked in a gravelly voice through the pain of split and peeling lips. "I think I hear it."

If his ears weren't playing tricks on him there could be a stream running along the base of that mesa. Because of the high, dry brush between him and the cliff he couldn't see if salvation was really there or it was just another of Mother Nature's tricks. As he turned Orion and Captain towards the sound, five Yaqui children slowly and cautiously emerged from the dead thicket, each holding out their hands.

"*Por favor*," they pleaded over and over.

They reminded him of the stick figures he used to draw when he was a kid, except he never included rib bones, swollen bellies, and dark, sunken eyes. He pulled a large strip of mule deer jerky from his saddlebag and tossed it to them. As he watched them scurry back into the brush to divide up the feast, death filled his nostrils. The threesome strode deeper into the high brush towards the cliff. A small village became visible and the foul odor became even stronger. It was a few dozen crude huts, an empty corral, and a couple of disintegrating stone structures that were too old to have been built by their current occupants. To the east he noticed an untended field from a former harvest.

It wasn't a trick. A small creek ran along the base of the mesa separating the village from its rocky wall, just beyond some stunted mesa oaks. As he slowly rode through the village toward the wet salvation he saw that many of the adults were so weak they couldn't even stand. Most were naked or wearing tattered *tilmas*. They were also too feeble to bury their dead. A stack of bodies was piled against the high cliff wall on the other side of the small creek. No smoke rose from any of the huts. There were no animals in the corral. The few Yaquis that didn't inhabit the pile across the creek would very soon become occupants. He had never seen such wretched helplessness. This was simply a place for dying.

He slipped off Orion and knelt by an old Yaqui braced against a rotting corral post. When he asked the man how the village got in such a bad state the Indian told him that a group of Mexican soldiers had come through and seized all of their harvest and animals to feed their troops. What little food that was left had been given to the children, but even that was gone. Then the old man showed Billy a piece of paper that said, in Spanish, "We owe you one thousand pesos, signed, Captain Flores Attendo."

Holding up the paper the old man said, "*No podemos comer papel!*"

He was right. They couldn't eat paper.

Kneeling at the stream, Billy filled his four canteens under the pleading stare of several children. When he glanced at them he could see beyond the hunger in their eyes to the point of the grey emptiness that welcomes death. The smell was even worse being that close to the pile of decaying bodies. With canteens filled and Orion and Captain watered he began to lead the animals back out of the *barrio*. The villagers who could still stand tried to walk towards him, hoping for any kind of handout. Many could only force a few steps before they'd simply collapse. It would've been more merciful if those soldiers would have put a bullet in the heads of every man, woman, and child in this village. He knew it wouldn't do him or the people here any good to share the very few supplies he had left, but he also knew he couldn't leave them in their current state.

He gave them Captain.

When he tossed his few remaining supplies and the filled canteens across Orion's rump, the horse didn't do his usual complaining about the extra weight. He just hung his head. The two weren't a hundred feet from the grotto when they heard Captain squeal as a few of the stronger villagers cut his throat. Not wanting to look back, Billy hoped they'd at least have the decency to cook him. He also knew it would be a far stretch of life before he stopped hearing that squeal. If ever.

The water helped shake his brain back into a calmer state and the dusty tabletop map slowly refocused. He recalled at least two small towns in their current direction, but when he arrived at each of their locations both had vanished from the earth. Either his map was wrong or the land had swallowed them up. The way his plan had gone so far he figured it was the former. A few beans and a handful of oats were all that was left of his supplies. Maybe a day's worth of each. The pain in his jaw was lingering longer before hiding away, but always returning with brain piercing jabs. Even his flask was down to only a few drops of *mescal*. Orion struggled to find any type of edible vegetation. When Billy could catch one, he would eat scrawny hare or rattlesnake. On a few occasions he was lucky enough to spot a chuckwaller. The lizard was chewy but large enough to fill his belly.

His clothing was turning into rags, weathered from the heat and slashed by the swirling dust and blowing sand that cut like little knife jabs. His Levi

Strauss' and chaps had dozens of small rips and slices courtesy of the wicked underbrush. His cotton shirt had lost all but two buttons and the fabric in its underarms was rotting. The hole in his John B, courtesy of Tomas Amador, had weathered away to the size of a half dollar. Only his Justins seemed to be surviving. He guessed, or rather hoped, they were somewhere between Sonoita and Los Indios. They could be north of the two towns, or south, or east, or west. Far ahead he could see the waves of heat rising from the sandy ground. Behind him he could see the waves they had just passed through.

"Funny," he mumbled. "Why can't I see them when I'm in them?" He sure as hell felt them.

Even Orion's keen sense of direction seemed to be muddled by the unchanging landscape. Every time they'd pass a tall, distinctive cactus, both man and horse would stop and study it, worried that it was the same one they had passed the day before. He knew they wouldn't last much longer like this. If he was right about their current location, the border town of El Papalote should be to the north. He hoped he was. He convinced himself that he had to be. He turned Orion north. The horse didn't balk. Three days later, hungry, tired and filthy, the two lumbered in to El Papalote. The way people gaped at him he figured he must look like death on a dead horse. But to his surprise he was also greeted by colored lights and nativity scenes everywhere. The fronts of *tiendas* displayed them, even small adobe homes had miniature ones in front. *Pastorelas*—little religious skits—were being performed in the streets. It was Christmas Eve. He had been wandering Sonora for close to a year.

"Some fuckin' plan!" he mumbled.

After stabling Orion in the livery he treated himself to a hotel room and a bath, his first since soaking in the Rio Yaqui. The steaming slate-colored bathwater quickly turned black. When he rose from the tub he took a peek at the full length mirror leaning against an empty rain barrel. It took him a moment to suck in the fact that the gaunt and gut-shrunk body in the mirror was his own. He wondered if his friend would've put his body through this kind of torture for him, then cursed himself for even thinking it because he knew Jeff would. As he stood there naked, dripping wet, he looked at his clothes then cursed himself again.

"Stupid, stupid, stupid!" he grumbled. Putting on the same duds made the entire bath a waste. "Fuckin' knothead," he said aloud as he climbed back into the flea-ridden rags.

He bought new clothes at a well-stocked *tienda* then took a second bath. Its water also turned black. After donning his new outfit he again stood in front of the bath house's mirror. It bothered him that he looked more like a *vaquero* than a Ranger, but he wanted and needed to better fit the surroundings. The new attire felt strange, especially the sombrero. It was awkward and unbalanced. The serape looped around his neck and over his left shoulder. Though it neatly hid his shoulder holster it was heavy. Fortunately the *tienda* also had a small selection of Levi Strauss jeans. But his most expensive purchase was a pair of calfskin *chaparajos*. He thought about getting some with silver studs down the legs like those worn by the *Rurales* back in...he forgot where...but decided they were too fancy for his taste. There was one item that he simply could not get used to: shirts with a collar. Every shirt he had owned before had no collar. It surprised him when he saw this new style of clothing. It also scratched and chafed his neck. Before the day was over he had cut off the irritating hunk of cloth.

A local *restaurante* was serving traditional Mexican holiday dishes. He indulged. It was a feast: deep-fried *bunuelos* drenched in brown sugar and guava; a large mug of warm *champurrado* that relaxed his jittery tooth; and, of course, many, many tamales. The people were friendly, the music was festive, but for the first time in years, he was alone on Christmas Eve.

As he sipped his second mug of *champurrado* and tapped his foot to the music, he longed to hear Freddie playing carols on his harmonica before his little friend caught the last train up to Bisbee to spend Christmas with his daughter and folks, and probably his "little dressmaker with the huge udders." He had dubbed her that because her breasts were the most ample he'd ever handled and she was barely any taller than his ten-year-old daughter. Being just a smidgen over five feet, it wasn't easy for Freddie to find a woman he could look in the eyes. But the idea of a little woman with large breasts seemed to fascinate Sparky the most.

"Just how big are they?" Sparky asked Freddie early one Christmas Eve afternoon in the barracks.

"More than a handful?" inquired Billy.

"They're big, that's all I can say," replied Freddie, obviously a little embarrassed, but still proud to let everyone know just who he was courting and what he was fondling. He pulled his harmonica from his pocket, tapped it on his jeans a few times and started to lift it to his lips.

"Size of a ripe tomato?" asked Jeff.

"Bigger," smiled Freddie.

"A big tomato?" chuckled Sparky.

"Bigger."

"Head a cabbage?" asked Billy.

"Bigger."

"Musk melon?" asked Jeff.

"Bigger," Freddie repeated and began playing "The First Noel" on his harmonica.

"Bigger than a musk melon?" an astonished Sparky repeated. "I ain't ne'er seen teats that big."

"They're tits, Sparky," responded Billy. "Woman have tits, cows have teats."

"Kiss yer grandma's butt. I was bein' polite."

"'Preciate that, Sparky," Freddie said to his big friend. Then he returned to his harmonica and continued "The First Noel."

Besides the two years Billy had spent with Anna, all the other Christmases were celebrated with Jeff, who would try to teach him the words to some carols. The only one Billy could ever recall was "Silent Night," and that was just the first few lines. Then they'd break out a bottle of bug juice, get drunk, and go to the whorehouse. Even though it was Christmas Eve, whores worked. Whores survive by numbers.

That night Billy lay on the bed in his El Papalote hotel room listening to the singing voices and popping fireworks outside. "Only one man dead," he thought. Tomás Amador. If that was the way it was going to be, one man a year, could he keep it up? He knew he had to. He had promised his friend.

"Ya got it."

He had no idea where he was going from here. The plan he scratched out on that dusty table in San Moise had cost him at least ten pounds. His lean six-foot frame could not afford losing anymore. A familiar tune drifted up from the streets and into the hotel window. It was "Silent Night," but sung in Spanish. Thinking the soft music would soothe him into a nice, restful sleep, he settled back, but sleep wouldn't come. He finally got out of bed, dressed, and walked down to the livery. Orion was munching hay when Billy opened the door to his stall.

"Merry Christmas, Shithead."

He curled up in the hay next to his friend and slept.

Orion was running so fast Billy felt like they were flying, but he could still smell the giant lizard's hot, rank breath close behind them. Its yellow teeth were a foot long and dripping with green drool. Its head was the size of two large rain barrels. Its tongue shot out and slashed across Billy's back, stinging like a bullwhip in the hands of a muleskinner. The monster smiled as it lowered its head, mouth wide open, ready to chomp Billy right out of his saddle. Suddenly a loud hee-haw exploded from the left. Captain was charging at full speed. A speed Billy didn't even know mules could reach. It was like his hooves weren't even touching the ground. The brave mule slammed its head into the monster's jaw, knocking it sideways before its teeth could clamp down on Billy and Orion. Then Captain hee-hawed loudly and ran off into the desert with the angry lizard hot on his tail.

He must been making noises in his sleep because Orion snorted and rudely nudged him awake.

January, 1910

He welcomed in the New Year at El Papalote and decided to stay through the month of January. Not only would it give him time to regain some strength, but it also felt good to be around friendly people for a change. And the town featured two inviting whorehouses. But before attempting to unload some baggage, he had to do something about his tooth.

Again, the local dentist was a barber. Again, he decided to risk it. He entered the shop and told the man his problem. The barber/dentist poked around in Billy's wide open mouth then, like the previous one, made an angle gesture with his hand.

"*Torcido!*" explained the barber.

Again, in frustration, Billy gestured for him to just pull the sumbitchin' thing. The man shrugged his shoulders then reached to his tray of tools and returned with a long, thin, double-edged sharp knife aimed at Billy's mouth.

114

"Stop!" Billy yelled and leapt from the chair.

"Ya don't pull no tooth with a knife, goddamn it," he blurted through the pain as he stomped towards the door. "Ya ain't diggin' fer gold, asshole!"

Back to *mescal.*

The local *policía* were both good men with no ties to any gunrunners. To Billy's surprise neither owned a piece of either whorehouse. They even sent out telegrams to other border towns asking for any information on policemen named "Amador, Quías, Alvarez, Pasco, Victoriano...Amador..." Every day for weeks he'd walk into the telegraph office, and every day the same answer: No one knew anything, or no one was talking.

He considered making a new plan, but decided it wasn't time. He had to hang with the one that got him here. He needed to map out a route that would take him back east and through other towns. Just like the one he mapped out on that table in San Moise that took him west. Surely there were some little towns he had missed. But what if that plan was just as worthless as his current one? Would he make another one taking him back west again, then another east again, then another and another until his ass was one, big, fat callous and Orion leg's were nubs?

"Think, knothead," he chastised himself.

Again he wished Jeff were here to help him wring out this damn problem. Again he realized if Jeff were here there wouldn't be a damn problem to wring out. He decided an evening at the whorehouse might help him think, but coming up on midnight he still hadn't thought of any way to improve his piss-poor plan. In a habit he got into when he was a respected Ranger he left by the back door, angry and drunk. In the darkness he stumbled over an old Yaqui sleeping in the alley. The Indian leapt to his feet, groggy-eyed, but with a knife in hand pointed square at Billy's throat.

"Whoa, whoa, ol' fella," Billy cried, backing away from the annoyed Indian. "Didn't see ya there, sorry 'bout that!" He pulled out his refilled flask. "Have one on me!"

The Indian accepted Billy's slurred apology. He sheathed his knife, grabbed the flask, and hogged down a long pull. That was when Billy noticed the scar across his neck where someone had botched a throat slitting. He also saw that the Yaqui was missing his left hand.

It didn't take them long to drain Billy's flask. Thinking their evening was over he said *adios* and started to leave the alley. The old Indian slurred, "No, no!" and pulled out a wineskin from under the blanket he had been sleeping on and offered it to Billy. Sniffing its contents made Billy's nose hairs retreat clear up and hide behind his eyebrows.

"*Pulque!*" stated the Yaqui. "Drink!" he demanded.

Billy had experienced *pulque* once at the Quechan reservation where he had also dined on the roasted tarantula. It's a powerful drink made from the *malquey*, an agave plant. Contrary to those who believe the evil white man introduced fire water to the Indian, *pulque* and *tiswin* had been getting the *rojo hombre* stewed long before the *blanco hombre* ever planted a boot in the west.

A half-dozen sips later and the two alley dwellers were soused and singing "Red River Valley." Well, Billy was singing. The Yaqui was chanting in more of a howling caterwaul. Several times a whore would stick her head out the back door and tell them to pipe down. He was surprised he could remember the words to his friend's favorite song. Even more surprised when he finally realized just how sad those words were.

The old Yaqui sported a face that mirrored a century of dried leather. Billy was shocked to learn the man named Tanok, meaning Sun, was only thirty-seven-years-old. When he asked him how he lost his hand, Tanok told a story that sucked Billy's cajones right up into his belly.

"Had hand 'til six months ago," the Indian replied in English clearer than Sparky's. "Chicano policeman say I steal bottle of wine. Tanok did not. But he say Christian Bible say thief lose hand. Two of his *compadres* hold me down. Quias chop off hand."

Billy sat up. His mind desperately tried to rinse away the strong liquor. Did he hear right?

"Quias?" he asked. "Did ya say Quias?"

"Si," answered Tanok and gulped down another mouthful of *pulque*.

"And he was a policeman?"

"Si."

"What was his first name?"

"No hear. No care. Someday kill."

Even though it was a rather common last name south of the border, it was the first time Billy had heard it hitched to a policeman.

"Where was this?"

"Pedro Conde. *La casa de putas.*" Tanok squeezed the last of the *pulque* from his wineskin.

Billy then repeated the names to Tanok. "Amador, Quías, Alvarez, Pasco, Victoriano...Amador..." but the only one the Yaqui could give him was Quias. That was enough though. It was his first real lead since Retta drunkenly slurred out Los Pozos as the location of the former Tomás Amador. Pedro Conde was also a border town. He had missed it on his trek west because he was so focused on the Yaqui villages. He began to think he might have misjudged General Torres. Maybe the greaser didn't send those men to Yaqui country. Those fellows are gunrunners and rustlers. To keep up their business they had to hang close to the border. He figured that ol' fart Torres could even be gettin' a cut of their illegal doings. He was angry he hadn't thought of that sooner.

Finding himself rapidly sobering he rose and brushed off the remnants of the dirty alley then handed the Yaqui a five dollar gold piece. The Indian's eyes grew wide as he grinned at the sight of such a fortune. Then the grin quickly turned to a frown.

"*Ten cuidado! Él es un gran mal hombre!*" he advised Billy.

Pedro Conde was about fifty miles southeast of that dark alley. From there he decided he would work his way back east towards Nogales, sticking to only the towns along the border. The next morning he got a week's worth of supplies and tossed them across Orion's hind quarters. After three unsuccessful attempts to snatch and pull the load off with his teeth, and after another reminder of the automobile, Orion accepted the load.

With the brutal Mexican sun darkening his skin, a beard and moustache, hair almost to his shoulders, combined with his new outfit, he was being slowly reborn into his surroundings. Even the local food and water had stopped stampeding his bowels. He figured dressed and looking the way he had been was another reason why Tomás Amador had spotted him so quickly. It could also be why he hasn't gotten any information from the hundreds of other people he'd questioned. But now he had a destination: Delores Quías, in the town of Pedro Conde. At least he hoped it was the same Quías. From Tanok's description it sounded like him.

"*A big, bad man!*"

It bothered him that he no longer looked like a Ranger...but he wasn't.

For seven years he was told "Show your badge, show 'em yer a Ranger. Be proud of it!" He was! He still was! Nothing meant more than being a Peace Officer. But was he still one? The Ranger star was not on his chest. He refused to defile it by pinning it to his current clothes, but inside he was still a Peace Officer. His pa used to say, "Yer brain might lie to you, but yer heart never will." Then his ma would add, "All good feelings and all good deeds come from yer heart. Pay heed to yer heart, Billy." He thought he was, but the thus far worthless plan came from his brain, catching him in his own loop. He wondered if that made it a lie. Was his brain tricking him into roaming forever around Sonora, Mexico?

"No!" he said aloud to the hot south wind. "So what if my brain thunk it up—my heart wants it. That makes it right. I'm seekin' justice, badge or no badge!"

The two made camp about twenty-five miles southeast of El Papalote. Although jerky played hard ball with his tooth, he didn't want to chance a fire. Being that close to the border made the area a common crossing place for renegade Apaches and any kind of bad man. Orion snagged a mouthful of grass from a patch the greedy, dry ground had overlooked.

"Don't chew so loud, shithead!" Billy scolded. "Ya want some assholes to find our nestin' place? They'd probably et you!"

Orion snorted in defiance and stomped his hoof.

"Hell yes they would! Don't argue with me!"

Orion snorted again, twice, and stomped his hoof even harder.

"No way! They'd et you 'fore they'd et me. 'Sides, what di'ference do it make? We'd both still be et."

Since the pain in his tooth seemed to be sleeping, he joined it.

October, 1906

Freddie and Langston Penny were several days overdue when Captain Wheeler received a telegram from a Mexican policeman in La Morita, a border town east of Nogales. The wire said a Ranger had been there for two days and no one could get him to leave the saloon. He wouldn't tell anyone his name, his clothing was covered in blood, and he kept drinking and threatening anyone who came near him. He refused to eat and had even been sleeping in the saloon. The telegram also warned the captain to get some help down here *pronto* or they might have to shoot him.

Wheeler had reports of an Indian raiding party that was killing white settlers in the area north of La Morita then skipping back down across the border. The strange thing was that no one could tell what these Indians were. Their markings and clothing were unknown.

"I think one of 'em might be dead," explained Wheeler to Billy and Jeff. "I sent the two, but only one's in the saloon. Somethin' happened. Better go check it out."

"Since these Injuns are unknown, how 'bouts we take Sparky 'long with us, Cap'n?" Billy suggested.

"Good thinkin'!" Jeff added.

The next train traveling east out of Nogales wasn't until the following morning, so the Rangers saddled up and headed southeast on a three hour ride to the small border town of La Morita.

"Ya think it be Freddie?" Sparky asked. He was very worried about his little friend. "Langston's ain't ne'er fought no Injuns," Sparky reminded them.

"So, ya sayin' ya think it's Langston who's dead?" asked Billy.

"Nope," replied Sparky. "If he ain't ne'er fought Injuns, he mighta run off at the sighta 'em, leavin' Freddie 'lone."

"If he did and it got Freddie killed," responded Jeff, "I'm gonna put a bullet in his brain."

Sparky frowned to himself. Now he had two worries, and that was a lot for Sparky. He was worried if his little pal was still alive, and if he'd have to stop Jeff from following through with his threat. The rest of the ride was as still as a bug-less night in January. Each man fretted silently to himself, worried about which Ranger lived and which didn't. They picked up their pace and arrived in La Morita in just under three hours, a little before five in the afternoon. The town featured two *cantinas*. They found the unknown Ranger in the first one they entered.

It was Freddie.

He had planted himself at a table in a dark corner. A near empty bottle of tequila rested in front of him. His head was tilted back and he appeared to be asleep. Drool was flowing from the corner of his mouth. His right arm was on the table with gun in hand. The three friends approached with caution.

Breathing a sigh of relief, Sparky spoke softly, "Freddie? Hey, Freddie, we're here."

Freddie slowly opened his eyes. They were glazed over yet darted from side-to-side. His cheeks were hollow. His face was grey and ghostly. The blood on his shirt was crusted and turning a rusty brown and mixed with dried, yellow vomit.

"Wansome'quila?" he slurred.

"What the hell are ya doin', Freddie?" asked Billy.

The bartender had joined the group. "Por favor, *Señor*, get him out!" he pleaded. "His smell, it is stinking up my place."

"Hace cuant hempo paso' el aqúi?" inquired Sparky.

"Dos dias!" answered the bartender.

Billy took hold of one of Freddie's arms as Jeff grasped the other. The two lifted him out of the chair.

"We gotta get some food in ya, Boulder!" stated Billy.

Suddenly Freddie jerked free of his two friends, staggering and waving his shooter. "NO!" He sobbed and screamed, "Ya ain't gonna make me eat him! Ya ain't..." His eyes rolled back in his head and he collapsed to the floor exhausted, drunk, starving, and terrified.

They got two hotel rooms and managed to get Freddie cleaned up and as comfortable as possible. Sparky had an extra shirt in his saddlebags. It fit the small Ranger like a night gown, but at least it wasn't caked with blood and puke. Freddie slept for close to twenty hours, interspersed with occasional screams repeating the same thing he yelled in the saloon, "Ya ain't gonna make me eat him! Ya ain't..." Finally his senses began to unscramble.

"I ain't ne'er seen nuthun like it," he explained as he sipped his third bowl of hot broth with shaking hands, spilling some on his shirt. "Them Injuns held that poor boy down and that chief cut out his heart. Right there, right in front of me...and Langston weren't dead when it was done. The screamin'...I can still hear his screaming." Freddie began to sob.

"Easy, Boulder," said Sparky.

Freddie was shaking so badly Billy had to take the bowl of hot liquid from his hands. After taking several deep breaths the sobbing lessened and he continued.

"Then the fucker rubbed Langston's heart all over my face and shirt and kept yellin', 'Like that, little Ranger, like that?' and laughin'...just laughin'... with this crazy look in his eyes. Then...then...he et it."

The other three Rangers looked at each other in silence.

"He et it!" repeated Freddie like he was still trying to believe it himself. "Then them other Injuns cut Langston up into pieces, just hacked 'im up. Then they started cooking them pieces. The smell! I can still smell it, fellas! I can still smell it!" The sobbing returned.

"Git some more rest, Freddie" ordered Sparky.

"No, no, I ain't done," Freddie frantically insisted and choked down his sobbing. "I gotta tell ya, I gotta tell ya the rest, gotta get it out. We gotta tell the Cap'n. That fuckin' chief...that fuckin' bastard...he started tryin' to make me et pieces of Langston. He kept stuffin' chunks of meat in my mouth and holdin' it shut and makin' me chew and makin' me swallow and I kept pukin' and gaggin' and...and...he kept yellin,' 'We do same to all Rangers. Rangers stay away, stay away, stay...' and shovin' more pieces of Langston in my mouth and..."

"Easy, Freddie, easy," stated Sparky as he touched his friend's shoulder.

"Then I guessed I passed out," Freddie said, his voice seeming to slightly calm. "The next thing I knew I woke up with my hands tied to my lizzy. My horse had wandered into this town. Where are we?"

"La Morita," answered Jeff.

"My head was spinning and poundin' and all I could think 'bout was getting' that...that taste outta my mouth." He looked up at his friends and tears filled his eyes. "It's still there, fellas, it's still there." Through the returning sobbing he spat and shouted, "The bastard took my harmonica."

"What 'em Injuns look like?" asked Sparky.

Freddy shook his head and reached for the bowl of hot broth.

"None I'd e'er seen! They had big cloth headdresses wrapped 'round them with all diff'rent colors of big feathers stuffed in them. Colors I ain't ne'er seen 'fore, and I mean BIG feathers. Ain't ne'er seen a bird that big!" He guzzled down the remaining broth.

"How many of them were there?" asked Jeff.

"Twenty, thirty, at least," Freddie replied as he held out the empty bowl for more broth.

"What'd ya think, Sparky?" inquired Billy, as he took the empty bowl and ladled in more broth from the small bucket they had taken from the local *cantina*.

Removing his hat and scratching his large head, Sparky said, "Well, I hear tell of a tribe called Karankawa in east Texas. S'posedly they et their enemies. Says it give 'em powers!"

"East Texas?" exclaimed Jeff. "What the hell are they doin' clear out here?"

"Maybe East Texans were too chewy," joked Billy.

No one laughed. They just looked at him.

"Sorry!" he added.

They gave Freddie another day of rest then returned to Nogales and relayed the story to Captain Wheeler. Without a second thought he decided to dump this job on the Army.

"Let 'em skin-hungry Injuns et a few soldiers 'stead a my men," he declared.

"Cap'n?" Sparky asked, "How ya gonna tell Langston's folks ya can't send home his body fer a Christian burial?"

"Guess I'll have to lie, Sparky," replied Wheeler. "No parent needs to get that kinda news."

For a brief moment Jeff tried to picture his grandfather's reaction when his son was returned to him as rotting chunks in a box. "Fuckin' savages," he muttered. "Sooner we kill them all the better this country'll be." He stomped out of Wheeler's office.

Nothing more was ever heard of these strange cannibal Indians with the large colorful feathers. The Army unit sent from Fort Naco did find an abandoned campsite near where Freddie had described. It did have a scattering of human bones. No live Indians. The killing of settlers stopped. There were no stories about people being eaten. If they were Karankawa maybe they went back to East Texas. Maybe down into Mexico, making them no longer a U.S. problem. Maybe they just ate each other.

Freddie bought himself a new harmonica, but it was close to a month before he could eat any kind of meat.

February, 1910

It was a little before noon of their third day when Billy and Orion arrived in Pedro Conde. The town looked like a hundred others. At first it seemed too little to even warrant a policeman, but then Billy figured maybe that was what Quias wanted. The asshole wouldn't have to work as hard and could spend more time at the whorehouse and *cantina*. He ate lunch at a small *restaurante* run by a friendly family named Salazar. When his meal of enchiladas and rice was served by their two young sons it made him think of his own boys. It had been two years since he had seen them. Born in '06 and '07 they'd be close to four and three by now.

"Maybe," he told himself, "when all this is over and done with, I'll go see how they turned out."

After the meal, he planted himself across the road from the *bordello* next to a small corral. He sat in the dirt under one of only five trees in the town and waited. First he had to see if this was the right Quías. He knew his face from the argument they had outside the ratty Mexican jail where Jeff lay dying. Shortly after sundown a large man in the usual soiled police uniform strolled towards the whorehouse whistling a tune Billy didn't recognize. It was him. It was the right Quías. Billy lowered his sombrero to appear as just another sleeping Mexican. He had forgotten what a brute of a fellow Quías was, or he was simply too angry during their past argument to even care. He decided it would be wise to wait until his prey left the whorehouse drunk and spent from hours of unloading baggage...Advantage...and more of the town would be asleep. Quías didn't appear to be armed, not even the standard issue *pistola*. "Strange," he thought, but another advantage. He settled against the corral fence post to wait. Soon a light breeze captured the pungent odor of the few cattle and horses in the corral and blew it up his nose. For an instant he thought he could even taste it. He spat.

April, 1907

"A ranch," Jeff suggested, "maybe in northern New Mexico, where it still snows. I do miss snow. Didn't think I would 'cause I got so sick of it back home."

The two Rangers were stretched out on their bunks listening to a thunder storm. At least three times they had to shift their beds to keep them from being drenched by leaks in the rotting roof. Sparky was stretched out on his two mattresses on the floor, snoring away, mindless of the water pooling at his stocking feet. Freddie had taken the train up to Bisbee to see his daughter, and probably his "little dressmaker with the huge udders." Usually on these down times Billy would spend some time with his wife and boys, but lately every time he came home Anna's head seemed to be in faraway places.

"We could pool our money," continued Jeff. "Buy some land, get us a horny bull and a few heifers, and in no time we'd have ourselves a herd."

"Ain't that easy," stated Billy. "I cut cattle fer years. They are stupid, smelly devils." He lit his pipe.

"Better than goats though, right?" Jeff stated with a grin.

"Ridin' herd on wild turkeys be better than goats," answered Billy. "Sides, we got us work here. Why leave it?"

"I'm not sayin' we do it first thing in the mornin', but sometime...in the future."

Outside, lightning flashed and thunder rumbled.

"Cattle are jumpy as hell, too," added Billy. "Night like this and they'd be stampedin' fer Mexico."

"Yer such a pessimist, Mr. Old!"

"A what?"

"Pessimist! A fella who always thinks on the bad side of things!"

"Ne'er said I wouldn't do it," Billy bristled.

Another loud clap of thunder shook the barracks.

"Well, it's just a dream anyway," said Jeff. "Every man needs a dream. You got one?"

"Got what?"

"A dream! What you'd like to do with your life!"

"I thought I was doin' it."

"No other ambitions?" asked Jeff.

"Just keepin' me and Orion fed and a warm place to sleep...maybe a 'cas'nal whore." It troubled him that he so quickly added those last four words seeing that he'd been hitched for more than two seasons, but deep down he knew it was true.

"Come on, Billy, there's gotta be more to life than food, fire, and fuckin'!" Jeff rose and crossed to the small stove, grabbed an old rag and opened the grill to toss in another small log.

"Well, goddamn it then, what about you?" Billy blurted. "Shit, Jeff, ya coulda been just 'bout anything ya wanted. Ya got brains, ya got schoolin', but ya come down here to this shit-saken place to get yerself shot at by a bunch of pus-buckets. You confound me, Jeff Kidder!"

Jeff chuckled then spat a wad of tobacco into the fire and listened for a moment as it sizzled and popped. As he closed the grill and returned to his bunk, a low roll of thunder covered the noise of the creaky floor boards beneath his feet. He sat back down on the bed, facing Billy.

"My grandpa was in the U.S. House of Representatives," Jeff stated. "For a spell he helped run this whole damn country, but it frustrated the hell out of him, gave him more white hairs than a snow fox. I asked him why he did it. Know what he said?"

"What?" asked an attentive Billy.

"'Jeffie,' don't you laugh, that was what he called me 'til his dying day!" 'Jeffie, this world is always going to have bad people, and some of us are put here to try and stop their evil doin's. This is the best way I know how to do that.'" Then Jeff tapped on his Ranger badge and said, "This is the best way I know how to do that, Billy. Hell, I'm not gonna do it forever, I know that!" He grinned and added, "Just 'til I get famous." His serious tone immediately returned. "But right now it needs to be done so I'll do it. It's necessary, and that makes me necessary—not just another asshole takin' up space."

Billy's head lingered on those words for a few seconds before he asked, "So, does that make me nes'sary, too?"

"Absolutely," answered Jeff as he lie back in his bunk. Following a few thunder claps he added, "It's a good dream though, ain't it? A ranch? A man with no dreams ain't worth a horse apple."

Billy remembered it was one of the few times he heard his friend use the word "ain't." Twice!

"Damn good dream, Jeff!" he answered as his friend began humming "Red River Valley."

Sparky raised his head in a sleepy daze and called out, "Ma, why'er my feet wet?" He curled up into a large fetal position and resumed his snoring.

February, 1910

It was a dark night in Pedro Conde. No moon. Billy looked up and saw Orion's namesake. He pointed and said, "That there's where ya'll go when ya leave this earth, shithead, right up to them three stars. Maybe Cap'n's on one of them already."

Orion snorted and stomped his hoof twice.

Several hours passed before Quías finally stepped out into the night, but with a fly in the ointment. In one hand he carried a bottle of nearly spent tequila. With the other he was tugging along a young whore who didn't appear to be in the mood for a moonlight stroll. Billy knew he couldn't stay in this town too long without drawing attention to the fact that a *gringo* was here, regardless of his appearance. He had to make his move. Hoping the whore would appreciate her freedom from the beast he stepped out of the darkness.

"Delores Quías!" he called.

The big man stopped and turned towards the stranger. *"¿Quién está pridiendo?"* he replied.

Billy removed the *sombrero*. "Remember me, *amigo*?"

Quías squinted through tequila and no moon then said, "Ah, *sí*," he answered, nodding his head and displaying a taunting grin, "The Ranger! Oh, I forget. No more Rangers, *sí*?" He laughed. "You look for job, Ranger?"

Billy slipped free of his *serape*, took the .45 out of its shoulder holster, and placed it and his Smith & Wesson on the ground.

"No!" he replied. "I'm lookin' fer you, asshole."

A Dime Novel would say he put aside his weapons because Quías was unarmed and it wouldn't have been a fair fight. Actually, he just didn't want a gunshot rousing any other Mexican policemen that might still be inside the whorehouse. Not being totally ignorant of the bulk facing him and still wanting an advantage, he pulled the long knife from the back of his belt. All the moves the Comanche breed taught him flashed through his head. He positioned his feet for the ever important balance. He cleared his mind of everything except where he wanted to sink the blade. Then Quías released the whore's arm and smashed his tequila bottle on a fence post, creating a nasty jagged weapon.

Advantage gone!

Through gritted yellow teeth, the policeman hissed, "Come get me, *hombre!*"

Finally, here it was, after all those years, a knife fight. Just as Billy was about to approach the hulking beast the whore flew out of the darkness and with both hands smashed a rock into the back of Quías's head. The big fellow collapsed at Billy's feet in a silent heap. For a moment he stood there stunned. Then the whore kicked the unconscious *hombre* in the ribs.

"*Puerco!*" she spat at the hulk in the dirt. Then she looked at Billy and said, "*¡Corton los cojones! Hienden ellos.*" Muttering even more obscenities in Spanish she stomped off into the darkness.

Whores usually liked Rangers. Mainly because they paid without question, didn't knock them around, and were often in a hurry, but Billy was pretty certain this one just hated Quías. He thought about thanking her with a silver dollar but, then again, she did ruin his first chance at a knife fight. Rather, a knife and broken bottle fight.

April, 1904

"That's it?" whispered Jeff. "One head?"

"Did ya see how skinny them Injuns were?" remarked Billy.

Two ranchers near the southern base of the Dragoon Mountains had complained about some Indians stealing their cattle. Since the places had been hit in succession, Jeff figured the Indians were stupid enough to hit the next one in line. The two sly Rangers hid out on a hill overlooking a herd of about two hundred smelly head. Side-by-side, prone in the high grass, they waited. Sure enough, an hour after sundown, four Indians slipped out of the heavy brush, two braves and two squaws toting papooses. They quietly cut one head from the herd and led the animal off into the bushes.

"Told ya they were dumb enough to hit the next one," grinned Jeff. "Let's go get them!"

"What?" exclaimed Billy. "We gonna chase four starvin' Injuns over one ol' moss back?"

"They're stealing, Billy! It's our job."

"Bullshit! It's only 'cause ther Injuns! One fuckin' cow? Go if ya wanna, I ain't!"

"Goddamn it, Billy, it's our job!"

"Chasin' rustlers is our job, not starvin' Injuns." He clamped his pipe stem into his mouth and defiantly crossed his arms. "I ain't doin' it!"

Jeff stared at his friend for a long moment then chuckled. "You remind me of my little brother, crossin' your arms like that! 'I ain't doin' it!'" he mocked. Settling back down in the grass he plucked a stem and chewed on it. After a few moments he said, "You're right. One ol' moss back isn't worth getting' our dander up with each other. Guess those Injuns have to eat, too." Then he grinned and asked, "But how am I ever gonna get famous if we keep doin' shit like this?"

"Hell, in just a year ya brung in seven rustlers and four beaner police-men gunrunners. Ya keep pissin' off them crooked Mexican *policia* and they'll make ya famous alright...as maggot meat."

"Can't just leave them to their dirty deeds, Billy?"

"Then stop givin' out yer name ev'ry time ya shackle them. Yer just lettin' their friends know who to hunt down."

Neither spoke for several minutes. They simply watched the Indians lead the one cow over a small rise and disappear into the night.

Finally Billy asked, "Wanna pickle our livers?"

"Why the hell not? It stinks out here."

The two rose from their prone positions and crossed to their mounts.

"What if we had a horse ranch 'stead of cattle?" asked Billy. "Wouldn't wake up ev'ry morn to that god awful stench."

"Wouldn't make as much money either. People need to eat and the automobile's gonna replace the horse anyways."

"Ain't gonna happen. Horses don't need roads."

"How many times I gotta tell ya, Billy, steel's our God now and automo-biles are made of steel. Either of these two critters we're perched on made of steel?"

"Well, then maybe we oughta get a steel ranch," suggested Billy.

The men's laughter was followed by a short silence as they slowly rode towards the nearest town.

"What 'bout a honey bee farm?" Billy finally suggested.

With a baffled look, Jeff asked, "Ya serious?"

"My pa had a couple of hives," explained Billy. "He'd put the honey in mason jars and sell it in town. Made a nice penny. We could invent dif'rent things made with honey. Ya know how folks like honey on their biscuits? We could invent a biscuit with honey already in it. Might be lotsa things that honey could be put inside of instead of folks buyin' it in a jar and puttin' it on them things...like...like griddle cakes and bread and...and...we could call it "Old Kidder Honey"

"Why not Kidder Old Honey?" asked Jeff, amused at his friend's excitement.

"Cause Old Kidder makes it sound like there's this old fella named Kidder with a secret concoction fer makin' things with honey."

Jeff looked at Billy and said, "You been ponderin' on this fer a spell, haven't ya?"

"Course, we might git stunged a bunch," added Billy.

"That's a reckon!"

"Ya think a honey bee knows that if it stings ya it's gonna die?" Billy asked.

"I doubt it. They're just bugs."

"Too bad that can't happen to people," stated Billy.

"What'd ya mean?"

"If a fella killsa 'nother fella, 'cept in self-defense or somethun, then he'd just drop over dead, too, right then and there, just like a honey bee that done stung someone. Make our job a lot easier."

"But boring," stated Jeff as he released a stream of juice through a tobacco-stained grin. "Can't get famous doin' borin' things."

A half hour later they were trotting into the small town of Pearce, Arizona. As they had promised themselves, the Rangers ended up in the local saloon. After several more than too many drinks, they figured it could a good night to unload some baggage.

"Where's the whor'house?" Billy drunkenly slurred at the bartender.

"Last buildin' south on the left," the man replied.

Billy thanked him and flipped him two bits.

With a wink the bartender added, "Have fun!"

The two soused friends staggered up to the front of the place indicated, threw open the door, boldly stepped in, and shouted in unison, "Who wants to fuck a Ranger?"

It took only a drunken instant to realize they had been duped. Four shirtless Apache bucks sky high on *mescal* beans jumped up with knives in their hands and a killing gleam in their eyes. Leaping between Jeff and Billy and the four braves, an Indian whore began hustling the two Rangers back out the door.

"You, you, Rangers!" she yelled, "You go! No trouble here! You go!" She pushed Jeff and Billy out the door into the night air. "GO!" She turned quickly to calm the braves and slam the door behind her. It's damn certain she didn't do this because she liked Rangers. Most fancy whorehouses wouldn't let an Indian set foot in them—of course, pretty squaws were a different story. But in a few towns, especially ones near a reservation, a squaw with some gumption would sometimes set up her own house.

For a moment the two men stood there shaking. Just split seconds apart both sank to a seated position. Luckily it was after midnight and the street was empty of wagons and livestock. Horrific images of what could've befallen them flashed through their heads. Finally Billy stood up and adjusted his gun belt.

"Whatcha doin'?" slurred Jeff, still seated in the dusty street.

"I'm goin' back to that saloon and shoot that bartender in both his knee caps," slurred Billy.

"Good thinkin', slurred Jeff.

As soon as those two words had entered his ears Billy passed out flat on his face. All he got that night was a broken nose.

February, 1910

The sun and Quías opened their eyes at almost the same time. For awhile Billy was worried he wouldn't. Having the *hombre* put under by a whore with a rock didn't fit his plan. Even with a hell of a headache it took the policeman only seconds to realize he was in deep shit. His wrists were tightly bound to his belt buckle. He was far from town, flat on his back with his legs in the air and his feet strapped to the inside stirrups of two jittery horses. Standing in front of the two restless animals holding both sets of reins in just one hand and a fancy pipe in the other was the ex-Ranger.

"Spit quick or die, Quías," Billy calmly stated between two puffs.

Not wanting to struggle and frighten the horses, Quías wisely became very cooperative.

"Sí, sí, *Señor Ranger, por favor*, what...what you want to know? I tell you anything, anything, just please, no let go reins, Ranger, *por favor*."

Leading the two horses in a slow, deliberate circle, leisurely bouncing the back of Quías'head off the rough terrain, Billy said, "You and Amador were inside that *cantina* back in Naco when Ranger Kidder came in. Moises Alvarez, Diaz Pasco, and a Victoriano were outside. I wanna know the whereabouts a them last three *hombres*!"

Without a moment's hesitation, Quías was spilling his guts.

"Moises is in La Bandera," he said, almost sobbing. "I know not where Pasco is..." Billy lightly jerked the reins causing the horses to slightly pitch and shuffle. Panic shot across Quías's face. "No, no, *Señor*, I beg you. *Por favor!* I know not where Pasco is. He no *amigo* of mine, *Señor*, no *amigo*!"

"Victoriano then," said Billy. "Where can I find him?"

Seeming surprised by the question, Diaz replied, "Uh, in his office I guess, *Señor*, in..."

His words were cut short by the hissing of an angry rattlesnake that had silently slithered into the area. The horses bucked and leapt, jerking the reins from Billy's hand. They shot off into the morn with Quías screaming for mercy. All Billy could do was stand and watch the man being skinned across the rocky Sonora ground. He really didn't plan on the *hombre* dying that way—like a wishbone from a Thanksgiving turkey—but he hasn't had much luck with plans lately. Feigning innocence the rattler continued on its journey into the bush.

"La Bandera," Billy thought. It was even further south than San Moises where his plan began, and nowhere near the border, and not in Yaqui country. Maybe General Torres did send them far away. Maybe he'll be following the assholes clear down into Mexico City. As he climbed on Orion he also grumbled over Quías's response to his question about the mysterious Victoriano.

"Office?" he groused.

He wondered what was this Victoriano fellow, some kind of businessman, banker or store keeper? He had never heard of some lazy "office sitter" throwing themselves into the middle of a gun fight. Unless it was a Peace Officer, Billy didn't think people in offices even packed guns. He couldn't make any sense of it.

"It'd make sense to Jeff!" he shouted aloud in frustration.

Orion snorted in agreement.

"Oh, and I suppose you know someone who has an office, shithead?" he snapped back at the animal and waited for a response. "I didn't think so. Hell, ya ain't even got the sense God gave a..." He started to say "horse" than quickly changed it to "goose!"

Angry and confused, he jerked Orion's curb straps and the two headed southeast for La Bandera.

September, 1904

"I tell ya, fellas, the man who sits in that office is important," explained Jeff to ears that would rather listen to Freddie's harmonica playing. "I voted the first time in ninety-six, then again in at the turn of the century. It's every American's duty. That's why I'm takin' some vacation days and goin' up to Colorado to vote."

Arizona was a territory so to vote Jeff had to go to a state. None of the other three Rangers relaxing in the barracks could understand why he'd waste good vacation days making that trip. None of them had ever voted and weren't about to start now.

Sparky was stretched out on his two mattresses when he said, "Too fer to go."

Then Freddie taunted Jeff by blowing "Dixie" on his harmonica.

"Everyone should vote, goddamn it," he chastised his friends. "You don't want just any fool sittin' in that office."

Billy sat up on his bunk. "There's a goddamn fool in that office now," he spat. "T.R. weren't no general and he ain't no damn President neither."

"Then go with me and vote against him," suggested Jeff.

Billy grunted and added, "Only ways he got the job in the first place was 'cause McKinney got hisself shot by that crazy ass Polock!"

"McKinley," Jeff corrected his pal.

132

"It's 'cause a that ol' Injun curse!" said Freddy as he pounded his harmonica in the palm of his hand to remove some lingering spit. "That's what done it!"

"What Injun curse?" asked Sparky. "Done what?"

"Something about some fella tippin' o'er a canoe," added Freddie. "That's all I can 'member!" He blew once on his harmonica. Satisfied it was spit free, he slipped it back in his shirt pocket.

Sparky was baffled, as usual. "Some fella got an Injun curse jist fer tippin' o'er a canoe?"

Jeff sighed and explained, "It was a curse put on Harrison when he was fightin' at the Battle of Tippecanoe. He whupped Tecumseh and his warriors. Tecumseh's brother, some asshole Injun they called 'The Prophet,' put a curse on Harrison and said every President elected at the same time as Harrison would die. It's a bunch of bullshit! That's all!"

"I don't know, Jeff. Em Injun curses hold some pow'ful medicine," warned Sparky. "My gramps done lost all his teeth 'cause a Injun curse."

"Oh, come on, Sparky!" scoffed Jeff.

"True as a hen lays eggs! My gramps done tol' me 'bout it! We be sittin' on the porch. I was a little shaver..."

"When were you ever little?" Freddie joked.

"Oh, when I was 'bout six I was yer height now," said Sparky, flipping the tease right back on his little pal.

Freddie chuckled and said, "Kiss yer grandma's butt."

"I asked him what happened to all his teeth, and he tol' me an Injun done cursed 'em and they all falt out."

"All at the same time?" asked Billy.

"That's jist what I said!" replied Sparky. "Gramps, I says, all at the same time I says, and he says, 'Oh, no, o'er a spell a forty-some years.' Can ya believes that? A curse that done hung 'round fer forty years? Nosireebob! Ya don't wanna mess with 'em Injun curses!"

A curious thought struck Freddie so he put a question to Jeff.

"Jeff, ya say this here 'Prophet' fella made up the curse when Harrison whupped him in some fight?"

"So the myth goes," replied Jeff. "But that's all it is, myth, just another stupid redskin legend!"

"When did Harrison fight in that Injun War and whup that Prophet fella?" prodded Freddie.

Jeff thought for a moment then spoke as if reciting the answer to a test, "Battle of Tippecanoe, eighteen eleven!"

The little man frowned then asked another question.

"What was a Pres'dent doin' fightin' in an Injun war?"

"He wasn't President yet," answered Jeff.

"So when did he get the job a Pres'dent?"

"Eighteen forty."

"That when he died?"

Impatiently Jeff replied, "Okay, here it is: Harrison in eighteen forty, Lincoln in eighteen sixty, Garfield in eighteen eighty, McKinley in nineteen hundred. All zeroes! All died! Okay? It was a coincidence! That's all! There is no goddamn Injun curse!! It's a buncha bullshit!"

"Now, my cipherin' ain't as good as yers, Jeff," admitted Freddie, "but don't eighteen eleven come afore eighteen forty? So that there curse was put on Harrison neigh onto thirty years afore he got to be Pres'dent, right? So how'd this here 'Prophet' fella even know Harrison was ever gonna be a Pres'dent?"

Jeff stared at Freddie. No words came to his mouth because no answer came to his mind. His harmonica playing friend had brought up a point he'd never considered, and it was so simple. He was embarrassed at his inability to provide an answer. He wondered why that question never occurred to him back in college. Would Professor Temple have had an answer?

After a short period of nothingness, Sparky laughed and said, "Looks like we done stumped the college boy." With that statement Freddy and Billy joined the mocking laughter.

Flustered, but trying not to laugh along with his friends, Jeff replied, "It's still bullshit and I'm still gonna go vote, goddamn it!"

"Well, if yer plumb set on makin' the trip," stated Billy, "then at least vote agin the damn fool!"

"He has done some good things since he's been in office, Billy."

Billy huffed and lit his pipe.

"Like what?" Freddie asked with genuine curiosity.

"Well, the Meat Inspection Act," Jeff explained, seizing the opportunity to regain his status. "The Pure Food and Drug Act, the..."

134

"Whoa, whoa now," exclaimed Sparky. "Chew 'em words finer. What be 'em 'Act' things?"

"Those two acts," Jeff explained, "means that it's safer to buy food without it being contaminated." The other three men just stared at him. "Poisoned!" he clarified.

Still not quite grasping the content, which was normal for Sparky, he asked, "What kinda fool'd et poison food anyways?"

Then Freddie had a recollection.

"My little girl got real sick from some bad baby food one time that we got in airtights," he claimed. "They said it was somethin' in the can that done it."

"Airtights have sickened a lot of folks over the years," stated Jeff. "T.R.'s act makes sure the people who make those airtights can't do that again." Feeling comfortable that his status had been reclaimed he added, "Nuthun they sell can hurt anyone. It all gets inspected before they can ever sell it. That's what the person in the office of President can do, should do; protect the people."

"The only office that goddamn fool should be sittin' in is an undertaker's," blurted Billy. "He done got enough deaths on his head." With that last statement he stomped out of the barracks.

Jeff didn't go to Colorado.

1910

La Bandera was a distance to his rear. Tomás Amador, Delores Quías, and Moises Alvarez were dead. Two to go: Diaz Pasco hopefully awaiting his fate back in Naco, if that gambler was telling him the truth. No reason for him not to. And the mysterious Victoriano perched behind a desk in an office somewhere. Billy figured he'd find a way to make Pasco tell him where that office was. Heading to Naco meant backtracking north. As usual, Orion bitched. Every five minutes for the first hour the plucky horse would try to turn east or west or south. Any direction besides the one from which they had just come. About every five minutes for that first hour Billy would have to yank the black's curb-strap and remind him of what a shithead he was. Finally, knowing he could get resupplied in Naco, he reached into his saddlebag and pulled out the last of his withered carrots. He split it in two with the bigger half going to Orion. It hurt to chew.

"Ya happy now?"

Orion snorted.

"Can we get back to headin' north now?"

Orion snorted.

"Ya'll do anythin' fer a carrot, won't ya?"

Orion snorted and nodded his head.

"Ya whore!"

It was cold that first night heading to Naco. Even the woolen *serape* wouldn't fend off the chill. He reckoned a fire would be too risky if some of Alvarez's friends were on his trail. If the asshole had any friends. The question of a "man behind a desk" still had him stumped. He wondered if even Jeff could figure that one out. A cold breeze forced him to tighten the blanket around his shoulders. A coyote howled in the distance. He listened to its long lonely bay. For some reason it brought his thoughts back to that gambler. Mexico had long been a haven for ex-patriots, bandits, rapists, murderers, renegade Indians, even former Confederate soldiers who refused to accept defeat. But the gambler's last statement had been bouncing around Billy's brain pan all day: "Ain't much to smile 'bout 'round here."

"That's the truth," he muttered to himself.

He couldn't remember the last time he smiled, the last time something made him laugh or feel good—maybe singing in that alley with Tanok. He was wearing down. He knew how this trek was changing him. He'd always considered himself a carefree man, just another fellow doing his job. Just another Peace Officer. When this was finally over would he be the same Billy Old? Even though he had no legal badge or had taken no oath, he still felt like a Peace Officer. It was in his blood. A Peace Officer was supposed to uphold justice. Isn't that what he was doing? Upholding justice and bringing it to a few who had escaped it? Sure, he had hardened, but he knew to finish this it was how he had to be. It didn't necessarily mean he had to stay that way.

"When this is over," he told himself, "I'll bring back the old Billy Old." He chuckled at his words. Orion moved over closer to him, lowered his large head, and nudged him with his nose. "Sorry, Big O," said Billy as he stroked the stallion's nose. "Ain't got no more carrots. We'll get some in Naco."

The horse released a frustrated snort but remained close to his friend. Billy sensed Orion's uneasiness and began humming "Red River Valley."

Three days later and only one away from Naco, Billy decided it was safe enough to build a fire and have a hot meal. He tossed the last of his saved bacon lard into the skillet, but before he added his remaining beans, he mixed a few of them in with the last small handful of oats for Orion and slipped on his nosebag. Since horses can't vomit, he knew the beans would probably make the stallion shit about every mile the next day, but Orion needed nourishment, too. He certainly wasn't getting any from the barren Sonora ground.

His tooth was almost to the point of unbearable. He had even considered trying to knock it out himself with the butt of his Smith & Wesson, but figured he'd probably end up knocking out the wrong one. Shaking his flask he could tell it was down to only a few sips. Orion snorted and stomped his hooves.

"If you gotta shit already," Billy told him, "do it downwind."

Emerging from the darkness as if they had just been born of the earth itself stepped seven Yaquis, all with rifles, and all aimed at Billy. He rose quickly but knew his Smith & Wesson would never leave leather before he would have seven slugs in him. One of the Indians slowly walked into the glow of the fire. In his right hand was a plucked and cleaned quail, ready for roasting. Then Billy noticed the man's missing left hand.

Tanok handed the quail to Billy and said, *"Gracias."*

All seven Yaquis then turned and disappeared into the night shadows as silently as they had come. Relief washed over Billy in a rush. His legs wobbled and his stomach churned. He was about to soil his breeches. He scampered off into the brush before he ruined his last pair of Levi Strauss'. As he squatted behind a bush, hoping a rattler didn't bite his ass, he realized he didn't have any paper.

May, 1902

Leaning against the side of an outhouse in the Mexican border town of Los Fresnos, Billy couldn't help chuckling at Jeff's exploding bowels inside. Eariler that day the two Rangers had swapped lead with three rustlers. Two were now feeding crows and one got away, but a blood trail said he wouldn't be long in the saddle. Before they herded the stolen thirty butt-heads back up across the border, they decided to enjoy the favors of the small town.

"I done tol' ya to not drink the water down here, ya Dakota dummy!" Billy yammered at the outside of the closed privy door.

With a voice that sounded strained and weak, Jeff exclaimed, "The goddamn whore told me it was a shot of tequila."

"At least it was only a shot and not a full glass," explained Billy. "Otherwise you'd be stuck in that little shack fer a week."

Jeff groaned then asked, "Why the hell'd she do that?"

"They like to pull that joke on knotheaded *gringo*s down here fer the first time."

"Why didn't you warn me?"

"I fergot you was new."

"Go back there and shoot her for me," Jeff demanded.

"Nope."

"Some friend you are!" A guttural eruption shook the outhouse so hard it caused a roof shingle to slide off and strike the ground. "Can ya fetch me some paper," Jeff grunted from inside the smelly half-moon shack.

"Ya mean there ain't none in there?"

"Would I ask if there were, goddamn it?"

"Well, seems to me that a smart college fella like you would've taken note a that 'fore he loosed his innards."

"Billy, yer pissin' me off!"

Billy patted his pockets then glanced around the ground. "Ain't got none; don't see none 'round."

"What the hell am I supposed to do?"

"Use yer bandana."

"Good thinkin'!"

"Jist don't put it back 'round yer neck."

1910

Naco, Mexico and Naco, Arizona were not old towns. Both were established in 1897 as a border crossing to connect the copper mines on each

138

side. Both had quickly petered out. The Mexican side looked as if it had been baking in the sand for a century. Coming from the south meant Billy would have to pass through it. He could've skirted it, but wanted to take another look at Lucheia's *cantina*. He paused for a moment in front of the small adobe structure that resembled a hundred others he had visited for the past...how long has it been? He imagined the gunshots as Jeff fought for his life. The empty, riddled water trough still sat rotting in the sun. Could Pasco be in there right now? Could he get this over with right now? No. He had to make a plan to get what he needed out of Pasco—the whereabouts of Victoriano. He also knew that common courtesy says first check in with the local Marshal on the Arizona side. Rangers always did that. Let him know that this stranger in town was not a threat. But he wasn't a Ranger. And he was a threat...to Diaz Pasco.

At first no one paid them any mind. The shoulder length hair, beard, and *serape* and sombrero made him part of the scenery. Then a tall, ugly policeman with a crooked eye noticed the white star on the black stallion's forehead. Soon four of them had gathered and were glaring at the twosome. Orion blew a contemptuous snort and sent snot in their direction.

"Easy, boy," Billy said as he patted the horse's neck.

While they maintained a bold bravado, that twelve foot stretch of bridge that crossed nothing but sand felt like one-hundred-and-twelve. As soon as the black's hooves left the wooden planks of the bridge, both deeply exhaled. They had entered Arizona Territory. Of course, that decrepit, sun bleached bridge that divided the two countries wouldn't stop a stray bullet from mysteriously crossing the border and finding its way into Billy's spine or Orion's ass. But it was the U.S., and it felt damn good.

To his surprise, they had to dodge several wagons and people as they made their way along the main street of the Arizona side of Naco. He didn't remember it being this cluttered. It still wasn't anywhere near the size of Nogales, but had certainly stepped up its energy. He wondered if this, like his Christmas Eve arrival in El Papalote, was some kind of holiday. What holiday? What comes after Christmas? New Years! No, he spent New Year's in an El Papalote whorehouse. Easter? Is it Independence Day already?

He stopped in front of the Marshal's office. Saddle sore and badly in need of a bath, he climbed off Orion, hitched him to the post, and walked into the small building. It was a typical Marshal's office, about ten-by-ten. A large metal door separated the office from the jail cells. A rifle rack dressed the south wall. Under it a small table held a tin coffee pot balanced over a single lump oil burner. A pot-bellied stove rested in a corner and a crank telephone hung on the wall behind and slightly to the left of the desk. To his shock, seated in a swivel chair behind that desk was former Ranger John Foster.

Even looking as grizzly as he did and dressed as he was, Foster immediately recognized his old friend. The man grinned, jumped out of his chair, and extended his hand.

"Billy Old!" he declared. "How the hell are ya?"

"John, what the devil ya doin' here?" asked Billy.

"They hung a deputy marshal badge on me and stuck me down here 'bout a year ago," he answered, gripping Billy's hand with both of his.

"Who in the government hates ya?" Billy asked with a grin.

"Who don't?" replied John Foster. The Deputy Marshal laughed and pulled a bottle of good whiskey along with two glasses from a desk drawer. "Ya look like you could use this."

It felt good to not only see a friendly face, but also a familiar one—one that had no hate in its eyes and could speak English, which had almost become foreign to his ears. And one that he could safely turn his back on. John Foster was also at Jeff's deathbed. This made him privy to the same story as Billy. John knew the names..."Amador, Quías, Alvarez, Pasco, Victoriano... Amador..."

"What's with all them folks in town, John? Some kinda holiday? Last time I was here this place was hardly bigger than a rabbit turd."

"Growth, Billy. Gettin' a lot of hay shakers and ranchers 'round here. Hell, we even got telephones."

"No shit?"

"No shit!" Foster pointed to the contraption hanging on the wall. "Wanna call somebody?"

"Don't know who that'd be, John!"

"Whatta 'bout Anna?"

"She left me a short time after Jeff went under," explained Billy, not wanting to make eye contact with his old friend. "Two years was all she could handle with bein' a Ranger's wife. Took my boys and moved back to Kelvin."

140

"Sorry to hear that, Billy." John replied with great sincerity. "She's a good woman."

"Yeah, that's why she shed herself of me," Billy sternly declared, hoping it would close the subject. And it did. Foster poured two shots of the good whiskey, then gestured at the crank phone on the wall.

"I hate when that goddamn thing rings," he declared. "Bout scares the shit outta me ev'ry time. I've took it apart and put it back together twice now to see if I could calm the clatter, but can't seem to figger the damn thing out."

Billy recalled how John liked to tinker. He was always taking his weapons apart and putting them back together. He'd clean them even when they didn't need it. The man had a natural curiosity for how things were made and worked.

"Gotta admit though it's come in handy a few times," the Deputy Marshal continued. "If some bad ass is on his way to town I sometimes know 'fore he gets 'ere."

"That's a good thing!"

"Yeah, yeah, it is!" agreed John Foster. "Now and then I even getta phone call up from Mexico. Matter-a-fact got one just yesterday." With a sly smirk John added, "Word has it that Amador and Quías are worm meat."

Apparently the telephone hadn't heard about Alvarez yet, but Billy knew John Foster well enough to know where this conversation was going.

"That the word, huh?" Billy casually remarked, then downed the shot of liquor. He grimaced slightly as the strong beverage burned his insides. It was a good burn though. The best he'd had since he and Tanok drained his flask of the "good stuff" back in that El Papalote alley.

"Yeah, it is!" the deputy replied, casting a keen eye on Billy, but still maintaining an indifferent tone. "Amazin' how the word spreads, ain't it, Billy?"

"Amazin', John."

"Even out in the desert," he added. "Ya think maybe the wind blows it up from the South?"

"I thought the telephone brung it," replied Billy as he smiled and helped himself to another shot of the very good whiskey.

John stared at his friend for a moment over the tip of his still full shot glass.

"Word is some *gringo*'s been roamin' around Sonora like an avengin' angel. He downed the shot in one smooth gulp.

"Sure a lot of words goin' 'round, John!"

Then the conversation went precisely where Billy knew it would.

"I ain't gonna allow no killin' on this side of Naco, Billy."

Billy started to pour himself another shot but figured if he did, he'd have to lie down. It's been too long since he put that good of whiskey into such an empty gullet. He pushed the cork back into the bottle.

"Didn't even cross my mind, John," he lied.

"Well, then I hope what I'm gonna show ya ain't gonna change yer mind." John Foster picked up his cell keys and said, "Come with me."

Billy followed the Deputy Marshal as he unlocked the heavy door to the cell area. Its rusty hinges emitted a screech that sounded like a hog being butchered. John grinned devilishly and gestured towards the hinges.

"I like to keep 'em thatta way. Sometimes I open and close the door a few times in the middle of the night just to listen to my company bitch."

"Ya devil you," said Billy with a big smile.

"Hell, it's a jail, not a damn rest home. Only got one fella in here right now, but ya might recall him."

They passed two empty cells. Each had a bunk bed, one sink, and one toilet bucket. What was in the third and last cell about made Billy dance a jig. There in the bottom bunk, flat on his back, sound asleep was Diaz Pasco. He was littler than Billy remembered. His feet didn't even reach the end of the short bed, and he was perfectly positioned for a quick throat slitting.

"He showed up back in Naco 'bout a month ago," explained John. "Wasn't here two weeks 'fore he crossed the bridge and landed himself a ninety day sentence for drunken disorderly and strikin' a peace officer."

Billy looked at John Foster.

"No, it weren't me he hit. My former deputy. I woulda hit him back... whole buncha times!"

Pasco stirred and rolled over.

"When's he get sprung?" Billy asked with his eyes fixed on the sleeping man.

"Now, Billy," said John with a grin, "the fact that ya asked that question tells me ya mighta already done changed yer mind."

John Foster left the Rangers right after Jeff's murder. The two had become good friends. Not as close as Jeff and Billy, but close enough for John to be just as angry over the half-assed investigation that led to no arrests. But that wasn't why he left the Rangers. He switched over to the local lawman side because all the traveling with being a Ranger angered his hip, which was injured in a showdown straight out of the Dime Novels while he was still a Ranger. It happened in the streets of Nogales. The three Tragship brothers had just killed Sheriff Donny Austin. Since the law was gone they decided to smoke up the whole damn town in a drunken rampage. They didn't know that an Arizona Ranger was in the barber shop at the time. John heard the shots, ran outside with lather still covering his face and found his friend Donny lying in the street. The brothers had stood over the dead sheriff pumping bullet after bullet into his head until there was no more head. John removed his vest and covered the mash that what was once Donny's face. Outraged, he dashed over to the sheriff's office and grabbed a pump-action twelve gauge. Outside in the street were five more bodies, one of them a woman, along with a couple of horses and an unknown number of dogs. John knew he'd have to get close enough for the street howitzer to be effective, so he waited alongside a building until the killers boldly walked by. With no fear for his own life he stepped into full view and calmly said, "Hi, boys!" When he told the story he claimed he owed his life to the shaving lather.

"Em Tragship boys were so shocked at seein' a lather-faced fella, they froze," he'd explain with a chuckle." "I think they done thought I was some crazy, rabid knothead, but that split second gave me the advantage."

He took an arm off one, the face off another, and sent the third to hell. One Tragship bullet managed to hit him in the hip and left him with a limp, but not enough to keep him from being a lawman only a lump-brained jackass would dare to rile. Since local lawman only had to protect one small territory, sometimes just within the city limits of a town, John appeased his hip by leaving the Rangers and becoming a Peace Officer. Somehow, someway, he ended up down in this shithole of a border town. The only thing that kept him from putting a bullet between Pasco's eyes was the oath he had taken as a lawman.

Having been both a local lawman and a Ranger, Billy felt the former was a bit less taxing. Not that he'd ever say that to John. He knew the damage that bullet had done to his friend's hip so he didn't blame John for making the switch. A Ranger's assignment could keep him in the saddle for days, if not weeks, and sleeping on cold, rocky ground. One bite from a scorpion or a rattler could put a lone man under so Rangers usually traveled in pairs. Many times those Rangers were teamed up with Indian trackers.

January, 1908

Resting just eleven miles north of the border and only a few miles northwest of Nogales, Arivaca had always been a hotbed of illegal border crossings and gunrunning. Captain Wheeler had gotten wind of a wagon load of stolen guns from the Mexican Army was heading north through that area. How Wheeler got that information, no one knew or dared to ask. The wily old captain always seemed to know things that others couldn't even have guessed. And one thing every Ranger knew was never question the captain's orders. But that didn't stop a hotheaded Jeff Kidder from opening his mouth.

"Why the hell are you teamin' me up with that fuckin' Pima, Cap'n?" Jeff demanded. "Why not Billy or Freddie?"

Wheeler's eyes tightened, but he decided to give his Ranger one more chance to back off. He calmly answered, "This assignment needs a good tracker."

Not reigning in his tone, Jeff spouted back, "Then team me up with Sparky, goddamn it, not that fuckin' fool who couldn't even get us the right information 'bout Trigger Point!"

"Did Feather Yank start that fire?"

"Smokin' them rustlers out was the best way to handle that situation. We were blind 'cause the lazy fucker didn't hang 'round long enough to..."

The captain rose quickly. "That 'lazy fucker' and I been friends for twenty years," he fired at Kidder, "clear back to when we was with Crook chasin' down that shitbird Geronimo. He can track a scorpion 'cross a flat rock. He keeps his mouth shut and I trust him with my life."

"That's all well and good," Jeff fired right back. "But why the hell do ya spect me to trust the fucker with mine?"

Wheeler leaned into Jeff's face. "Ya don't know shit, Kidder!" he declared. "Ya got all that college learnin' and ya don't shit! Lemme tell you something 'bout the Pima. In all their history they never attacked no white settlers. Fact is they actually helped 'em. They're a decent, good people with a proud heritage. You're goin' with Feather Yank! Now git yer finger outta yer ass and git yer gear! I'm done talkin' to ya!"

The tough captain didn't turn away from Jeff's face. He held his gaze until the Ranger clicked his heels in a steamed turn and stomped out of the office.

Normally whenever Wheeler assigned a Ranger to a duty with Feather Yank he would tell the story of how the Pima got his name, but Jeff had put a burr so far up the captain's ass he didn't bother. It was a funny tale—to everyone except Feather Yank's uncle, the tribal Medicine Man. When he was two-years-old and yet to be named, the toddler crawled into his uncle's tepee and yanked every feather out of one of his ceremonial headdresses, about one-hundred-and-fifty eagle feathers. His uncle was ready to skin the boy until Feather Yank's mother told her brother he was stupid for leaving the headdress within reach of a child. Then she reminded him that he had three lazy squaws who needed something to do besides give him babies and baths. Let them put the headdress back together, she told him. From that day on, much to the chagrin of his Uncle, the boy was known as Feather Yank.

Sparky and Billy were sitting on the porch of the barracks when Jeff stormed past them, threw open the door, and entered the building without saying a word.

"What's he all horns and rattles 'bout?" asked Sparky, letting a wad of tobacco spittle spew out into the dirt.

Before Billy could even rise Jeff kicked the door back open and started towards the corral toting his bedroll.

"Jeff, what's goin' on?" inquired Billy.

Without even glancing at his two friends Jeff groused, "Wheeler teamed me up with that fuckin' Pima."

"Kiss my grandma's butt," exclaimed Sparky. "What's the Cap'n thinkin'?"

Feather Yank was standing in the corral feeding his Paint a carrot. Jeff dropped his bedroll and began walking to the Indian. Rising, Billy and Sparky froze their eyes on the encounter, ready to jump to action. Even though the Pima dressed like a white man, in long breeches and a twill shirt, he refused to abandon his moccasins, long hair, and fancy necklace of over a hundred large colored beads of red, white, and blue. The colors were not for the sake of Ol' Glory. Each one had its own sacred meaning to his people. In the center of the necklace was a medallion with the figure of a man playing a flute.

"Feather Yank," Jeff shouted before he even reached the man.

Sensing the Ranger's hostility and not bothering to turn toward the approaching man the Pima said, "Whatchu want, Jeff Kidder?"

"Look at me, goddamn it! I wanna talk to ya."

Feather Yank turned to face Jeff. Knowing their friend's temperament, Billy and Sparky decided to head towards the corral. The Pima and the Ranger stood toe-to-toe, almost the exact same heights, both primed and ready to lock horns. Although Jeff had at least fifteen pounds on the lean Indian, Feather Yank had twenty more years of killing under his belt.

"When ya scouted those rustlers at Trigger Point what'd ya see?"

"Cattle," Feather Yank coldly replied.

"No shit! What the hell else?"

"Small fire with branding stick."

"No people?"

"People?"

"Yeah! Ya know, those things that walk 'round on two legs?"

"No people," the Indian replied with a snort and turned back to his Paint.

"How long'd ya eyeball the place? Look at me, goddamn ya!"

The Indian slowly turned to Kidder. His eyes were formed into two narrow slits. "Why you ask, Jeff Kidder?"

"Cause a woman and children were there!"

"You kill?"

"Yeah, goddamn it! We kill!"

"Many woman and children killed out here, Jeff Kidder," the Indian started to again turn away.

Jeff grabbed Feather Yank's shirt and pulled the Indian towards him. They were eye-to-eye and all four eyes were blazing red.

"Hey, fellas," Sparky called out as he and Billy hurried to the corral.

"Not by me, goddamn it," Jeff snarled. "Maybe if you'd have scouted better they wouldn't..."

146

Jeff's words were cut short by the recognizable sharp side of a knife blade pressing against his belly. He looked down and saw the large weapon in the Pima's hand. He knew the strong Indian could quickly slice him clean through to his backbone.

"No grab Feather Yank, Jeff Kidder," hissed the Indian, his eyes steely and cold.

Jeff released the shirt and stepped back, his hand on his Colt.

"Jeff!" Billy yelled as he entered the corral.

"He pulled a knife on me, Billy! The fuckin' injun pulled a knife on me!"

Sparky's long legs brought him to Jeff before Billy could get there. He squared up his six-foot-ten-inch frame directly in front of Kidder.

"Fer a college boy ya ain't none too smart!" declared Sparky. "Don't ne'er pull an Injun up close to ya!"

"That's twice today I've been told I ain't smart, Sparky and I don't like it." He tried to shoulder his way past Sparky but the big man stepped from side-to-side blocking any further foolish action Jeff might be pondering. "Get outta my way, Sparky!"

"Too much hate in yer eyes right now, Jeff. Ain't gonna do it!"

Kidder backed away from Sparky and squared his body for a confrontation.

"Ya gonna pull on me, Jeff?" asked Sparky.

"No Injun's gonna press a blade to my belly!"

In one quick stride Sparky was chest-to-chest with Jeff. With huge hands he grasped Jeff's shirt and lifted him a good foot off the ground. Billy saw the shocked expression on his friend's face. Apparently he had no idea of Sparky's real strength.

"That gonna make ya famous?" Sparky growled, their noses almost touching.

Jeff could smell the tobacco juice in Sparky's mouth and feel his legs helplessly dangling in the air. Then as fast as he was lifted, his feet were back on the ground, and he found himself stumbling backwards.

"Chief Wheeler say find stolen cattle," Feather Yank blurted. "I find stolen cattle, go back and tell him. Job done!" He sheathed the knife. "Always do what Chief Wheeler say." After the last statement the Pima climbed on his Paint. "We go now, Jeff Kidder!"

Again Sparky leaned into Jeff's face. "They be a simple people, Jeff," he hissed. "Ya tell 'em go get wood, they do it, but they ain't gonna jist build a fire without ya tellin' 'em that, too."

Sparky's homespun explanation was like someone had lit a candle in a dark room. Billy saw it in his friend's eyes. Jeff glanced at Feather Yank, then back at Sparky. The latter's words actually sunk into the stubborn South Dakotan's head. He recalled the Arikara tribe near his hometown. They were peaceful Indians, but dumb as dirt, or so he thought. He recalled telling one of them who was working on his folk's farm to take a bucket down to the creek. Fifteen minutes later the Indian had not returned, so Jeff went looking for him. The Indian was just standing by the creek with the bucket in his hand.

"What're you doing?" he asked the Arikara.

"Take bucket to creek," the man answered.

Feather Yank did as he was ordered. He found the stolen cattle. If Wheeler would've said stick around to see how many rustlers were there perhaps he would've. Jeff wondered if that made Wheeler responsible for the deaths of that woman and the children. Or should Feather Yank have used initiative and stuck around longer to gather more information? Maybe Indians don't have initiative. Maybe it's not in their nature. He wondered why he was putting all of this effort into trying to figure out this particular Pima. What's the point? He's just another dirt worshipper. Sure, Jeff knew it was his plan to set fire to the buildings, but how was he to know the woman and children were in there? He couldn't see through walls. Still, no matter how many excuses he'd conjure up, the guilt remained. It was his plan. He also knew he had to cool his heels. He'd be on the trail with this Indian for several days. Finally he tied his bedroll across Vermillion's butt and said, "Let's go."

As the two rode off towards Arivaca Sparky said, "Wonder whichen will make it back in one piece."

The captain was right about the Pima keeping his mouth shut. Regardless of how many times Jeff tried to make conversation with the stoic Indian on the short ride to Arivaca, all he got was an occasional grunt. Of course, everything he said was on the prickly side. Common sense finally began to sink back into Jeff's head. To ease the tension he knew he had created he tried to make peace with the Pima over the next few days, or his version of peace.

The Indian still merely grunted in response. Every time Jeff would ask where they were headed next, the Indian would respond with the same frustrating two words, "Find guns!"

"Ya know, Feather Yank," Jeff suggested one afternoon, "when ya retire you should become one of those wooden Indians that stand outside of stores holdin' cigars. They never talk either!"

"No like cigars! Smell like horse shit!"

On their third night while again sitting silently around a small campfire in the foothills of the San Luis Mountain range, Jeff knew he had to find a way to put a crack in the wall between them.

"Feather Yank, I ain't never apologized to an Injun, but I figger I owe you one," he quietly stated. "I'm truly sorry I got in yer face like that back in the corral. I just don't appreciate havin' the death of a woman and a baby on my head."

The Indian looked at him and said, "Not on head, Jeff Kidder, in heart. This heart heavy with deaths of much women and children; Must live with it."

Jeff knew it was something he would have to learn to live with, but how? It was his plan. He tried changing the subject. "What's that figure on your necklace, that fellow playin' a flute?"

"Kokopelli," replied Feather Yank.

"What's a kokopelli?"

"When the Kokopelli play flute in village, next morning all squaws in village be with child."

Jeff sneered. "You believe that shit?"

"You believe stork bring baby?"

Jeff chuckled to himself. He was surprised to actually hear a sense of humor coming from an Injun. Then he recalled a night in a Quechan camp with Billy and two young squaws. They heard a flute playing outside the tepee they were given to stay in. He wondered if he might have a half-breed kid running around that reservation. But at least now he had the stoic Indian saying more than just "Find guns," so he decided to push a little more.

"What's your story, Feather Yank? The white man's got his Bible and story of how everything began, ya know? What's yers?"

Without hesitation, Feather Yank poured out his proud history.

"*Juh-wert-a-Mah-kai* make world from sweat off chest. Take four times to get right. From his eye he make *Noo-ee*, 'nother man, to help make more people. *Juhwerta Mahkai* take ball to make sun. He put ball in North, no good! He put in South, no good! West no good! East good! From more sweat *Juhwerta Mahki* make more people, man, woman, and they make more people, but these people no good, so *Juhwerta Mahki* kill them. He bring down sky."

"The sky?" Jeff stated skeptically.

"*Si.*"

"How could he bring down the sky?"

"Fire, stone come from sky. Kill all! Happen four times. On last try he get earth right and people right. Then *Juhwerta Mahki* tell people big flood come and they must go under earth."

"Under? Ya mean like in caves?"

"Hole in ground!"

"Hole in ground? Ya don't get away from a flood by goin' in a hole, fer crissake! Hell, the water would flood a hole in the ground! Ya sure they didn't climb to the tops of mountains where they'd be..."

"No, no! Water too high!"

"Water was too high to go up a mountain yet they were safe in a hole in the ground?" asked Jeff in a condescending tone. "Don't make sense!"

"My people story, Jeff Kidder! I tell it!"

"Okay! Okay! Calm down! Your face is turning red!"

For a second Jeff thought he saw the flicker of a smile flash across Feather Yank's face.

The Indian continued, "People who not go in hole die. After water go 'way, people come out of hole and make all other people and all animals from wet clay."

As he watched the Pima gently stir the twigs in their small fire, he recalled a story from his childhood, something about a "hundred pounds of clay."

"A big flood destroyed the world in the white man's book, too," he remarked.

"Flood come to many peoples."

"Ya think it was the same flood?"

"No matter!" replied Feather Yank. "World still have bad people."

With that last statement the Indian rolled over and was asleep in seconds.

The San Luis Mountains are a low range running about nine miles. The next morning Feather Yank led Jeff to a certain point of high ground overlooking a deep, dried river wash that could easily hide a traveling wagon. They knelt in the tall grass. From ground level, they couldn't see into the wash, wouldn't even know it was there, but from their current height, it was a cinch.

"Wash go northeast. Chief Wheeler say wagon go Tucson. Tucson northeast!" The Indian refused to use the term Captain. He felt "Chief" was more respectful.

"He told you that? About Tucson?" That was news to him.

"Chief Wheeler say we follow wagon to Tucson, see who buy guns."

"So he wants us to find the buyer, too? Why the hell didn't he tell me all that?"

"Indian talk less," the Pima stated and started to rise, but suddenly stopped. "No move, Jeff Kidder!" he warned.

"Huh?"

"No move!"

Jeff froze. Feather Yank pulled his knife from its sheath and whisked a small red scorpion off the back of Jeff's shoulder, dangerously close to his neck. "Little red ones plenty nasty!" He crushed the scorpion under his moccasin.

A chill forced sweat beads to pop out on Jeff's forehead as he managed to stammer, "Thanks."

"We camp here," stated Feather Yank as he stripped his Paint. Early the next morning the Pima was shaking Jeff awake. "Up!" he ordered. "Wagon in wash!"

Jeff rubbed the sleep from his eyes, rose, and hurried to where the Indian was prone in the high grass, peering down into the wash. Sure enough, three men, one driver and two escorts were taking a wagon up the wash. Even though its contents were covered by a tarp, it was easy to make out their shapes—cartons of rifles. Six, Jeff believed.

"No wear *policia* clothes," said Feather Yank. "Wear Army clothes."

"I don't get it," mumbled Jeff.

"Soldier safer in U.S. than *policia*."

"So you think they're really *policia* dressed as soldiers?"

"Find out in Tucson!"

With that, the pair saddled and mounted their horses and started the slow crawl to Tucson, staying out of sight on the high ground over the wash to keep an eye on the wagon. It took two days for the sluggish vehicle to finally cover the rugged sixty-some miles to Tucson. The soldiers drove it directly to the town's crowded railroad yards.

Hidden a few standing railcars away, Jeff whispered, "We need to take them before they get those guns loaded onto a train."

"No! Chief say need know where train go."

"I thought we were supposed to stop the shipment of the guns."

"I not say that!"

"Wheeler wants to know the buyer AND where the guns are going?"

"*Si!*".

"Why didn't he tell me any of this?"

"Indian talk less! When guns on train, we look in crates."

"Why? We know they're guns!"

"You see through wood, Jeff Kidder?"

This Indian was growing on him and gnawing at him at the same time. Knowing Feather Yank was right about making certain there were guns in those crates grated at him, but the way he said it had amused him. It was clever. No, he decided. It couldn't have been meant that way. Indians aren't witty.

"What about the gunrunners?"

"If there, we kill."

The sun was sinking when the three soldiers finally off-loaded the crates and left the boxcar. Jeff and Feather Yank waited another half hour so darkness would help cover their way to the target. The boxcar door scraped loudly as the Pima pushed it open. The grinding sound bounced off nearby cars. The smell of past cattle shipments rushed up their noses. Rancid hay and dried cow chips covered the floor. The two climbed inside. Feather Yank flipped back the tarp, pulled his large knife from its sheath and began prying open one of the crates. It was creaking even louder than the boxcar door. Suddenly it popped off, striking the wall of the boxcar with a clanging sound that made them feel like they were inside a bell. Then the lid crashed to the floor.

"Most Indians I've known are quieter!"

"We no all look same either!"

Jeff chuckled. Perhaps this Pima does have a sense of humor, he thought. He pushed aside some straw packing and pulled out a strange looking rifle. It was too dark in the boxcar to read the weapon's marking so he took it to the door and held it up to the twilight.

"Gewehr?" he exclaimed. "Shit! These are German rifles! What the hell are they doing....?"

"May we help you, gentlemen?" came a voice from outside the boxcar.

Jeff and Feather Yank froze as they stared at four men, all with heavy moustaches and dressed in black suits, white shirts with dark string ties, and bowler hats. It was like each had been stamped out of a mold in some factory. The sight would've been humorous except for the sobering fact that each toted a shotgun. They matched, too.

"Please return the weapon to its crate and climb out!" ordered the voice.

"We're Arizona Rangers," explained Jeff.

"That's fine! Do as I ask please!"

As soon as Jeff and Feather Yank's feet touched the ground all of the men lowered their shotguns. One short man stepped forward.

"Thank you. Nathan Zimmerman, Pinkerton Detective Agency," the short man grinned and extended his hand.

Confused but relieved, Jeff shook the man's hand. "Jeff Kidder, Arizona Rangers. What the hell's goin' on here, Detective?"

"What are you two doing here, Ranger?" inquired Zimmerman, still smiling.

"Uh, our Cap'n ordered us to follow these weapons."

"Why?"

Briefly glancing at Feather Yank then returning to the Pinkerton, Jeff replied, "To be honest, Detective, I'm not really sure!"

"You saw what the weapons are?" asked Zimmerman.

"German rifles, but what the hell are they...."

Feather Yank decided to speak. "They go to White Father in Washington."

A stunned stillness passed among the men. Finally the detective replied, "Smart Injun, ya got there, Ranger."

Jeff took a step closer to the short Pinkerton and brusquely said, "He's a Pima! And ya bet yer ass he's smart!"

Momentarily taken aback from Jeff's stern reaction, the Pinkerton recovered his congeniality and said, "Of course!" He looked directly at Feather Yank and extended his hand. "My apologies, sir!" The Pima reluctantly shook it and grunted. "He's right," the detective continued. "These rifles are going to the War Department in D.C."

"Why?" Jeff inquired, still confused.

"For some time we've believed Germany has been shipping arms to the Mexican army and the Mexican police. This could be our proof. The three soldiers you followed here are Mexican policemen working with us. One of them is a Pinkerton."

"So why all the fuss? Other countries sell weapons to Mexico. Hell, even the U.S."

"Not at the rate Germany has! Although we haven't seen them until now our sources tell us that over forty thousand of these new Gewehrs have been delivered over the past six months. Working near the border like you do, and with all the unrest down in Mexico, do you really think their government has the money to buy that many fancy German weapons?

After wrapping his mind around the moment, Jeff said, "Are you tellin' me Washington thinks Germany is arming the Mexican Army? For what?"

"That's what the President needs to find out," answered Zimmerman. "But first, we needed proof. Looks like we got it."

"We got proof, too," stated Feather Yank as he turned. "Come! We go tell Chief Wheeler."

Feather Yank simply walked away. Jeff momentarily studied the four armed men. "Uh, that it, Detective Zimmerman?"

"That's it!" the Pinkerton answered with another grin.

As Jeff hurried to catch up to Feather Yank he heard the grinding of the boxcar doors being closed, followed by the distinct sound of a metal lock securing the contents. Before he could even form a word, the Pima spoke first.

"Good we no kill soldiers."

"Just what goddamn proof do we have?" The question shot from Jeff's mouth.

"German arm Mexican army, maybe invade!"

"Invade? Invade what?" Jeff asked. Then a thunderbolt shot through his head and he stopped dead in his tracks. "The U.S.?

"Chief Wheeler," Feather Yank explained and kept walking, "he wise man. Have visions, like Indian."

Jeff struggled to catch up with the fast walking Pima. "That's the craziest notion I ever heard. Germany is not gonna invade the U.S."

Feather Yank stopped and turned to Jeff, looking him straight in the eye.

"You no listen, Jeff Kidder! Not what Chief Wheeler say! Not what Feather Yank say! German have Mexican do it."

The Indian turned and kept walking, leaving a stunned Jeff Kidder standing alone. Finally capable of forming some words he hurried after Feather Yank.

"Why didn't he tell me this?" he shouted. Then as he reached Feather Yank's side he found himself mumbling, "Yeah, yeah, Indian talk less!"

When the two returned to Ranger headquarters Jeff once again decided to climb into his captain's face. Horn tossing mad he demanded to know why he wasn't privy to the information given to Feather Yank.

"Sit down, Ranger!" the captain demanded. He lit a cigar, blew out of long stream of blue smoke as Jeff impatiently squirmed in the hard-backed chair. "There's a lotta shit goin' on o'er in Europe. Them damn fools always seem to be fightin' each other, stirrin' up trouble. 'Specially 'em godless Huns and Turks! Who's our main pal o'er there?"

"Uh, England," answered Jeff, wondering where this conversation was going.

"Ya know yer politics. Good," smirked Wheeler. "If the Brits had to go to war, don't ya think we'd give 'em a hand?"

"I suppose...maybe...if we had a reason!"

"How 'bout this reason:" exclaimed Wheeler. "What better way for the Huns to disrupt our helpin' the Limeys than to have an invasion from Mexico?" Wheeler stared at Jeff for a moment. "I can see by yer expression ya think that's a pretty far-fetched notion, right?"

Jeff shrugged. "You're the Cap'n, Cap'n!"

Sitting on the corner of his desk and leaning towards Jeff in an obvious position of authority, Wheeler chided, "Then humor yer Cap'n, Ranger! Imagine it did happen! Who'd be first hit?"

Jeff stirred as if in the defendant's seat facing a stern district attorney. "Well, us, obviously."

"Ain't it better to be safe than sorry?"

"I suppose so, but...!"

Wheeler rose from the desk, towering over the seated Jeff.

"Ain't no supposin' 'bout it, Kidder. The fact that ya thought it was a far-fetched notion is exactly why I gave Feather Yank the details and not you. If a Ranger don't believe in his mission, he'll prob'bly fuck it up. Maybe get hisself killed. Feather Yank has ne'er questioned any orders I've given him. As ya know, he's still breathin'." Turning his back to Jeff, the hardnosed captain returned to the swivel chair behind his desk, but not without one more reminder of precisely who was in charge. "Now get the hell outta here and grab some hot grub!"

Jeff rose, turned in a huff and stomped out of the room, his pride bruised by the captain trusting an Indian scout more than him. Wasn't his stint as a lawman in Nogales proof enough to Wheeler? Hadn't his completion of dozens of successful missions warranted the man's trust more than some Indian? He knew Wheeler was right about one thing—he would've thought, and still did think, that Mexico invading the U.S. was about the most ridiculous idea he'd ever heard. Would hearing that absurd notion ahead of time have made him less cautious, less of a Ranger? "Hell no!"

As he left the office, Feather Yank was waiting outside the headquarters door, standing in a stiff pose with his arms crossed. With one hand he held an object out to Jeff.

"Cigar?"

1910

"I need a deputy, Billy," John Foster said. "Cinco de Mayo's comin' up next month. Even though we're a bit more civilized now, ya know how wild things can get 'round that time." The idea immediately appealed to Billy.

156

He had worn a star for so long he felt naked and unbalanced without one. "Besides, word has it a revolution is brewin' down there, which pro'bly means we're gonna get us a shitload of refugees crossin' the border. I'm gonna need help with that, too. I swear, Billy, I ain't ne'er seen a place as fucked up as Mexico. They got all 'em players down there—Diaz, Zapata, Huerta, Madero, Carranza—all a 'em wantin' power."

Billy recalled a night in Quitovac and said, "I hearda that Madero fella." He also thought of the young bartender and hoped he was staying clear of the fray.

John continued, "Ya 'member that *bandito* you were chasin' a few years back? Uh, Dorotéo Arango?"

"Yeah! Asshole gave us many a hairy chase!"

"He's even part of the revolution, but he done changed his name to Pancho Villa. Guess he thinks that'll make up fer all he done afore. Ya don't wanna go back down there and get caught up in that shit storm." Then John added with a devious grin, "Iffin that's where ya been, that is! Stay on as my deputy and we could watch each other's back, know what I mean?"

Billy knew exactly what he meant. John wanted to keep an eye on him, see that he didn't go after Pasco. At least on this side of Naco. Billy also knew that when he did go after Pasco, John wouldn't know a damn thing about it. The last thing he would want to do is have to go through a friend to get to an enemy, especially one as dangerous as John Foster.

"One-hundred-and-seventy-five a month."

"John, what's the date?"

"April ten."

"Still nineteen ten?"

"Yep," John said, wondering if the Sonora sun had scrambled his friend's brains.

Mexico had burned away over a year of Billy's life. A stay-put lawman would mean good food, a warm bed, and whorehouses. Then Jeff's words flew through his head, "There's gotta be more to life than food, fire and fuckin'!" Yes, there is, thought Billy—being a Peace Officer.

"Got yerself a deputy, John!"

"Good," replied Foster and tossed him a tin star. "I think ya know the oath!"

Billy clasped the star in his palm. It felt good. It felt right. The tin was cool in his palm. He started to pin it on but stopped. Attaching it to his soiled Mexican clothing would do it a dishonor. He kept it tightly gripped in his hand.

"There's a decent boarding house on the high hill to the east. No bedbugs and good food. The old lady who runs it's named Castle, and she is built like one."

"What about the barracks at old Fort Naco?" asked Billy. "Wouldn't there be some room there? They ain't bad."

"Army left and they tore the place down. It was fallin' apart anyways—in worse shape than our barracks back in Nogales. The wood, at least the pieces without termites, was used to build the apothecary down the street."

"The what?"

"Apothecary! Fancy name fer the drug store and soda shop. They sell medicines, ice cream, stuff like that!"

"Medicines? They got anything fer a toothache?"

"Hell, we got a dentist fer that."

"Ya mean some four-fingered barber who yanks them out?"

"Nope! A real live dentist from back East. He's even got one of them 'lectricy drills."

"No shit?"

"No shit! Look at this here!" John flipped a switch on a device on his desk. "This here's my Crocker and Curtis 'lectricy fan," he shouted over the noise.

"Purty nice, John," Billy shouted back, feeling the air blow across his face.

"Told ya, Naco's changed, Billy! We're growin'!" He shut off the loud, spinning device. "Wish it weren't so damn loud. I took it apart and put it back together, too, tryin' to make it quieter. That telephone, the fan, why do all them new 'ventions gotta be so noisy?"

"Boardin' house, huh?" Billy said with a bit of apprehension.

"They even got a bath house with hot and cold runnin' water," stated John. "Take advantage of it!" Sensing Billy's reluctance he asked, "Ya short of cash? I can spot ya a little if...."

"No, no thanks, John. 'Preciate it, but I got some stoved up. It's just...

well...no barracks, all 'em folks in the street, a boardin' house—lotta changes I gotta get my head 'round!"

"While yer at it git yerself some clothes that ain't filled with Mexican critters. Haircut and shave'd be fittin' too."

Billy chuckled, "I hear ya!"

John was dead right about the barracks at old Fort Naco, but Billy didn't agree that they were worse than the ones back in Nogales. Baking under the Arizona heat, the roofing shingles in Nogales would dry up and crack. When it rained, they got a shower on their bunks. On cold nights, the walls had splits so wide they'd let in enough breeze to blow off their blankets. The flannel mouths up at the territory seat were keen on paying men to risk their lives and protect their fat asses, but couldn't give a hoot where those men ate and slept.

February, 1908

It was the smell of rain and a dark grey sky with a rumbling belly that had sent Billy and Jeff to the roof of the old barracks with two hammers, a box of nails, and a burlap bag stuffed with shingles.

"Where is Vermillion?" Billy asked Jeff, as they squatted on the roof repairing potential leaks. "I heard a Yankton and Deadwood, but ain't ne'er heard of Vermillion."

"After all these years yer finally asking me that? Why?"

"I don't know. Just tryin' to make talk while we fix this shitty roof, I guess."

"Southeastern corner of the state," replied Jeff, speaking loudly as he hammered in a fresh shingle. "On a bluff over-lookin' the Missouri River. Lewis and Clark camped there August twenty-fourth, eighteen four. Shot their first buffalo there. John Audubon stayed there, too."

"Who?"

"John Audubon. He drew birds."

"Huh?"

"He drew pictures of birds. Hand me some more nails!"

"Why?"

"Cause I'm out of them! Why'd ya think?"

"No! Why'd that Awd'bon fella draw birds?" Billy slipped Jeff a handful of nails.

"So folks would know the different kinds of birds in America."

"Folks wanna know that?"

"Sure."

The fact that someone actually took the time to draw birds amazed Billy. He wondered how the artist got them to stay still long enough to be drawn.

"Did this Awd'bon fella get paid to draw them birds?"

"He put his drawings together in a book and sold copies of it. That's how he made money."

"And folks truly spent their money fer that bird book?"

"Just like I did for that goat book, remember?" They both laughed then Jeff continued, "Spirit Mound is right outside Vermillion, too."

"What's that?"

"Ya never heard of Spirit Mound?"

"Nope!"

"Bet Sparky has!" remarked Jeff.

"I ain't Sparky!"

"It's a sacred place where the Injuns are 'fraid to go."

"Why?"

While pounding in another shingle, Jeff said, "Somethin' about little devils livin' there. I don't know. Ask Sparky!" He chuckled with his next statement. "Couple of pals of mine and I used to make Indian Whiskey then sell it to the local Injuns to get drunk on so they'd get brave enough to climb Spirit Mound."

"What's Indian Whiskey?"

Jeff stopped pounding and grinned as he explained, "Ya take a barrel of Missouri River water and pour in two gallons of alcohol. Then you toss in a couple of drops of strychnine to make them a little crazy, along with a couple of plugs of tobacco to make 'em sick. An Injun won't believe it's whiskey if it doesn't make 'em crazy and sick. Then a few bars of soap to make it foam up at the top, a good half pound of red pepper, stir in some sagebrush and boil it 'til it turns brown. Strain it into another barrel—Walla!—Indian Whiskey. I tell ya, Billy, the fools loved the stuff! Made a lot of that shit, especially after

160

they killed my friend Richie Fuller. We were hiding in the grass one evening, watchin' the drunk idiots circle all around that mound, trying to get the guts to climb it. I finally got bored and went home. Richie stayed. Next morning they found his body—stabbed seven times. Apparently they spotted him hidin' out, watchin' them and...well, many a day I wish I would've stayed with him... he might still be around if I had." Jeff went silent for a long moment and Billy saw his friend drift to somewhere far away. "Richie Fuller. Good fella," Jeff finally continued. "We grew up together, use to swap the latest Dime Novels." He chuckled at the memory then looked straight at Billy and stated, "Over the next few years I mixed up seven barrels of that shit, one for every stab in Richie's body. Never killed any Injuns...wanted to...God knows I wanted to... but never could get myself to put in enough strychnine. Until you, he was the best friend I ever had." He sent a stream of tobacco juice violently sailing off the roof then slammed the hammer down so hard on the next shingle that it splintered.

"Ain't we gotta 'nough holes in this roof without ya makin' more," Billy joked, hoping to cool his friend's fiery mettle. He watched his friend stare at the ruined shingle for a moment then toss it aside. Then he gave Billy one of his patented grins exposing his tobacco-stained teeth and grabbed a fresh shingle.

"Okay, now I got one for you."

"One what?" asked Billy.

"A 'why are ya asking me that now' question. Why haven't you ever told me about the whore who shot you?"

Billy bristled and said, "She weren't no whore."

"Oh," Jeff said softly, hoping he didn't just light a firecracker. "Sorry."

"She was a crazy bitch."

Jeff breathed a sigh of relief, chuckled, and said, "Oh, well, hell, that explains it...'cause it'd take a hellava lot to piss off a whore enough to shoot a fella. They can't afford to kill off their customers."

Both laughed. Jeff let loose another stream of tobacco juice which gave Billy a craving. He pulled out his pipe and lit it.

"Don't catch the roof on fire," Jeff warned him. "The government would probably charge us for the damage. Up here 'round all this dry wood it might be a good idea to chaw it, not smoke it."

"Gives me the hiccups somethun fierce!" answered Billy in a voice that carried over his hammering. "I'll be careful. 'Sides, if this worthless hunk of horse shit burnt down maybe we'd get us a decent one."

"Oh, right!" chided Jeff. "I'm sure that fat ass Henry Ashurst and his cronies would spring for the money to do anything fer us."

"We sent him that 'pology letter."

"*I* sent him that apology letter!"

"I helped," Billy claimed with a grin.

"Yeah?" replied Jeff, stopping his pounding and looking at his friend. "Spell apology!"

"Fifth fuckin' grade," Billy said with a smile and pounded in another shingle.

The sky rumbled, grunted, and flashed all that day but was only teasing. It squirreled away its treasured moisture. After dinner Freddie said he was feeling lucky and Jeff said he was feeling bored. Jeff knew Freddie wouldn't visit the whorehouses because of his intentions with his "little dressmaker with the huge udders," so the two decided to go into town, see the vaudeville show, and play a little poker. With no current assignments, Billy and Sparky perched themselves on the porch of the sort-of-repaired barracks to enjoy a quiet evening. Billy lit his pipe as Sparky cut off a half dollar sized plug of chaw and stuffed it in his mouth.

"Yer pipe 'minds me a flapjacks soaked in maple syr'p," Sparky remarked as he sniffed the air, stretched out his long legs, and planted his feet on the porch railing. "My ma made 'em fer us ev'ry Sunday mornin'. Then she'd tote us off to church. Most time by our ears!"

"Yer ma must be one helluva lady to reach yer ears," teased Billy.

"She got long arms," laughed Sparky. "I seen her reach plumb 'cross the supper table and whack my brother up side his haid and ne'er even lift her fanny outta the chair."

"Ya went to church, huh!"

"Had to! Pa'd whup us silly iffin we dint. But he ne'er went. Always thunk that twern't fair—put on shoes and go to church whiles Pa got to rock on the porch. Or go fishin'."

The distant sound of single gunshot stirred the night air. Billy rose and said, "Where'd that come from?"

Still seated Sparky replied, "Towards town. Pro'bly some drunk."

Billy listened for a long moment then replied, "No follow up." He relaxed and sat back down.

"Like I says, pro'bly a drunk."

"Ain't no drunks in Nogales," kidded Billy.

"Ain't no fleas on hounds either," replied Sparky.

After another long moment Billy asked, "Ya still a churchgoer, Sparky?"

"Not so much...been meanin' to though. We used to go to the Presb'terian Church on the east of town, but it burned down some time ago and they ain't ne'er builded it back, so's I ain't been fer awhiles now." Sparky laughed with his next statement. "Ma always says 'em damn Catholics pro'bly torched it." He yawned and stretched his body, surely reaching close to seven feet, then let loose a wad of tobacco spit a good eight feet into the air, over the railing, and onto the dirt, kicking up a decent sized cloud of dust. "Always thought that'd be a good job," he added.

"What?" asked Billy, a little confused but laughing, "Burnin' down churches?"

"Kiss yer grandma's butt! No! Bein' a pastor. Ya only gotta work one hour a week, on Sundays, and ya jist read from the Good Book. Course, ya gotta knows how to read real good. Ain't got that one down yet!" Sparky wiped a few droplets of tobacco drool from his chin.

Billy had never set foot in a church, even as a child. His mother's great grandparents were from Persia and she still practiced Zoroastrianism. He never understood it or could even pronounce it, but would watch her on certain nights praying by the hearth. When he was twelve years old, she finally tried to explain her religion to him and why she always prayed by fire light.

"It brings us closer to our god," she explained.

Billy wondered if it was the same God other people prayed to, but never asked. His father didn't cotton to anything about any religion and had little tolerance for those who did. That was why his mother never prayed in front of him. So Billy was left to make up his own mind. Growing up he'd hear his friends repeating their versions of Good Book stories they were told in church, and in almost every bunkhouse there was a Bible thumper ready to bore everyone. So it wasn't as if he was a stranger to religion, or resented it. He just never had any interest in it. Never felt the need. When he enlisted in the Rough Riders there was a line on the enlistment papers to write in his religion. He simply scribbled "dont no." Now he told himself if he did set foot in a church it might get him to thinking twice about having to kill someone and give that fellow an advantage. So he stayed clear of them. Jeff wasn't much of a churchgoer either. He said he preferred a whorehouse to God's house. He knew what to expect in a whorehouse and never left one feeling guilty.

"Sparky, ya ever heard tell of a place called Spirit Mound up in the Dakotas?"

"The Little People," Sparky replied in an ominous tone.

"Huh?"

"They're a buncha little devils that live on that thar mound. Tales say 'em little folk be fierce fighters and'll kilt anyone who comes near their mound."

"Little Devils?"

"Yup! The Omaha and Otoe won't even go near the place. Claim 'em little people kilt over three hun'derd warriors and left hund'derds others crippled fer life!"

"No shit?"

"How'd ya hear a the place?"

"Jeff!"

"He been thar?"

"He lived by it, up in Dakota."

Billy puffed his pipe a few times and Sparky let fly another wad of tobacco juice. A long moment passed.

"Ever hear tell a Indian Whiskey?" Billy asked.

Sparky momentarily stopped chomping his plug and looked at Billy.

"That's killin' stuff, Billy. In the ol' days Frenchy trappers mixed it up to poison off the Injuns so they could git all the skins and furs. Bad stuff, Injun Whiskey!" The two sat quietly for a few moments as Billy puffed and Sparky chewed. "Jeff tell ya 'bout that, too?" he finally asked.

"Yeah!"

Sparky shook his head, spewed out another mouthful of spittle, and said, "Gotta have a powerful lot a hate to mix up that poison."

Billy took a deep breath then exhaled slowly. "Yeah!" he sighed. "Guess so." He wasn't worried about Jeff trying to make Indian Whiskey now, not down here. He knew the Missouri River didn't run anywhere near Arizona.

"Powerful lotta hate," Sparky repeated more to himself than to Billy.

Sparky was about as far from a mean person as Billy had ever known, but he heard the disgust in the tall man's voice with that last statement. He knew Sparky took issue with Jeff's feelings towards Indians. It wasn't that Sparky was fond of all Indians he knew or met. The big man just had a warm place in his heart for all people in general. Billy often fretted about that. He had seen many fellows with warm hearts end up in cold boxes.

Sparky's ears heard it first: two horses slowly approaching the barracks gate. Billy heard it seconds later. Soon both saw the silhouettes of two horses entering the gate, but only one rider. They recognized it as Jeff. A few seconds later they saw the body of Freddie Rankin draped across the saddle of the second horse.

"Someone shot him," Jeff called out, very distressed.

Billy and Sparky hurried over to the two horses. With Sparky's long legs, he arrived before Billy was half way across the open area of the barracks.

"No, no, no," bellowed Sparky. "Not Freddie! Not Freddie!" His eyes filled with tears. For a moment Billy thought the gentle giant was going to collapse.

"The shot just came outta nowhere," explained Jeff. "Couldn't even get a bead on where."

Billy could see the trails of tears that had cut through the dust on Jeff's face.

"He said he was feelin' lucky," Sparky sobbed, gently placing his hand on his friend's body. "Po' little guy," he added with tears rolling down his large face. "I'll tote him to the hospital."

"Lemme help ya," insisted Jeff.

"No!" snapped Sparky.

Billy hoped Jeff didn't read the look in Sparky's eyes that said, "Wish it had been you."

"I'll do it 'lone," Sparky insisted.

With great ease and reverence Sparky slid his small friend's body off the horse, cradled him in his arms, and walked towards the infirmary. Freddie looked like a child in the big man's arms. Billy had never seen Sparky so sorrowful. He and Jeff led the two horses to the corral and began to strip their saddles.

"Bullet just came out of nowhere," Jeff explained again as he pulled off Vermillion's saddle. His voice was shaking and his eyes were still watery.

"Ya didn't see a muzzle flash?" asked Billy.

Jeff sniped at his friend, "Don't ya think I'd be out there lookin' if I did, goddamn it?" A moment passed in silence. "Sorry! Didn't mean to piss at ya! I just...I just feel worthless right now. We had come outta the vaudeville theater and were standin' by the barber shop, just standin' there talkin', and the shot came outta nowhere."

Billy pointed to the blood on Jeff's shirt. "You hit?"

"Huh?" Jeff looked down at his shirt. "No. No. I...I caught him when he fell. He was dead before I even caught him, Billy."

Billy stared at his tense friend then asked, "What'd ya wanna do?" He was ready for anything Jeff would suggest. "I'm with ya whatever ya wanna do!"

"Nuthun we can do tonight. Got him square in the heart, Billy!" He yanked off his hat and threw it to the ground. "Outta nowhere! Square in the goddamn heart!"

"Ya think it was just a stray bullet from somewhere?" asked Billy.

"A gut feeling tells me it wasn't."

Since the time Jeff and Freddie caught those two gunrunners who implicated the Mexican police, they knew they were potential targets, but not even Jeff thought the greasy assholes would stoop to bushwhacking on the U.S. side of the border. Certainly not in the town that housed the Ranger's headquarters. So not only was Freddie's death painful, it was insulting.

The next morning Freddie's body was shipped by train to his parents in Bisbee. Sparky rode with it in the boxcar. Billy made sure his harmonica was placed in a special package and sent to his daughter Isabel. He wondered how she would handle the news and was glad he wasn't the one who had to deliver it. He had met her twice: a year ago when Freddie's folks brought her down for a visit, and again just a few weeks ago when he and Freddy visited her school in Bisbee. She was a pretty little thing, not a bit shy, and definitely her daddy's girl. He wondered if his two boys would mourn him going under. But how could they, he thought. "They don't even know me."

Jeff and Billy watched the train disappear into the distance.

"We got some detective work to do," Jeff finally said. "We gotta figure out where the hell the shot came from."

"Then what?"

"We'll see when we find it." Soon they were standing in front of the barber shop. Jeff looked at the ground and calculated precisely where Freddie was standing. "The bullet hit him square in the heart. We were both facin' thataway. "He placed his hand on his heart then stretched it out straight, trying to trace the angle of the shot. "I figure from the sound it had to come from about a hundred yards," he added, gazing down the length of his arm to the end of his pointed finger.

"That'd mean a long rifle," added Billy.

"Yep!" replied Jeff, and pulled a spent bullet from his pocket. "I took this out of him last night."

Billy could tell by his friend's voice that that had to have been painful. He had dug a few bullets out of friends...but never a dead one...and never one as close as Freddie.

"Looks like a fifty," observed Billy, "maybe a Sharps."

Jeff's eyes were scanning a ridge overlooking the buildings across the street. "Since we were facing north, it couldn't have come from a rooftop. Too close! The round would've passed through him. Let's take a look up on that ridge."

Billy eyeballed the location. "Be one hell of a shot at night."

"That barber shop light outlined us perfectly."

They both stood in silence for a long minute, staring at the ridge.

Finally Billy said, "You know this was an assination!"

"I know!" agreed Jeff, not bothering to correct his friend's pronunciation.

"Means they ain't got no qualms 'bout crossin' the border and dry gulchin' you, too!"

"I know. When Freddie fell into my arms I dropped to my knees, cradlin' him. That took us both out of the light. Otherwise there might've been a second shot. If he hadn't fallen towards me, you might've been plantin' both of us."

"Knowin' Freddie he pro'bly did that on purpose to get ya outta the line of fire. Ya know they won't stop at doin' ya in the back!"

"Guess you're just gonna have to watch it for me." With a forced half grin Jeff added, "Ain't exactly how I imagined bein' famous."

"I told ya to not spit out yer name to ev'ry crooked beaner policeman ya harnessed."

"Okay, fine!" Jeff shot back at his friend. "I fucked up! And it got my friend killed. Don't ya think I know that? What I don't know is why the sumbitch didn't target me?"

The two Rangers tethered Orion and Vermillion to a tree near the top of the ridge and hiked to its crest. They strolled among the craggy rocks until Jeff finally stopped and stared down towards the buildings.

"Good line of sight from here," he stated and pointed towards the barber shop in the distance.

Both men knew this was the work of a killer with the eye of a hawk. Billy tried to imagine how Jeff was feeling at that moment, knowing he was being targeted by someone who could make that kind of shot. Someone he couldn't even see, that it could come from anywhere at any time. It would be like living on the edge of cliff in earthquake country. It angered him that he didn't know how to protect his friend. Then he spotted something glistening a few feet away.

"There!" He picked up a spent cartridge.

Glancing at the piece of brass, Jeff said, "You called that one right, Billy! Sharps! Bushwhacker's weapon!"

After a long moment of just standing and staring down the hill at the barber shop, Billy finally said, "Ya know, he ne'er told us her name."

"Who?"

"His little dressmaker."

The only funeral Billy had ever attended was for his pa, so he hated them. At least it wasn't raining at Freddie's. Any Ranger not on assignment made the trip up to Bisbee for the service. It was more crowded than Billy thought it would be. Freddie had a lot of friends in the town, or his parents did. As he scanned the black-dressed mourners he noticed the school marm Miss Hannipy among the group. She caught his eyes, smiled sadly, and subtlety waved. Her hair was piled up, not hanging loose like the first time he saw her in Isabel's classroom. She still reminded him of a pretty dove with a broken wing. He also searched for anyone who might resemble a dressmaker, but then wondered how he could even tell. "Maybe the huge udders," he thought, then chastised himself for having that thought at such a dour time.

With the exception of the sobbing coming from Freddie's mother and daughter the crowd was mostly silent. A preacher who was too young to even have known Freddie read from the Good Book and talked about what a wonderful father, son, and God-fearing man he was. Captain Wheeler presented Freddie's parents with a plaque recognizing their son's service. Billy wondered which star his little friend would end up on. It wouldn't have to be a big one. He also kept a close eye on Jeff, knowing it was tearing his friend's guts apart that the killer picked Freddie and not him. He was the one who had the most run-ins with the crooked police. He was the one who had ventilated most of them. He was the one who constantly upset their flow of *pesos*. And when Jeff saw Isabel sobbing on her daddy's casket, his guilt was so powerful he had to walk away. Billy followed him.

"Ya can't let this shit et you up inside, Jeff," stated Billy when he caught up to his friend. "Where ya goin'?"

"I'm bad medicine, Billy. Best you steer clear of me."

"That ain't gonna happen! We done had each other's back fer six years and I ain't 'bout to shy away now."

Jeff stopped walking and turned sharply to his friend. Through gritted teeth and angry eyes he hissed, "Then yer gonna die." He turned and walked towards the nearest saloon.

Later that day when Billy and the other Rangers boarded the train back to Nogales Jeff wasn't there.

"He said he wanted to stay here 'nother day," Wheeler explained. "He'd catch tomorrow's train."

"Why?" Billy asked.

"Dint say and I dint ask," replied Wheeler. "Ya know how hard he's takin' this. I figger maybe he wants to spend some time with Freddie's folks, since he was there when it happened."

The next day Billy went to the station to meet Jeff, but he wasn't on the train from Bisbee. He went straight to Wheeler's office.

"Ain't heard nuthun," stated the captain. "Billy, ya know sometimes a fella's gotta handle things in his own way.

"Ifin ya mean by bein' 'lone, Cap'n," all that's gonna do is get him kilt."

Over the years Billy had seen his share of fellows deal with pain in many ways. Not the kind of pain from a gunshot or knife wound, or broken arm or leg from getting thrown from a testy mount, but the kind of pain that leaves a hole inside of them. A hole they try to fill with alcohol, or whores, or solitude, none of which do the job.

Two days later Jeff returned to Nogales. He had rode a freight wagon back and said it gave him time to think.

"Ya, well, whiles ya was thinkin' I was growin' grey hairs! Fraid ya was laying in a ditch somewhere with a fifty caliber round through yer goddamn stubborn head."

After the two had found an empty table at the saloon closest to the freight station and were nursing a beer, Jeff explained, "I talked with his folks...told them how it happened...told them it was my fault."

Billy was angry. "Why the hell'd ya do that? It weren't yer fault."

"They're gunnin' for me, Billy, and that makes anyone near me a target, too. Freddie was alongside me. And I tell ya this right now, I will not let another friend die because of me."

"Freddie didn't die because of you. He died because he was a Ranger doin' his job."

Jeff was silent for a long moment before he replied, "You remember our first night on the trail together, back in o-three?"

"When we was haulin' Calvin Small Toe?"

"You told me you lose a bit of your soul with every man you kill. 'Member that?"

"Yeah."

"You also lose a good chunk of it when a friend goes under. You want vengeance. You wanna reap some damage...and it's so damn frustrating when you can't."

"We'll find him, Jeff. We'll get him."

"I think you better change that 'him' to a 'them.'

"Then we'll kill 'em all!"

Jeff looked at his friend. Billy saw the usual tobacco stained grin slowly spread across Jeff's face. They clanked their beer mugs together.

Unless they were on separate assignments, for the past six years hardly a day had gone by without the twosome at least having a palaver, even a short one in passing. For the next few weeks after Freddie's funeral Jeff had been shying away from everyone, including Billy. He requested only missions he could handle alone. Most nights he'd return to the barracks long after the others were asleep. Some nights he wouldn't return at all. It was after midnight on the last day of March when he finally crept into the barracks. Sparky was snoring away on his two mattresses on the floor and Freddie's bunk had yet to be filled with a new recruit. Jeff quietly sat on his bed and removed his Justins, wiggled his freed toes, then stripped down to his long johns. He stretched out on the thin mattress and stared at the ceiling. Suddenly he felt a hard poke push through the mattress from under his bunk and jab his back. Knowing it was a gun he froze.

From beneath the bed a voice asked, "How the hell can I cover yer back if I ain't got no fuckin' idea where yer goddamn back is?"

The first emotion that swept through Jeff was anger, but it was quickly replaced with a long exhale coming from the knowledge that he wasn't about to have his spine blown in two. He sat up on his bunk as Billy slid out from beneath. "You haven't anything better to do then scare the shit outta me?" asked Jeff with a relieved laugh.

"Gotta get the message through that thick skull of yers some how."

"What the hell ya doin' here? Anna kick you out again?"

"Why ya been shunnin' me?" asked Billy as he sat down on Freddie's empty bunk and purposely ignored Jeff's question.

Jeff bit off a chunk of chew and replied, "I been trying to find Quias and Amador."

"Four eyes are better than two."

"Gotta do it alone, Billy. I'm not going to get another friend..."

"Goddamn it, Jeff, stop sayin' that!" yelped Billy. "You did not get Freddie kilt! An asshole with a Sharps did it, and from the distance of his shot he pro'bly couldn't even tell who the hell he was aimin' at—just knew it were two Rangers."

"Then why did he pick the smaller target, and how did he know where the hell we were to begin with?"

Billy strained his brain for an answer. Finally he said, "Ya say you and Freddie just came outta the vaudeville show?"

"Yes."

"Did ya notice anyone? Ya know, anyone seedy in there? Any pepper bellies?"

"This is Nogales, Billy. Besides, we were too busy laughin' at the skits and gapin' at the nudie dancers." Jeff chuckled and added, "Freddie kept whisperin' to me 'bout how his little dressmaker had bigger tits than any of them." Again he sat for a long silent before finally saying, "If those shitwads get me before I get...."

Before Jeff could finish his statement Billy said, "Ya got it. I'll finish it, but there's a better chance of them not getting' ya at all with me around. I done lost one friend by not being there. It's a shitty feelin' I don't want agin."

Jeff looked straight into Billy's eyes and said, "Neither do I."

That statement should have been a hint to Billy of what was to come, but it flew over his head like a bat at twilight.

"We been doin' this job together fer neigh under six years, Jeff. Ya ain't got me kilt yet. And I don't aim to let ya."

The two friends talked and laughed until around three in the morning. Sparky continued to snore away. After Jeff promised to stop being so reckless Billy finally relaxed and dozed off on Freddie's old bunk. The next morning Jeff was gone again. Already dressed, Billy quickly headed into Wheeler's office. It was early and the captain hadn't made coffee yet, so Billy did.

"All he said was he had some 'vestigatin' to do," explained Wheeler.

"Where 'bouts?" asked Billy as he waited for the coffee to brew.

"Wouldn't tell me."

"Thought we was all su'posed to let ya know where we was all the time."

"Sometimes fellas take on guilt that ain't really theirs, Billy. Ain't nuthun ya can do to stop 'em."

"So yer sayin' he's out lookin' fer them two Mex police gunrunners, thinkin' one of them mighta put Freddie under?"

"That'd be my guess." The captain whiffed the freshly brewed coffee and poured himself a cup.

"Why the hell'd ya let him go 'lone?"

"Hey, don't jump up my ass, Billy!! That's how he called it. Said ifin I don't let him do it he'd take some pers'nal days off and do it anyways."

172

Billy crossed to the window, and gazed at the rusted gate for a long moment. "Think he crossed to the Mex side of town?"

"That's where I'd go."

"And I thought I was the fuckin' dumb one," declared Billy as he started to leave the office.

"If yer goin' down there grab a street howitzer from the armory, 'cause I ain't got no one to send with ya. Advantage, Billy!"

"Yessir!" With that last statement he was just about to close the office door behind him.

"Grab two!" Wheeler called out.

Billy stopped at the door. "Thought ya said there ain't no one to go with me."

"There's me. I could use a little sun."

Billy smiled and left the office. He found himself excited. He didn't know the old captain still had the urge.

Wheeler took a sip of the fresh coffee. "Holy shit," he mumbled. "This could kill a sidewinder!" He dumped it out the window and watched a cactus gasp and shrivel into dust.

Fifteen minutes later the two Rangers were crossing over to the Mexican side of Nogales. No one gave them a second gander as they walked towards the closest *cantina*, but when they entered the smelly place, all heads turned their way. The two pump action shotguns each housing a fine collection of twelve-gage rounds kept any stares from holding too long. The little old men went back to their checkers game, the whores returned to their usual customers, and the *hombres* turned their bellies back towards the bar. Only a Mexican policeman badly in need of a shave, haircut, and bath, and dressed in the typically soiled uniform approached them. He didn't wear a pistol, but sported a very fancy black belt about three inches wide and studded with silver coins. Tucked into it was a machete.

With a surly tone in his voice he asked, *"Problemo, pelados?"*

"Habla inglés?" asked Wheeler.

"Si," the man answered with an irritated grudge.

"Any Rangers been in today?"

"No!"

"Ya know two *policia* called "Tomás Amador and Delores Quías?" asked Wheeler.

"No," answered the policeman. He turned and bellied back up to the bar.

"The fuck he don't," stated Billy and started to step towards the man.

Wheeler grabbed Billy's arm and said, "Good relations, Billy!"

"Cap'n, ya know what a *pelado* is?"

"Can't say I do."

"Low life scum. That's what the fuckin' pepper gut called us."

"That a fact?" stated Wheeler. For a moment he looked at the chuckling policeman who was bellied up to the bar with his back towards the two Rangers. He said something to his *amigos* and they all laughed. Wheeler whipped out his knife and stepped up to the back of the unsuspecting policeman. In a flash, faster than Billy thought the old Cap'n could even move, he turned the blade sideways and slithered it up between the man's breeches and fancy belt. With a jerk upwards he slashed the belt in half. The first thing to hit the floor was the machete, followed by the fancy belt. After that came the policeman's breeches. The cantina erupted in laughter because he wasn't wearing any skivvies. The flustered *hombre* pulled up his breeches and glared at the captain. For a moment Billy could see revenge in the *hombre's* eyes and his hand start to reach for the machete, but he quickly realized how difficult it would be to wield a blade in one hand and hold up his breeches with the other. He hurried out the door spewing a trail of Spanish curse words.

"Feather Yank taught me that trick," explained the captain. "Finally got to try it."

Five *cantinas* and four whorehouses later they were right back where they started. As they crossed back into the Arizona side of Nogales Wheeler said, "At least I got outta that stuffy office fer awhile."

The next time Billy saw Jeff was three days later, dying in that shitty Mexican jail.

April 10, 1910

The air in the dentist office was oddly pleasing. Since Billy wasn't familiar with the odor the only word that came to his mind was "clean." A large apparatus with many cords and skinny metal arms resembling a big praying mantis hovered over a high backed leather chair. The strange machine was

174

intimidating, but not enough to make him turn and skedaddle or the pain to mysteriously vanish again. Dr. Steven Rollins was seated reading the paper. He jumped up to greet his new patient.

"Welcome, Sir," he stated cheerfully. "What can I do for you today?"

"Been fightin' a bad toothache for months, Doc."

"Have a seat, please," invited the dentist. "Let's take a look."

Billy removed the sombrero and eased into the high backed black chair, not only suspect of the threatening metal arms suspended over his head, but also the large electrical cord running from the metal insect straight into an oversized plug in the wall.

"I'm Doctor Rollins, Steven Rollins," the friendly young man stated.

He hardly looked old enough to shave. Billy figured the fellow must be fresh out of dentist school. At least he supposed and hoped dentists went to some kind of school.

"Billy Old. Forgive my smell, Doc. I been out on the trail and ain't been in town long enough to get a proper bath."

"No problem, Mr. Old," Dr. Rollins replied with a smile, then slipped a white mask over his mouth and nose.

Billy gave a soft but painful chuckle and asked, "Ya gonna rob me, Doc?"

The dentist laughed and explained as he crossed to a sink, "Germs are our enemy, Mr. Old."

Then Billy knew the fellow was definitely from the East—he actually washed his hands before he began probing around in his mouth. It took less than thirty seconds for the young dentist to find the problem.

"Mr. Old, you have a wisdom tooth that has grown in at an angle, putting pressure on your molar. That's what is causing your pain."

Billy remembered the two Mexican barbers and how they gestured with their hands at an angle.

"The position of the wisdom tooth makes it impossible for me to simply extract it. I'll have to cut the gums around it so it can be shifted to a proper position for extraction. That will eliminate the pressure on your molar and stop the pain."

"Will it hurt?" asked Billy, trying to decipher every word the man just said.

Dr. Rollins reached to the counter on his left and held up an awkwardly shaped thingamajig with a big black cup on the end.

"This is called The Clover. It was invented by an Englishman named Joseph Clover. It's for applying ether."

"Applyin' what?"

"Ether! It's a gas that renders the patient unconscious." The dentist pointed to a specific part of the unusual device. "Liquid ether is placed in this reservoir. When I pump this, water rotates in this jacket around the ether, which keeps it from getting too cold and helps create a vapor. You breathe in the vapor through this large cup. In just moments, you're in a deep sleep. You won't feel a thing, Mr. Old."

"It's safe?" inquired Billy.

"Absolutely!"

"How much?"

"I can do the entire procedure for three dollars, sir."

Billy woke up over two hours later. It was the deepest sleep he had ever experienced. He dreamed he was on the stage of a packed opera house receiving a thunderous applause for something he had no idea he had done. He dreamed his pa was sitting on their porch smoking his hand carved ivory pipe with a cougar skin rug wrapped around his bare feet. He dreamed Orion and Captain were singing Red River Valley in strange harmonic human voices. Three Man was laughing and playing patty cake with Freddie's daughter. Not one dream with skinny whores and anthills, or fat policemen and severed limbs, or giant man-eating lizards. When he awoke, he felt content and refreshed, but confused by his surroundings.

"Welcome back, Mr. Old," smiled Dr. Rollins. "How do we feel?"

"Uh, rested," he found himself saying.

He wondered why his hand hurt. He opened his fist and saw he was still grasping the tin star, which had made five deep impressions in his palm from its five points. His toothache was gone, but now there was a fire in his gums. He touched his cheek and it felt large and puffy.

"Please keep the cotton padding in your mouth for at least two or three more hours," explained Dr. Rollins. "For the next few days eat only soft foods. If you can survive on just soup, it would be wise." He handed Billy a small bottle of pills. "If the pain gets too intense take two of these. In one week I want you to come back so I can make sure there is no infection and the stitches are dissolving correctly."

"Dissolving?" Billy thought he knew what the word meant.

"Yessir! After the gums were cut they had to be stitched back up. The stitches I used are made from cat gut so they'll dis..."

"Ya put cat guts in my mouth?"

"Mr. Old, I assure you, they are sterilized and safe, and will completely dissolve over the next several days."

"Will they...taste like...cat?"

"I don't know," laughed the dentist. "I've never tasted cat."

It was a shaky and slow walk from the dentist office to the boarding house, especially the climb up the tall hill. Several times he had to stop and let his brains tumble back into place and sturdy himself on any item that was nearby. When he finally reached the door, a very large woman greeted him.

"Ya Billy Old, young fella?" asked the woman.

"Yes'um," he mumbled.

"John Foster told me ya was a comin'. I'll show ya the room."

Old Lady Castle was exactly as John had described her. Take three boulders, stack them on top of each other, put a head on top and add two arms and two legs and that would be Irene Castle. Billy stood at an even six foot, but still looked up to meet her green eyes. She had a high, raspy voice that always seemed to have a smile buried in it. He liked her immediately. If she wasn't so old, he figured she'd be a good, big match for Sparky. He chuckled as he imagined the size of their babies.

"Do ya chew?" Mrs. Castle asked as she led him up the stairs to his room.

"No, ma'am!"

She squinted at Billy's jaw and demanded, "Then what's in yer mouth?"

Struggling to speak through cotton packing, Billy replied, "Got a tooth pulled!"

"Oh! Good! Damn tobacco spit stains my carpets. My second and fourth husbands chewed, rest their souls!" She crossed herself. "Had to replace six carpets. Damn nasty habit. Lord knows my fifth sure as hell ain't gonna be a chewer, soon as I hook him, that is." She laughed from her toes up. "If ya womanize, do it at the whorehouse or in a hay loft! Don't bring them back here to my place, savvy?"

"Yes, ma'am!"

"All my boarders are good folks. Treat them decent and they'll do the same, savvy?"

"Yes, ma'am!"

"And stop the goddamn 'ma'amin' fer crissake! Name's Irene!"

"Yes, ma'am!"

"Breakfast at seven, supper at seven," Irene Castle explained as she opened the door to the room. "Yer on yer own fer lunch!"

The room was small, but had a welcome feel to it. The bed looked plumper than anything Billy had ever experienced or could even remember seeing. A white doily covered a small table placed by the bed. A three drawer dresser was against the wall beneath a painting of a waterfall.

"Three drawers?" he thought. "I ain't got enough stuff to fill three drawers."

"Here ya go, Mr. Old," said Mrs. Castle as she dropped the skeleton key into his hand. "Privy's at the end of the hall. Ya pull the chain to flush it. Bathhouse is out back; plenty of soap and towels and hot water. 'Preciate it if you'd take advantage of it 'fore ya put them clothes down on that bed quilt, savvy?" With that last statement she was stomping away down the hallway. Billy felt the floor slightly tremble with each of her steps. Nearing the staircase to the parlor below Irene Castle tossed one more statement over her shoulder. "I'll be in the kitchen if ya got any questions...like precisely where that bathhouse is!" She laughed and disappeared down the steps.

"I must really stink," he snickered to himself, which sent a twinge of pain through his jaw.

After tossing his saddlebags on the bed he remembered the mistake he had made in El Papalote—taking a bath then having to climb back into the same filthy clothes. He refused to be that stupid again. He walked back down the high hill to take a gander at Naco's new stores. He had three drawers to fill.

For the next few days he survived on soup and soft bread. Each morning Mrs. Castle made him a special serving of warm milk toast.

"Ya know," she bellowed one morning, "if ya weren't so goddamn young I'd be aimin' at makin' ya my fifth husband! Course, maybe that's what I need—a young one—to keep up with me. Won't kill 'im off so fast!" Then she'd laugh from her toes up.

The stitches in his gums had dissolved with no taste akin to cat. Of course, he had no idea what cat tasted like anyways. The pain in his jaw was quickly becoming a nasty memory. His new clothes made him feel like an American again. Once again he had to cut the scratchy collars off the three shirts he had purchased. The two pairs of Levi Strauss' were stiff and needed breaking in, but at least they didn't have holes in the knees and backsides. He kept the chaps he had purchased in El Papalote, but burned the *sombrero* and *serape*, along with the critters they housed. His most expensive item was a John B. 10X Felt Shiner in black, much fancier than the one Tomas Amador had put a bullet through. He also treated himself to a haircut and shave, but kept a moustache and goatee.

Settling into a boarding house was easier than he figured, probably due to the pleasant nature of Irene Castle. The house offered four rooms for boarding. The fifth one was Mrs. Castle's personal living space. One room belonged to a widowed school marm. Her hair was always pulled straight back so tightly it made her eyes look like one of Billy's Angora goats, and her favorite word seemed to be "humph." She reminded him of every marm he had ever had and how they all seemed to feed on prunes and proverbs and have a natural dislike for children.

Another room went to the flamboyant owner of Naco's new Vaudeville theatre, a fellow who called himself Benny Cohan and claimed to be a distant cousin of some Broadway star with the same last name. Billy had no idea who he was talking about. The man was obsessed with neck scarves and waist sashes. At every meal he'd sport a colorful matching tandem. He would blurt out funny things like, "My eyes smell onions," or "I am such a tender ass." Billy couldn't get a handle on a single word of it. He figured Jeff would've, though.

One room went to a retired traveling salesman whose diarrhea of the jawbone consisted of his many past exploits in lonely housewife seduction, flavored with details that made the old school marm humph and Irene Castle chuckle. Billy figured the bragging salesman had been sipping from Arizona's legendary Hassayampa Creek. Anyone who drank from it could never tell the truth. It wasn't long before he started taking many of his meals at the local café.

Just three days after Billy took the deputy job, John Foster had to make an overnight trip to a nearby small town to help identify a suspected bank robber. At least that's what he told Billy who figured his shifty friend was testing his word about not putting a bullet in Pasco's brain pan. He probably went fishing. Taking advantage of his time alone with Pasco, late that night he unlocked the heavy, screeching door to the cell area and walked down to the greaser's temporary home. Pasco was asleep.

Very softly Billy said, "Wake up, fucker!"

Either the prisoner was a light sleeper or the screeching door had served its purpose and already stirred his senses. He blinked a few times, sat up on his cot and coughed. After realizing it wasn't morning he rubbed his eyes into focus.

"What you want, *gringo?*" he managed to grumble.

In a cold, flat tone Billy replied, "When you get outta here, I'm gonna plant ya!" Then he turned, walked out of the cell area, closed the heavy, noisy door behind him, and locked it.

Stunned and angered from this late night surprise visit all Diaz Pasco could do was shout from his iron home, "*¿Quien chingados es? Hey?? ¿Quien chingados es?*"

Billy knew it would be fruitless to ask the beaner about the mysterious Victoriano. Knowing he was being sprung in sixty-some days, Pasco would just lie. Even if he did tell him who or where Victoriano was, Billy had no idea of how long it would take to find the man. That might give Pasco the chance to squirrel away under another rock when he got out of jail. So he decided to put those sixty-some days to use by coming up with of a good way to make the killer talk, and a good way for him to die. He also figured since it had been a fair spell since he had unloaded some baggage, what better way to pass some of those sixty-some nights than in a whorehouse?

Naco only had one whorehouse left on its side of the border, so it didn't surprise Billy to find it a bit loud and busy. What did surprise him, though, was who he spotted shopping her wares across the crowded parlor.

"ABBIE!" he shouted over the clamor of clinking glasses, giggling whores, and whooping men.

She immediately recognized the smiling face across the room. Abbie Crutchfield squealed, ran over to him, leapt into his arms, and wrapped her legs around his waist. Laughing, the two turned circles before collapsing onto, fortunately, a vacant love seat.

"What the hell ya doin' in Naco?" he asked.

"Too many bad men in Nogales," she explained. "Life's a bit more toler'ble here. Not as busy, but what the hell, I'm eatin'!"

For a good hour they sipped the coffin varnish the place called whiskey and reminisced about Jeff. She cried in his arms and he in hers. It felt good. For over two years he had bottled up his remorse and corked it with hatred. He knew crying was supposed to be unmanly or cowardly, but he didn't care. The liquor excused it. Neither had truly mourned their friend's passing. He had kept himself too angry and she had kept herself too busy.

"Truth is, Billy," admitted Abbie, "another reason I come to Naco is 'cause this is where he got kilt. Don't know what I was thinkin.' I mean, I couldn't do nuthun 'bout it. At first I thought I could. Thought I could lure one of 'em bastards up to my room and slit his throat. Deep down I knew I couldn't. Hell, I ain't even sure what they look like." She wiped away a tear and tried to cover her loss with humor. "Guess I did love the hotheaded jerk."

He didn't know how to respond to her declaration so he just nodded and lowered his head. He knew a man wasn't supposed to love another man, unless it was his pa, but couldn't think of any other way to describe his feelings. He cursed himself for not knowing more words.

As the place began to get even more crowded and louder she suggested they go up to her room. Every whore has her own room in which to live and conduct business. The walls were purposely thin so customers could hear their neighbor's lusty grunts and groans. The animal noises seeping through the walls usually helped speed up the time with their current customer. Whores survive by numbers.

The room was small and dingy. Not much different than any other whore's room he had visited, except for one thing. Hanging on her wall was a painting of a horse. She noticed Billy staring at it.

"Ya like it?" she asked.

"Yeah," answered Billy.

"I painted it," she replied with much pride. "It's Lavender."

"Lavender?"

"My Bay," Abbie responded as if he should know that. "Her name's Lavender, my fav'rite color."

Then Billy remembered. A few years ago Abbie had saved up enough money to buy herself a horse. It was a pretty Blood Bay. She housed it at the livery in exchange for servicing the blacksmith once a month. She must have worked out the same deal here with the local smithy. At least once or twice every couple of weeks she would take it for a run, just so the animal would remember it had legs and she could feel like the fresh breeze was temporarily cleansing her soul. Jeff had told Billy that one day he expected her to just keep going, not look back, not even say goodbye. Go to California, New Orleans, anywhere. He felt she didn't belong in this part of the country. But she always came back. Now Billy knows why.

"Tried to get the boss to lemme paint my whole room lavender," Abbie continued, "but she wouldn't—gave me some half-ass excuse 'bout the only beauty in yer room should be yer own. Ain't that a crock-a-shit? As if any a 'em drunken cowpokes care what a whore looks like 'bove her tits!"

Still studying and growing more impressed with the details in the painting, Billy said, "Yer a good painter."

With mock arrogance Abbie replied, "The keerek term is Arteest!"

They sat on the bed. Very quietly, so his words wouldn't seep through the thin walls, he told her the whole story, from the time he left Nogales to his mystical experience with the ether. The towns he'd been in, the people he'd seen. The things he'd seen. The things he'd done, the suffering, the one-handed Yaqui, the giant lizard bone, Captain, and Three Man. Although he had vowed never to, he even told her about the Indian squaw and the infant. He knew he could trust this woman to not judge him. Once again, just like the night he had told Jeff about his time with the Rough Riders, he realized that some things are just better getting shed of then letting them eat up your innards.

After his story Abbie said, "That's a lotta hell to drag yerself through, Billy."

"It ain't over—still two of them to account for. One of them's sittin' right here in John Foster's jail."

"Why ya doin' this, Billy?"

"Cause I told him I would. And he would've done it fer me."

"Yeah, yer pro'bly right. He was as shit brained crazy as you."

They didn't fuck. They both felt Jeff would be watching. Later Abbie introduced him to her friend Henrietta, a peppery little blond with a shifty sense of humor. He unloaded some baggage. Several times.

May, 1910

Naco had become so tame it was damn near boring. Billy was surprised how it had happened just shy of two years. Farms and ranches surrounded the area. Telephone lines were strung. A woman could phone an order into the Sears Roebuck wish book and not have to wait as long for it to arrive. Electric lights lit the streets and most of the small buildings. An occasional automobile would even roll in from Bisbee or Tucson and scare the hell out of the horses and send the peasants on the Mexican side of town into a state of wonder. A movie house opened and he saw his first moving picture, "Pride of the Range," with a fellow named Tom Mix. He laughed at the size of the actor's huge white hat and the fact that it never came off in a fist fight.

When the mines were producing they were twelve saloons operating in Naco. Only three managed to survive the demise of the copper and they shut down at midnight. One no longer allowed gambling. He figured the whorehouse would be the next. That usually happened when "civilization," meaning churchgoers and do-gooders, started bleeding into the area. The one thing a tamer town did give the two lawmen was some spare time to catch up on the whereabouts of friends. His most shocking news was about Sparky.

"Ya ain't heard?" asked John, as he reassembled a very clean Winchester.

"Heard what?" replied Billy.

"About a month after the Rangers got broke up, Sparky's ma died so he moved back in with his pa. The big fella spent damn near a whole year studyin.' "

"Studyin'?" Billy had a tough time imagining Sparky studying anything except Indians. "Studyin' what?"

"The Good Book. He became an ordained pastor. Got hisself a little church up in Oracle."

"I'll be damned! Sparky done got his dream job."

"Married some little dressmaker from Bisbee," added John. "I went to the weddin'. Strangest sight I'd ever seen: Giant ol' Sparky all decked out in a fancy store bought suit, and standin' next to him was this tiny little lady that barely rose 'bove his belt buckle, but she sported the biggest bosoms I've ever seen in my life. I tell ya, Billy, I thought she'd tip over."

Billy almost fell out of the chair laughing. He knew one day he would have to ride up to Oracle just to see this amazing change in his friend and finally feast his eyes on the "little dressmaker."

John returned the cleaned and reassembled Winchester to its resting place then hesitated as he stared at the rack.

"I ain't gonna clean that sumbitch's piece," he declared.

"Huh? What piece?" Billy asked.

"This Sharps," answered John, pulling the confiscated weapon from the rack. "Belongs to that asshole Pasco. I ain't gonna clean it!" He rudely returned it to its resting place. "Let it sit there and rust. Maybe it'll blow up in his face."

Billy knew there was more than one Sharps in the territory, but there was only one Diaz Pasco. He now knew who took Freddie Rankin from his young daughter. Three days had passed since his last visit to the scum bucket so he figured another one was due. After John went out for some supper Billy unlocked and opened the noisy, heavy door and strolled down to Pasco's cell. The prisoner was standing, looking out of the small window in the back wall.

"When you get outta here, I'm gonna plant ya!" he calmly repeated.

Once again, Pasco yelled as Billy walked away, "*¿Quien chingados es?*"

He smiled as he closed the noisy metal door behind him. It felt good messing with the brain of the jailed killer. It made him feel clever, even a little smart. He figured Jeff would've been proud.

January, 1908

"Billy, I'm beggin' ya!" pleaded Freddie. "Her whole class is 'spectin' it!"

"I ain't ne'er talked to a buncha kids, Freddie!" explained Billy. "I'd look dumber than I am."

"Ya don't gotta say nuthun, Billy," explained Freddie. "All ya gotta do is stand there and lemme show them how to handcuff someone, or rope them, ya know, the kinda things we do on the job."

"Why not bring Sparky?"

"His ma took sick. He took a few days off to tend to her," answered Freddie. "And Jeff's off chasin' down some gunrunners with Feather Yank. Besides, Isabel knows ya."

"I only met her once, Freddie."

"That's more than anyone else."

"But them kids are in the fifth grade, Freddie."

"So?"

"That's how old I was when I quit my schoolin'!"

"So?" repeated Freddie.

"So, well, hell, Boulder, what if...what if they're smarter'n me?"

Freddie laughed and said, "Hell, Billy, they're pro'bly smarter than the two of us clumped together, but it don't matter none...they're kids!"

Billy paused for a moment, pondering Freddie's request. Then he shook his head and said, "I'd just put an onion in yer apple pie."

"I told ya, ya don't have to talk, just be there with me. I'll do the talkin'. "

"Whatcha gonna talk 'bout?"

"Just tell them some stories!"

"What kinda stories?"

"Stories 'bout what we do as Rangers, that's all!"

"Them stories ain't fittin' fer little kids, Boulder!"

"'Well, then...I'll water them down a skosh. Ya know, 'stead a sayin' blew his brains out, I'll say, uh...sent 'im to Heaven. Yeah, that's a good one, sent 'im to Heaven. Tell ya what, I'll buy ya a week's supply of pipe tobacco."

Billy shuffled his feet then walked in a few tight circles before he finally asked, "I don't gotta say nothun?"

"Not a word."

"Two weeks supply," demanded Billy.

"Deal!" Freddie spit in his hand, held it out, and they sealed the bargain.

The next day the two Rangers took the morning train to Bisbee. It was a good walk from the station to the small schoolhouse. Along the way Billy reminded Freddie at least a dozen times that he had to do all the talking. He asked Freddie that since they were in Bisbee, was he also going to introduce him to his "little dressmaker with the huge udders?"

"Hell, no," Freddie responded. "I ain't gonna let anya ya fellas 'round her 'til we're hitched. Then when ya tell her a bunch lies 'bout me it'll be too late fer her to change her mind."

Isabel's fifth grade class was waiting anxiously to meet two Arizona Rangers in the flesh. When they walked into the classroom it exploded with applause and shouts. Billy almost turned around and ran out. Upon seeing her daddy, Isabel ran up to Freddie and leapt into his arms.

"Hey, Peaches!" he exclaimed as he held her high and kissed her four times. Once on the nose, once on each cheek, then right back to the nose, and counted "One, two, three, four" as he delivered each smooch. She giggled. He beamed. The class shouted, laughed, and whistled. For just a second Billy felt a tinge of envy pass through him. He figured his two sons would be walking by now, perhaps even running. Would they greet him like that?

"Naw," he thought, "boys don't do that kinda stuff."

Written on the blackboard in huge letters was "WELCOME, ARIZONA RANGERS!"

"Take your seats, class!" ordered a young woman, also smiling.

Billy couldn't remember ever seeing a school marm smile. He thought she looked too pretty and too young to even be a school marm, at least compared to the ones he remembered. Her hair wasn't pulled up in a tight bun, or forced back to make her eyes squint like a coolie. It flowed to her shoulders and was a deep auburn color. Even her dress was colorful and not something that reminded him of an undertaker. As the children scrambled back to their places behind the small desks, the woman turned to Freddie.

"Thank you so much for coming, Mr. Rankin," she stated with genuine appreciation and an even bigger smile. "This whole idea of having a parent come speak to our class is very new. We're still testing the waters, so to speak. As a matter of fact, you're the first one to actually show up." Then she turned to Billy and said, "Hello. I'm Miss Hannipy."

As Billy started to tip his hat, the young woman extended her hand like a man would do when being introduced to a stranger. Having never shaken a woman's hand in greeting he was taken back for a second, not quite sure how firmly he should grasp the dainty paw.

"Billy Old," he replied shyly, lightly taking her hand. "I, uh, work with Freddie."

He was surprised at her firm grip. It was strong and forceful. Then he noticed her withered left arm that denied her its use, but had strengthened her right. She reminded him of a pretty dove with a broken wing.

"It's very nice to meet you, Mr. Old, and thank you for joining us!" Turning to the class she announced, "Class, this is Mr. Rankin, Isabel's father, and this is his friend Mr. Old. What do we say?"

Together, in one loud voice, the entire class erupted with, "HELLO, MR. RANKIN! HELLO, MR. OLD!"

Billy chuckled.

"Mr. Rankin, Mr. Old," stated Miss Hannipy, "the floor is yours!"

The next hour was filled with oohs and ahhs as Freddie explained just what it was the Rangers did, without the gory details, of course. He handcuffed Billy then asked the class for volunteers to see what it was like to be handcuffed. The entire room raised their hands in unison and started calling, "Me, me, me!" So Billy took out his cuffs and he and Freddie went around the room, cuffing and releasing all eleven children.

"Any boyfriends and girlfriends in this here class?" Freddie asked with a devilish grin.

Several of the kids started hooting and pointing at two kids seated next to each other—a blond haired boy and a brown haired girl. So Freddie cuffed a hand from each together and said, "Yer now hitched!" Everyone laughed and made cat calls at the two children. They took it in stride.

Freddie demonstrated lassoing a steer by using Billy as his cow. To Billy's surprise, Freddie tossed him on the ground and began to hogtie him. In a moment of spontaneity that he didn't even know he had, Billy mooed, grunted, and kicked like a roped steer. The classroom ignited with laughter. Freddie played a few tunes on his harmonica and the kids sang along. All-in-all, Billy actually enjoyed himself. He also witnessed a side of Freddie he had never seen: a father. Isabel ran up and hugged her daddy goodbye. Tears began to form when she asked when he was coming back to Grandma's.

"Soon as I can," answered Freddie, giving her the "One, two, three, four" kisses again.

Miss Hannipy lightly tapped a ruler on her desk and said, "What do we say to Mr. Rankin and Mr. Old, class?"

Again an eruption took place. "Thank you!"

Billy was impressed with the way Miss Hannipy handled her class. It was nothing like what he remembered about his fifth grade class. The kids actually seemed happy to be there. As the two Rangers were returning to the station to catch the late afternoon train back to Nogales, Billy was still smiling.

"Guess that weren't as bad as I thought'd be," he stated.

"Kinda fun, weren't it?" said Freddie with a smile.

"Yeah, was!" answered Billy, also grinning. "Kinda makes ya feel important."

That was the last time Isabel would see her father alive.

May, 1910

When a new lawman was in town, it was wise to let folks get accustomed to his face. So Billy spent some free time just roaming the area surrounding Naco, meeting the new settlers, making friends. The ones who respected the badge appreciated the gesture. The ones who didn't now knew who to fear. It was on one of those days of roaming that he discovered the empty, rotting shack about five miles northwest of town. Checking with the land office he found it was abandoned property, which made it a perfect place for a future planting.

It was early Friday morning of the same week he had stumbled on the abandoned shack that Abbie took her ride. He had slipped the blacksmith a half dollar to inform him of the next time she asked to have Lavender prepped for a run. The smithy told him she always rode east on the trail towards Pirtleville and was usually back in about three hours. He needed to speak to her in a safer place than within the thin walls of her depressing room.

About a mile outside of town the trail crossed a small creek. Knowing she would slow to ford it, he parked himself and Orion on its east side in some cottonwoods. When he stepped out of the trees in front of her, Abbie jerked Lavender to a sudden stop. The Blood Bay whinnied and reared. As fast as he'd ever seen a man pull one, Abbie had her boot gun drawn, cocked, and aimed straight at his johnson. Knowing there are few things more dangerous than a pissed off whore, Billy threw his hands in the air and shouted, "It's me!"

"Whoa, girl! Easy!" She calmed Lavender but continued to chide Billy.

"Ya scared the shit outta me, Billy Old! Jesus Christ! Almost gimme a god-damned heart 'tack!"

"Sorry," Billy declared, stifling a chuckle. Then he held up a small bag that had been hanging from the lizzy on Orion's saddle. "Got some fresh biscuits here," he said. "Could ya handle a little breakfast?"

Still mad enough to melt snow, but hungry, Abbie replied, "Why the hell not!" She slid the boot gun back into its nesting place and hopped off Lavender . "Yer lucky I dint blow yer head off," she added.

"It weren't my head ya were aimin' at."

Abbie laughed. He knew her anger was cooling. She tethered Lavender next to Orion, who took an immediate interest in the pretty Bay. He nudged her with his nose. She replied with a loud fart.

"Whatcha doin' out here?" asked Abbie. "All 'em days down in that Mexica' heat ain't baked yer brain pan, has they?"

"I need a favor, Abbie," Billy stated with reluctance.

"A favor?" the girl repeated as she quickly devoured one of the fresh biscuits. "I don't do favors, Billy."

"It's worth a twenty dollar gold piece," he added.

"Jesus, who do I gotta kill?" she devilishly grinned, exposing a mouthful of fresh biscuit.

Not certain how Abbie would react to a plan that included her being friendly with one of Jeff's killers, he considered treading lightly, but then figured there really was no way to tread lightly with what he needed to ask of her. At first he thought about asking Henrietta, but she had no stake in the game. Abbie did. They took her customer, her lover, her potential husband and escape from the life she was living. So he decided the best route was straight to it.

"In about thirty days Diaz Pasco gets sprung. I need ya to get him passed out drunk and fucked senseless 'fore he crosses the bridge." He waited for her to spit at him, cuss him out, claw at his face, anything. She just looked at him for a long moment while continuing to nibble on her second biscuit.

"Is that all?" she finally asked.

"Uh, yeah," he answered, exhaling.

"He one of Jeff's killers, ain't he?"

"Freddie's, too."

Abbie turned and gazed off to the north. The morning sun lit up the right side of her face as Billy watched her eyes travel far away. When she spoke, it was a soft voice he had never heard before. He thought of his mother.

"Ya know," she finally said, "I used to dream that someday Jeff and me mighta got us a little house, with windows...real windows that open up and let in fresh air...not some stuffy little room with four ugly walls I can't even paint. Might not ne'er have happened, but I liked to dream it. Them skunks that kilt him kilt that dream." Then the harder Abbie voice he was accustomed to returned and she added, "Fuckin' right I'll do it."

"I been kinda iffy 'bout askin' ya to take on someone who had a hand in Jeff's killin'."

"A dick's a dollar, Billy," she replied coldly and chewed her biscuit. "It don't matter who it belong to...'cept a gambler...stay clear a their kind. Fuckin's lot like ridin' a horse. Same movin,' ya know, thrust, push..." Her hips moved so perfectly, so smoothly that Billy momentarily forgot who he was with and felt an awakening in his member. "...ya know, all that shit," she continued, oblivious to Billy subtly adjusting his Levis to the tightness in his crotch. "So when I got me a customer and he's a gruntin' and a pumpin' 'way, I ain't even there. I'm out ridin' Lavender." She bit off another chunk of biscuit. "Didn't bring any molasses, did ya?"

"Uh, no, sorry," Billy answered as the minor disturbance in his Levis calmed. It amazed him how quickly she had turned it on then just as quickly shut it down, but that was what he liked about whores: they were always ready. He figured that was why he wasn't upset when his marriage fell apart. He expected a woman to want it as often as he did. Otherwise, what's the point?

As Abbie downed the last bite of her third biscuit she asked, "Ya gonna kill the sumbitch?"

Billy smiled and replied, "Now why would I go to all the trouble of gettin' the man drunk and havin' his baggage unloaded, plus payin' ya to do it, if I was just gonna kill him anyways?"

Abbie looked straight into his eyes. He thought he saw a little sparkle in them as she answered, "Pleasure?"

Late that night as he lay in the plump bed at the boarding house,

190

Abbie's single word was still twisting around his head: "Pleasure!" Is that why he was doing this? Tomás Amador, Delores Quías, Moises Alvarez. Just names of dead men, that's all they were; men who deserved to die. He didn't think he felt pleasure from their deaths. Satisfaction maybe, accomplishment absolutely, but he felt no remorse. Should he? Should he be asking God for forgiveness? Why? He'd never asked God for anything before. Can't start now! That would make him...? "What was the two dollar word Jeff used?" he asked himself. "Uh, hippo...hippo...crick? Crate? Crit, like grit...hippogrit! That's it! An asshole that pretends to have feelings he ain't really got!" He rolled over on his side and bit down on his unlit pipe. "No!" he heard himself say aloud. "This ain't pleasure! They took my friend. I'm takin' them." Then another one of Jeff's two-dollar words popped into his brain and he spoke it aloud: "Vindickive!" He thought about it for a moment then added, "Yeah, that word fits me best. Like that ol' Missouri River, fuck with me and I'll vindickive ya! Ain't pleasure, it's justice."

Proud of himself for remembering those words, he chewed on the pipe stem for a few moments then put it back on the white doily covering the small table by the bed. He stared at the ceiling, wishing he could see the stars. Then more of Jeff's words slowly floated down and covered him like a warm blanket.

"This world is always gonna to have bad people, and some of us are put here to try and stop their evil doin's."

August, 1907

"Make no mistake, fellas," warned Captain Wheeler, "Dave Shepherd ain't nothun but a splinter in the ass of life—an animal, a rapin', killin' monster that eats from the trough. He's livin' to git dead and he knows it. At that last farmstead, he and his two *compadres* raped and killed an eleven-year-old girl."

"Jesus!" Freddie winced. "That's only a year older than Isabel."

Captain Wheeler used his carved willow stick to point out locations on the wall map of Arizona territory.

"That farm was just north of Three Points. Right here!" The willow whacked a specific point on the map. "Dave knows ever'one's after his ass, includin' the Army, so he's gonna skirt fer Mexico. He's got the Papago

Nation to his west, so I figger he'll ride along it, headin' south, and try to cross the border at Sasabe." Again, but with much more deliberation, the willow whacked a point on the map where Sasabe sat. "Here!"

"Ouch!" whispered Billy to Jeff. "Bet they felt that!"

Jeff chuckled quietly, not wanting to experience the wrath of his very determined captain. Billy always wondered where Wheeler got his information, but every time he asked him the captain would just grin and say, "If I told ya I'd have to shoot ya."

Everyone knew when Sparky had a question. First, his face would contort into the expression of a constipated man struggling to expel a huge log, then he'd dip his left shoulder, then dip his right, then ask his question at the exact same time he was raising his hand.

"Cap'n, Three Points is 'bout fifty miles from Sas'be and we're a good thirty from it. Iffin 'em *hombres* are already on the trail, we could be cuttin' it close to git thar on time."

Wheeler looked at Sparky and said, "They have this new contraption, Sparky. It's called the train."

Sparky chuckled and said, "Aw, shoot, Cap'n, the train ain't new."

Sometimes Sparky made Billy feel smart.

"Ya all know what the ugly bastard looks like,"continued Wheeler. "We been eyeballin' pitchers of him for six months now and this is our first good lead." Then he glanced at his pocket watch. "Jeff, Billy, Freddie, ya got fifteen minutes to make that train to Sasabe. Bring the asshole in or take 'im out, don't much matter which."

With their mounts housed in a boxcar the train ride from Nogales to Sasabe took less than thirty minutes. Usually Freddie would fill the time playing his harmonica, but on this trip all he did was talk about his daughter. Billy and Jeff learned more about Isabel then they ever imagined they could. He didn't even make one mention of his "little dressmaker." Understanding that what Dave Shepherd had done had truly rattled Freddie, the other two Rangers let him ramble. By the time the three arrived in Sasabe, they knew his daughter's school marm's names from kindergarten up to her current fourth grade one. They knew how much she weighed at birth, how tall she was now, when she was toilet trained, and the hell Freddie's parents went through to do it.

"My folks got them flushin' toilets put in," Freddie laughed as he explained. "She thought it was gonna suck her down and spill her out into the ocean to be et by a big fish."

May, 1894

Greeting him was a sculptured and highly decorated golden throne-like stool resting on a small platform. Next to the grandiose device was a long brass chain hanging from a tank overhead. A sign on the wall said, "Please pull chain when finished."

Having a few days off, Billy's friend Henry Anderson suggested they ride down to Las Cruces and crony around the whorehouses. Rumor had it that the town featured some of the finest brothels in the territory, a whole street lined with them.

"We'll be like two kids in a candy store," declared Henry.

They treated themselves to a dandy room in a fancy Las Cruces hotel. They marveled at the large bed, but wondered why it had a frilly roof.

"Ain't no sun in here fer it to block," remarked Henry as he studied the strange lacy cover.

"Maybe the roof leaks," suggested Billy, staring at the embossed tin tiles above.

"Better not," stated Henry, "fer the price we paid fer it."

A fancy table with two chairs rested in a corner next to a window that allowed the tempting night lights of Las Cruces to glow through. There was a dresser for their belongings, which neither brought, and a tall mirror framed in gold mounted to the wall. Both stood in front of the mirror for several minutes, having never seen such a clear view of themselves from head to foot.

"I think we cut quite a figger," Henry stated with a proud grin.

"'Them whores ain't gonna know what hit 'em," added a smiling Billy as he studied his reflection.

Continuing to admire himself, Henry stated, "Ya know, I think I oughta go into politics. I look purty damn good."

"Now why would ya wanna let yer ass grow fat?"

"No, no," added Henry. "I mean sumthun like, say, runnin' fer sheriff. They ain't got fat asses."

"No, but they sometimes get their asses shot off."

"We can't ride fence all our lives, Billy," Henry removed his hat and turned sideways to admire himself from a different angle. "Shed yer hat and turn sideways," he instructed.

"What fer?"

The two stood back-to-back and stared into the mirror. "Don't ya see it?" asked Henry. "We could be brothers; same height, same hair color and eyes."

" 'Cept I'm purtier," exclaimed Billy with a grin.

"Yeah, well, we'll let 'em whores decide that."

They ordered room service and filled their bellies with things to eat that they didn't even know a fellow could eat. They smoked a couple of expensive cigars. They took another look at themselves in the long mirror.

"Yessir," declared Henry, "I'd make a dandy fine sheriff."

"Ya get 'lected sheriff, Henry, and I'll be yer deputy," Billy teasingly scoffed.

Then right as the two horny cowboys were ready to set off on their tour of the local candy stores, Billy's stomach reminded him of just how much he did eat. He had to use the hotel facilities. *Pronto*! He hurried down the hallway and opened a fancy door with the word "Lavatory" engraved above it in glittering gold. Carefully he sat down to do his business. Unlike the wooden outhouses he was used to, this metal fixture was cold. He quickly raised his butt in fear of getting stuck there.

"How embarrassin'," he thought, "if someone had to get ya unstuck from a privy seat."

Slowly, one butt cheek at a time, he eased his fanny down on the cold throne. He was relieved to feel how quickly it warmed up. Once he accomplished his mission, he obeyed the sign and reached up and pulled the chain. The fixture beneath him shook and trumpeted like a circus elephant. Water swirled and gushed, frightening him so badly he leaped up to escape the ass-eating monster. Forgetting his britches were still around his ankles he tried to run from the water beast, but it got him. He fell and cracked his forehead on the gold sink, knocking him out cold.

After what seemed like an hour of thumb-twirling and anxious glances out the window at the beckoning night lights of Las Cruces, Henry decided to check on his missing *compadre*. He walked down the hall to the door marked "Lavatory," and knocked on it. No reply.

"Billy? Ya in there, Billy?"

Henry slowly opened the door. There was his friend on the privy floor with his pants down around his ankles and blood oozing from his forehead. Fortunately the hotel had a doctor on staff who stitched up the gash in Billy's head. Fearing a concussion he ordered Henry to keep Billy relaxed for the rest of the night, but not let him fall asleep. After the doctor finally left, Henry plopped down in a chair and gazed longingly out the window at the taunting Las Cruces lights.

"Sorry, Henry," mumbled Billy, avoiding eye contact with his frustrated friend.

Henry just sat staring out the window, shaking his head. Finally he said, "Billy Old, only you could put an onion in a apple pie."

August, 1907

Sasabe was a border town that might as well have a pair of swinging saloon doors dividing the two countries. It was vigilantly protected by a fat, slumbering guard oblivious to the flies feasting on the leftover *burrito* in his moustache. It was an easy location for scum buckets like Dave Shepherd to pass back and forth between Mexico and the U.S. The Rangers wasted no time finding a good location to establish a proper greeting for the three outlaws. Just north of town was a sharp turn in the trail from Three Points. Being the only trail from that town the Rangers figured, or at least hoped, Dave and his pals would use it. High rocks about thirty feet tall on each side made it a tight passage. By waiting just around a natural bend, they wouldn't be spotted until the three men were right in front of them. The rocky walls also carried the sounds of hooves, so they would hear anyone coming from quite a distance. They settled in and waited. Once again, all Freddy could talk about was Isabel.

Sure enough, late that same afternoon Dave Shepherd and his two saddle buddies came trotting around that rocky bend simply to be warmly greeted by three Rangers, weapons drawn. His two partners immediately threw up their hands. Dave decided to scoot.

"I got 'im!" cried Freddie, spurring his mount.

In a matter of minutes, the other two cretins were on the ground and cuffed without any resistance. Then Billy and Jeff heard a shot, followed by the painful scream of a horse. Then silence.

Billy turned to Jeff, worried. "What'd ya think?" he asked.

"Go check it out! I'll keep these two company!"

Billy leapt on Orion and circled around the rocky bend. Another shot rang out, followed by a short pause, then another shot, a pause, another shot, pause, another shot. Seven more shots each followed by a brief pause led Billy to the site. Freddie was straddling the riddled body of Dave Shepherd slowly pulling the triggers of two empty weapons.

"I think you got him, Freddie," declared Billy.

Freddie bent at the waist to get his face closer to the very dead Dave Shepherd. With a pinch of piss and a pound of pleasure in his voice he said, "No more little girls fer you, asshole."

May, 1910

Cinco de Mayo came and went with no killings. To Billy, it was just another testament as to how tame the area was becoming. The jail did collect a few drunks, mostly men who had never celebrated the holiday before— meaning the American settlers new to the region. There was one shooting. A whore named Rachel put a hole through a farmer's cheek with her parlor gun after he had cut her leg with a knife.

"Justifiable," claimed John Foster.

The farmer lived, but won't have much fun explaining the hole in his face to his wife. Rachel was stitched up and immediately returned to work. Whores survive by numbers.

There was the usual parade, which always amazed Billy. These were peasants, people with nothing. Yet once a year they managed to come up with fancy, colorful costumes. He knew they kept them stored away for the celebration, but how? Where? To live in such squalor yet keep these clothes so clean, so fresh, so exciting, made him marvel. The parade and *mariachi* band passed from the Mexican side to the U.S. side, then back again to the Mexican side. The drunks had sobered by the next morning so Billy released them after each put forth a two dollar fine. He saw Pasco staring at him, obviously still trying to figure out just who was this tormenting *gringo*.

He couldn't resist. "When you get outta here, I'm gonna plant ya!" He turned and walked away.

"*¿Quien chingados es?*"

Billy closed the screeching, heavy door behind him, smiled, and locked it.

"*¿Quien chingados es?*"

He crossed to the rifle rack and removed Pasco's Sharps. It felt warm, like it still held the heat from the round that took Freddie. He slid it back in the case next to other long rifles. For a moment he studied them all: a Henry, two shotguns—one double barrel and one pump, and a Winchester 30-30. He recalled the latter being Jeff's choice for hunting. Jeff was one of the best shots Billy had ever seen with a long rifle, yet he seldom used one. Billy didn't own a rifle. When he needed one for assignments, he'd sign it out from the Ranger's armory. Truth was he never considered himself that good of a shot with a rifle, but for what he had planned for *Señor* Pasco, he'd need to be.

"This here's the Winchester eighteen ninety-five Second Model Sporting Rifle, complete with a Malcolm Model number three hunting scope," explained the salesman in Naco's gun shop. The fellow was about the same height as Billy, but sported a pot belly that couldn't be hidden under his vest. His mutton chop sideburns fed into a neatly trimmed moustache to make up for the fact that he had no hair on the top of his head. "This gem is the first Winchester rifle with a box magazine underneath the action instead of the old tubular one."

"What's that mean?" asked Billy.

"Means it's safe to chamber a variety of different military and hunting cartridges, but I'd stick with thirty-eight to seventy-two rounds. Best penetration! Twenty-four inch round barrel, crescent butt plate. Punch the eye out of a flea at over a hundred yards. Goin' huntin'?"

"Yeah," Billy answered as he handled the long beauty.

"What are you usin' now?"

"Winchester thirty-thirty," he lied.

"Good weapon," stated the clerk. Even though Billy was the only other person in the store, the mutton-chopped man leaned in towards him. "Not many folks know this, friend," the salesman whispered, "but this here model is Teddy Roosevelt's favorite huntin' rifle."

"You don't say!"

"I do say!"

The man looked as though he might pop his vest buttons so Billy said nothing. He knew T.R.'s favorite hunting rifle was the Model 1895 Lever Action .405 Winchester. Besides, an argument might agitate the fellow into bumping up his price.

"How much?" Billy asked.

"Just seventy-five dollars, friend, and that's includin' the scope!"

"Would you take sixty-five?"

"Tell you what," replied the man, rubbing his chin. "Since you're my first customer today, make it an even seventy and I'll throw in a couple of boxes of thirty-eight seventy-two cartridges."

At thirty-six years of age, Billy Old bought himself his first hunting rifle.

October, 1884

"I told ya 'fore, Billy," Cleaver Old reminded his ten-year-old son, "ya ain't gonna hunt with me 'til yer eleven."

"That's only three months 'way, Pa."

"More like six months. Yer in the fifth grade, boy. Ain't ya s'posed to know how to cipher better 'an that?"

"I won't git in yer way, Pa."

"Ya ain't goin' wit me, Billy! Ain't nuthun more to say!."

Cleaver Old had established his rule of an age limit for hunting long before Billy was even born. When he was eleven, his pa took him and his little brother Ethan on a fall hunting trip. They camped out in the woods just a few miles walk from their farm. Up bright and early the next morning they were poised and hid, awaiting the first signs of deer. Soon enough, a buck roamed into range. Ethan had begged his pa all night to let him fire the weapon. The man agreed if the opportunity arose. Here it was. Young Ethan carefully sighted up the old black powder musket and squeezed the trigger just like he was taught to do. It backfired, killing him instantly and sending small pieces of metal into the cheeks of Cleaver and his Pa. The scars left on their faces were a constant reminder of the tragedy. Cleaver vowed to never let any of his children hunt before they were eleven-years-old.

"Now ya stay here and help yer ma wit chores. I'll be back 'fore supper."

"Shoot!" exclaimed young Billy, kicking up a cloud of dirt.

But Cleaver Old didn't return home that night. The next morning Billy and a few neighbors went looking for him. With Uvalde resting at the southern base of the Texas Hill Country, those hills were the logical place for folks to hunt. That's where Billy and the neighbors found his mutilated body under a six-foot Mesquite tree, the work of a cougar. Apparently he had tried to hop into the tree to escape the angry cat, but the Mesquite trees in that area didn't grow to an escapable height.

"Must've been a fair sized cat," commented Haskin Pike, the Old's nearest neighbor. "Must a yanked poor Cleaver right outta that tree."

When Billy saw the sight he threw himself on top of his father's body, hysterically pounding on the man's chest..

"Why didn't ya take me with ya?" he screamed through sobs and tears over and over. "I coulda been there! I coulda been there!"

Haskin Pike grabbed the boy's flailing arms.

"Come on, Billy Boy, come on," Haskin shouted over Billy's wailing, "ya don't wanna 'member him like this."

Before Haskin could finally pull the sobbing boy from the mangled body, Billy had ripped the blood stained, hand carved ivory pipe from his father's pocket. Two other men led him away.

They buried his father on the land he had worked since he was a boy, alongside his brother Ethan and Billy's grandparents in the small plot to the north of their home. A dark time followed for him and his ma, who was not a strong woman. The farm was too much for her, so Billy gave up his schooling. A year later Daria Old married that neighbor Haskin Pike. He was a widower with no children and a good man with a kindly spot in his heart for his newly acquired stepson. The addition of the Haskin property doubled the size of both farms, doubled the size of their goat herd, doubled the work, and doubled the stench. Everything everywhere smelled like goats. He had never told his mother about his pa's pipe. He kept it hidden under his mattress. Late at night he'd pull it out and just sniff in the maple aroma. Not only did it help him fall asleep, it helped stem the smell of goats.

Over the next three years, each morning became more of a struggle for Billy to rise and face the chores needed to tend the goat herd and work the farm. There were even times when he wished he was back in school. Haskin Pike had to occasionally remind his stepson to not abuse the goats for simply being goats. For his mother's sake he tried his best to settle into what appeared to be his destiny, but deep inside he knew he wasn't meant to be a goat herder or a farmer. But what he was meant to be, he had no idea.

One morning he woke up to the usual clamor of the bells from the goat's necks. Instead of covering his head with a pillow to drown out the noise he sat up, realizing what he had to do. Daria Old was nursing his second half-sister when he sat down at the table.

"My brain's sayin' I ain't a farmer, ma. I ain't no goat herder. I hate them goats. Haskins makin' enough money from the herd, he can hire some help, so me goin' won't be a burden on ya'll, and ya got the two girls to care for...ya don't need me 'round to worry 'bout, too."

"You can dislike goats, Billy, but you shouldn't ever say ya hate anything," she said in her normal soft voice. "Ya say yer brain's tellin' you ya ain't a farmer, so what's it tellin' you ya are?"

"It ain't had the courtesy of doin' that yet."

"Don't you think ya being gone, out of my sight, would make me worry 'bout ya, too? Even more? Yer only fourteen, Billy."

"Almost fifteen, and I'm tall, ma, I can pass fer sixteen and get a job."

"Doin' what? What do you have to offer someone? Goats are what ya know, Billy."

"I'll go somewhere where there ain't no goats."

"And where's that?"

"West! A cattle ranch, maybe."

Daria Old forced a tearful smile and said, "Ya think goats stink, wait 'til yer 'round a herd of cattle." She stared at her son for a long moment then took his hand, sighed, and said, "But no one can keep a person where they don't wanna be."

October, 1897

The Dempsey's bunkhouse door clamored open and shut and Henry Anderson stomped over to Billy's bunk with a huge grin on his face.

"I'ma doin' it, Billy, just like I said I would."

"Doin' what?" asked Billy as he lie on his bunk puffing on his pipe.

"I done thrown in my hat for the Alamogordo deputy sheriff job. Election's in two weeks. Ya gonna vote fer me?"

"Well, I don't know, Henry," teased Billy. "Who ya runnin' agin?"

"No one! No one else wants the job. I'm a shoe-in! Ya know what that means, don't ya?"

"What?"

"Yer gonna be my deputy. Yer gonna be workin' fer me."

"Whoa, whoa now, Henry! I admire ya fer doin' it, but I ain't no..."

"Ya white liverin' on me, Billy Old?" Henry asked, leaning down into his friend's face. "Ya done tol' me in that fancy ass Las Cruces hotel room that ifin I got to be a sheriff ya'd be my deputy."

"I was just funnin' with ya, Henry. I ne'er thought..."

"Ya got sumthun agin lawmen, Billy Old?"

"No, no, it ain't that. I like lawmen. I just...just..."

"Just what, goddamn it?"

"I ain't got the smarts to be a lawman," Billy shamefully admitted. "I quit my schoolin' in the fifth grade."

"And I quit mine in the sixth. That makes me a year smarter than ya so I'll be doin' the thinkin' and you'll be at my right hand. Can't cut cattle all yer life, Billy boy."

About a week before the election a letter from Haskin Pike finally found him. His mother had died six months ago giving birth to their third child, another girl. Too late to even attend her funeral and to give a final goodbye, he got very drunk. Henry's offer was still bouncing around his head. One soused night in the bunkhouse while staring at the flame in the stove, an empty bottle of cheap rye at his feet and another in his hand, he suddenly blurted out his mother's words.

"I praise good thoughts, good words, and good deeds," he slurred. "I reject all bad thoughts, bad words, and bad deeds."

He'd always believed those were good words to live by, and he figured becoming a lawman would've pleased her. He accepted Henry's offer. As soon he was sworn in and pinned on that badge he knew he had made the right decision. He stared at the piece of metal on his vest. He wiped it to a soft glow with his sleeve. Suddenly he was filled with self-respect and confidence. He felt taller, stronger. That little chunk of tin had given him balance and purpose. Billy Old had become a Peace Officer.

Except for jailing drunken cowboys and breaking up saloon brawls, his close to a year stretch as an Alamogordo deputy was uneventful, until he met Bessie Mae Hampstead. She was a member of the local vaudeville troupe and as wild as a mustang in season. The hot-tempered daughter of a local farmer, she and Billy were night and day, boot heel and horseshit, but moved into a small shed together anyway. Even though they didn't have a pot to piss in, the baggage handling was the wildest and craziest Billy had ever had. On many a night the walls of the old shack would rattle and shake so loudly they could probably be heard clear back to her daddy's farm.

But they also had their dark times. Many nights, long after her show was over, he had to come to the small theatre and drag her out kicking and screaming and calling him names that would make a bullwhacker blush. When she didn't get her way she'd holler and spit in his face and sabotage his meals with excess salt or pepper or castor oil. Just three months into their volatile cohabitation the young woman put a bullet in his chest. Even though the slug was a horse hair away from putting him under and laid him up for months, he wouldn't press charges.

"She done headed out, Billy," a sorrowful Henry informed him about two weeks into his bed-ridden recovery. "She got hooked up with a travelin' actin' troupe and headed for parts unknown. Ya should've pressed charges, Billy. Least that'd kept her here."

Billy lowered his head and softly said, "No one can keep a person where they don't wanna be."

About a week after Henry delivered the news about Betsy, Billy was visited by a trio of grim looking town councilmen. Clarence Hopper was the owner of the largest dry goods store in Alamogordo and second in importance to a Mayor that was rarely sober enough to stand up, let alone lead any type of meeting. Clarence was a decent, no-nonsense fellow from South Carolina.

"Billy, Henry's been killed," Clarence stated flatly in a strong southern accent that he refused to shed.

Billy was stunned and angered. The first and only words out of his mouth were, "Who did it?"

202

"We got the culprit," exclaimed Clarence. "No need to fret yo'self 'bout that."

Rabbit Taylor was the next councilmen to speak. Believe it or not, contrary to most folk's opinion of bankers being fat and lazy, Rabbit was far from it. His real name was Randall, but there wasn't a man in town that could best him in a footrace at the Fourth of July picnic games, so everyone called him Rabbit.

"We tried to get him to hire 'nother deputy," explained Rabbit with genuine remorse. "But he insisted that he could handle trouble 'lone 'til you were back on yer feet. He went into the saloon to break up a fight and a drunken cowhand belly shot him. The fella was so close it set Henry's shirt on fire. Took the poor lad near two days to pass on. We're gonna hang the sumbitch, though, Billy, don't ya worry 'bout that!"

Billy didn't say a word.

"Billy," added Clarence Hopper as he sat on the foot of the bed, patting Billy's leg. His Carolina accent was dripping with as much sincerity as he could arouse. "We're truly sorry 'bout this, but we had to hire another Deputy Marshal and he's brought on another deputy. Now, we are gonna cover yo' medical expenses until y'all are up and better, and we'll give ya a sev'rance when ya are."

Even though he didn't understand the word "sev'rance," Billy didn't say a word.

After a brief moment of silence, Clarence stood up and said, "Well, sorry it had to turn out like this, Billy. We hope ya understand—for the sake of the town—we had to move on."

Billy didn't say a word.

As he reached for the door handle, Rabbit said, "Billy, ya take good care a yerself now, ya hear?"

The third councilman, who had never said a word, threw three words over his shoulder as he left.

"Git well, Billy," the man stated with a sad smile.

Clarence was the last to leave. He stopped at the door, turned to Billy and nodded, then shut the door behind him.

Billy slammed his fist down on the bed and felt a couple of stitches pop loose in his chest. He told himself he should've been there, covering Henry's back. He cursed his stupidity for ever getting involved with Bessie Mae in the first place. She was the reason he was in this bed. She was why Henry had to go into that saloon alone. She was why he lost the first and only job that made him feel proud, made him feel like he actually mattered. It took a solid two months for him to completely recover from the wound and regain his strength. Too much liquor and too many whores quickly depleted the severance pay from the town council. The Dempsey's offered him his cow cutting job back, but his heart wasn't in it. He knew he could still do the job, but just didn't have the fire. Henry's death and Bessie Mae's departure had left a hole in him that he didn't know how to fill.

"Remember the Maine," was the cry on the street. Figuring Cuba was far enough away to help him shake off some bad memories, he joined up. Little did he know about the new memories that war would create. It was also during this time with the Rough Riders that he realized he didn't miss riding fence. He didn't miss cutting cattle. He didn't miss being a hired hand. He didn't even miss Bessie Mae. He missed being a Peace Officer.

Cuba was a hot, nasty, mosquito-filled shithole. Although the war hardly lasted long enough to dig enough graves, his unit was stuck there as part of an occupying force until September '99. The fighting had stopped, but men were still dying of malaria, dysentery, and yellow fever. A few just simply blew out their brains. Finally he and the surviving men he had enlisted with in Texas were put on a boat and shipped to the port of Galveston. In November of that same year they were officially mustered out of the Rough Riders with only a pitiful amount of discharge money and no words that even came close to a thank you.

Galveston was a pig sty filled with unemployed, maimed, and angry soldiers. Finding a job there was like barking at the knot. He hoped that since crime was wild in the port city, maybe he could land a position as a Peace Officer. He soon found out that the city officials weren't interested in pinning a star on a former Rough Rider.

Without the world exploding as many people had predicted, the twentieth century rolled in without a whimper. By March, Billy decided he'd had a gut full of Galveston. It had been twelve years since he left his hometown of Uvalde, Texas. It was close to April, a blooming time back home and a good time for a visit. He could see his mother's grave, maybe even meet his half sisters. Two days later he was stepping off the train in San Antonio. From there he would buy a horse and make the ride southwest to Uvalde. But at the San Antonio station he was greeted by a poster hanging on the depot wall that read, "Good men wanted in Nogales. Join the soon-to-be-formed Arizona Rangers."

"Gimme a ticket for Nogales," he told the bald agent in the ticket office window.

Uvalde would have to wait.

May, 1910

Billy and John were just finishing lunch at the café when they heard the calliope music coming from the north side of town.

"Can't be the circus," declared John as the two lawmen stepped out of the café, both still toothpick-mining for food remnants. "They come by train and I didn't get no call from that damn loud contraption."

The music stopped and was immediately followed by a crackling, muddled voice speaking through a megaphone. As Billy and John walked north towards the noise, followed by curious town folk, the voice became clearer.

"Right here in black and white, folks," blurted the voice. "This is scientific proof from some of the most famous scholars in the world."

When Billy and John turned north onto third street they found a crowd already gathered around a medicine wagon parked in front of the Imperial saloon, Naco's most popular watering hole. Painted across both sides of the wagon in large letters were the words "Doc Lionel Davenport." A fancy dressed midget in a bowler was scurrying about the crowd handing out newspapers. A natty dressed, gangly fellow with a beard and bushy black hair partially covered by a tall stove pipe hat was perched on top of the wagon, megaphone in hand. He reminded Billy of the tintypes he had seen of Abe Lincoln.

"Poison gases, friends," declared Doc Davenport. "That's right, friends. Poison gases raining down on God's green earth from that devil comet."

Most folks already knew that Hally's Comet would be flying by around May 19, but they didn't know about the poisonous gases in the comet's tail that were going to snuff out all life on the planet.

"Read for yourself, friends," shouted Doc as held up a newspaper and continued, "Los Angeles Times...'Doom and gloom coming to earth.' He replaced that paper with another. "Phoenix Sun...'Poison in the comets tail will kill all life on earth.' Tucson Citizen...'Poison air, Poison Air.' Just read what my assistant Hercules is handing ya, folks! It's all there in black and white."

The crowd mumbled, stirred, and gasped at the news. John grabbed one of the papers from the passing Hercules. Billy couldn't help but stare at the little man. The only midget he had ever seen was in a circus, and that one was dressed as a clown. He stared at the dwarfs features, watched his wobbling legs scurry through the growing crowd of people, wondered how his thick, stubby fingers could dole out the papers so rapidly, never dropping one. It took Hercules' vanishing amongst the legs of the crowd to pull Billy's attention back to the newspaper.

"What's it say, John?"

"Scientists say the world could be endin'."

"No shit?"

"They think there's poisonous gas in the tail of Hally's Comet and we're all goners."

Everyone had just nine days to live...unless they bought Doc Davenport's patented Comet Poison Protection Pills, of course. For the remainder of the day the wagon stayed put right there in front of the Imperial Saloon. The town came to it in damn near a panic. While Hercules was busy handing out pills and collecting dollar bills, Doc continued to preach death and doom from his wagon. A lot of folks bought the pills, including every whore in the whorehouse, most Naco business owners, many farmers and ranchers, Billy and John, and the congregations of both churches, which all downed the little tablets together during an all night prayer vigil on May 19. Not wanting some strange poison to disrupt his plan, Billy spent an extra dollar for a pill to crumble up in Pasco's hash.

Doc and Hercules made a killing. The comet didn't. Everyone in Naco woke up on the morning of May 20 alive and thankful to be breathing the same air from the day before.

"Guess them pills worked," declared Billy as he poured himself a cup of Irene Castle's weak coffee.

"Told ya they would," she stated and continued frying eggs and bacon.

June, 1910

The first day of June was hotter than a fart in a glove. John Foster's noisy Crocker & Curtis electric fan was simply spinning the same air around the stuffy office. Billy decided that the outside heat was better than the inside heat. He was sitting in a rocker in front of the office, smoking his pipe and fanning himself with his hat when four ragged *cabrónes* crossed the bridge from the Mexican side of Naco. One of them was riding an Appaloosa. He sat up. The usual tingle shot up his spine and rested on the back of his neck. This time he got a better look at the quartet: two white men, one black, and one breed. And this time they took a look at him. The star on his chest was reflecting the sunlight. The breed on the last horse held his stare the longest. There were no pigging strings with scalps hanging from their lizzys, so Billy figured they were on their way to one of the peaceful reservations to gather some. Reservation Indians didn't put up as much of a fight. He watched them turn right off Towner Avenue and onto fourth, which meant they were most likely heading for Fat Frank's place, an establishment that still welcomed and fed off their kind. John Foster was stealing an afternoon nap in one of the empty cells when Billy shook him.

"John, we got some scalp hunters in town."

John sat up, rubbed his eyes and asked, "One of 'em ridin' an appaloosa?"

"Yeah! Ya know them assholes?"

"Been through three times this year, always headin' north, never see 'em comin' back south though. The nigger's Willie Shoso. The two whites are a couple of idiot brothers named the Farleys. The breed calls himself Jack after his hero, that murderin' Modoc Captain Jack. Funny, two white men and a breed and they let the darky run the gang....and that curly wolf was raised on sour milk! How'd ya know they was scalp hunters?" John rose quickly from the bunk, excited. "They got scalps on 'em? Iffin so we can arrest 'em."

"Didn't see any, but I ran 'cross them down in San Moise. They had piggin' strings fulla hair."

"They go down to Fat Frank's?" asked John as he strapped on his gun belt.

"Headed that way."

"Guess we better take a stroll o'er there. Git the smoothbore!"

"Pump?"

"Double barrel! It looks meaner and I like the nasty sound it makes when ya cock it."

The first thing that violated the senses in Fat Frank's was a combined, putrid odor of stale beer, vomit, overflowing spittoons, and pickled hard boiled eggs. Second was a large, bullet-ridden, blood stained Confederate Stars & Bars flag hanging behind the bar with two crossed Calvary sabers suspended in front of it. All the rest of the walls were bare. Fat Frank wouldn't allow any other décor to draw attention from his Stars & Bars. It was also one of the darkest saloons in town with only two small windows in front facing the north. While most of Naco featured electric lights, Fat Frank still preferred the yellow haze of the lump oil lamps. Maybe it was because they created shadows for his questionable patrons to fade into, but probably because he was just one cheap, low life, bastard.

Fat, mean, and old, Franklin Aberdeen Trudeau still hated Yankees and considered anyone who wore a badge to be one. But he had one blind eye and was too obese to back up any of his belligerent guttural bursts. So he'd just be surly whenever possible, which was all the time. In his younger days though, he was on the winning side of six Alabama duels. Since his aiming eye was not the blind one, and even as mean as his customers were, they had no desire to face the lard-bucket if he had a shooter in his chubby hand.

John Foster fisted open the saloon doors and cheerfully stomped in.

"Hello, Willy!" he chortled. "Welcome back!"

Billy stepped in behind his friend and positioned himself to the right of the door, shotgun aimed up and resting on his shoulder. He chuckled to himself, "Jesus, John's still got cajones the size of melons!"

Without turning from his leaned stance on the bar the black *hombre* said, "Hello, John! Ya gots 'ere quicker than I thoughts ya would; only gots one drink down me."

"Got me a sharp-eyed deputy now; younger eyes than mine. He sees things *poco pronto!*" John casually walked up to the bar and muscled one of the

Farley brothers aside so he could stand next to Willy. The brother scowled but gave ground. "Ya just passin' through our lovely town, Willy?" John asked as he took the Farley brother's shot glass and downed its contents. "Or ya gonna stay and maybe open a nice little business here?"

Billy couldn't hold back. "Like a wig shop?"

The heads of the breed and both brothers snapped to Billy. Willy turned his head slowly and stared. "We know ya, Deputy?" he asked.

"I don't know. Ever been to San Moise?"

"Matter a fact we like it down thar!" answered Willy. "You?"

"I was there awhile back," Billy answered and took the scattergun off his shoulder. "Didn't like it though! Place smelt like burnt locusts."

"Who the hell e'er smelt burned locusts?" asked one of the Farley brothers.

"Ever leaned o'er a campfire and accidently set off a little a yer hair?" Billy added. "Smells like burnin' locusts." Knowing all bad men were not stupid, he could tell by the look in Willie's eyes that he got the message.

Then Fat Frank decided to weigh in, his voice still carrying a deep Alabama draw.

"Foster, why ya and yer hot shot deputy gotta be such shitboxes and harass my customers?"

"Oh hell, Frank," responded John Foster. "This ain't harassin'!" With his back still to the scowling Farley brother, John lifted his boot and stomped his heel down on the man's toes. Billy leveled the shotgun.

"Shit!!" the brother squealed, grabbing his foot and hopping from the bar on one leg. "Ya sumbitch!"

"That's harassing, Frank!"

The angry Farley's hand instinctively reached for his belly gun, but the sweet sound of a cocking shotgun changed his mind. The second Farley helped his cursing brother into a chair.

John looked Willy square in his ugly face and said, "Willy, ya know that I know what ya fellas are up to and soon I'm gonna catch ya with the goods, but I ain't gonna arrest ya. Nope! No sir! I'm gonna turn ya over to the Injuns. Might even stick 'round and watch 'em skin ya, too. Ain't had no good entertainment in months."

"Maybe ya needs to git out more, John," suggested Willy with a grin that displayed three missing front teeth.

Foster smiled. "Well, Willy, until ya fellas haul yer dirty asses outta my clean town I'll be doin' just that.

"We be outta here at daybreak, John," Willie turned to the bar.

Smacking Willie on the back with the palm of his hand, John replied, "Glad to hear that, Willy!"

Billy could see every muscle in Willie's body stiffen, but the tall black man wisely kept his composure. John turned and showed his back to the four skunks. He left the saloon with Billy slowly backing out behind him with the shotgun again resting on his shoulder. As they were walking back to his office John slapped Billy on the back.

"Damnation, Billy Boy," he gushed. "I ain't had that much fun since I got this here job!"

Billy wondered why John even allowed a greasy shit pit like Fat Frank's to stay open. Suddenly the Deputy Marshal stopped walking and said, "What was all that jabber 'bout 'burnin' locusts?" Billy told him about the San Moise incident. "Shouldn't flapped yer gums 'bout that," chastised John. "Em are bad *hombre*s. I'd watch yer back 'til they're long gone."

"Lemme tail 'em, John!"

"Huh?"

"Gimme a few days to tail 'em."

"Ya got a death wish?"

"Ya know they're headin' up to one of the rez's fer scalps!"

"Ya can't do nuthun 'less ya catch them with the goods," John reminded him. "It's the time of the lawyer! Sleezy bastards are gettin' scum buckets like them off on little twisty things in the law. Hell, we got two a them blood suckers right here in Naco. I tried to get Pasco on assault with intent to kill, but the leech got it down to strikin' an officer. 'Stead of five years, he got ninety days. That's why my last deputy quit. Shit, I miss the ol' days," grieved John. "Ya did what ya had to do, no blood suckin' lawyers."

"Come on, John, I need to feel like a Peace Officer."

Foster stopped walking, gave Billy a hard stare, and said "What the hell ya think ya are now?"

"No offense, John, but I ain't used to sittin' 'round waitin' fer somethun to happen."

John looked at his deputy for a long moment then finally sighed and continued walking. "Yeah, I know what ya mean!" he admitted. "It took me some gettin' used to, too."

"Once I see where they're headed I'll get back to you and ya use yer telephone to warn them."

"Let the reservation police be ready fer them. Let them take care of 'em?" John stated, intrigued with the idea. "They spot ya, Billy, they'll kill ya quicker than flies to shit. 'Specially now that ya opened yer trap and let 'em know what ya did."

"I've tracked assholes 'fore, John."

They continued their walk back to the office in silence. Billy knew John was letting the idea ferment.

Finally Foster said, "Okay, three days! No more! If ya think they be even sniffin' at ya, ya hightail it back here."

"Thank ya, John."

"Wish I could go with ya!" He patted his hip and said, "Older I git, more I feel that goddamn Tragship gift."

"Someone's gotta hold down the fort."

Early the next morning he tossed a few days of supplies across Orion's rump. The black didn't complain. He figured the horse was just glad to be getting out of that stable and back on the trail. Any trail!

Billy was a decent tracker. Not as good as Sparky, but neither was anyone else in the Rangers. Due to all the people growth in and around Naco, he had to stay within eyeshot of the scalp hunters until they reached ground that wasn't so cluttered with tracks. Then he could drop back to a safer distance. The four men left shortly after dawn, heading west. It looked as though they had set their sights on the Papago reservation, but after a couple hours of riding they turned north at the small town of Palominas and began following the San Pedro River upstream. Now Billy thought he had a pretty good idea where they were headed—the San Carlos Apache Reservation. The river ran straight to the secluded southwest corner of the Rez, a perfect place to ambush some peaceful Apaches and fill up their pigging strings. He considered heading back to Naco and giving John the news right then, but it was a ten day ride up to San Carlos. What if the scalp hunters changed their minds, trashed their trail, and veered west towards the Papago Rez? It was closer. Since John had given him three days, he decided to stay on their trail for at least another day. Knowing he could follow the river allowed him to pad the distance between him and his quarry.

An hour before dusk the four men made camp under some cottonwoods alongside the river. When Billy got within sight of them they had already unsaddled their mounts, laid out their bedrolls, and built a fire. Prone in the high dry shrub on the crest of a small hill, he watched through his spyglass. They were down for the night. A few minutes later he could smell the coffee and almost hear the sizzling bacon. It made him jealous because he knew his night would be fireless with no coffee, and his dinner would be jerky and hard sinkers. Orion was hidden in a small clump of trees about fifty yards further back, so he couldn't snort and stomp to warn Billy about the breed creeping up behind him.

Something slammed down between his shoulder blades. The air blasted from his lungs. A kick in his ribs flipped him over just in time to see the butt of a rifle coming straight at his face. Then more pain was followed by welcomed darkness.

The sun had just about finished its work day when he awoke. He couldn't breathe through his nose. It was smashed and caked with dried blood. He could barely see. Both of his eyes were almost swelled shut. What fretted him most was the strange position in which he was bound: flat on his stomach, his right arm twisted behind him and tied tightly by a rope to his ankles. Another rope went from his ankles to the stump of a dead tree several feet back. His left arm was stretched straight out in front of him with his hand resting on a flat rock. A rope went from his left wrist to a stake in the ground. Four fingers of his left hand were bound together with his little finger splayed out from the others. He couldn't move anything. It was like he was a deer placed on his stomach and ready to be gutted from the back.

"What the hell is this?" he thought. Then he noticed the breed standing over him grinning, sporting his shoulder holster and .45.

"Have a nice rest, Hair Burner?" asked one of the Farley brothers. The question was followed with another kick to his ribs.

"Don't bust him up too bad now, Lucas!" Willy Shoso chuckled. "We gots ten days a fun 'head of us!" Willy knelt down next to Billy's face and said, "Ya like to burn hair, huh, does ya, white boy? Smells like burnin' locusts, huh?"

Billy grunted defiantly and said, "Smells better than yer breath!"

"Since we got him on his tummy," stated Leon, the other Farley brother as he began to unbuckle his britches, "I wanna do his ass up good!"

"Pin it up, Leon!" said Willy. "We gots ten days fer that! Ya'll git yer turn! We gonna takes our time with this hair burner." Still kneeled down next to Billy, Willy gently rested the blade of his scalping knife at the point where Billy's little finger knuckled to his hand. The realization of why he was secured in that manner sent a chill through his body. Willy leaned close to his ear. "Now here's what we gonna do, Hair Burner. Sincen we gots us a ten day ride up to San Carlos Rez, I'm a gonna take me one finger a day durin' that ride. After we git up thar and git our hair, I'm a gonna set yers on fire and watch ya try to put it out with no digits, just yer stubby palms. After my boys have thar fun, that is!" The other three men hooted and howled.

Willy pushed his blade down hard and fast. For a split second Billy struggled to realize what had happened. Then the pain shot through his hand, up his arm, into his brain, and came screaming out his of mouth.

"Hot blade!" demanded Willy, extending his hand behind him. The breed pulled a second knife from the coals and handed it to Willy. "Can't let ya bleed out on us now, can we?" smiled Willie.

Another scream exploded as the red hot knife was pushed against Billy's hand to curb the bleeding. Sweat was pouring from his forehead, tears streaming from his eyes. Welcomed darkness came again.

When consciousness returned, his head was filled with a rushing noise. It took some time before he realized it was the river. Birds were chirping. It was morning. He had been out all night. His eyes strained to open but could only manage two small slits. Bloodshot and swollen they were barely able to see a tree over his head. Then the pain attacked. First his ribs ached with every breath. Then his hand felt like it was roasting in a fire. He could take in no air through his broken nose. Thankfully his ass didn't hurt. He raised his left hand to observe the damage.

"Why?" he thought. Why was he was able to raise his arm? Through the narrow slits he saw himself also raise his right arm. Neither was bound. Then he noticed the dressing covering the vacant spot where his little finger once lived. He looked down at his feet. They were also free. He slowly raised his head and strained to see the four Scalp hunters still asleep on their bedrolls.

"This is crazy," he thought. "They left me loose while they slept?"

Every part of his body screamed in pain as he raised himself up, quietly as possible. He strained to get to one knee, trying not to let his mouth reveal just how much it hurt, and all the time keeping a constant eye slit on the sleeping men. Stifling a grunt by biting down on his good hand, he stood and froze. Dizziness batted his brain in circles. Somehow he managed to keep his balance, but certain one of those sleeping assholes would stir and spot him. He squinted to locate their horses and was shocked but pleased to see Orion tethered among them. He turned slowly to creep over to his friend, keeping a swollen eye on the sleeping Farley brother closest to him. His head started to soar so he stopped and waited for it to land. Stealing another cautious glance at the sleeping men he noticed the blood oozing from and pooling about the neck of the Farley brother closest to him.

"What the hell?" he thought.

Then he looked at the other brother sleeping to the left of his sibling— same pool of blood in the same place. Confused he carefully stepped around the two Farley brothers moving a few feet closer to Willie and the Breed. All the time he kept his damaged hand pressed against his throbbing rib cage. Fighting through clouded eyes he saw that their necks also featured wide grins and were bathed in pools of blood.

"You like trout, Billy Old?" came a familiar voice from near the river.

Billy couldn't believe his swollen eyes. Feather Yank was walking up from the river bed with two wiggling trout on a stick. He was so overwhelmed, he collapsed to his knees. Every emotion in his body exploded together in a laugh that hurt his ribs, but he didn't give a damn.

"You bad tracker, Billy Old," stated Feather Yank. "Too many noise!"

Like a surgeon the Pima split the two ten-inch rainbows down the middle and scraped out their guts with the same knife he had used to slit four throats. Billy tried to speak, but his mouth felt like the bottom of his boot. His throat just rasped out something even he couldn't understand. Feather Yank tossed him a canteen. It hurt to catch, but it was a grateful pain. He downed three long swigs. The water was cool and delicious. The best he'd ever tasted. He swished more around in his mouth and spat it and blood into the dirt. Then he poured some on his head and face. While Feather Yank was busy wrapping the fish in some large leaves, Billy used his bandanna to dry and clean his face as best he could. The Pima nodded his head towards the ripening bodies in the hot sun.

"Bad men!" he stated. "Take scalp of any Indian, say it Apache for bounty. I track two moons. Miss many times. Slip'ry men, very slip'ry." Then with a sly grin the Indian added, "Catch now!" He pushed the wrapped trout deep into the coals of the fire.

"Ya saved my life. Obliged!" Billy was finally capable of choking out. "They was plannin' on havin' some nasty fun with me!"

"I hear!" Feather Yank replied, kneeling by the fire, poking at the cooking trout.

"They was gonna cut off my fingers," added Billy. "One by one, each day until they reached San Carlos, then that, that...that goddamn nasty ass Farley brother..."

"I hear, Billy Old!" Feather Yank adamantly repeated.

Billy was stunned. Did he hear right, or did the Indian misunderstand him? "Ya hear? Ya hear? What he hell ya mean ya hear?" He got up so fast it made his head spin and sent a shot of pain through his ribs and hand all at the same time. He collapsed back to his knees, but anger overpowered the pain as he spat out his next words. "Ifin ya were close enough to hear why didn't ya step in and save me a finger?"

"Four bad men, one Feather Yank, ten Billy Old fingers—I no dumb Injun!"

"They took my goddamn finger!"

Feather Yank quickly stood up and stomped over to a blood-stained flat rock mostly embedded in the dirt. He bent over, picked something up, and crossed to Billy.

"Here!" He tossed Billy's little finger to the ground in front of him. "They no take!" He returned to cooking the trout.

Billy stared at the shriveled object at his feet. It looked like a dried-up dog turd. He wondered if he should save it.

"Put on necklace and wear," suggested the Indian. "Then no lost!"

Billy picked up his little finger and tried to wipe off the caked blood and dirt then realized how silly that was. "Where was ya hidin' when they did this?" he asked the Indian as he held up his severed finger.

"In tree!" Feather Yank turned and pointed out a thick pine about half way between the camp and the clump of trees where Billy had tethered Orion. "Too far to help Billy Old keep finger. Dark best for throat cut. Do Jack first, then black skinned man. Brothers big sleepers, do last!" Using a stick he shuffled and rearranged the hot coals around the trout.

"Ya been trailin' them fer two months, ya say?"

"Si!"

"Did ya know I was trailin' them, too?"

"You make many noise!"

"Yeah, ya said that!"

Billy tried to rise but the pain in his ribs was actually worse than that in his hand. He groaned and clutched his side then layed back flat on the ground. Feather Yank studied him for a moment.

"Watch fish!" he ordered. Billy wondered how the hell he was going to do that when he could hardly stand. Feather Yank walked down to the river, scooped up a handful of mud, and carried it back to where Billy was laying. "Lift shirt!" he said. Billy did, with great difficulty. The Pima smeared the cool mud across his rib cage. "Let dry!" He returned to the fire and prodding at the trout.

The mud felt good. Very good! It reminded him of the healing moss. But it didn't quell his frustration.

"How long ya known I been trailin' them?" he asked. "How long ya been back there watchin' me watchin' them?"

"Billy Old make..."

"Many noise, yeah I know! How long, ya goddamn shifty Pima?"

"Hour after you leave Naco," Feather Yank replied with a chortle.

"Hour? Hour?" Billy bellowed. "Then why the hell didn't ya join up with me; might still have my damn finger?"

Feather Yank pointed at the little finger still in Billy's hand and said, "Do still have damn finger!"

"You know what I mean, goddamn ya!"

Feather Yank looked straight at Billy and grinned. "They catch you they slow down to have fun with you...not so slip'ry...then I catch them."

Billy's jaw dropped. "Ya sumbitch!" he gasped. "Ya used me as bait! Oh, that's low down, Feather Yank, even for a damn Injun."

"Fish done!"

216

The Rainbows were delicious. Even though chewing them sent sharp pains through Billy's cheekbones and second broken nose, he devoured every part of it. He groaned in disgust as he watched the Indian suck out their eyeballs.

"Best part," declared the Pima with a big smile.

Feather Yank retrieved Billy's shoulder holster and .45, along with his Smith & Wesson which was lying next to Willie's body. He placed them in Billy's lap. Then he stripped the four scalp hunters of their clothing, belongings, and weapons. Billy said nothing. He just watched the Pima gather the riches of his hunt, knowing they would be distributed among his people. With his bounty loaded, Feather Yank helped Billy mount Orion. Then the Indian turned his horse to the west and Billy turned Orion southeast for Naco. He left his severed digit by Willy Shoso's bare feet as a tasty appetizer for whatever might come along to dine on the unburied lot.

As he began to ride away the Pima shouted over his shoulder, "Goodbye, Billy Old."

It stopped Billy in his tracks. He had parted company with the Indian many times over the past five or six years and this was the first time he had ever heard him say goodbye. It made him wonder if the stories were true: did the Pima see the future? Now, along with every inch of his body, his heart was hurting, too. He watched the old fellow ride away.

When John Foster heard Billy's story and how Feather Yank had used him as bait, he laughed so hard he almost pissed his pants. Figuring he could at least get some much needed sympathy at the whorehouse he walked in to the parlor. The moment Henrietta spotted him she started laughing and said his enlarged nose and black eyes made him look like a raccoon. Abbie came in and just added insult to injury.

"I think I once skinned somethun that looked like ya," she said with a laugh.

At least Irene Castle was sympathetic to his plight. She wrapped his rib cage tightly with a long stretch of cloth, slapped two cuts of beef on his eyes, and kept him on her sofa for the rest of the day without a drop of whiskey—which was really the worst of the insults. Every day for a week she cleaned and doctored his hand and pampered him until she was certain her favorite boarder wasn't getting blood poison or gangrene.

"Ya'd think a fella'd get extry pay fer losin' a finger!" Billy complained to John Foster everyday for about two weeks. Truth is after a short time of being minus the little digit he didn't even miss it, except when it came to cupping his hand on Henrietta's breasts. The missing left little finger allowed a bit of her right tit to elude his grip. He could live with that. He also found the missing finger had no effect on his shooting skills, especially the one he was still honing.

The deserted shack he discovered northwest of town belonged to an old prospector who went out searching for silver and never returned. That was seven years ago, so he was either living rich or in a buzzard's belly. The shack wasn't livable, except for spiders, rats, lizards and snakes, but the well pump still worked so he had water. A small, half-collapsed lean-to provided shade for Orion while he practiced his marksmanship. Every day over the next several weeks he made time to spend sixty-minutes there. Thirty were for honing his skill with his new Winchester 1895 Second Model Sporting Rifle with the Malcolm Model #3 hunting scope. The other thirty were spent slowly digging a hole. At the end of his self-training course, he could split a pea pod at seventy-five yards and had dug a hole a little over five feet deep.

June 17, 1910

Twenty-two days and Pasco would be sprung.

John hadn't arrived yet so Billy was alone in the office. Over the past seven weeks he'd come to enjoy sitting in John's swivel chair and putting his feet up on the desk. It felt good. As he relaxed, leaned back and put his arms behind his head he smiled to himself.

"Wonder if I could get used to this?"

Then the ringing telephone shattered the quiet room and made his ears want to fold into his skull. He flung his feet off the desk causing the chair and him to spin and topple backwards. Now he knew why John said the damn thing scares the hell out of him. This was only the second time he had heard it ring. The first time he was back by Pasco's cell reminding the fellow of his upcoming planting, so he didn't get the full grating impact of the loud contraption until now. He lifted and placed the listening piece to his ear then softly spoke into the horn in front.

"Hello?" There was a stretch of silence until he repeated himself a little louder. "Hello?"

"John?" a voice came plowing into his ear.

Billy moved the listening cone a little further away from his now throbbing ear and replied, "Uh, no! He ain't here yet!"

"To whom am I speaking?" asked the loud voice from somewhere deep inside the contraption.

"I'm the deputy."

"This is former State Representative Henry Ashurst. Can you pass along a message to Marshal Foster, Deputy, uh, Deputy....?"

Feeling it wise to fib, Billy answered, "Smith. William Smith, sir."

"Are you capable of passing along a message, Deputy Smith?"

"Yeah, yessir, I'm cap'ble."

"Okay, listen carefully, Deputy. First, tell John that yesterday the U.S. Senate approved a bill to make Arizona and New Mexico the next two states. You got that?"

"Arizona and New Mexico are gonna be states."

"Now this next part is very important. You listening?"

"Yessir!"

"Tell him Henry said," then in a childish voice Ashurst chanted, "Nah, nah, nah, nah, nah, nah! Told ya so! Got that, Deputy Smith?"

"Uh, I think so."

"Repeat that last part, please!"

Feeling foolish but obeying Billy chanted, "Nah, nah, nah, nah, nah! Told ya so!"

"That was only five 'Nah's', Deputy!"

"Huh?"

"There's six 'Nah's!' Nah, nah, nah, nah, nah, nah! Now try it again please."

Billy rolled his eyes and said, "Nah, nah, nah, nah, nah, nah! Told ya so!"

"Very good, Deputy! Thank you." The line went dead.

Billy waited a long moment. "Hello? Ya still there? Hello?" He hung up the contraption. "Now that was fuckin' strange!"

John arrived fifteen minutes later and Billy relayed the message precisely as Ashurst had given it. Foster laughed.

"What the hell was that 'bout?"

"Back in ninety-three I was a deputy up in Flagstaff," explained Foster. "Henry Ashurst was a turnkey at the same jail. He was just nineteen but had a fire in his ass to get into politics even back then. Well, he didn't take kindly to how we'd treat some of the more rambunctious prisoners. When we'd rough them up a bit to get answers to things that needed bein' answered, Henry'd get all upset and warn us, 'Ya know when we become a state yer gonna have to stop that shit! It ain't right!' I'd tell him they ain't gonna make this pisspot place a state, too much desert and too many damn Injuns. 'When they do,' Henry told me, 'I'm gonna laugh in yer face.' O'er the years when we'd cross paths he'd remind me, 'John, I'm gonna laugh in yer face one day,' he'd say." Then a concerned frown crossed John's face and he added, "Come to thinka it, how'd that fat ass know where I was? Ya know, I wouldn't be surprised if he was one a them assholes that stuck me down here in the first place! Here's to yer statehood, Henry!" John raised his hand towards the telephone and extended his middle finger.

"I ne'er knew you was a deputy up in Flagstaff," said Billy.

"Dark time fer me, Billy." explained Foster as he poured himself a cup of coffee. "Lost my wife to cholera." He sipped the warm brew. "Damn, Billy, I swear I could paint a house with yer coffee."

"Ne'er knew ya was married either."

John sat down at his desk, pulled out a cigarette and lit it.

"Only fer six months. She was part Hopi, 'bout a quarter was all, but she had a special place in her heart for them people. Bein' a nurse she spent a lot of time in their camps, treatin' them and things. Caught cholera and...and up and died on me."

"Sorry, John."

"Aw, that was my younger days, long gone, long forgotten; try not to let my head go there."

"Any kids?"

"Not together long enough. Like to have some though...maybe some-day...ifin I don't get too old to make 'em. Always wondered what a kid I made would like like." He chuckled and took a deep pull on his store bought cigarette then followed it with another sip of Billy's strong coffee.

Images of his own two boys flashed through Billy's head. If his ciphering was right they'd be four and three by now. He wondered how they looked.

June 25, 1910

Fourteen days and Pasco would be sprung.

It was Billy's turn to clean the rifles. John had just received his weekly copy of the *Tucson Citizen* and was pouring over every word. Suddenly he jumped up, wadded up the paper, and threw it across the room.

"Goddamn fat asses are at it agin," he yelled.

"What's a matter?" Billy asked, startled by the man's outburst.

Pointing to the crumpled paper he spat, "That! That piece a shit news! Oughta wipe my ass with it!"

Billy picked up the crumpled paper and searched for what had upset his friend. "What am I lookin' fer here, John?"

"Gimme that piece of shit," John demanded.

He snatched the paper, crossed to the trash can, lit the paper on fire, and dropped it in the container. "That's what I think of yer fuckin' parole," he spat at the flames in the trash can.

"Who's been paroled?"

"Ev'erone, goddamn it," John bellowed. "Em fat asses up in Washington started a Parole Commission so them scum buckets convicted of a federal crime could be paroled 'fore their sentences are up."

"I'm in the dark here, John!" He opened the door of the office and tried to fan out the smoke with his John B.

"Use to be," explained John jabbing his finger towards the burning paper, "afor that thar fuckin' commission they be makin,' them assholes convicted of federal crimes had to serve their whole sentence with no chance of parole. Now them bleedin' heart fat asses are gonna give 'em the chance to go free early." John kicked the trash can. Fortunately it didn't fall over and spread its flaming contents across the dry, wooden floor. "Why do we even do this job, Billy? What the hell good are we? If it ain't some shifty ass lawyer gettin' the scum buckets off, it's the goddamn government givin' 'em paroles. I need to retire. No, I need to get drunk."

221

He stomped out of the office. Billy took the trash can with its smoldering contents outside before the entire office was engulfed in smoke. He turned on the noisy Crocker & Curtis electric fan and aimed it at the open door. Three hours later John still hadn't returned and Billy was worried. Foster was not a high lonesome drinker. Billy hadn't seen him drunk one time since he arrived in Naco. He figured it was time to find him and the best place to look for a man who wanted to get drunk wouldn't be the ice cream parlor.

The first saloon he visited was the Imperial. No John. Then he peeked in the other two, but still no John. As he stood on the corner of Tower and Fourth Street scratching his head and worried about his missing friend, two gunshots came from the direction of Fat Frank's.

"Oh, shit!" he mumbled, drawing his Smith & Wesson and making tracks towards the ratty establishment. Two more shots rang out followed by what he thought was laughter. He crept up to one of the small windows and squinted inside the dark room. Two more shots erupted, followed by the sound of something shattering, then whooping and laughter. He couldn't believe what he was seeing in the dimly lit room. John and Fat Frank were seated in two chairs side-by-side. Both held a smoking shooter in one hand and a bottle of liquor in the other.

"What the hell's goin' on in there?" Billy yelled from outside.

"That you, Billy boy?" slurred a very drunk John Foster.

"Yeah!"

"Git yer ass in here!"

"We ain't gonna shoot ya!" laughed a very drunk Fat Frank.

Billy carefully stood in the doorway allowing the swinging doors to stay between him and the drunken men, "What's all the shootin'?"

"I'm gettin' 'lectricity put in tomorrow," answered Fat Frank.

"So we're gettin' rid a all them damn ugly lump oil lamps," John added, firing again and shattering a lamp across the room.

"Pull up a chair, Deputy!" suggested Fat Frank. "Join the fun!"

"I told Frank 'cause a them fat asses' parole thing he's gonna be seein' a lot of shifty ol' friends and he'll be seein' them lots better in 'lectric lights."

"Don't want none a 'em sumbitches sneakin' out without payin'," explained Frank as he destroyed another lamp and downed a long swig from the bottle in his chubby hand.

"Yeah," stated John. "Can't trust convicts!" He fired again and missed a lamp. "Damn!"

"Ha!" taunted Frank.

"I'm still 'head of ya by one!"

Billy pushed aside the swinging doors and stepped into the room. It was littered with shattered lump oil lamps. Fortunately, since it was daytime, none were lit. Otherwise the two drunken sharpshooters might be sitting in the middle of a burning building.

"Ya say yer gettin' 'lectri'cy tomorrow?" asked Billy.

"Fellas are gonna start stringin' the wires first thing in the morn," Fat Frank proudly slurred. "Place'll soon be lit up like a Christmas tree." He fired at another lamp, missing it. "Shit!"

"Like the Fourth of July," John proudly added as he fired and hit the lamp Fat Frank had just missed. "HA!"

"What'd ya gonna do 'bout tonight's customers?" Billy asked.

Fat Frank and John paused their shooting and looked at each other for a moment.

"Gonna be awful dark in here," Billy added.

"Dint think a that!" replied Fat Frank, looking at John.

"Me neither!" said John, looking at Fat Frank.

"What the hell!" said Fat Frank, and shot at another lamp.

"Yeah, what the hell," said John, and shot at another lamp.

Billy shook his head and left the two inebriated fellows to their fun.

That night John Foster did another uncharacteristic thing: he showed up at the whorehouse. Billy was sitting on a tattered love seat in the parlor with Henrietta in his lap when John stumbled in, still drunk, but not so drunk that he couldn't spot Billy.

"Billy Boy," the Marshal shouted and staggered through the medium-sized crowd.

"'Cuse me, pard'un me, 'cuse me, pard'un me, 'cuse me..." he kept repeating as he shouldered his way towards Billy. Suddenly he stopped and tried to focus as he stared into the face of a certain man in passing. "Jimmy Wasko? Do yer wife know yer here?" Then he laughed, smacked the fellow on the back, and stumbled on over to Billy and Henrietta.

"Billy Boy," he slurred and removed his hat, "please innaduse me to yer lady friend"

Billy smiled and said, "Henrietta, John Foster. John, Henrietta."

John squeezed in with them and the two person love seat released a groan.

"Charmed!" he slurred. "Got a friend?"

"John, ne'er seen ya here," stated Billy, trying his best not to laugh at the very drunk Deputy Marshal. "Sure ya ain't lost?"

John reached over and took Billy's beer from his hand, helped himself to a long pull, wiped his lips with his sleeve, and handed the brew back to Billy.

"I figger with all 'em felons 'em fat asses are gonna be turnin' loose, I best git re'quainted with visitin' whorehouses." He turned to Henrietta. "No offense."

"None taken," she replied with a giggle.

"Now," John slurred to Henrietta, "regardin' my earlier inquire...Got a friend? I got lots a baggage to unload."

Henrietta called out, "Cassie Lou?"

For a little woman she featured a strong voice that bounced off the four walls of the whorehouse parlor. In a flash a good sized raven haired, worn beauty with ice blue eyes that could freeze a man solid was in John's lap. The two-person love seat was putting up one hell of a fight.

"Now that's service," stated John. "I cain't even git that kinda service at the café I et at ev'rday." Once again he tried to focus his eyes as he studied Cassie Lou. "No offense, darlin' but ya look likes ya might well have some Injun in ya."

"Quarter Pueblo," replied Cassie Lou, starting to rise from John's lap. "If that bothers ya, Marshal, I can get..."

"John! Quarter, huh?" Foster replied with a grin as he pulled Cassie back down onto his lap. "That's jist fine, darlin,' jist fine."

The two person love seat held its own.

June 30, 1910

Nine days and Diaz Pasco would be sprung.

Running short of thirty-eight seventy-two rounds Billy paid another visit to the gun shop. The eager clerk who thought he was an expert on T.R.'s hunting habits greeted him.

"How's the huntin' goin,' Deputy?"

"Ain't been yet. Just been honin' up my skills. Need 'nother box of thirty-eight seventy-twos."

The clerk reached up on the shelf behind him and removed a box of cartridges. "Ya know, it's funny," he explained. "I was just thinkin' of ya the other day."

"Why's that?"

"It was on Saturday, June twenty-fifth, thirty-four years to the day that them heathens wiped out Custer and his men. My second cousin on my mother's side was one of them men—proud member of the Seventh Calvary."

"Why'd that make ya think a me?"

"Well, not so much you as yer weapon—The Winchester eighteen ninety-five Second Model Sporting Rifle with the Malcolm Model number three hunting scope. If Custer and his men would've had a weapon like that, whoo doggies, that battle would've had a whole 'nother outcome."

"S'pose so."

"Ya know the Seventh only had single shot breech loading Springfield's, don'tcha? Them damn Injuns all had repeatin' Winchesters." Then he leaned in towards Billy and said, "Ya know where they got them?"

"From a gun salesman?"

The salesman dropped his smug smile and Billy thought he could hear the hairs on the back of the man's neck bristle and stiffen. Then the fellow tried to puff himself up to a height he could never reach and blurted, "Sir, I would never sell weapons to Indians."

"Where'd they get them then?"

The man regained his composure, glanced around the shop that he already knew was empty but still wanted to place a little drama on his next spilling of wisdom. He leaned in close to Billy and whispered, "The Krauts. Them damn Huns been sellin' guns to Injuns for years. They want this country. They want our resources."

"The Germans?" asked Billy, doing his very best to not laugh in this fool's face.

"Yessir, Deputy! Them godless Huns are gonna make war on us. Ya wait and see!"

Billy paid for the thirty-eight seventy-twos and slipped the box in his pocket.

"Mark my words, Deputy," the clerk insisted as Billy turned to leave the shop. "We are gonna have us some trouble with them huns."

Billy returned to the Marshal's office. John was sitting in a rocker out front. He relaxed next to him. The two just sat and rocked for several minutes, not even speaking. Again Billy thought to himself, "I might be able to get used to this." Several people strolled by and nodded a hello. A few wagons lumbered through, causing both Billy and John to chase away the dust with their hats.

Billy lit his pipe, took a couple pulls then said, "John, ya know what that crazy ass gun shop clerk done told me?"

John lit a cigarette and said, "What?"

"That Germany's gonna make war on the U.S?"

John laughed and stated, "Sounds like the fool's been drinkin' from Hassayampa Creek. Sides, how the hell'd they get here?"

"Boats, I guess!"

"Hell, our Navy'd blow 'em outta the water 'fore they even reached the shore."

"Think so?"

"Now if you be sayin' them Huns are gonna do somethin' o'er there 'cross the pond then, yeah, hell, yeah. Them Europe assholes are always killin' off each other's kings and queens and such. Ya'd think they could learn by our example!"

"What example?"

"Ya don't have as many wars when ya ain't got a bunch of rich kings and queens callin' the shots, tryin' to collect taxes from folks that ain't got them, arguin' over whose gonna marry who, who owns that castle, who owns this castle, and so on. That's what's good 'bout a democracy: Fewer damn wars!"

"We done had wars!"

"But we had reasons fer 'em, Billy! They were nes'sary...well, 'cept fer that fuckin' Civil War; weren't no reason fer it! Goddamn waste of lives! I tell ya this though, if 'em dumb ass Europe folks get 'emselves into a war, it'll be a humdinger. All them new weapons and ways to kill folks...shit! Billy, they got guns that fire hun'derds a bullets a minute, and cannon that'll shoot o'er five miles? Hell, they got gases that'll rip up yer lungs and make them bleed right inside ya, make ya choke on yer own blood. Nosiree, Billy Boy, the next war o'er there ain't gonna be nice. Let's hope we're smart 'nough to stay clear of it."

Just as Billy was about to ask John what he meant by there not being a reason for the Civil War, Walter Simmons, the tubby bartender from the Imperial Palace came huffing and puffing up the street.

"Marshal," he managed to gasp out. Coming to a halt in front of Billy and John and panting to catch his breath, he managed to huff out, "It's Clara Silvers, John! She's at it again!"

John let out a chortling sigh and told Billy to fetch a blanket from one of the cells and meet him at the Imperial Palace. Then he and Walter hurried off down the street. When Billy was within eyesight of the saloon, blanket in hand, he saw a woman standing stark naked in front of the Imperial Palace. She wasn't doing anything, like dancing or parading around, just standing there in a stiff upright position like a soldier ready for morning inspection. Several people, especially men, had gathered around laughing. The woman refused to move or speak and John was obviously reluctant to force her inside by touching her naked body. Then the door to the tailor's shop down the street flew open and Billy saw a frantic man run out and head towards the crowd.

John grabbed the blanket from Billy and draped it around the woman's shoulders. She still didn't say a word, didn't even bother to grasp and close it up, just stood there, arms still hanging at her side, the blanket open in the front for all to see. The tailor ran up and closed the blanket. The naked woman's face went into an immediate scowl. Her hands began making wild gestures. The man just nodded his head and led the woman back to his shop. The crowd, still laughing, began to disperse.

Walter Simmons looked at John and laughed.

"Third time this year, Marshal," he said. "Think Abner'll ever learn?" Then he wobbled back inside the saloon.

"What the hell was that 'bout?" asked Billy.

"That's the tailor's wife Clara Silvers," explained John. "She's a mute. She likes to go visit her mother back in St. Louie. Abner don't like payin' fer the train ticket, 'specially since she likes to go a lot. Since she can't nag and bitch at him 'bout it, that's her way of fin'ly gettin' the tightwad to give in. It's worked three times this year."

227

"Why don't he just move his biz'ness to St. Louie?" asked Billy.

"He's the only tailor in town," explained John, "makin' too much money here. Wouldn't be so bad if she were decent to look at. Them Jew women are a bit too hairy fer my taste." He looked up at the front of the saloon and licked his lips. "Well, since I'm here, think I'll have a beer. Wanna join me?" Seeing the bewildered expression on Billy's face, John grinned and said, "What? Just 'nother day in the life of a stay put Peace Officer, Billy Boy."

July 4, 1910

Five days and Diaz Pasco would be sprung.

John was pacing the floor as Billy walked in from late afternoon rounds.

"Lot of fellas gettin' drunk fer the fireworks tonight," warned Billy. "We may be in fer a few overnight guests." John kept pacing. "Still no telegram?"

"The goddamn fight was close to three hours ago," Foster snapped. "My pal up in Reno said he'd wire me soon as it was over."

"Why ya so worked up o'er one ol' prize fight?"

"Ya know who's fightin', Billy?"

"Ain't got no in'trest."

"Ya should in this one! It's 'nother damn darky name a Jack Johnson. He's a beast! He's goin' up agin James Jeffries, the man Jack London called 'the chosen rep'sen'tive of the white race.' Iffin Johnson beats Jeffries, he done beat the best of the white man. That ain't good, Billy. Nosiree, ain't good at all!"

Billy suddenly realized why John said the Civil War was a "goddamn waste of lives." It also became clear why he had never chased Fat Frank and his stars and bars out of town.

Young Orin Stample burst through the open door with the telegram. John snatched it from his small hand.

'Bout damn time, boy!" he barked.

Orin turned three shades of white. Billy gave him a dime and the boy scampered back to the telegraph office for his next delivery. For a long moment John just stood there, holding the yellow piece of paper, afraid to let his eyes settle on it. He took a deep breath then read the words he had feared for hours.

"Shit!" he exclaimed, wadding up the cable and throwing it in the trash. "Gonna go see Cassie Lou!"

Billy didn't see him again until the next day. He even missed the fireworks. No matter how he tried to figure it, Billy couldn't get his head around how one prize fight could mean the end of the white man. Then he remembered what Sparky said about Jeff and the Indian Whiskey: "Takes a powerful lot of hate." Now here it was again—another friend who just lumps a certain kind of folks into one big pile of hate.

July 7, 1910

Two days and Pasco would be sprung.

Ever since Henrietta introduced John to Cassie Lou, Billy had been arriving at the office ahead of him. John had been keeping some late nights with his quarter Pueblo. Billy figured she reminded him of his dead wife, and that's okay. He deserved some good times. John's late arrival also gave Billy the opportunity to pay another visit to the *cabrón* in cell four. After the heavy door screeched its' customary good morning, he ambled down to Pasco's cage.

"Two days...then I'm gonna plant ya!"

He turned and left with the usual bellows following him out of the cell area. The heavy screeching door finally covered the screams. John showed up ten minutes later.

"Mornin'," he said and poured himself a cup of coffee. "I gotta talk to ya, Billy."

"Okay!"

"Serious stuff now," John added with a frown. "Ya better sit down."

"What ya gonna do, fire me?" asked Billy with a grin.

"Ya should be so lucky!" John hesitated, trying to figure out how to form the words into what he needed to say. He sipped the strong coffee. Billy watched his eyes widen and his lips pucker. Then he shook his head as to rattle his eyes into focus.

Sensing his quandary Billy said, "Just spit it out, John! Festerin'll twist up yer bowels!"

John sat down and sighed deeply. "How'd ya think the town would take it iffin I married a whore?" He rose quickly and began to pace again. "Not only a whore, but a breed!"

Billy was so stunned he didn't know what to say. After just twelve days his friend was ready to marry? Finally words came to him. "Uh, John, a lot of fellas done hitched up with whores. Ain't nuthun new. I bet if Jeff were still 'round, he'd of hitched up with Abbie."

"Jeff wouldn't have to worry 'bout a mayor and a town council or what 'em scrubby clean, mealy-mouthed church folk'd be sayin'."

"Ya ain't even known her fer two weeks, John."

"Only knew my first wife fer a month."

"Month's longer than bein' shy a two weeks."

"Billy, I ain't sayin' we gonna get hitched tonight or tomorrow, fer crissake! I just need yer 'pinon 'bout what ya think towns folk'd say."

"A fellas gotta do what makes him happy, John. Do Cassie Lou make ya happy?"

"I'm a good twenty years her elder."

"Do she make ya happy?"

"Like a bee in a honey pot!"

"Then fuck 'em!"

"I'm gettin' too old to go huntin' fer a new job."

"Ya crazy?" laughed Billy. "They got a good man here willin' to take on a shitty job. They ain't gonna find no one else to do it. Ain't that many knotheads like you 'round."

"They could always offer you the job!"

Billy looked him in the eye and said, "And they can go shit splinters!" For a second Billy studied his perplexed friend then said, "My ma and pa always told me 'listen to yer heart, not yer brain. Yer brain'll lie to ya, yer heart won't.' That's what helped me get through all that shit down in Sonora. I listened to my heart 'cause I knew it was right, and that made what I was doin' right, too. If ya wanna hitch up with Cassie Lou, just fuckin' do it. It's yer heart that deserves to be happy. Yer brain'll learn to live with it."

July 9, 1910

Diaz Pasco's ninety days would be up at midnight.

230

That afternoon Billy had told John he was going to make the ride up to Bisbee to visit Freddie Rankin's folks and see how his little girl was doing. John hoped that he had forgotten Pasco was being sprung that night, or he simply wanted to avoid the temptation of blowing his brains out by not being in town. Either way, the Marshal was relieved.

Orion was finally going to get a good run. Billy could tell the black was growing restless just circling a corral. He needed some stretch in his muscles and sweat on his back. So he turned the horse's head north and leaned down into his ear.

"Fog it, Big O!"

The stallion leapt into action. They made the twelve mile ride to Bisbee in less than thirty minutes arriving around four PM. Billy registered for a room at the hotel then found the local general store and purchased a doll. Having attended Freddie's funeral two years ago, finding his grave was easy. A tombstone that wasn't initially there was now at the site. It read "Frederick B. Rankin, 1872-1908. Arizona Ranger, Father, Loving Son." Billy wondered what the "B" was for. He chuckled at the thought of it being "Boulder." He stood for a moment just staring at the stone.

"I know ya ain't in there, Freddie. Yer up on one of them stars flyin' 'round the skies. Ain't figgered whichen yet. I just wanted ya to know that I found yer shooter...and I'm gonna plant him!"

Eldridge and Janelle Rankin were surprised and pleased to see Billy. Since Isabel was on a hay ride but would be home for supper, they convinced him to stay. After what he had heard about Janelle's home cooking from Freddie it didn't take much convincing. As they awaited Isabel's return, Janelle fixed and served tea on a fancy silver tray.

"Oh, I forgot the sugar," she said.

As soon as she returned to the kitchen Eldridge put his finger to his lips and made a soft shushing sound. He pulled a small flask from his pocket and spiked his and Billy's cups with a shot of rum. Billy considered telling him he knew who killed his son, but feared Eldridge might want to see the man brought to justice with a trial. He had no intentions of wasting that much time on Diaz Pasco. When Janelle returned with the sugar she also carried a large book. It displayed several neatly placed tintypes of Freddie at various ages, along with the same of Isabel.

"Look at these two, Billy," stated Janelle. "This is Freddie at one year old, and this is Isabel at one year old. Don't they look alike?"

"Sure do," Billy replied courteously, but didn't really see the resemblance.

"She is her daddy's girl!" Janelle smiled.

As she continued to turn the pages of the book and give the details of each and every tintype, Billy began to think of his own family. He had no tintypes of his mother or father, only the pictures in his head. He wondered if Anna had any of his sons. Maybe someday he'll find out. He thought that looking at tintypes was supposed to make a person happy, but these didn't. Maybe it was the way Janelle described them. Even though she appeared to be excited about showing them to someone new, her voice said different. It seemed to come from a sad place. Fortunately Isabel walked in the door and Janelle's face lit up. Much to Billy's relief she closed the depressing book.

Isabel squealed and giggled at the sight of Billy, recalling the day over two years ago when he was hogtied in her classroom. She also ran up and gave him a hug, something he did not expect, but enjoyed. She was taller than the last time he saw her and had longer hair. He could see she was going to be a very pretty young lady. Freddie would be proud and worried about boyfriends. After hearing how well she was doing in school and how much she loved her new seventh grade school marm, he felt he should've brought her a book or pencils or a ruler or something, anything besides the childish doll. But she seemed to like it, or pretended to.

After a supper the likes that lived up to Freddie's bragging, Billy and Eldridge went out on the porch for a smoke. Billy tamped down his pipe as Eldridge opened a small package, pulled out a cigarette and lit it.

"Sorry 'bout the tintypes!" whispered Eldridge. "Like to burn those damn things! Sometimes I'll wake up in the middle of the night and Janelle won't be in bed. She's downstairs looking at that goddamn book. No tears, not cryin,' just...just starin' at those tintypes. 'Bout the only thing that'll bring her out of her dark place is Isabel. The girl's her life now."

Something with Freddie's birth had messed up Janelle's insides. He was the only child the couple had, or could have. When Freddie joined the Rangers it gave his parents the chance to take in their granddaughter, for which they were elated. Now they would raise her to womanhood. Something Freddie would never see. When the Rankins asked Billy to stay the night he told them he already had a hotel room in town, which he did, even though he never intended to use it. It was all part of his alibi in case John Foster asked of his whereabouts during Pasco's sudden disappearance. Yes, he felt guilty about using these fine folks like this, and even a little white lie to a man like John Foster felt like betrayal, but it had to be done and he had to do it alone. Once again he gave Orion his head and the two were back in Naco in a little under thirty minutes, shortly after ten Saturday night. Any remaining guilt had been left somewhere back among the pages of that tintype album.

As usual, the hotel clerk was snoring away on his small cot in the little room just off the lobby of the only hotel in Naco. It was a two story building with six rooms on each floor. Billy quietly entered, took the key to Room 11, and wrote the name Diaz Pasco on the registry. He placed two silver dollars by the signature, enough for one night's stay. He crept out as quietly as he came in, leaving the desk clerk in snoring slumber. A few minutes later he peeked in the whorehouse door to be certain John Foster and his quarter Pueblo were nowhere in sight and that Henrietta wouldn't see him enter. Soon he was alone with Abbie in her tiny room.

"He can't cross that bridge," Billy reminded her in an anxious whisper.

"I know, Billy" she impatiently answered. "I ain't stupid. Ya done tol' me hunderd times."

"Whatcha gonna say to him?"

"Aw, fer shit's sake, Billy..."

"Abbie, ya gotta mean it! He's gotta believe ya!"

She sighed and whispered in a lustful tone, "Victoriano sent me to pleasure ya."

Billy held up a key. "Room eleven, second floor," he explained. "It's just inside the backside steps and doorway, so use them. No one should see ya that way." The last thing he wanted was to have Abbie tied to Pasco's intended demise.

"Damn, Billy," she exclaimed, excited and pleased and her eyes wide. "Ya know how long it's been since I fucked in a fancy hotel room?" As if it unlocked the greatest treasure in the world, she snatched the key and quickly stuffed it in her corset. The two of them left the small room and went downstairs to the parlor. Since it was Saturday night, business was good. The high pitched sound of clinking glasses rose above the laughter and conversation.

He found Henrietta and she told him John and Cassie Lou had left for the night.

"John gonna marry that girl?" Henrietta asked as she lightly stroked Billy's privates. "He should! Won't cost him as much."

Billy chuckled but never took his eyes off Abbie as she shopped her wares, moving from man to man, laughing, flirting, touching, and making every hombre in that room feel like a king. She had a little less than two hours to kill before Pasco's release, might as well make the best of it. Whores survive by numbers.

October, 1907

It was the second time this week Jeff had found Billy in their favorite whorehouse instead of at home with Anna and their two baby boys. He wasn't surprised or angry, just disappointed. He had seen his folk's marriage fall apart, but not in such a short time as this. Of course, Billy spending drunken nights in this place certainly didn't help bandage the bleeding union. He and Retta were occupying the same chair at a table for four when Jeff strolled over to them.

"Retta," Jeff stated coldly, "take a walk!"

Knowing Kidder's volatile reputation the whore didn't argue. She was up and mixed in with the crowd in seconds, much to the anguish of a soused Billy. He sprang to his feet and knocked over the chair.

"What the hell ya doin', goddamn it?" he shouted. The sudden clamor caused the bouncer to take notice.

Tarley Jefferson stood six-inches over six feet and was the son of a former slave who was given his freedom from a west Texas plantation after he saved the town from a rampaging bull. The animal got loose and was running through the streets goring anything and everyone in sight. Tarley's pa was standing in the back of a wagon loading supplies for his master. When the crazy bull passed by the wagon the former slave leapt on its back, grabbed its horns, and twisted its neck until it snapped. Although his master was reluctant to do it, the whole town insisted on the man's freedom. He got it, but his wife didn't. It's said he waited close to a year just across the border from El Paso in the New Mexico hills and survived on cactus roots and coyote meat until his wife could escape her bondage and join him. How the couple ended up in Nogales no one knows, and Tarley's grizzly attitude didn't welcome any questions about his ma and pa. But the baby they birthed was a bull himself.

"There be a problem chere, Rangers?" asked Tarley in a voice deeper than a hoarse bullfrog.

Jeff was shocked with how fast the big man made it through the crowd and to his side.

"No problem, Tarley. Right, Billy?"

Billy fuzzy-eyed his friend then turned to Tarley and begrudgingly said, "No problem, Tarley."

"Den have fun, Rangers," Tarley replied with no smile and returned to his normal sentinel post, but both Rangers knew the bull would be keeping an eye on them.

"I ain't goin' home, Jeff!" declared Billy still rather loudly.

"Didn't tell ya to, did I?" answered Jeff, taking a quick glance and nod towards Tarley to assure the man that all was still hunky-dory.

"I'm just sayin' I ain't doin' it." He plopped himself back down at the table.

Jeff chuckled and said, "This is kinda switched 'round, isn't it?"

"What'd ya mean?" Billy spat as he poured himself a shot of whiskey.

"Ain't gonna offer me one?" asked Jeff.

Billy hesitated for a moment then poured Jeff a drink. "Only 'cause ya said ain't. And what's switched 'round?"

"Usually I'm the one who's a loud drunk."

"Ya ain't drunk," Billy replied in a lower volume.

"Guess we'll have to remedy that, huh?" Jeff downed his whiskey, poured himself another one, and joined Billy at the table.

"I want my whore back," slurred a disgruntled Billy. "And why ain't ya with Abbie?"

"She's gotta stay up in her room for a few days...women folk stuff."

"Hate that!" stated Billy.

"Nature runnin' its course, that's all."

"That was the one good thing 'bout when Anna was carryin'—none of that nature stuff goin' on. Made fer a lot of good times."

"I don't know 'bout that. Unloadin' yer baggage while she's carryin' might make me a bit too cautious to enjoy it."

"Ya only do it durin' the first six months or so," explained Billy. "I tell ya, some of the best baggage handlin' Anna and I had was when she was carryin' our first born. We did it almost ev'ry night with no worries 'bout women folk stuff." Billy poured himself another drink and gulped it down then just stared at the crowd. Finally he looked at his friend and said, "And that's when it all but stopped...right after our first boy was born...the fuckin' just went right out the window. It's like...like she don't have no interest in it no more." He poured another drink and continued, "Even more so after the birthin' of our second boy."

"Maybe it'll pass," said Jeff. "Maybe sooner or later she'll get back to the old Anna."

"I ain't holdin' my breath."

Jeff glanced around the room and said, "I can see that."

"Don't you go gettin' holy roller on me. You like this place as much as me."

"That I do, my friend. That I do."

"Then get Retta back here!"

Jeff cut off a chunk of chew and slipped it into his mouth. "I don't know how many times I had to chase my pa outta the one and only whorehouse in our town," he said. "Got so sick of hearin' my folks shoutin' and bitchin' at each other that my little brother and I would take our blankets out under the big willow tree 'bout twenty yards from the house so we wouldn't have to listen to'em. In the wintertime we'd go down in the storm shelter. Some nights, though, we couldn't get far enough away. I think the best thing they ever did was get that divorce."

"Ya tellin' me to do that?"

"Nope, just statin' a fact. 'Neath willow trees and down in storm shelters ain't fun places fer kids to spend their nights."

"Yer sure liken the 'ain'ts' tonight."

Jeff smiled and poured another drink for both of them. "Guess you're rubbin' off on me. The other day I even stopped a couple of frisky colts from pickin' on an old Injun woman. Surprised myself with that one." He laughed. Then the two raised their glasses, tapped them together, and sat quiet for a spell. Finally Jeff said, "I almost got hitched once. Back up in Vermillion. Her name was Molly Thompson. I tell ya, Billy, she was the girl of my dreams."

236

He waited for his friend to continue the story, but Jeff just released a long stream of tobacco juice into the spittoon a few feet from their table and sat there. Finally Billy asked, "What happened?"

"Well, when my folks got divorced and sold the farm I didn't know whether to stay in Vermillion or go to Los Angeles with my ma or Oregon with my pa. I knew Molly wanted me to stay." He looked at Billy and gave him a big tobacco stained grin. "She had her own plans for me."

"Molly. Good name," stated Billy, only so it would spark his friend to continue with his story.

"Molly Thompson...hair as black as night and eyes like two chunks of coal." He smiled at a memory and added, "She had one dimple, in her left cheek, just like her ma. Truth is, though, I was kinda partial to Oregon—never seen that part of the country. One night we were lying out in a field watchin' shootin' stars" He looked at Billy and added, "She was wearing my favorite mohair sweater. I told her that I was considering Oregon. For a long spell she didn't say anything. Then she sang me a song."

"A song?"

"Yep! Red River Valley. When I heard those sad words comin' from her heart I knew I'd be stayin' in Vermillion."

Jeff stopped talking. Billy watched his friend's eyes drift to a faraway place. Before they got too far to bring back Billy asked, "Well, what happened?"

"She drowned before we could tie the knot," Jeff replied "Flash flood! I was off hunting with some fellas. That was when I had that great shot on that mule deer I told ya 'bout." He lowered his head and slowly moved it from side to side. "Should've been there, mighta been able to...but...well, shoulda, coulda, woulda don't mean shit now, does it?" Trying to lighten the mood with a chuckle that didn't even make a scratch in the sadness of the moment he added, "Sometimes that ol' Missouri River can be a vindictive son-of-a-bitch."

"What's that?" asked Billy. "That "vin" thing?"

"Vindictive?" said Jeff as he poured them both another shot of whiskey. "Means, uh, hold a grudge, won't let bygones be bygones."

"How can a river hold a grudge?"

"Rivers aren't patient things. We dam them up, cut channels off of them, change their courses to irrigate our crops, courses they been running for thousands of years. After awhile they just get pissed and say enough's enough, and they flood, just to remind us whose boss. Then just as I was about to pack up for Oregon I got wind of the Rangers. I told myself this was my chance to do something." He smiled and added, "Maybe even get famous. So here I am."

Billy stared at his friend for a moment, letting all he just heard sink in. Finally he said, "That's the saddest fuckin' story I ever heard. I ain't even in the mood to get drunk now."

"You're already drunk."

"Drunker then!" The two laughed. After it quelled Billy looked straight at Jeff and asked, "You gonna marry Abbie?"

Jeff smiled and turned his shot glass over and plunked it down on the table. Billy waited a moment then followed suit.

"Come on!" said Jeff, rising from the table. "I'll walk you home."

July 9, 1910

Hidden in the shadows he watched Abbie greet the newly released Pasco five minutes after midnight. She had stopped the man in front of the hotel just like Billy had instructed, not giving the *cabrón* a chance to even draw near the bridge to the Mexican side. He couldn't hear what either was saying, but with Pasco's grinning teeth standing out against his dark skin, he knew the shitbird was pleased. Abbie smiled, stroked his chest, stomach, and privates, all the time slowly swaying her own hips and allowing them to lightly brush against the member that had been caged for ninety days. She pulled the key from her blouse and brandished it. Arm around each other's waist they sauntered up the back stairs of the hotel.

The side window of the dentist's office was easy enough to jimmy open and big enough for Billy to climb through. Knowing no one would be there late Saturday night, he wasn't worried about the clamor when his leg bumped the mechanical praying mantis and it spun and clanged against the high backed chair. Besides, he figured, who the hell would want to rob a dentist's office? He scooped up the Clover and its accompanying pieces, climbed back out of the window, and returned to the blackness behind the hotel.

Room 11 was perfectly located with a window looking out onto the corral. A lit candle in that window for ten seconds was to be Abbie's signal for when Pasco would be spent and asleep. Billy anxiously lurked in the shadows behind the building. He kept Orion saddled alongside another mount he had taken from the livery. After ninety days of no whores and no liquor, he figured it wouldn't take Abbie long to wear Pasco down to a limp bag of bones.

He was wrong.

With every hour that passed the night air got colder and his concern for Abbie got hotter. He had smoked almost all of his tobacco. He smacked his pipe on his boot to drive the last of the red ashes onto the ground then slipped it into his vest pocket. The heat warmed his chest. It was just a few hours until dawn. Did something happen? Surely the man would've been spent in that amount of time, or had the asshole hurt her? Right as he decided to risk it and go up the steps to check, the candle lit, burned for ten seconds, and went out. He grabbed the Clover and hurried up the backstairs of the hotel. Lightly rapping on the door of room eleven he expected a quiet entrance.

"Ya owe me 'nother five bucks," she howled right as she threw open the door.

"Sssshhhh!" Billy demanded.

"Oh, he's dead to the world. Ninety days in that cell and the sumbitch wore me ragged. I'm too damn sore to work fer at least two days. Ya owe me 'nother five bucks, goddamn it."

"Okay, okay. Hold this!" He shoved the Clover into her hands than fished a five dollar gold piece from his pocket.

"What the hell's this?" asked Abbie as she studied the strange object.

Retrieving the device and handing her the coin he explained, "It's a Clover. I took it from the dentist's office."

She stuffed the gold piece into her corset and said, "Don't look like no clover I e'er seen. Ain't got no leaves! What's it fer?"

"Givin' a fella ether!" answered Billy as he poured the liquid ether into the device. "I done tol' ya 'bout it afore! It makes ya sleep real deep."

"Whata ya mean real deep?"

"Damn it, Abbie, real deep is real deep! Now get on outta here!" Just as he had seen the young dentist do, he poured the liquid ether into the Clover and began to pump.

"Huh? The woman was stunned and wounded. "Ya mean I can't stay in this here fancy hotel room, at least fer the night?"

His impatience melted when he saw the longing in her eyes. He remembered what she said. "Ya know how long it's been since I fucked in a fancy hotel room?" How often is this woman offered luxury? How often does her room smell like lilacs? How often does she get to sleep on clean sheets? Well, not so clean anymore, but the bed was still bigger and fluffier than what she was accustomed to.

"Only if ya get outta here early and leave by the back steps," he relented. Abbie giggled like a little girl and spun in a circle. "I mean it, Abbie, Early!

"I know, I know," she responded, grinning.

"I don't want no one tyin' ya to this asshole."

Abbie looked at Billy for a half moment, teasingly ran her fingers along his shoulder in a flirtatious manner.

"Ya worried 'bout me, Billy Old?" she asked coquettishly.

"I don't want nothun happenin' to you that should be happenin' to me!" he answered in a curt and serious tone.

Realizing he was truly referring to only her safety, two unfamiliar feelings crept through Abbie, two emotions that had been buried for years. She found herself grateful yet deflated. She had forgotten what it was like having someone actually be concerned about her well-being, and being a whore, rejection had always been just part of the business. So why did this rejection sting her?

"Okay," she replied softly.

The Clover was prepped and ready. Billy placed it over Pasco's face.

"What did he say when ya told him Victoriano sent ya?" Billy asked.

"Nothun'special!" Abbie answered quickly. "Ya gonna smother him? Here?"

"I told ya, damn it, this lets out a gas that knocks ya cold. Now what did he say about Victoriano?"

"Uh..." She had to think; it had been a long night. "Uh, he just said... Ahh, the Chief! He still love me!' That stuff smells funny!"

"The Chief?" replied Billy, pumping the Clover. "What the hell's that mean?"

240

"Pretty plain! That stuff gonna make me pass out, too?" she asked, more fascinated with the Clover than the question at hand.

"No! What's pretty plain, damn it?" demanded Billy, still holding the black cup over Pasco's face.

"That Chief Amador still loves him." She pointed to the Clover. "How long do ya keep...?"

"Who?"

"Chief Amador. How long do ya keep that...?"

"Naco Chief of Police Amador?" He stopped pumping.

"Yeah," answered Abbie.

Billy was stunned. "His name is Victoriano?"

"Why the hell else would ya have me tell Pasco that Victoriano sent me?" an exasperated Abbie asked. "I swear, Billy Old, I truly do think yer brain was fried out in that desert!"

A stampede thundered through Billy's skull. All this time he thought Jeff was repeating names in his delirium, starting his list over..."Amador, Quías, Alvarez, Pasco, Victoriano...Amador..." but he was saying there were two Amadors–Tomás and Mexican side Naco Chief of Police Victoriano Amador. Billy never knew his first name, only addressed him as Chief Amador. How simple it would have been, he thought, if he'd known that at the beginning–Chief Amador and gunrunning. It makes perfect sense. All those other policemen couldn't have been so ballsy unless their boss knew what they were doing and was getting his cut...and the asshole has an office. He began pumping again, vigorously. Why didn't he think of it? Jeff would've! Maybe he did! Sure he did! Jeff was smart!

"Fifth fucking grade," he whispered. A few moments later he removed the Clover and broke his angry self-deprecation with a question, "Got a pin, something pointy?"

Abbie reached for a pearl nestled between her bosoms in the center of her corset. With her thumb and forefinger she unsheathed a four-inch hat pin and held it out to him.

"Jesus," he muttered, eyeing the deadly spear. He had thought it was merely a pearl for decoration.

"What?" she asked. "It's quieter than my boot gun and jabbed in the right place, does the job."

He took the pin and plunged it into Pasco's arm. Abbie stifled a shriek.
"Good lord, Billy!"

Pasco didn't even flinch. Billy handed back her pin. She studied it momentarily, making certain it was still wickedly straight.

"That is some deep sleep," she mumbled.

Billy heaved the limp body of the killer over his shoulder and grunted, "Told ya!" With his free hand he scooped up the Clover. "Get the door fer me, will ya?"

"Where ya takin' him?"

"Gonna plant him just like I told him and just like I dreamed."

"Dreamed?"

"A man without a dream ain't worth a horse apple," he said with a smile. Knowing she would keep asking questions he cut her off quickly. "Enjoy the room, Abbie!"

He was out the door and down the steps before she could open her mouth again. Now he knew about Victoriano, so he could just put a bullet in Pasco's brain pan. Simple! Clean! No! That's not the way it was supposed to happen. He'd worked very hard at digging that hole. Suddenly he wondered if anyone ever dug a hole for Alex MacDougal's burned body in that box canyon. Just as suddenly he knew no one did. Billy had a lot of practice digging holes during his time with the Rangers. Surprisingly though, only a few Rangers were in those holes. Most of the ones he, Jeff, Freddie, and Sparky dug were for lost prospectors who got themselves butchered by the few remaining hostiles. Or families of farmers and ranchers who'd been killed by marauders and border bandits. It was dirty duty, but it had to be done. He just hated digging the small holes.

February, 1902

The train ride from Flagstaff to Yuma Prison was slow, hot, and dirty. Leave the windows closed and they roasted. Open them, and they'd choke on black soot from the smokestack. The prisoner Jeff and Billy were transferring was Calhoun Small Toe, a murderer and rapist who had somehow escaped the noose but would be spending the rest of his days in a Yuma iron cage. After discarding the criminal, the two Rangers were on another slow, hot, and dirty train ride from Yuma to Nogales. Billy was gazing out the window. The track ran parallel to and slightly above a long stretch of green river bottom. The scenery wasn't anything he hadn't eyed before, but this time it had a more peaceful feel to it. Maybe it was because their tedious mission was finally over and they were on the way back to headquarters in Nogales, or maybe because he and this new Ranger from Dakota were beginning to become good friends. He had decided he liked this fellow, despite some of his views.

Jeff was reading the *Yuma Sun* newspaper and would occasionally mumble "Shit" to himself. It made Billy chuckle.

Somewhere within the droning and clacking sounds of the train Billy thought he heard coughing. After a while the sound grew louder. He realized it was coughing, the cough of a child, and more than one child. The few people in the passenger car began to move to vacant seats further from the hacking noise. Soon the conductor entered the car and a woman passenger stopped him and pointed towards the seats from where the coughing was coming. The conductor stepped over to the area, looked down, then recoiled and pulled the overhead brake cord. The train jerked violently and began to squeal and grind to a halt.

Billy rose and asked the conductor, "What's goin' on?"

"Just remain seated, sir!" responded the conductor. "We got the problem under control."

"What problem?" Billy asked as he started towards the conductor, balancing and bracing himself on the backs of seats. The train continued to screech and jerk its way to a stop.

The conductor held up his hand and said, "I wouldn't go near 'em, sir."

"Near who?"

Billy inquired as he pushed his way past the conductor.

Huddled together in one seat were three Indian children aged about six to ten, all dressed in their finest white man apparel, obviously a school uniform. They were sweating and chilling and coughing.

"That's typhus!" stated the frightened conductor. "I seen it hun'erds a times!"

"Ya didn't notice they was sick when they got on?" asked Billy.

The conductor frowned and said, "I don't pay no 'tenshun to their kind!"

"Why are we stopping?" Billy asked in a foreboding tone as if he knew what was on the conductor's mind.

"Ya crazy? They're infected! We gotta get 'em outta here!" The train was still slightly moving when the conductor opened the door that led to the small platform between the connecting cars. "Ya kids git on outta here, now!" he ordered.

Billy couldn't believe what he was hearing. "Ya can't put them off here!"

"Damn right I can! I'm responsible for the folks on this train. They could infect us all!"

"There ain't nuthun out there."

"That's their problem." When the train had finally groaned to a complete stop the conductor shouted his orders at the shivering children again. "Git now!"

Terrified and slightly delirious the three children rose and crossed to the open section between the cars. The two older ones had to practically carry the youngest.

Billy hurried over to Jeff and said, "We can't let this happen!"

"Not our train, Billy!" Jeff calmly replied. "And they're Injuns!" He went back to reading his paper.

"They're kids, and they're sick."

Without lowering his newspaper Jeff replied, "Then their folks shouldn't have put 'em on the train in the first place."

If Billy's eyes could've shot fireballs Jeff's paper would've been blazing in his hands.

"I ain't leavin' them out there 'lone!" he said, then walked up to the conductor and told him he was getting off, too.

"I tell ya, fella, it's typhus!" exclaimed the conductor. "Ya wanna die, too?"

"No! I want my horse outta yer fuckin' boxcar!" He was angry at both the conductor and his new friend. He and Jeff had just spent ten days together picking up and delivering Calhoun Small Toe. He thought they were getting to know and respect each other, but figured he must be wrong. No decent human being would do this to children.

Frustrated at Billy's stubbornness, Jeff tossed the newspaper aside.

"There's nothing you can do for them, Billy," Jeff said. "Come on back and sit down!"

Billy took one quick, hard glance back at Jeff then hopped off the standing train behind the three sick children.

"Ya kids stay right here!" he told them.

He hurried to the boxcar, forced open the door, and carefully removed Swiss, his chocolate gelding.

The conductor leaned out from the platform and waved to the engineer. This was followed by two quick toots of the train whistle. Jeff was now standing on the platform watching his friend lead his horse to where the three children clung to each other in the dirt.

"Billy," Jeff shouted, "Get back in here! They're Injuns for crissake!"

"I'll meet ya in Nogales!" Billy shouted back.

"Aw shit!" muttered Jeff as he hopped off the train. He turned and spoke to the conductor. "Hold it a minute," he ordered. Then he hurried to the boxcar to getVermillion.

The conductor leaned out and held up his hand to keep the engineer from moving the train. After Vermillion had left the boxcar the conductor waved the engineer forward. Two more toots came from the engine's whistle. The train's wheels spun and sparked on their steel road to regain traction, then slowly strained to move.

"Yer crazy!" the conductor shouted as the train began picking up momentum. "Both a ya! It's typhus, I tell ya! Ya gonna kill yerselves o'er some damn injuns?"

Jeff listened to the conductor's voice sink under the noise of the train. Soon he was staring at the butt end of the caboose as it grew smaller.

"Shit!" he mumbled again.

Billy had already taken a shirt from his saddlebags, ripped it into three strips and was dousing it with water from his canteen. He placed it on the foreheads of the children.

"We gotta make a litter."

Jeff looked at his new friend for a long moment then said, "I swear to god, Billy Old, if I catch typhus and die, I'm comin' back to haunt yer ass."

It took them close to an hour to find and gather enough wood to make a sizeable litter and stretch and secure the tarps from their bedrolls across its frame. The children's coughing had grown worse.

"Ya know it's twenty miles back to their rez," Jeff reminded him, "and we're runnin' outta daylight!"

"I saw some arrowweed shelters 'bout five miles back 'long the river bottom," Billy stated. "We'll take them there fer the night!"

"What the hell's that?"

"The Quechan live in them during their harvest time, make them outta arrowweed."

"Then what, Billy? Huh, then what?"

For a moment he wasn't sure how to answer that question. "Then we... we doctor them."

"With what?" demanded Jeff. "We don't have any medicines and typhus is caused by lice."

"Then we...we gotta bathe them real good in the river. Ya still got that fancy smellin' soap in yer saddlebags?"

"That's expensive stuff. You 'spect me to use it on them...them?"

"Kids, Jeff! Kids! They're fuckin' kids!"

The going to the arrowweed shelter was rough and long. Five miles felt like five hours. By the time they reached it, the youngest of the children had gone under.

Jeff frowned as he entered the small, dark, domed shaped thatch hut.

"They live in these pieces of shit?"

"Take those two down to the river and put yer fancy soap to work! I'll take care of the little one."

Shit!" Jeff muttered again.

"Would you rather dig the grave?"

"No! I don't wanna bury a kid, even an Injun kid."

Billy started digging his first small hole.

Bitching and mumbling most of the time, Jeff stripped the other two Indian children and soaked them and their discarded uniforms in the river. He scrubbed them down hard with his fancy, expensive soap then started to lather their clothing.

"Don't bother with the clothes," Billy shouted from the tiny gravesite. "Burn 'em! We'll wrap the kids in our camas."

"Our what?"

"Bedrolls!"

"Aw, come on, Billy, not our bedrolls!"

"Just do it, goddamn it, Jeff!"

"Means we'll have to burn them, too."

"Supply will give us new ones. Ain't no big deal."

Jeff grumbled to himself, "Goddamn new ones itch like hell."

After he buried the little one Billy built a fire inside the small domed shelter and the Rangers burned the children's clothing. It warmed up fast as the smoke drifted out of the hole in the center of its roof. Soon they had the two remaining children wrapped in the bedrolls and as close as they could get them to the heat, hoping it would help break their fevers. The coughing was ugly and deep. A couple hours after dusk, a second child died.

Billy dug his second small hole.

The Indian girl was the oldest of the three and the strongest. She managed to make it through the night. At dawn the Rangers placed her on the litter, burned their bedrolls, and started the slow ride to the Quechan Reservation outside of Fort Yuma. Since they could follow the river back to the reservation, about every half hour they'd stop and soak the rags on her head with fresh, cool water.

"Thank you," the girl exclaimed as Jeff placed the cool rag on her forehead.

He was shocked. "Did ya hear that, Billy? She thanked me, in perfect English."

Billy reminded him, "Them clothes they was wearin' meant they was prob'ly on their way to the Injun school in Nogales. They're mission Injuns."

"Learnin' the white man's ways, huh?" replied Jeff, pleased that these Indians were at least making an effort to conform. "Good for them. For her. That's what every goddamn one of them should be doin'!"

Billy fixed his eyes on his new friend and decided it was time to impart a bit of wisdom. "I ain't gonna claim to know what it's like up in them Dakotas, but down here, Jeff, in this part of the country, there's just too many Injuns to try hatin' them all. Ya'll use up all yer hate in a day. Yer gonna need some fer the assholes who really deserve it."

It was late afternoon when the Quechan reservation came into view. Billy fired a shot to get their attention. Four braves quickly rode towards them. One spoke Spanish so Billy was able to explain the situation. They isolated the girl in a sweat hut. The two Rangers were greeted with gratitude and fanfare.

"They wanna treat us to a pansaje," said Billy.

"What's that?"

"It's a sit-down dinner, outside, on blankets with the chiefs and elders."

"Is it safe?"

"Oh, yeah!" answered Billy. "We're heroes, even if we did only save one of them."

Several blankets were placed on the ground. The tribal elders seated themselves in a circle around them, gesturing for Billy and Jeff to join them.

Jeff leaned to Billy and whispered, "I've seen these gut eaters up home wolf down nasty beef entrails. Is that what we're gonna have to eat?"

"If it is, smile and chew!"

The first item passed around was a small bowl of salt from which each man took a pinch and placed it in his mouth. Before the bowl reached Jeff he leaned over to Billy.

"We don't sprinkle it on nothing?" he whispered.

Billy whispered back, "Salt's like gold to the Injuns 'round here. It's a big honor that they're sharin' it with us."

When the bowl reached him, Jeff took a pinch of the salt, licked it from his fingers, nodded and smiled at the elders and passed the bowl to Billy. Next was the peace pipe. It, too, was passed around the circle as each man took a toke. Several squaws appeared from nowhere with platters of tarantulas deep fried in bear fat. Jeff stared at the serving for a long moment then looked up at the Indians happily devouring the eight-legged delicacies. They smiled and nodded at him. Billy was breaking off spider legs and eating them like candy. It took another couple of moments and some inner fortitude for Jeff to finally sample the strange treat. After one bite he was hooked. His face lit up as the spider's flavor exploded in his mouth.

"These are mighty tasty," he declared. "I thought they'd be crunchy, but they're chewy." He ate the entire platter and snatched two more from Billy's plate.

A tray of prickly pears heavily seasoned with cayenne pepper came next. To calm the fire from the pepper each man was given a cup of *pulque*, which can get a man drunk quicker than a lightning strike. The final serving was a very tasty rabbit.

"What'd ya think they season this jackrabbit with?" asked Jeff as he discarded bones cleaned of any and all meat back onto his plate. "It's mighty tasty, too."

"Rattlesnake venom," Billy casually answered.

Jeff stopped eating and looked at his friend, wide eyed.

"Just kiddin'!"

After the feast they were entertained by a Squaw Dance then given their own tepee furnished with enough buffalo hides and various animal skins to put Jim Bridger to shame. As both men plopped down on the comfortable and soft hides a flute began playing somewhere in the distance.

"What the hell's that?" asked Jeff.

"Kokopelli," responded Billy, sitting up.

Before he could explain the meaning of the word two young squaws crept into the tepee, giggling.

Jeff's hand instinctively reached toward the holster lying next to him.

"What the hell?"

"Relax," stated Billy. "I kinda expected this."

"Expected what? What do they want, our hair?"

"Think lower! After one a them Squaw Dances the women folk can choose any partner they want. Looks like we done been chosed."

Jeff was shocked, mortified, and curious.

"You mean they want to...to fuck us?" he managed to stammer with both concern and arousal.

"Yep," Billy answered with a big grin. "Which one ya want? That one's got bigger tits, but the other's got a more toler'ble face."

"But they're...they're savages," he whispered.

"No need to whisper. They don't know what we're sayin'."

One of the squaws giggled and said something to the other.

"What'd she say?" Jeff asked.

"Don't know fer sure, but I think she said she ain't ne'er had a white man afore."

"That makes two of us," responded Jeff. "Uh, what if we catch some ungodly disease?"

"Hell, Jeff," Billy chuckled, "em two are prob'bly cleaner than any Nogales whore. Besides, turnin' them down would be an insult—might have to fight our way out of here."

That was bullshit and Billy knew it. He figured these two squaws were just out to satisfy their own curiosity and have a little fun. But he also figured sex with an Indian may be something Jeff Kidder should experience.

Jeff grimaced and whispered, "What if she smells? I know male Injuns smell somethin' fierce."

"Oh, she will! She'll smell like a woman, 'stead of a whore."

Billy knew the fellow from Dakota frequented the whorehouses and had had his share of baggage handlers, but when he glanced over and saw the squaw gumming Jeff's johnson while tickling his ball sack with a quail feather, he figured his new friend was in a place he had never been before. The kokopelli played on somewhere outside the tepee.

The next morning Billy sketched out a crude map to where he had dug the two small holes. He gave it to the Chief so the children's families could retrieve the bodies for their ritual ceremonies. As the two Rangers saddled their mounts, Jeff was noticeably quiet.

As they rode back to Yuma to catch another slow, hot, filthy train to Nogales, Billy finally asked, "Okay, what's buggin' ya? Spit it out!"

"I want you to know that if my dick falls off I'm gonna have to shoot you."

They both laughed long and hard. For the rest of ride Jeff couldn't stop talking about the the squaws, the piles of animal skins in their private tepee, the tasty tarantulas, even the way the Quechan elders winked and grinned at him as they ate the delicious meal. Billy just smiled and let him ramble.

They never learned if the young Quechan girl survived.

July 10, 1910

Diaz Pasco woke in a haze and with one dandy headache. From the first lifting of his eyelids to the time the haze cleared enough to appreciate his situation had to have been a long minute.

"*Qué es esto?*" he managed to choke out, "*Qué es esto?*" He couldn't move his arms or legs. "*Qué es esto?*" He couldn't even wiggle. He felt as if his body was wrapped in a very tight blanket. And it was: a blanket of earth. "*Qué es esto?*"

He had half of the same sentence out of his mouth when a rattle cut off his words. To his front, slightly to the right, and about ten feet away he saw a stake in the ground. Attached to the stake was a five foot long leather strap. Tied by its tail to the end of the strap, barely a foot from his face was a very angry four-foot Diamondback.

"*Qué es esto?*" he screamed again and again and again.

The Diamondback hissed and twisted and jerked and struck at the man's head, but couldn't empty his dripping fangs, which seemed to get the serpent even angrier. As Pasco's eyes began to bring more of the world around him into focus, he realized they were level with the hooves of a black horse standing about twenty feet away. With the back of his neck scraping against hot sand, he strained to tilt his head upward until his limited view ran up the horse's legs to the saddle. Silhouetted in the dawn sun, seated on the horse, holding a long rifle with a scope pointed in the air and its crescent-shaped butt plate resting against his hip, was the *gringo*.

"¿*Quien chingados es? ¿Quien chingados es?*"

"Told ya I was gonna plant ya." He gave Pasco a face full of Orion's ass and the two began a slow walk from the buried man.

"Fuckin' *gringo*, fuckin' *gringo*," the man shrieked in a dry, raspy voice as the snake tried like hell to break free of the leather strap and quiet this screaming nuisance. "¿*Quien chingados es?*"

At close to seventy-five yards Billy pulled Orion to a halt. A second after he did, Pasco stopped screaming, wondering what the *gringo* was doing. Billy slid off Orion and dropped to one knee. Resting his left elbow on his left knee, he steadied the Winchester 1895 Second Model Sporting Rifle and lowered his eye to the Malcolm Model #3 hunting scope to take careful aim at the stake holding the leather strap.

"Just like splitting a pea pod," he whispered to himself.

Pasco screamed.

As Billy's finger began to tighten around the trigger it suddenly felt like he was shaking. He couldn't seem to steady the Malcolm Model #3 hunting scope. He wondered if his brain was trying to stop his heart from finishing the job. He wouldn't let it. Again lowering his eye to the scope he tried to focus in on his target. But the target wouldn't hold still. It kept quivering. Then he realized it wasn't the target that was quivering and it wasn't him that was shaking. It was the ground. A tingling sensation shot through the knee resting in the dirt and up his leg until his whole body seemed to tremble. The earth under him was coming alive, churning and crawling in circles like it was stirring from a deep sleep. Bushes shook, rocks moved, and cactus twitched. A hard gust of hot wind and sand stung his face and jarred his body. Looking to the west he saw a huge sandstorm explode from behind the small mesas and swallow them up as it rumbled towards him at lightning speed. Orion reared and whinnied. Billy could see brush and cactus and sand and small stones twisting and swirling in the raging brown and black mass. The dawn sunlight made it all sparkle and blink, reminding him of the Christmas lights back in El Papalote. For a long moment the sight of the roaring beast had him frozen solid. But this was death blowing its hot, foul breath at him. Breath filled with sand that had turned itself into millions of razors that would rip and shred the skin of anything in its path.

He hopped on Orion and cried, "Fog it, Big O!"

The duo sped off for the shelter of Naco, leaving the screaming pleas of Diaz Pasco swallowed up in the throat of the storm.

June, 1904

A band of normally friendly Papago Indians were hot on their asses. Billy and Jeff were high-tailing it east towards Fresnal Canyon with hopes of losing them in the twisting rocks. But just beyond the canyon and heading straight for them was a sandstorm. A big one. They jerked the reins of Swiss and Vermillion, causing the animals to skid to a halt and kick up dust and pebbles. Both whinnied angrily at the sudden pain from their bits. The two Rangers had only minutes to pick their poison: pissed off Papagos or a pissed off Mother Nature.

Having never seen a true southwest sandstorm Jeff was almost hypnotized by the sight. He thought it looked like a spinning, pulsating mass of dirty cotton candy. It was his disdain for Indians that had caused their plight. They were tracking some stolen cattle and found a dozen head on the Papago Gila Bend reservation. That was evidence enough for Jeff to pull his fancy Colt on the tribe's Medicine Man while Billy took a closer look at the moss backs. The Medicine Man, fed up with this stupid white man, turned to walk away. Jeff yelled at him to stop but the man kept walking. Not allowing a snub like that to stand, especially from an Indian, he sent a round into the dirt between the man's legs. The Medicine Man stopped.

"Ya hearin' me now, asshole?" shouted Jeff.

The Indian turned and glared at the Ranger with hate in his eyes. Then he suddenly looked to a hillside beyond and his face formed into a devious smile.

Hearing the shot and expecting the worse, Billy galloped back yelling, "These ain't the cows! They ain't jingle bobbed."

It was too late. A returning hunting party of peaceful Papago Indians on the crest of the hill had just seen a white man take a shot at their Medicine Man. They poured down the hill, firing wildly.

"Do we go through it?" Jeff shouted over the roar of the approaching storm.

"Hell no! Blind our horses. Keep for the canyon!"

They spurred their mounts and rode like hell. Seconds before the storm would whip them both out of their saddles Billy spotted the cave. Big enough to ride into, they bolted into the natural shelter. The grotto was only about thirty feet deep, but enough to escape Nature's blast furnace. Luckily the storm drained the anger from the Indians and they hurried back to their village for shelter. The two men hopped off their mounts, held the reins tightly, and watched the storm howl and churn and shriek by the cave.

"Why the hell'd ya shoot at that Med'cine Man?" Billy shouted over the noise.

"I shot 'tween his legs," snapped Jeff, as if that made it okay.

"That's still shootin' at him, goddamn it!"

"The sumbitch turned his back to me."

"So?"

"He was ignoring me, goddamn it!"

"So?"

"We're the goddamn law, Billy!"

"He's an injun, for crissake! He don't un'erstand our laws. Pro'bly didn't even un'erstand a fuckin' word we was sayin'!"

"Then it's time he learned!' declared Jeff, leaning into Billy's face and still having to shout above the passing storm outside their small refuge. "This is our country, Billy, not some giant godless happy hunting ground anymore. There are laws, there are rules! There's baths for crissake, and that includes a bunch of fuckin' dirt worshippers!"

"Still ain't no call to shoot at his feet like that! All ya did was pepper up them other Injuns. Ain't ya e'er heard the old sayin' 'Ya git more bees with honey then vinegar'?"

"It's flies!" Jeff corrected Billy in a condescending tone.

"Ya still ain't always gotta pull that fancy ass Colt a yers, and ya sure as hell ain't gonna 'git famous' fer shootin' some old medicine man!"

"They're a goddamned conquered people, Billy! Don't you think I know we're killin' off a way of life? But it's happened for thousands of years to millions of defeated peoples. They had to bend to it or die. It's in the history books, Billy! It's life, Billy! It ain't always fair, but it's life, ya stupid shit!"

As soon as his tongue pushed those last three words from his mouth Jeff wished he could suck them right back down his throat and choke on them. Hating something or someone so hard can eat up a man's insides and turn his heart black. It can make him say things that shouldn't even be in his mind, much less coming out of his mouth. For thirty minutes they sat in silence, watching the storm inch by. It was the longest thirty minutes of Jeff's life.

"I'm a shit, Billy," Jeff finally said as the world outside calmed. Too ashamed to even make eye contact with his friend, he continued, "Nuthun but a shit! Hit me, ya hear! Bust me in the rotten mouth that deserves what it spewed."

"I ain't gonna hit ya, Jeff," replied Billy, tightening his saddle cinch.

"Callin' ya that was the lowest thing I could do, Billy. I didn't mean it. I was pissed and I ain't worth a bucket of pox puss. I'm ashamed, Billy."

Inside, Billy smiled at his friend saying "ain't." Outside, he stood motionless for a few more seconds then turned and extended his hand.

Jeff looked at him, shocked that the man could be so forgiving. Embarrassed and humbled, he finally managed to stammer, "Ya sure 'bout this?"

"Hell, ya think yer the only knothead that ever said somethun that he later regretted? If I had a nickel fer ev'ry dumbass thing I said I'd own the biggest whorehouse in New Orleans." Jeff grinned and tightly grasped his friend's hand with both of his.

Then Billy added, "But don't 'spect us to kiss and make up."

The two men laughed, looked at each other for a short moment then hugged. It was a quick embrace, like two brothers who had just been in a fist fight with each other, both knowing it was wrong and they had to make it right.

"Glad no one was here to see that," laughed Jeff after they broke the embrace.

"Me, too," laughed Billy. "But our horses did!"

Jeff drew his Colt and said, "Guess we'll have to shoot 'em!"

"How'll we get back?"

"Good thinkin'!"

July 10, 1910

Feeling frisky, Mother Nature blew the storm to the north towards Bisbee, but much to her dismay it petered out a few miles from the town. Billy returned the Clover to the dentist's office, knowing no one would be there on Sunday morning. Exhausted from the previous evening's work, he slept most of the day away in his plump bed. It was close to supper when some knuckles pounded on his door, startling him into consciousness.

"Billy it's me, John, lemme in!"

Hearing the urgency in Foster's voice, Billy unlocked the door and opened it. Foster thrust a piece of paper at him.

"Some Mexican kid ran in the office, tossed this to me and ran out. What the hell's goin' on, Billy?"

Billy read aloud, "Pasco for whore. Lucheia's." Just four words, but they stung like a nest of yellow jackets.

"Did ya kill him, Billy?"

"No," A half truth as he quickly slipped on his pants and shirt.

"What'd ya do? Did ya take him? Why do they have this whore? What whore? Abbie? Where the hell is Pasco, Billy?"

"He's dead, John!" Billy replied as he whipped his gun belt around his waist.

"You just said...."

"He's dead. That's all there is to it," Billy answered as he slipped on his shoulder holster. "Now I gotta get Abbie outta there."

"Why did they take Abbie?"

"Ain't got time now, John." He started for the door. Foster stepped in his path. "I gotta cross that bridge, John!"

John saw the determination on his friend's face and stepped aside. "I can't go with ya, Billy."

"I know." He left his friend alone in the room.

He rode Orion as far as the bridge than tied him to a post. No sense getting his horse all shot up, too, when he could easily walk the distance across the bridge to the Mexican side. It was late Sunday afternoon and the sun was setting, so he figured there wouldn't be any bystanders.

"Wait here, Big O, and don't do nothun stupid like come after me."

Sensing the danger Orion snorted and lowered his head to feel Billy's palm on it at least one more time, which he did.

"Now don't go gettin' morbid on me either, shithead!"

He stared at the wooden structure for a long moment thinking of Jeff, Freddie, Henry, and his ma. He prayed Abbie was still alive.

"No more," he thought. "This time I'm gonna be there."

He began the walk across the weathered bridge. About halfway Captain Wheeler's words bounced around his head again, "Only a fool walks into a hostile environment alone." Then he heard Jeff's voice, "You're not stupid, Billy!" It stopped him dead in his tracks. He thought, "Why go into Lucheia's at all?" He knew Abbie would be in there with them, but they didn't know where Pasco was. If he could get them out in the open...maybe...just maybe...a slight advantage.

"Them?"

How many of "them?" He continued walking and just as his first boot left the bridge and touched Mexican soil, he stepped to the right. The main street of the Mexican side of Naco ran east and west. The *cantina* sat to the south. Billy was crossing the bridge from the north. By stepping to the right, or the West, he had put the setting sun at his back and in the faces of anyone leaving Lucheia's. Advantage! He pulled his Smith and Wesson. There were five beans in the wheel so he slid a sixth one into the empty cylinder under the firing pin. He checked the clip of his .45. Full! He touched the small of his back and realized he had left his knife at the boarding house. He took a deep breath and walked out to the middle of the dusty street. It was still empty. That probably meant they were all inside waiting for him to step through that door like Jeff did. That's fine! They can wait until hell freezes over.

"Hey assholes!" he shouted. "I'm here! Bring out the whore!"

There was a long silence before a voice finally responded from somewhere inside the dark *cantina*.

"Come in for drink, *amigo*," it taunted. "We talk!"

"Not a chance in hell, *amigo*!" Billy shouted back. "Ya want Pasco, bring out the whore!"

Another long silence was finally broken when four Mexican policemen clamored out of the *cantina*'s door, but none were Victoriano. *Four!* Billy wondered if this was what Feather Yank had seen when he said "Goodbye, Billy Old." From the stagger in the policemen's walk he knew they had been doing some heavy Sunday drinking. *Advantage!* The same tall, ugly one with the crooked eye was dragging Abbie. He had one arm tight around her waist to keep her standing. His other hand held a knife to her throat. Her face was swollen and bloody. Her nose had a slight crook to it. Her arms and legs were covered in bruises. She wore the same corset from last night, but it was streaked with blood and tattered, ripped, and allowed her left breast to hang free, on which Billy could see red threads of blood coming from nicks and slices. *Four!* God only knows what else they did to her.

He quietly said, "Forgive me, Jeff."

The man with the crooked eye shouted, *"Donde está Pasco?"*

"Speak English, *Pelado*," Billy shouted back.

One of the policemen stepped forward with a bit of a stagger which told Billy that most of the man's courage was coming from what he had consumed in the *cantina*. *Advantage!* Billy could see him squint into the setting sun. *Advantage!*

"Where is our *amigo*, my friend?"

"Long as ya got the whore, I ain't yer friend, *amigo*."

"All we want is trade, *Señor*," slurred the policeman with a sadistic grin.

257

"The whore for our *amigo*! Even Steven, as you *gringo*s say!" He chuckled at his attempt at humor then looked around with a mock expression of wonderment. "But I do not see him. You try to cheat us, *amigo*? All four of us?"

The policemen laughed at the odds.

A shot rang out from the north and the crooked eye exploded out the back of the tall, ugly man's head. Both he and Abbie collapsed to the dirt. Not certain what had just happened, everyone, including Billy, glanced in the direction from which the sound had come. It was like time had frozen everything. Another shot rang out and a second policeman's chest opened like a large blooming rose as he, too, fell to the dirt. Then time thawed and all hell broke loose. The mouthy policeman closest to Billy drew his *pistola*. Billy quickly planted four rounds into the man's torso. The fourth policeman fired several wild shots as he ran back into the *cantina*, chased by the last two bullets from Billy's gun. He hurried over and knelt next to Abbie, checking her pulse. Still pumping.

"Sorry, Billy," she gasped. He wondered how she could even tell it was him through her swollen and bloody eyes. "I stayed in that fancy hotel room too long."

He bedded the empty Smith & Wesson, awoke his seven-clip .45, and ran over to the side of the *cantina* door.

"Sorry, Cap'n," he whispered. "Goin' in!"

He entered with the .45 leveled, holding it steady in both hands. It was dead quiet in the *cantina*. Billy scanned the room. The bartender's hands were stretched so high his dirty fingernails almost scraped the ceiling. The two old checkers players had managed to flee by the side door into the alley, leaving their game unfinished. The whores must have taken Sunday off. No sign of the other policeman. To his surprise, at a corner table sat the same gambler he had encountered in La Bandera. The man gave Billy a subtle nod towards the upright piano. Billy noticed the instrument wasn't quite flush against the wall. He aimed his .45 square at its center.

"Play Red River Valley!" he whispered.

Six shots exploded from his seven round clip into the piano. The old upright chimed and clanked and pinged in agony as pieces of wood and wire flew from it. A few seconds later came a thud, followed by a limp hand still clutched around a *pistola* flopping out from the space behind the instrument.

He turned to the gambler and said, "Hope he didn't owe you money, too."

The gambler smiled.

Billy ran out of the *cantina* and back to Abbie. It took muscles he had forgot he had to lift and carry her to the other side of the bridge. She was heavy. Not fat, just thick and sturdy. A light breeze blew back her hair and he saw that the animals had cut off her ear.

John Foster was waiting on the U.S. side of the bridge.

"Sure wish we could do somethun 'bout them stray shots 'cross this border!" remarked the grinning Deputy Marshal who was walking toward the bridge on the Arizona side carrying Billy's Winchester 1895 Second Model Sporting Rifle with the Malcolm Model #3 hunting scope. "Someone might get hurt."

"Couldn't let 'nother friend die o'er there, John," Billy stated, groaning as he tried to lift Abbie onto Orion's back.

Foster stepped over and helped him hoist her into Orion's saddle. The black had patiently stood perfectly still, sensing that he needed to.

"Neither could I," the deputy marshal added as they settled Abbie into the saddle. She swayed and Billy knew she was about to pass out.

"Ring up the doc, John," ordered Billy. "Tell him I'm headin' to his place. And why didn't ya tell me Chief Amador was in on it?" asked Billy.

"Ya heard Jeff say the same names I did," replied John.

"I didn't know his name was Victoriano," Billy said. "I always called him Chief Amador.

"That's a powerful asshole to be goin' after, Billy," John Foster warned him. "Ya know he's prob'ly already rattled his hocks south."

"I ain't goin' nowhere 'til I know Abbie's gonna be okay," Billy stated. He took hold of Orion's reins, stood on the left side of the horse, and supported Abbie with his right hand. "Ifin she don't make it, I ain't gonna let them town assholes give her a pauper's burial just 'cause she's a whore." In a voice a little louder than a whisper he added, "Walk slow, Big O."

Sensing their destination Orion lowered his head and began a slow, smooth walk towards the doctor's office.

Abbie's first few days were the worst. Her nose had a slight but permanent hook to it. She had lost two jaw teeth and, of course, an ear. Three ribs were cracked, but none had punctured a lung. The knife slashes on her arms and legs and breasts weren't deep enough to warrant stitches so they wouldn't scar. She was lucky. It also turned out that the big, tough landlady Irene Castle had a heart as huge as her body. She admitted to Billy that in her younger days and prior to her collecting of tobacco chewing husbands, she had also been a "fallen angel" as she liked to call it. She allowed her favorite boarder to place Abbie in the spare room abruptly vacated by the traveling salesman. One of the man's previous "lonely housewives" had tracked him down with a child in hand. That same night he headed out for parts unknown.

Just four days after Abbie was left in the capable hands of Irene Castle, a strange box arrived at John Foster's office. Billy walked in to find John studying the curious object.

'Bout time ya got here," stated John. "I been itchin' to see what's in this here thing."

Billy saw a wooden box wrapped in several rabbit skins and tied with twine.

"Why din't ya open it then?"

'Cos it's got yer name written on the skins, and I think it was writ in blood. "Besides, it's agin the law to open another man's mail."

"My name? What is it?"

"Now how the hell am I su'pose to know that?"

"Where'd it come from?"

"It was just sittin' here on the desk when I came in. Well, ya gonna open it?"

Billy cut the twine, removed the skins, and pried off the wooden top.

"Jesus," he said, recoiling from the box's grotesque contents and foul odor.

All John Foster could manage to stammer was, "Holy shit," three times as he backed away from the container. Packed neatly in its wooden coffin was the severed head of Victoriano Amador. A sharp stick had been plunged into its right eye socket to secure a note with just two words scribbled on it in blood.

"Even. Tanok."

"Who the hell's Tanok?" asked a confused and disgusted John Foster.

Closing and rewrapping the box, and relieved that he wouldn't have to haul his ass back down into that shithole of Sonora, Billy simply said, "A friend." He also remembered something Sparky had once said: "Make a friend of a Yaqui and he's yer friend fer life." He left the office with the box snuggled under his arm. The next morning when the remaining Mexican police began to arrive for their daily assignments, they were greeted by the head of Victoriano Amador perched on the steps of the Naco police station.

September, 1910

It was a Sunday morning and Billy had planned to sleep in, but his slumber was disturbed by an early knock on the room. Groggy and slightly hung over he hated to leave his soft bed.

"Who is it?"

"The smitty," answered the deep voice from beyond the door.

"Just a minute."

He climbed out of bed and slipped on his britches. A second before his hand touched the doorknob the Peace Officer in him stirred. He pulled his Smith & Wesson from its bed, too.

"What'd ya need?" he inquired before opening the door.

"Got sump'um here fer ya from Miss Abbie, Mr. Billy," replied the deep voice with a thick Mississippi accent.

He slipped the weapon back to bed, turned the deadbolt, and opened the door. With his typical toothy grin the smitty's large muscular arm thrust a flat item out to Billy. It was about one foot by one foot and wrapped in newspaper.

"What is it?" asked Billy.

"I ain't a nosy man, Mr. Billy. Din't ask. Miss Abbie jist says give this to Mr. Billy one day after she be gone."

"Gone? What'd ya mean gone?"

"Like I says, Mr. Billy, ain't a nosy man, but the girl be long gone, both she and that purty horse a hers."

Billy began to dig around in his pockets for a coin to give the smitty but the man raised his hand and backed away.

"No need, Mr. Billy. Miss Abbie done gimme two shiny silver dollars fer my trouble." As the big man turned to leave he tossed one last statement over his shoulder. "Sure gonna miss our monthly visits though."

Puzzled and curious, Billy shut the door and twisted the deadbolt. He sat down on the bed and removed the newspaper surrounding the flat item. There was no note, no letter, just a beautiful painting of Orion standing on a small mesa almost in the exact pose as the first time he and Jeff spotted the black stallion. She had signed it "A. Crutchfield."

"I'll be damned," he muttered with a smile, realizing that his friend must have described the whole encounter with Orion to Abbie in great detail. She had captured almost all of it, right down to the blue moon and the eerie light it spread across the land, even the challenging look in Orion's eyes. The sleep finally left his head and things began to tumble into place. Abbie had done exactly what Jeff said he thought she might one day do—got on Lavender and just kept riding, didn't even say goodbye. He hoped she went off somewhere to become an "arteest." All those whorehouses could use a new painting.

Just to be certain no fat asses from the Territorial Government were going to come down on John Foster for the incident on the Mexican side of Naco, Billy stayed for another two months. John married Cassie Lou Blue-field the day after Thanksgiving. Billy was his best man and Henrietta her bridesmaid. As John and Cassie stood before the altar, Henrietta gave a subtle gesture with her thumb towards the preacher reading the verses and leaned into Billy's ear.

"Until you come along he was one of my regulars," she whispered. "The toad faced vulture playin' the organ is his wife. Now ya know why he was a regular."

Billy swallowed a belly laugh so hard that he almost farted it out the other end.

Pretty certain that the whole shooting incident was dead and buried he reluctantly returned his deputy badge and traded John his fancy Winchester 1895 Second Model Sporting Rifle with the Malcolm Model #3 hunting scope for the Winchester 30-30 in the rifle rack. The two men's goodbyes were short but sincere. Both had the feeling their paths would probably never cross again. Later Billy found out that after Congress finally did pass that parole act

John quit his job. He and Cassie Lou moved to Santa Maria, California, where he opened a small fix-it shop. John Foster loved to tinker.

December, 1910

After supper, retired Ranger Captain Harry Wheeler liked to sit on the porch of his small ranch outside of Benson and watch the sun set while enjoying a good cigar. Between puffs of blue smoke, he saw a distant figure on a black horse approaching his house. As the twosome grew closer, he recognized the white star on the horse's head.

"I'll be dipped in sheep shit," he muttered and stepped down off his porch to greet this long lost *compadre.* "Billy Old, ya ol' shitwad," the former captain called out with a huge smile. "Where the hell ya been hidin'?"

Billy patted Orion's neck as he came to a halt and simply said, "They're all dead, Cap'n!"

"Huh? Who?" asked the confused captain, fearing Billy was talking about more ex-Rangers. "Who's dead, Billy?"

"Them assholes who put Jeff under," answered Billy. "They're all dead. I couldn't walk this earth knowin' they still was."

Captain Wheeler lowered his head and sighed, "Well, Billy, I can't condone what ya done..." then he lifted his head and let loose a toothy grin locked around the big cigar, "but I sure as shit ain't gonna mourn the sumbitches."

Billy tugged on Orion's reins and said, "Just wanted ya to know, Cap'n!" He started to turn the horse.

"Billy, yer welcome to stay the night. Supper's still warm."

" 'Preciate that, Cap'n, but I gotta get to Los Angeles."

"Los Angeles? Why?"

"Gotta tell Jeff I got them!"

He turned the black northwest. Harry Wheeler watched the twosome fade into the darkness.

"Got a long ride 'heada us, Big O," said Billy as he patted his friend's neck. At first he had thought about taking the train, but the idea of having so many star-filled nights ahead of him made him figure he'd have plenty of time to decide which stars Jeff and Freddie were on.

A half a mile from Wheeler's ranch he got a hankering to stop in and see his old pal Sparky on the way to Los Angeles, and finally get a gander at the "little dressmaker with the huge udders." He jerked Orion to a halt as he struggled to recall the name of the town where his giant friend was preaching the gospel.

"What the hell was the name of that town?" he asked Orion, who simply snorted. He wanted to smack himself on the side of the head to see if the name would pop back into the right place. He did. It didn't.

"Fifth fuckin' grade."

Epilogue

October, 1934, Taos, New Mexico

"It belonged to my father," the man replied. "Then you are the A. Crutchfield who painted this?"

She found it difficult to take her eyes from the painting of Orion. First she saw the flaws. Next came the memories, both painful and pleasing. Why this young man was so oddly familiar became suddenly clear.

"Yer...yer Billy Old's boy?"

"Yes ma'am," he grinned. "William."

Looking at his smile made her feel she had just jumped back in time twenty-four years. Her hand started to touch the hair covering her missing ear, but she didn't.

"How's yer pa," she managed to ask.

"He died back in nineteen fourteen."

"Oh, sorry to hear that," responded Abbie. Wondering if Billy's past had caught up with him, she knew she had to ask the next question. With a measured tone she asked, "How?"

"He was shot."

"By Mexican police?"

"Uh, no," replied the man, baffled by her question. "Why do you ask that?"

"Cause he pissed off one hell of a lot of 'em."

"My mother and father split up a few years before that. My father married another woman and, well, I guess she was a little crazy or something. They got into an argument one night and she shot him. He was a peace officer down in Pearce, Arizona at the time so that's where they buried him. I take it you two were friends...or something?"

"Friends," Abbie firmly stated. "How'd ya find me? How'd ya make the connection?"

"I'm a deputy sheriff in Bernalillo County, down in Albuquerque. I saw the name A. Crutchfield in a newspaper story about the artists up here in Taos. It said you painted horses. When my mother died a few months back my brother and I were cleaning out some stuff and we found the only two things we could tie back to our father: a pipe with a buffalo head carved out of ivory and this painting. My brother's a smoker so he took the pipe. When I read the article I remembered this painting was done by an A. Crutchfield. So I took a day off to come up here to see if it was you that did it."

"Why?" Abbie asked. "It ain't worth nothun. I ain't famous."

"Well, it's not really the painting I'm curious about. It's my father. I was only two years old when he and mom divorced. I only saw him once in the few years before his death. I barely remember him, let alone know anything about him. Mom refused to talk about him; even went to court and added an "S" to our last name, making it Olds." He chuckled and continued, "Made us sound like we belong to the rich automobile family, she'd say."

"Yet you drive a Ford."

They laughed. He liked her laugh. It was deep, from the gut. She winched a little at hearing so much of Billy in his laugh, but still enjoyed it. Her mind flashed back to that night in the fancy hotel room when she felt the strange feeling of rejection.

"All I know is he was an Arizona Ranger and a Peace Officer," he added, stepping into the middle of her memory. "I was hoping you could, well, light up a dark room, so to speak."

Abbie smiled, looked at the man for a moment then asked, "How much time ya got?"

"Whatever it takes," he answered with a smile.

The next morning William Kidder Olds climbed into the old Ford full of stories and free of baggage. Before he had even sparked the car's ignition, Abbie was seated at her work table ciphering out what bills she could pay with the twenty dollars he had insisted on leaving her.

Whores survive by numbers.

Historical Background

Jeff Kidder was born on a farm in Vermillion, South Dakota in the early 1870s. He was college educated and an avid reader of dime novels and he constantly practiced the "quick draw," at which he became proficient. When his folks divorced, sold their family farm and moved away, Kidder went down to Arizona to join the Rangers. Not being completely sold on the man, the Ranger Captain assigned him to the streets of Nogales where he served as a deputy for close to a year before finally being admitted into the Rangers. He proved to be an excellent Ranger, making many arrests, so many in fact that the crooked Mexican police involved with gunrunning and rustling actually put a bounty on his head.

While pursuing Tomas Amador and Delores Quias, Mexican police-men involved in many illegal activities, into a cantina in Naco, Mexico, he was ambushed by two other policemen and seriously wounded, but managed to kill the two ambushers and wound both Quias and Amador. While trying to make it back to the safety of the Arizona side of Naco, he was attacked by three more policemen, one of them being Chief of Police Victoriano Amador. After running out of ammo he surrendered and was severely beaten, suffering a cracked skull while being hauled into a nasty jail cell and was left there without medical aid. He died the next day in the company of Billy Old, John Foster, and the Ranger Captain.

None of the five policemen involved in Kidder's killing were convicted. They were sent to various locations around Sonora. Kidder's grandfather served in the U.S. Congress and his Uncle Lymon was the namesake of the infamous "Kidder Massacre" mentioned in this book. Kidder was also known for being a rather loud drunk.

Billy Old grew up on a farm in Uvalde, Texas in the early 1870s. The area is known for goat farming and producing mohair. He worked as a farmer, cowhand, Peace Officer and Arizona Ranger. After a short two-year marriage, his wife Anna left him and took their two infant boys to her hometown of Kelvin, Arizona. She later changed her last name to "Olds."

While serving with the Rangers he became close friends with fellow Ranger Jeff Kidder. After political influences caused the Rangers to be disbanded, Billy vanished into Sonora, Mexico for close to two years. Upon his return he informed a former Ranger Captain that the five men responsible for Kidder's murder were now dead. In April of 1914, while serving as a Peace Officer in Pearce, Arizona, he was shot and killed by his second wife. His tombstone is the largest in Pearce's old cemetery and even encircled by a short iron fence. The tombstone reads: Peace Officer.

Freddie Rankin, William "Sparky" Sparks, John Foster, and Captain Harry Wheeler are the actual names of Rangers who served at the same time as Old and Kidder. Anything else about them is fiction. Henry Ashurst was the Coconino County District Attorney and known as "The Silver-Tongued Sunbeam of the Painted Desert." Doroteo Arango was the real name of Pancho Villa.

With the exception of Trigger Point, all other towns and locations exist. All the rest is fiction.

Readers Guide

1. What realization did Billy come to while serving in the Rough Riders?

2. Why did Billy feel that Jeff's killers would be transferred to areas primarily occupied by Yaquis?

3. Why was Billy so enamored with whores?

4. Why was Billy's sacrifice of Captain necessary?

5. What unusual type of bones peaked Captain's curiosity in the desert?

6. What was Sparky's main concern about Jeff?

7. Why did Billy's rather bizarre dreams seem to cease once he reached Naco, Arizona?

8. How did Jeff and Feather Yank's assignment together effect Jeff's opinions of Native Americans?

9. What was John Foster's concern about his relationship with Cassie Lou?

10. Why didn't Billy and Abbie ever become lovers?

11. What do YOU think Abbie did from the time she left Naco in 1910, until she volunteered for the Red Cross in 1918?

12. What was the significance of the star symbol throughout the story?

13. Even with the age difference Abbie and Billy's son were physically attracted to one another. What other reason(s) could there have been for them deciding to spend the night together?

14. Both Billy and Jeff suffered from the same symptoms of a form of Post Traumatic Stress Disorder (PTSD). What was it?

CPSIA information can be obtained
at www.ICGtesting.com
Printed in the USA
FFHW02n0949210918
48521201-52392FF